Maxim Jakubowski is a London-based novelist and editor. He was born in the UK and educated in France. Following a career in book publishing, he opened the world-famous Murder One bookshop in London. He now writes full-time. He has edited a series of fifteen bestselling erotic anthologies and two books of erotic photography, as well as many acclaimed crime collections. His novels include *It's You That I Want To Kiss, Because She Thought She Loved Me* and *On Tenderness Express*, all three collected and reprinted in the USA as *Skin In Darkness*. Other books include *Life In The World of Women, The State of Montana, Kiss Me Sadly* and *Confessions Of A Romantic Pornographer*. In 2006 he published *American Casanova*, a major erotic novel which he edited and on which fifteen of the top erotic writers in the world have collaborated, and his collected erotic short stories as *Fools For Lust*. His latest novel is *I Was Waiting for You*. He compiles two annual acclaimed series for the Mammoth list: *Best New Erotica* and *Best British Crime*. He is a winner of the Anthony and the Karel Awards, a frequent TV and radio broadcaster, a past crime columnist for the *Guardian* newspaper, Literary Director of London's Crime Scene Festival and now edits the MaXcrime imprint.

THE MAMMOTH BOOK OF BOOK OF BEST BRITISH MYSTERIES

Volume 7

MAXIM JAKUBOWSKI

ROBINSON

RUNNING PRESS
PHILADELPHIA · LONDON

Constable & Robinson Ltd
3 The Lanchesters
162 Fulham Palace Road
London W6 9ER
www.constablerobinson.com

First published in the UK by Robinson,
an imprint of Constable & Robinson, 2010

A copy of the British Library Cataloguing in Publication
Data is available from the British Library

UK ISBN 978-1-84901-197-6

1 3 5 7 9 10 8 6 4 2

First published in the United States in 2010
by Running Press Book Publishers

9 8 7 6 5 4 3 2 1
Digit on the right indicates the number of this printing

US Library of Congress number: 2009929935
US ISBN 978-0-7624-3846-4

Running Press Book Publishers
2300 Chestnut Street
Philadelphia, PA 19103-4371

Visit us on the web!
www.runningpress.com

Printed and bound in the EU

CONTENTS

ACKNOWLEDGMENTS

"MR E. MORSE, BA OXON (FAILED)" by Colin Dexter © 2008. First appeared in the *Daily Mail* as "THE MYSTERY OF THE DRUNKEN DRIVER". Reprinted by permission of the author.

"GHOSTS" by John Harvey © 2008. First appeared in *Il Giornale* (Italy). Reprinted by permission of the author.

"THE BLOOD PEARL" by Barry Maitland © 2008. First appeared in the *Newcastle Herald* (Australia). Reprinted by permission of the author.

"THE COMMON ENEMY" by Natasha Cooper © 2008. First appeared in *Ellery Queen Mystery Magazine*. Reprinted by permission of the author and the author's agent Gregory & Co.

"BLOODSPORT" by Tom Cain © 2009. First appeared online at THE RAP SHEET. Reprinted by permission of the author.

"THE RAT IN THE ATTIC" by Brian McGilloway © 2008. First appeared in the *Sunday Express*. Reprinted by permission of the author.

"ENOUGH OF THIS SHIT ALREADY" by Tony Black © 2008. First appeared online at PLOTS WITH GUNS. Reprinted by permission of the author.

"HOGMANAY HOMICIDE" by Edward Marston © 2008. First appeared as a chapbook published by Crippen & Landru. Reprinted by permission of the author.

"FRUITS" by Steve Mosby © 2008. First appeared online at SPINETINGLER MAGAZINE. Reprinted by permission of the author.

"A PLACE FOR VIOLENCE" by Kevin Wignall © 2008. First appeared online at STORYGLOSSIA. Reprinted by permission of the author.

"FOUR HUNDRED RABBITS" by Simon Levack © 2008. First appeared in *Ellery Queen Mystery Magazine*. Reprinted by permission of the author and the author's agent Gregory & Co.

"HISTORY!" by Toby Litt © 2008. First appeared in '68. Reprinted by permission of the author.

"THE MASQUERADE" by Sarah Rayne © 2008. First appeared in *Crime Scenes*. Reprinted by permission of the author.

"TAKE DEATH EASY" by Peter Turnbull © 2008. First appeared in *Ellery Queen Mystery Magazine*. Reprinted by permission of the author.

"THE PARSON AND THE HIGHWAYMAN" by Judith Cutler © 2008. First appeared in *Ellery Queen Mystery Magazine*. Reprinted by permission of the author.

"SPECIAL DELIVERY" by Adrian Magson © 2008. First appeared in *Crime Scenes*. Reprinted by permission of the author.

"A BLOW ON THE HEAD" by Peter Lovesey © 2008. First appeared in *Ellery Queen Mystery Magazine*. Reprinted by permission of the author.

"CHICAGO" by Jon Courtenay Grimwood © 2008. First appeared in *Sideways in Crime*. Reprinted by permission of the author.

"THE HOUSE THAT GOT SHOT" by Barbara Nadel © 2008. First appeared in *Ellery Queen Mystery Magazine*. Reprinted by permission of the author.

"THE OCTOPUS NEST" by Sophie Hannah © 2009. First appeared in *Criminal Tendencies*. Reprinted by permission of the author.

"WALKING THE DOG" by Peter Robinson © 2008. First appeared in *Toronto Noir*. Reprinted by permission of the author.

"THE VELOCITY OF BLAME" by Christopher Fowler © 2008. First appeared in *The 2nd Humdrum Book of Horror Stories*. Reprinted by permission of the author.

"SOMEONE TAKE THESE DREAMS AWAY" by Marc Werner © 2008. First appeared in '68. Reprinted by permission of the author.

"ANIMAL INTELLIGENCE" by Alexander McCall Smith © 2008. First appeared in *The Strand Magazine*. Reprinted by permission of the author's agent David Higham Associates Limited.

"12 BOLINBROKE AVENUE" by Peter James © 2008. First appeared in *Women's Day*. Reprinted by permission of the author and the author's agent Blake Friedmann.

"APPETITE FOR MURDER" by Simon R. Green © 2008. First appeared in *Unusual Suspects*. Reprinted by permission of the author.

"THE OTHER HALF" by Mick Herron © 2008. First appeared in *Ellery Queen Mystery Magazine*. Reprinted by permission of the author.

"SWORD LILIES" by Sally Spedding © 2008. First appeared in *Bluechrome Publishing*. Reprinted by permission of the author.

"LOVE HURTS" by Bill Kirton © 2008. First appeared online at SHORTBREADSTORIES.COM. Reprinted by permission of the author.

"FUNERAL WEATHER" by Kate Ellis © 2008. First appeared in *M.O.* Reprinted by permission of the author.

"A YEAR TO REMEMBER" by Robert Barnard © 2008. First appeared in *Ellery Queen Mystery Magazine*. Reprinted by permission of the author and the author's agent Gregory & Co.

"TIME OF THE GREEN" by Ken Bruen © 2008. First appeared in *Killer Year*. Reprinted by permission of the author.

"VIVISECTION" by Bernie Crosthwaite © 2008. First appeared in *M.O.* Reprinted by permission of the author.

"STAR'S JAR" by Kate Horsley © 2008. First appeared online at STORYGLOSSIA. Reprinted by permission of the author.

"THERE'S NO SUCH THING AS A VICTIMLESS CRIME" by Paul Johnston © 2009. Written for Victim Support Scotland. Reprinted by permission of the author and the author's agent Broo Doherty.

"AND HERE'S THE NEXT CLUE ..." by Amy Myers © 2008. First appeared in *M.O.* Reprinted by permission of the author.

"FRECKLES" by Allan Guthrie © 2008. First appeared online at SPINETINGLER MAGAZINE. Reprinted by permission of the author.

"HAPPY HOLIDAYS" by Val McDermid © 2008. First appeared in the *Daily Mail*. Reprinted by permission of the author and the author's agent Gregory & Co.

INTRODUCTION

Another fruitful year has passed by in the world of British crime and mystery fiction, which has witnessed the end of Ian Rankin's wildly popular Inspector Rebus Edinburgh-set series, as well as the Crime Writers' Association annual Dagger awards' achievement of a major new sponsor and television exposure, which should provide the genre with much increased visibility.

But, in the world of crime, you never say never, as the return of Sherlock Holmes from his fall at the Reichenbach Falls once ably demonstrated, and I'm most proud, in this seventh volume of our own series, to lead off with a brand new Inspector Morse story by Colin Dexter, years after the demise of the legendary Oxford cop. In addition, Val McDermid closes the book with a new tale featuring her main character Dr Tony Hill. And a genuine pleasure it is to be able to feature these much-loved characters.

A sterling year, then.

The health, vigour and imagination of the field in the UK continues to amaze me, and after poring through magazines, anthologies, newspapers, the internet and beyond, I have again been confronted by an embarrassment of fictional choices for this selection. Many writers make a welcome return but I am also pleased to greet the arrival of those authors who have not graced our pages before. They include established writers whose reputation needs no introduction: Sophie Hannah, Peter James, Tom Cain, Paul Johnston, Barbara Nadel, Barry Maitland and, from the fantasy field, the estimable Simon R. Green – accompanied on this occasion by another talented genre transfuge who makes a second appearance in the series, Jon Courtenay Grimwood – with also still relatively unknown newcomers such as Bernie Crosthwaite, Marc Werner, Kate Horsley and Tony Black.

Alongside them are many recidivists, British writers who make it a wonderful habit to contribute to our cornucopia of outstanding crime and mystery stories on a fairly regular basis and are most definitely worthy of being listed amongst the best: (in no particular order) John Harvey, Christopher Fowler, Ken Bruen, Alexander McCall Smith, Peter Robinson, Peter Lovesey, Amy Myers, Adrian Magson, Kate Ellis, Peter Turnbull, Simon Levack, Natasha Cooper, Robert Barnard, Judith Cutler, Edward Marston, Brian McGilloway, Allan Guthrie, Sally Spedding and Kevin Wignall. In addition, we also are pleased to offer a spot to established authors who've never before climbed aboard our ongoing project, such as Bill Kirton, Steve Mosby, Sarah Rayne and Mick Herron. A powerful line-up, I think you will agree, and none disappoint.

Ingenious plots, mysteries, thrills, puzzles, memorable characters, much food for thought and brilliant storytelling in both cosy and hardboiled moods – as ever, the crime and mystery short story has it all.

It's been another delightfully criminal year to remember.

Maxim Jakubowski

MR E. MORSE, BA OXON (FAILED)

Colin Dexter

In summer 2008 I returned to the UK after teaching for many years in the USA, having now been appointed Ancient History tutor at Lonsdale College, Oxford. Only then did I learn, with sadness, of the death, several years earlier, of the man with whom in 1968 I had spent one year in undergraduate digs in North Oxford – a man who remains a legend in the Thames Valley Police Force: Chief Inspector E. Morse. The Bursar of Lonsdale had decided to collect, in book form, a series of articles and anecdotes about the great man, and he invited me to contribute my own chief memory of him. For obvious reasons, I have changed the names of those principally concerned (except for myself and Morse) together with the house and the road of which I shall write. My memory of the incident that occurred there is still very vivid, and I have tried, for example, to recapture the spirit of the original dialogue by frequent use of direct quotation marks, although such a practice can only afford approximate, not verbatim, records of the conversations reported.

WE HAD FIRST met, both aged eighteen, in November 1967 when sitting the Oxford Entrance examinations. Physically Morse was of medium height, with a palish, slightly dolichocephalic face, and full light-brown hair, with the merest hint of ginger. Mentally, as I realized from the beginning, he had an extraordinarily gifted and subtle brain. We spoke together after leaving a three-hour English essay stint in the examination room. The paper we had tackled had given us all a wide range of topics, arranged in vaguely alphabetical order: Assyrian Archaeology; Buddhist Beliefs; County Boundaries and so on.

"Ye gods!" I said. "I couldn't write more than a couple of relevant sentences on any of them. Could you?"

"One or two of them, I suppose."

"Which one did you choose?"

"County Boundaries."

"Honestly? What do you know about *them*?"

"Nothing. I wrote about cricket."

"You must know a lot about cricket!"

"Very very little," Morse said, with a grin.

I knew at that point that some of us have been given a fifth gear in life, and that some others of us haven't. And it was no surprise to me to learn later on that Morse had been awarded a Major Scholarship in Classics at Lonsdale College – where we met each other again at the Michaelmas Term Freshers' party in October 1968, discovering that we had been allocated digs together in leafy North Oxford.

The childless Mr & Mrs Lloyd, with whom Morse and I spent our first year, lived at The Firs, a largish detached house in Daventry Road, off the Banbury Road, and just below the A40 Ring Road. Truth to tell, the property seemed not so well furbished and furnished as most of its neighbours, but it had plenty of space both inside and out; and Pagan and I each had a fair-sized bed-sit at the rear of the house, with a shared loo-cum-bathroom. Why "Pagan"? Well, it was the soubriquet by which he was known to his fellow under-grads, since it had leaked out that in the "Religion?" section of his University Application form he had written "High-church atheist". If we had rooms in College (which Morse, as an open scholar, would have for the next three years) we would have profited from the services of a "scout"; but things were quite satisfactory. Mrs Lloyd did virtually everything herself – cleaning, cooking, washing, ironing – and although the loo was not exactly given regular five-star treatment, we agreed not to complain. Mr Lloyd was a rather superior car-salesman at a Banbury Road garage, but his real pride and joy were the lawns at the back and front of the house which he treated (well, so I thought) with rather more affection than he did his wife; and most weekends saw him marching up and down with the lawn-mower. How did we all get on together? Pretty well, really. I took the majority of my lunches and dinners in the College Hall; Pagan, just dinners, preferring a liquid lunch in one of the city-centre hostelries. On Sundays, however, we had a regular lunch with the Lloyds, and one such occasion I recall with unusual clarity.

There were just the three of us, since Mr Lloyd was away in London at some jumbo second-hand car sale: just Pagan, myself, and Mrs Lloyd – she looking particularly attractive; and I swear I noticed Pagan glancing appreciatively more than once at the décolletage of her skimpy white blouse, its top button (by accident or design, I know not) left rather provocatively unfastened. When after the main course she had returned to the kitchen, Pagan asked:

"What's your favourite present-participle in the English language, Philip?"

For once, I was ready for him: "I'd go for 'bird-hatching'", I think. Remember when Tess sets off for the Vale of the Great Dairies? 'On a thyme-scented, bird-hatching morning in May ...' Lovely sentence."

Morse nodded. "Chapter sixteen, isn't it?"

But I was not prepared to congratulate my friend on his knowledge of Hardy's novels. Instead, I asked him what his own choice would be.

"I'll go for 'unbuttoning'," he said quietly, as Mrs Lloyd came in with the stewed plums and custard.

I mention this incident for a reason the reader may soon appreciate. Each week in term-time, either on the Monday or the Tuesday, Morse would receive a pale-blue envelope, its flap always firmly sellotaped, from someone in Lincolnshire. Morse never mentioned her – for of course it was a "her"! – not even her Christian name, although I did eventually learn it. Oh, yes!

During our first few weeks as co-lodgers, only one thing was a matter of initial discord. Morse had an ancient portable gramophone, on which continually, and sometimes continuously, he played high-lights from Wagner's *Ring* Cycle. I would myself have preferred the Beatles to Brünnhilde; but after Morse had one day given me a tutorial on the story and structure of that extraordinary work, fairly soon I began to appreciate, and later to love it. As Morse had explained: Wagner's music was never half as bad as it sounded.

We were both reading Classics, a four-year course, requiring success in two major public examinations: "Mods" after two years; "Greats" after a further two. Mods involved, mainly, translation *from* Greek and Latin, and composition *into* those languages. In these particular skills, Morse was paramount, having the facility to read each language with the fluency and speed of an average English ten-year-old following the fortunes of his favourite football team. On the other hand, Greats was centred more generally upon the history and philosophy of Greece and Rome, neither of which areas kindled much interest in Morse's mind. What fascinated him was the study of the manu-scripts of the classical authors, frequently corrupted in their transmission to future generations. He fervently believed that if only he was given the chance of considering many of the puzzling problems in these fields, he would usually make some better sense of virtually anything, like his great hero in life, A. E. Housman. It was so often a bit like making sense of a story where many of the key facts have been misreported and muddled up.

Like this one.

I had not seen much of Morse during the Michaelmas Term of our second year in Oxford. Although I was myself still with the Lloyds, he now had rooms in College; and in any case his former accommodation was in the slow process of some refurbishment. He had, I suspect, attended no more than two or three lectures in the latter half of that term; and although we occasionally sat together in Hall, we now appeared to be going very much our separate ways. Yet we did meet one morning in mid-December at the Gardenia Café in Cornmarket, quite unexpectedly, since coffee was hardly his favourite a.m. beverage. We chatted briefly, expressing mutual surprise that neither of us would be spending Christmas at home. I explained that my parents were on a Saga cruise in the Med, and that in any case I really ought to catch up on some much needed study.

Morse had nodded. He had helped me considerably during our first year together, and was clearly aware of my limitations.

"And you're staying with Helen?" he'd asked.

It seemed to me surprising that he'd referred to Mrs Lloyd by her first name – something I myself had never dared to do.

"Yes," I said. "But I'm going to Coventry for a couple of days just before Christmas. What about you?"

He had ever been reticent about his home, his parents, his siblings (if any), although I knew his father was a taxi-driver. And now, too, he was as vague as usual:

"Staying in college or burying my head in the Bodley," he said, tapping the two books beside his empty coffee-cup: *The Oxford Text of Homer*, and Autenrieth's *Homeric Dictionary*.

"I thought the College was closed over Christmas."

"Only the 22nd to the 26th. I've booked in at The Randolph those nights."

"Well, well. Not many of us could afford that."

He got to his feet and picked up his books.

"Dad's had a win on the gee-gees, Philip. *And*," he spoke very quietly, "if I can be of any help again ..."

"Thank you," I said, equally quietly, feeling strangely moved by his offer, perhaps because I'd noticed a certain sadness in his eyes as he turned to leave.

I'd noticed something else, too – no doubt about it! Acting presumably as a book-mark in the Oxford Text, there was an envelope, a pale-blue envelope. And I knew who that was from. Or, as he would have said, "from whom that was".

I was to see no more of Morse until much nearer Christmas.

On December 22 I left Oxford by rail for Coventry, where one of my best pals had arranged a party that evening – girls included, me included – and had invited me to stay overnight at his home. I was anticipating the outing with relish; but as I returned to Oxford earlyish the following morning, I was feeling sorely disappointed. The girl I was looking forward to seeing again ... Augh! Forget it! I could only recall Jane Austen's observation that often it was the *expectation* of happiness which turned out to be better than the thing itself. Anyway, I'd soon be seeing Mrs Lloyd again, although my expectations in that quarter were sadly very low.

I took a taxi from the railway station, and as I stood outside The Firs taking out my wallet, I saw immediately that something was terribly wrong. Twenty or so feet of the recently creosoted fence which ran along the front of the wide property were down, lying flat, smashed and splintered across the lawn. And clearly the stout left-hand gatepost had received a hefty bash from something, and was now leaning drunkenly a good many degrees from the vertical. As for the precious front lawn itself? Oh dear! It was churned up with sundry indentations, and criss-crossed with tyre-marks, reminiscent of an aerial photograph of the railway-tracks at Crewe station.

"What on earth …?" I began, turning to the driver.

"Dunno, mate. Some drunken sod, I s'pose."

"You hadn't noticed it before?"

"Wasn't out yesterday, was I? Shoppin' with the missus for Christmas."

For a few seconds after he had gone I stood staring at the mutilated lawn, but noticed that Mrs Lloyd's red Mini was standing in its usual place, apparently undamaged, in front of the equally undamaged doors of the double garage. Of Mr Lloyd's old Rolls Royce, which was normally parked alongside, there was no sign. I slowly walked halfway up the drive, and stopped. Pretty obviously the intruder had driven in, managed to stop, and promptly reversed out again. QED. I turned back towards the house, and there, framed in the doorway, stood the slim figure of Mrs Lloyd.

Five minutes later, we were sitting opposite each other at the kitchen table, and as she passed over my coffee, for a few seconds her delicate fingers rested upon my wrist – magical moments! – before looking at me steadily with sad, sad eyes, and told me the story.

On the previous evening she had been alone in the house. Jeff had been picked up at about 7 p.m. to go to a Christmas party in Linton Road. His own car was in for something to do with the gaskets, she thought – whatever they were. She had been watching a sit-com on

TV; and, yes, she *had* heard some sort of bang or crash at about 9.30 p.m. But it hadn't worried her much – probably the temperamental central-heating, or a firework perhaps. Anyway, she'd kept watching the rather good programme until the news at 10 p.m. Jeff had promised (almost!) to be home by just after 11 p.m., and she decided to go upstairs to bed. But before doing so, she'd put the light on in the front porch (for Jeff to find the keyhole!) and stepped outside to make sure she'd locked the Mini. "And you've seen, Philip, what's happened! Some – drunken – irresponsible – vandal – has ..."

Twin tears, like a pair of synchronized Olympic divers, were slowly sliding down her cheeks.

I reached forward and put my hand over her wrist – knowing immediately that I had overstepped the mark, for she withdrew her hand, got to her feet, dabbed her eyes, and blew her nose noisily as she reached for the kettle again.

"Did you ring the police?" I asked.

She shook her head: "Not then, no. The duty bobbies would all be out breathalizing the boozers."

"Let's just hope they breathalized that wretched man—"

"Or woman, perhaps."

"I wish you *had* rung the police immediately, though," said a new voice – that of Jeff Lloyd, who now stood at the kitchen door, unshaven, with slightly bloodshot eyes, wearing a pair of grubby beige trousers, and a new-looking flat cap, appearing more like a council road-sweeper than his usual smart-suited self, and carrying a pair of gardening gloves. He poured himself a coffee and came to stand behind his wife. "I mustn't blame the old girl, though, and I *don't* blame her. My fault, Philip," he said, "not Helen's. It's *shock*, you know, at the time. It disorientates you. If only I'd got in earlier ..."

"Anyway," Helen said as she turned round to look up at his tall figure, "we *did* ring this morning, didn't we?" Then she turned to me: "Said they'd be round asap."

Jeff Lloyd grinned weakly: "Probably early in the New Year!" He swallowed his coffee quickly and kissed his wife on the top of her head. "I'm just going to nip down to the garage. Tom's promised to try to fix the Rolls, bless him, so I'll need your car, darling." Helen dipped into her handbag for the keys, and he was gone.

I wondered, yet again, what she saw in that man. I'd read recently that seventy-five per cent of American women would willingly marry just for money, and perhaps it was the same with English women. And in this case, what if *she* had the money? That would make things even worse. But a few kindly words can go a long way; and a minute later he put his head round the door:

"Hope you'll still be joining us for Christmas dinner, Philip?"

I waited until I heard the front door slam, and the Mini spurt into life.

"Won't he be back to talk to the police?" I asked.

"They couldn't say when they'd come, and in any case *he* couldn't tell them anything. He wasn't here. Forget it, Philip! But if he's not here when the boys in blue decide to arrive, will you be prepared to stand by and give me a bit of moral support?"

I nodded happily.

It was half an hour later when the boy (singular) in blue appeared on the semi-tidied gravel drive, and when Mrs Lloyd called me through to the lounge, where for a few moments we watched the single policeman, in a black-and-white checkered hat, standing importantly beside what had formally been a splendidly carved gate, writing something with a stubby pencil on a clip-boarded sheet of paper. And a minute or so later, the three of us were standing on the front-doorstep, where our investigating officer introduced himself as Constable Watson – not exactly the best of omens! Perhaps subconsciously I had envisaged someone named "Holmes", carrying a bucket full of plaster of Paris, duly to be poured into the (admittedly) adulterated indentations of the tyre-marks. But Watson had no bucket. For myself, I could still imagine Holmes, after the merest glance, announcing to an astonished Watson the manufacturer of the tyres, their approximate mileage, and, in all likelihood, the make of the vehicle responsible.

Fanciful foolishness, of course, because Constable Watson, after a cursory look at the lawn, seemed to have reached an investigative conclusion:

"Made a bit of a mess of your lawn, hasn't it, Mrs Lloyd?"

"Not done much good to the fence, either!"

"Hope you're insured on that, madam?"

"Yes." She proceeded to recount her story, and one or two notes were added on the clipboard.

"Would the neighbours have seen or heard anything?"

Mrs Lloyd shrugged. "We've not asked, I'm afraid. You have to be in North Oxford for about ten years before you speak much to your neighbours."

Watson had clearly finished with his clipboard, and now held it by his side in his right hand whilst he removed his cap and scratched his head with the other. "Look, I ought to come clean with you, madam, and tell you that I very much doubt we shall ever have the faintest idea who was responsible for all this."

"Really, Constable? But you'd be quite wrong, you know. You see, I know exactly who was responsible for this wanton vandalism."

These were just about the most surprising words I'd ever expected to hear.

She re-opened the front door, reached behind the coat-stand, and picked up an object which she now held in front of her. "This, officer, is a whopping great clue for you. It's the number-plate, without a shadow of a doubt, which was knocked off the front of the vehicle whose owner decided to visit me last night – and who had *not* called in for a pre-Christmas sherry!"

Watson at last found his voice. "Thank you very much, madam. That may well be of some considerable value in our enquiries." He reached forward, but Mrs Lloyd drew it back from his intended grasp.

"No! My husband is in the car-business himself, and he's advised me to keep it here. He knows a great deal about car accidents, and any physical evidence required by insurance companies. Make a note of it by all means, of course, but I'm keeping it here, understood? I'm certain that you'll have little difficulty in finding the matching miscreant ... And a happy Christmas to you, officer!"

I confess to feeling sympathy with Constable Watson as for the last time he reached for his stubby pencil, and slowly and with great care, transcribed the number on to his clip-boarded sheet:

54LLY D

Was it just a coincidence that the four *letters* on the plate virtually spelled out the surname of the troubled householders?

"Well?" said Mrs Lloyd after the door had closed on our detective. "Hardly the brightest wattage bulb in the Thames Valley Force ... I just wish your pal, Pagan, was here – be good to have him around, and he'd probably invent some weird and wonderful tale for us ... Perhaps I should ring him, Philip? He *is* in Oxford, you told me."

"Yep. Not in College, though – that's virtually closed down completely from the 22nd to the 26th. Just a single porter in the Lodge, and I believe he's booked in at The Randolph, is Pagan."

"Alongside booze and books in the bar, like as not!"

"I suppose so."

"Funny, isn't it? Never seems to have much effect on him, booze. Not like me! Couple of glasses of red plonk, and I'm a tipsy little girl again. He once told me that too many double Scotches usually gave him *single* vision."

I let it go. Truth to tell, I was a bit miffed she hadn't told me earlier about the number-plate; and when she asked me if baked beans would be OK for a spot of lunch, I decided to leave her to it. But not before asking her one question:

"Where did you find the number-plate?"

"Just behind the gate-post, in the hydrangea patch. Jeff saw it when he started clearing up."

At the door I hesitated: "Would you like *me* to ring Pagan and ..."

"... put him in the picture? I'd like that very much, yes."

In the early afternoon I heard the phone ringing in the front lounge; and very soon Jeff Lloyd pushed his head round my door. "For you, Philip: Doctor Russell Hughes, he says. Not being rusticated, are we?" He grinned, and I followed him up the passage.

Dr Hughes, the Mods tutor at Lonsdale, was supervising both Morse and myself, and I'd found him a kindly and learned soul. He was so sorry to disturb me during the vac, etc; he wasn't sure if I could help, etc; but ... The burden of his call was as follows: Morse had a brilliant mind – probably the best he'd known in a decade; but the standard of some of his recent work, which he was at that very moment marking, was sadly far below expectations. Did I know any reason why this should be? Disappointments, illness, girlfriends, family, drugs, booze? I had no cause to lie to Dr Hughes – not at that point anyway – and I told him that I hadn't the faintest idea. He then told me what he saw as the stark truth of the matter: if Morse went on like this, he wouldn't even finish up with a "pass" degree, let alone a pedestrian third. And if I could in any way help, etc. With almost complete honesty, I told him that I would try very hard to do so. He gave me his direct home telephone-number, and rang off.

The only thing I had not referred to was Morse's sympathy with the widespread disillusionment and dissent of so many of his University peers. But although he attended a good many lengthy protest meetings, the only sign I witnessed of any active participation was in the Hilary Term when I observed him marching – silently – at the rear of a large and vociferous demonstration against the Vietnam war. Perhaps, at heart, he was a crypto-pacifist. But that was a personal matter, and no concern of Dr Hughes.

During that telephone conversation I had been looking around the lounge again: furniture, photographs, bookshelves, pictures; and on the lower surface of the coffee-table I spied two books a-top each other: the dark-blue hardbacked *Oxford Text of Homer*; and the paperbacked *Homeric Dictionary*. Inside the former was a slim envelope, a pale-blue envelope, addressed, in handwriting I recognized only too readily, to E. Morse Esq.

How on earth did those books get ...?

Jeff Lloyd, still in his gardening cap, was coming down the stairs as I made for my room.

"Finished on the phone, Philip?"

"Yep – all yours."

"Nothing, er, serious?"

"No. Just reminding me I'd promised him an essay on Virgil before Christmas," I lied.

"Fancy a coffee?" called Mrs Lloyd, as I walked past the kitchen, where she was making mince-pies. I went into the kitchen, sat down, and put the two books on the table.

"These are Pagan's," I said simply.

"Ah, yes, I remember. I found them in his room when the deco-rators came in. I keep trying to remember ..." she lied. "Anyway

I'm going to have a bath and a lie-down. Don't you think I deserve it?"

That day, all roads it seemed, were leading to Morse, and I went along with the traffic.

"And don't you bother *your* head – *I'll* ring Pagan."

"Today, perhaps?" she suggested quietly, as I took my coffee, took the two books, and walked back to an empty lounge.

I rang the College immediately, being told by the solitary porter that they would be open again on the 27th. At least Morse had not lied there.

"Oh dear! It's Mr Morse I was hoping to—"

The porter interrupted me. "I think I may know where he is, sir."

I too thought I knew where he was. And indeed, when I got down into Oxford, he was there, seated in the main bar of The Randolph, doing *The Times* crossword, with an almost empty glass of beer in front of him, alongside a completely empty tumbler of what (I doubted not) had been a whisky chaser.

He looked up at me: "Philip!" He pointed to the glasses: "You're just in time to replenish things. Make the Glenfiddich a large one, please."

With a half-pint of beer for myself, I sat opposite him at the round, glass-topped table, and told him simply and succinctly that Mrs Lloyd wanted to see him, adding only that there was no great rush because she was going to have a bath and a lie-down for a while.

Morse's eyes gleamed as he took a swallow of Scotch: "Lovely stuff! On Olympus they used to call it nectar, you know."

"Really?"

"Lovely *thought*, too – Helen in bed! She once told me she always slept in the altogether."

I could so easily have thrown my beer across his smiling face.

"Do you know what she wants to see me about?"

So I told him all about the felony inflicted on The Firs, and about Helen's imbecilic interrogation by our vacuous detective. And (what a strange man Morse was) he interrupted only once, querying, with a grin, whether Watson had brought a tape-measure along with him. As a climax to my tale, I took out a postcard on which I had written the details of the give-away number-plate. But Morse seemed strangely unimpressed, merely echoing Watson's words virtually verbatim: "Could well be of value to police enquiries."

I raised my eyebrows.

"Could equally well be stolen, though," continued Morse. "I just hope she had enough nous not to hand it over to your dumb detective."

He handed back the postcard, and wrote in the final clue in the grid. "Good clue that!

'It's nice is scrambled eggs (7)'. Anagram of 'it's nice'—"

"Thank you, Pagan! I just thought you'd be interested in knowing why Mrs Lloyd wanted—"

"I *am*, Philip. And we'll get a bus this very minute. Well ..." he hesitated. "Perhaps we don't want to find her in the bath, do we?" (Or *do* we, I wondered.) "Time for one for the bus-route?"

"No!" I said.

After a visit to the Gents, we walked down the broad front steps of the hotel, where Morse was stopped by the senior concierge, Roy, and was handed the two items he'd inadvertently left on the small table: *The Times*, and *A. E. Housman: Collected Poems*.

The bus service up and down the Banbury Road must be the best of any road in any city in the UK; and barely a quarter of an hour later the pair of us stood in front of The Firs. There, by the light of an adjoining street-lamp, Morse bent down briefly to examine the damaged gate-post, a white chip of bare wood showing through the creosote, before turning, in the ever-darkening dusk, to survey the indentations on the lawn.

"Should have brought that tape-measure – *and* a torch," he said.

I possessed one of these items, anyway. And when I got back from my room with it, I stood around, feeling vaguely helpless, as Morse flashed my torch's beam randomly hither and thither, on the lawn, on the drive, on the Mini ...

"Somebody washed Helen's car recently," he said quietly.

I shrugged. "Must have been Jeff Lloyd, I should think."

"Where's *his* car?" he asked, peering through the garage windows.

"Convalescing down at the garage – blown a couple of gaskets."

"I wonder what they are," mumbled Morse, as he turned to me.

"Any thoughts about things yet, Pagan?"

"Certainly! The car that came through the fence, you mean? The tyres were Michelins, comparatively new, and done about 8,000 miles, no more; driven by a left-handed lady who rides the clutch a little too much; and purchased in Reading about two years ago. That puts your PC to shame, agreed?"

"Don't take any notice of him, Philip!" Mrs Lloyd stood at the front door, a winter coat covering her bathrobe; and Morse walked up to her and put his arms around her in a bear-hug; and she, in turn, put her arms around him tightly. Fortunately, the scene was fairly short-lived.

"Come in, both of you! And stop your teasing, Pagan!" She turned to me.

"He's no genius, Philip! He's just noticed the make of my tyres, looked at my mileometer, remembered I'm left-handed, saw which year the car reg letter is, as well as the Reading garage sticker on the rear-window. QED. Forget it all, Philip – he was just trying to tease you. We *know* whose car it was – and you've told Pagan all about *that*, I'm sure." I felt very silly about it all.

"Shan't be long," I said, as I left them in the lounge and got back to my room. I was missing something, lots of things, here. For example, why had Morse spoken so flippantly, as I now realized, about Mrs Lloyd's own car? What, above all, had Morse's classics volumes been doing *in her lounge*, since I was absolutely certain that Morse had been studying those same two books a week earlier? Yet Mrs Lloyd said she'd had them the whole term! I shook my head. You lied to me, Mrs Lloyd! There was just the one thing that I knew, and that Morse didn't know (or *did* he, perhaps?): that I had found the letter. Not that I felt anything but guilt about it ever since Dr Hughes's telephone call. But, yes, I still knew something about that secretive soul, Pagan, that he had never mentioned to anyone else in the world (or *had* he perhaps?). The books were now safely installed with *me*, and I took the letter out and read it yet again.

SALLY DOWNES

12.xii.69

My dearest,

Read those first two words again – for you
will ever be my dearest. We both knew that
I would soon have to make the biggest
decision of my life – between you and
mother, and it's with despairing sadness I
write to tell you that it must be mother.
She is now so terribly handicapped with
this devastating MS, so fragile, so
vulnerable, that had you seen the joy that
leapt into her old eyes when I told her
she would always – *always* – have me with
her, you would have begun to understand.

Our days together this Christmas in
Oxford would have been the happiest of
my life, and of yours, I know that, my
darling. Please don't write to me or ring
me – that would be too much for me to
bear. Just remember the Kipling lines you
taught me: "Thou wast allus my lad – my
very own lad, and no one else".

S.

And *then*, suddenly and almost miraculously, the light dawned on
my bemused and second-class brain. I looked a last time at the name
that headed the letter, before refolding it and replacing the envelope
in the Oxford Text. It explained a lot – not everything of course, but
such an awful lot.

I had been sitting staring into space for several minutes when I
heard a soft knock at my door. I knew who it was.

"Can I come in?" said Morse quietly, holding the *Collected
Poems* in his hand. I gestured towards the other chair and he sat

down, placing Housman on top of Homer: "I get pretty careless, don't I, about leaving books around."

There was a minute or so of silence between us before he came out with it: "I know you've read the letter."

I nodded: "Lots of times, I'm afraid. I'm so sorry, Pagan. It's like breaking a trust and—"

"I'd have done the same myself, Philip. Sally might have blamed you, but I don't."

"There's something else, though," I said, as I took the white card from my pocket. But he waved it away.

"I guessed you'd twigged, Philip, because *I've* got a higher opinion of your intelligence than you have."

"Doesn't explain all that much, though."

"No, it doesn't ... Do you want me to tell you what happened?"

Of course I did. And he told me.

His father was in the car-business, and he'd seen in one of the Auto mags a list of personalized number-plates, amongst which was one that quite clearly would have been of considerable interest and pride to Sally Downes. And Morse went for it, clearing his worries about a Christmas present, and simultaneously clearing his own bank-balance. He had planned to give it to her on Christmas morning in their room at The Randolph.

On the night of the "incident", he had received a telephone call at The Randolph from Helen telling him, quite truthfully, that Jeff was out at a staff party at The Linton Lodge Hotel and wouldn't be back till, well, "pretty late" – thankfully to return, as he'd gone, in a taxi, because the Rolls was undergoing some minor mechanical operation. So! So she wondered why *she* shouldn't have an enjoyable evening, too. *She* was game, if *he* (Morse) was.

He was.

She'd parked momentarily outside The Randolph, poked her head inside the bar, seen him sitting there reading his Homer, and off they drove. Where to? The Trout Inn out at Wolvercote – no more than two or three miles away. Super time together! He, having drunk perhaps a little too much earlier, had resolutely stuck to beer; she, a little irresolutely, perhaps, had been rather more liberal; and each had taken a goodly share of complimentary counter-top canapés. In short they'd been mellowing gently and sentimentally; and, yes, he'd told Helen about the "Dear John" letter, and about the intended Christmas present for his beloved. Indeed, he had *shown* her the letter safely ensconced in the Oxford Text, which for once he'd remembered to pick up when Helen had called for him, but which later that same evening he'd forgotten to retrieve from the back of the Mini. Just after 10 p.m. they had agreed they should be getting away. But Helen had declared herself, she thought, incapable of driving back safely the short distance to The Firs.

"So," finished Morse, "*I* drove back here, pissed as the proverbial Triturus vulgaris. And … I don't think you'll need me to continue, except to say that I wasn't *really* teasing you, was I, Philip? Helen was quite adamant about *not* ringing the police that night. They'd be sure to breathalize the driver – *me*. And that would hardly be good news, would it? Driving without a licence, drunk driving, dangerous driving – all three, like as not. Anyway, that's all there is to say."

"No, it isn't. You've not told me about the next bit."

Morse frowned. "Ah, yes. You mean the number-plate business. It would have been bloody stupid *not* to have thought of that. And Helen agreed. We'd both sobered up a lot by then, and it was Helen now who reversed the Mini over the lawn – twice! – to make a real muck-up of things. Then straight down to The Randolph again, where I took the lift up to my room, put the number-plate into an Elliston's bag, got back into the car. So quick it all was, Philip! Helen parked the Mini in its usual spot, got a couple of buckets of water and washed down the front of it in case there were traces of creosote, whilst I sluiced down the mud from the tyres. Helen wasn't worried at all about any dent in the front: said she'd acquired enough of those already! Then I walked up to the Banbury Road bus-stop and – *voilà*! You now know as much about things as I do.'

Even more keenly than earlier I sensed that he was lying to me. It might all add up in a fairly logical way but … So I put my thoughts into words: "Why didn't you leave everything just as it was? You tell me you'd both already decided not to ring the police until today

– when *you'd* be back in The Randolph, and when Mrs Lloyd would be back to her customary sober self – unlike you!"

Morse was pained by my outburst. "You don't understand, do you? It's one helluva shock – *shock* – when you do something like that. It's dark and you're jolted and frightened and panicky, and all you're thinking about is how—"

Before he could finish, the door had opened and Mrs Lloyd walked in, sparkling and sweetly scented. "What cock-and-bull story has he been telling you now, Philip?"

"Just about, er, you know, how ..."

"Did you believe him?"

I said it quietly but firmly: "No!"

She smiled at me. "Don't be cross with him! I think I know exactly the line he's taken, the lies he's been telling you. But please understand why he did it. He did it to paint me as a completely blameless person in all this. But I'm *not* blameless, Philip, far from it. You want to know who was driving the Mini? It was *me*."

The news sank in. Was it so much of a surprise? "But why all this rather silly subterfuge? I was just asking Pagan the same thing when you came in."

"Let me tell you. In six weeks' time I've agreed to stand as a Conservative councillor for the Wolvercote ward. If any rumours – or facts! – get out about this, it will be curtains for my chances, my licence will be endorsed, and I can see the article in the *Oxford Mail*: 'Mrs Helen Lloyd, unsuccessful aspirant to municipal honours ...'. So I shall be eternally grateful to Pagan here for what he did. But it's no great shakes, Philip: no one's been injured; the Mini got off lightly; no one's suffered, not even the insurance company, because Jeff, bless him, has refused point blank to put in any claim; and he tells me he's going to dig up the lawn and re-seed it."

She said all this so genuinely and quietly that I knew I would probably be on her side whatever she did.

"There's one thing, Mrs Lloyd. If it's any consolation, *I'd* vote for you – if I had a vote, of course."

"*I* wouldn't, Helen," broke in Morse. "But if you've got a glass of anything going? Glenfiddich, say, or ..."

Mrs Lloyd turned to me and placed her hand on my shoulder: "Would *you* like a glass of something, Philip?"

Jeff was in the lounge just finishing a phone call to a fencing-firm as the three of us trooped in. "… No, only about four, five yards … Fine! … Second week in Jan, then … Fine! Thanks, Jim … Bye."

"Is that our punctured palisade?" his wife asked.

Jeff smiled and took her hand. "Yep. Soon be all tickety-boo again."

"Has Tom fixed the Rolls yet? I'm out all day on the 28th, you know."

"All in hand, darling." He turned to Morse and me. "Wonderful mechanic, Tom is. One of the old school. Pride in his work and all that. His missus hates going on holiday with him, because whenever he sees some poor sod parked in a lay-by with his head stuck under the bonnet, he just *has* to stop. Can't help it!"

Morse looked down with displeasure into his glass ("So sorry we've no Scotch, Pagan.") as we sampled the red plonk, and said he must soon be going. But before he left, Jeff Lloyd had asked him a question.

"What's the etymology of 'tickety-boo'?"

"Dunno. But you can spell it with either one 't' or two in the middle."

"How on earth do you—?"

"Crosswords," said Morse as he left. "Been wasting my time with 'em since I was eleven."

And, yes, I knew all about that. In College, his fellow undergrads would always go to him when any cryptic clue defeated them. Some of the dons, too.

I slept badly that night of the 23rd, falling into the arms of Morpheus (as Homer would say) about 5 a.m., and only waking well after eight o'clock. The room seemed very cold to me, and I stayed a-bed reading for more than an hour before getting up and dressing. The whole house was as cold as hotel toast, and empty, with the only sign of activity the flat-capped owner still raking the disfigured hash-marks on the lawn, and clearly, earlier, having stacked the pieces of cracked fence neatly within the borders.

It was almost eleven when I finally ventured out that bright and blustery Christmas Eve morning, where I saw that the concreted area in front of the double-garage was empty.

"No cars?" I said.

"No. Helen's at the Tory Club. And perhaps I'll get mine back today. Not that worried, though – time I bought a cheaper chariot. High time!"

"Gaskets, you said."

"*And* pistons *and* ... you name it."

I left him still energetically pulling the rake back and forth, and knowing, doubtless, that he'd need *some* automobile if he was to continue surfing the locality for bargains he could snap up for Grove Street Garage to sell at a decent profit.

I walked slowly down the Banbury Road, calling in at the Summertown Newsagents for *The Times*. Both Morse and I had been sorry when the Lloyds cancelled the paper-boy delivery – especially Morse. He could sometimes complete the cryptic crossword before the timer pinged for his boiled egg. I walked further on to The Dewdrop, had a pint of Courage beer, and then another with a baked potato; and thought of my father's life-long interest in classic cars ... just wondering perhaps whether he might be interested in a shaky but shiny old Rolls.

On my way back I would be passing Grove Street Garage; and I decided to call in and see if Mr Lloyd had been lucky yet. But very few cars were in the large, open space where all repairs were carried out; and very few signs of life either. I walked up to a grimy-faced young lad changing a tyre.

"Mr Lloyd around?"

"No."

"Tom?"

"Got the 'flu, aint 'e – back next week 'e 'opes."

The Rolls was there though, and I sauntered across to it: classy lines still, and clearly in the past the recipient of much TLC.

My head was whirling as I began to retrace my steps to Daventry Road. Something, somewhere, was terribly wrong.

It was on the morning of the 27th, Christmas now over, that from a public phone-box in Summertown I rang Lonsdale College.

"Back in business?" I ventured.

"Certainly, sir. Can I help you?"

"Just wondering if Mr Morse is back with you."

"Half an hour ago. I'll put you through to his rooms. Who shall I say's calling?"

I put the phone down guiltily and walked to the bus-stop, almost immediately lucky.

"City centre, please."

Lucky again at The Randolph, where at the Porters' Lodge on the right, Roy emerged from some inner sanctum, and without any apparent suspicion answered my carefully rehearsed questions about "Mr Morse" and his recent nocturnal attendances there.

"Yes, sir, I know him well," he grinned.

"Keeps your bar-girls up latish, he tells me."

"Ailish – she's our bar-boss – she's always had a soft spot for him."

"Not Christmas Day, surely?"

"Nor Christmas Eve, I don't think. I was off both days. But he was definitely around the two previous evenings."

"Monday the 22nd?"

"Yes, I remember that evening well. He *did* go out, but that was latish."

"Ah, that's just what I thought. Oh dear! We'd arranged to meet here at about, oh, about er ..."

"It was about tennish, sir. But he came back about eleven, I think. Can't really be sure I'm afraid. But I do remember he left a Christmas card for Ailish –" he reached into a pigeon-hole behind him – "and I put it ... here it is."

He showed me a sealed envelope addressed to AILISH, and dated 22.xii.69.

So! My old buddy Pagan had been lying to me consistently.

What it all amounted to, I wasn't at all sure, but I was getting a somewhat clearer picture of things as I began to walk back up to North Oxford. And just before I reached Summertown, my vision crystallized quite beautifully. Unlike Morse, who boasted that he never took any physical exercise "on principle", I had put on some surplus avoirdupois over my four terms in Oxford, and on several occasions on my long walk I resisted the temptation offered at the regular bus-stops. Most definitely my mind was profiting as I gradually reached what for me was a strange and wholly original conclusion, with the focus of my thoughts now centred quite firmly on – yes, on the Lloyds.

What was it that had struck me so suddenly and so forcefully concerning the Lloyd household? It would have struck even a dullard within a few weeks: no gardener; no cleaning lady; no laundry collection; no coffee mornings; no dinner parties; no drinks-cabinet; no paper-boy; little heating; one telephone; one TV set; two undergrads; and the likely sale of a vintage Rolls. In short, and quite unexpectedly, I knew, almost for certain that the Lloyds were pretty hard-up. There were one or two things I needed to check up on, if that were possible, but to be honest I felt rather proud of my own belated brilliance. Quickly, as yet another bus passed me, I looked in at the garage workshop where the greasy youth was seated on an outsize tyre eating a cheese sandwich. No one else.

Head in the clouds, I had almost reached the turning into Daventry Road when I heard a voice behind me: "Philip?" I should have known! Morse was seated on a public bench with Housman on his lap. "Come and join me," he said.

I stood my ground. "What for?"

He hesitated momentarily. "I know you want to get on but ... well, I just don't want you to make a fool of yourself, that's all. You've been a good pal to me, and I want ..."

Slowly I sat down beside him: "Please explain yourself, Pagan."

He nodded. "The College porter told me he had a call from someone for me, and I guessed it was you when you wouldn't give your name. Then Roy at The Randolph has just told me that someone had called in and asked some strange questions about me. And again I knew it was you. I know something else too, Philip. You thought I'd done something dishonest and dishonourable, and perhaps you were right, of course. Want to talk to me about it?"

"Not really, no."

"Do you want *me* to tell you what it is?"

"Not really, no."

So he told me then and there.

"It's probably occurred to you, a bit late in the day, what the situation is between Jeff and Helen – not just maritally but financially."

Well he was half right, wasn't he? I don't know how he knew, but he always tended to know things before anyone else. So I surrendered and told him (though not everything) and gave him my reasons. "In short, Pagan, I think the Lloyds are seriously short of cash and that this perhaps explains one or two things, things that so far seem pretty inexplicable."

"You're right," said Morse. "So short of cash they'll not be able to catch up on their mortgage payments until my old room is ready again."

"Won't he get quite a bit for the Rolls?"

"What makes you think he'll ever sell that?"

"Well, he sort of suggested ..."

"Would you believe him or me?"

"Neither of you."

"Wrong answer, Philip. Jeff Lloyd is a very fine fellow, please believe me."

"If you say so," I said, nonchalantly enough, but Morse's confident assertion was troubling me slightly. "Tell me, come on! Who's your source of information for all this stuff?"

"Helen, you know that."

"And I suppose you'll be asking dear Helen if you can have your old room back when—"

"Wrong again!" snapped Morse. "She did ask me if I'd like to come back, but I told her I had to be in College – if that's OK with *you*!"

It was the only touch of genuine anger I'd ever seen in his face. And it was my turn now to show my own exasperation and, yes, a fair measure of anger, too.

"Doesn't worry me either way, Pagan. What does worry me and disappoint me such a lot is that you *lied* to me about the 22nd. You were never at The Trout! You were in The Randolph till about ten o'clock that night, when you went off with Mrs Lloyd. Or am I wrong yet again?"

"Carry on, Sherlock!"

"Two possibilities, Pagan. First, Mrs Lloyd had been out earlier that evening, to a party perhaps, where she had too much gin or whatever, drove herself home, and *into* her home – with consequences that are getting too tedious to repeat. She couldn't have been all *that* tipsy because she knew she had someone who could be absolutely guaranteed to help her – you! She picked you up, drove back here, where you sorted things out for her, and still sober enough to have the bright idea of your number-plate. That was your plan, and you both stuck to it. Yes?"

"Is it my turn to speak now?" asked Morse quietly. "You said there were two possibilities."

"Yes, there are," I blurted out, "and I'm perfectly sure you know what the other one is: *Mrs Lloyd had never been out drinking at all that night.*"

"Well, well—"

A sudden squall of rain swept sideways across the street. We got to our feet, and quickly and silently walked down to The Firs, where the lawn was looking pretty neat, with parallel rake-marks across the now-levelled churn-up.

Mrs Lloyd's voice rang down the passage as we entered the rear door: "That you, Philip?"

"Only me, yeah."

Morse and I sat opposite each other in my room, our rain-sodden coats hanging behind the door.

"Carry on, Sherlock!" Morse repeated.

So I told Morse of my two discoveries. First, that Jeff Lloyd had lied to me about Tom What's-his-name already sorting out the blown gaskets at the garage, because Tom What's-his-name had been in bed with flu all over the Christmas period, and there was no other competent mechanic in the workshop. Second, that there was (is!) a dent low down on the passenger-side bumper of the Rolls, and the front grill was (is!) still showing signs of being in contact with something recently creosoted.

For about thirty seconds Morse sat staring at the threadbare patch of carpet beneath his wet shoes. "What are you going to do about it?" he asked finally.

"I just don't know, Pagan. Nothing, I suppose. What I *do* know is that I deserve better than being lied to by you, by Mrs Lloyd, and by Jeff Lloyd."

"So you think, Philip," said Morse slowly, "that it was Jeff who drove the Rolls through the fence. Right?"

"Yes, and I *know* it was, because it explains everything, which is far more than do your own puerile and futile fabrications. Mrs Lloyd heard the crash – of course she did! – and found her husband a bit dazed and shaken sitting in the driving seat. He didn't know what to do, and she didn't know what to do – except to go to you, Pagan. Which she did. And remember one key fact: she was completely sober. What was absolutely vital was that the police should not be informed straightaway about what had happened. Why? Because he had everything to lose that night. Had he been breathalized then, he would at the very least have had his licence endorsed, and much more likely lost his licence completely. *And certainly so if he had a previous endorsement.* Lost his job and—" But Morse had got to his feet and stood by the door. "He *does* have an endorsement, Philip. Say no more." Then he stepped into the passage and shouted: "Jeff? Jeff? Come down to Philip's room, will you?" Sometimes I used to be amazed that Morse was only six months older than I was.

At Morse's behest Mrs Lloyd had already joined us, taking one of the seats, whilst I sat on the floor. Almost immediately Morse had taken the main chair, both literally and metaphorically. Mr Lloyd was with us, but only for a minute or so: "Can't stay. Just had a call from Tom. The old girl's ready to come home, he says." He was his usually snappy, well-groomed self once more, blue-suited, with highly polished black shoes, and the flat cap incongruously perched on his head. Had he observed my curious glances? *Must* have done, for he tapped the cap and smiled. "It's OK Philip – on Helen's strict instructions. She says she's not going to see me forget her latest present. It'll be off as soon as I get out of the house, though." Neither Morse nor I had said a single word to compromise the apparently promising prospect of the day before him. Mrs Lloyd explained to us: "Prematurely-opened Christmas present! Now Jeff's gone," she turned specifically to me, "Pagan says I ought to fill in the few things you don't know, Philip. I won't bore you with all the details because you already know them. It's just what happened immediately after my tiny universe was shaken by the Big Bang. All right?"

She proceeded to tell me how she remembered every small detail of
the Rolls and of finding him, still silently stonkered behind the
steering-wheel, safety-belt still round him, with a nasty-looking cut
at the top of his forehead just below the hair-line. Concussed at the
time, that was for sure, but thank heaven he'd managed to jam on
the brakes and bring the car to a standstill. She'd switched off the
head-lights, brought him a mug of steaming black coffee, and sat
beside him in the passenger-seat, dabbing his forehead with a flannel.
Not half as bad as it looked, really; and gradually he'd become
slightly coherent and stupidly apologetic. *And* stinking of whisky.
After a second mug of black coffee, he was sobering up considerably; and after a few minutes he was able to get out of the car and
to stagger along with her support to the front lounge, where she put
an old sheet over the settee, gave him two Codeine tablets, and told
him to lie back, and to close his eyes. And (Helen finished) very soon
he had fallen into a deep, drunken slumber, with an absurd, strangely
contented smile around his mouth.

I had been listening attentively, and could not really expect much
more, except to ask what had happened to the Rolls.

Helen gestured to Morse, and it was he who finished off the story.

"Well, after all the – you're right, Philip! – the rather childish
machinations which you know all about, I got into the Rolls, and
with considerable diffidence and difficulty – it's one of those double-
de-clutch cars – managed to back it out and drive it to the Grove
Street Garage – Helen had the keys and followed me in the Mini—"

"Cleverly going backwards and forwards a couple of times over
the lawn first," interrupted Helen.

"—and Bob's your avunculus!" concluded Morse.

Helen got to her feet. "I must be off. Awful lot of ironing to do.
And there's nothing more to say, Philip, except to thank you all over
again. But you will promise, please, PLEASE, never to say a word to
anyone about all this while Jeff and I are still around."

She placed a kiss on the top of my head, and at that moment she
could have asked anything of me and I would have obeyed.

"Promise, PROMISE!" I echoed gladly.

"Fancy a quiet glass down at The Dewdrop?" asked Morse after
she had gone.

But I declined. "I've not finished my Virgilian masterpiece yet."

"You satisfied with things now?" asked Morse, rather hesitantly I thought.

I mused a while: "I'm just glad I didn't ask Mr Lloyd to take that wretched cap off!"

"Mm!"

Again Morse seemed strangely hesitant. Then what he said surprised me completely.

"Can you keep a big secret, Philip? *Can* you? After what you just said to Helen, I—"

"Course I can! What—?"

"I'm afraid it wouldn't have been very enlightening for you to have a look at Jeff's forehead."

"I ... I don't think I understand."

"*There isn't any cut on Jeff Lloyd's forehead.*"

"You can't mean ...?"

"You gave me a splendid run-down on the Lloyds' economy drive, didn't you? Do you honestly think that Jeff would have ordered a taxi there *and* back to that party of his on the 22nd at the Linton Lodge, only a twenty-five minute walk away? If a taxi had brought him *back* late that night – about half-past eleven, Helen tells me – there would have been some immediate and almighty kerfuffle – etymology again uncertain, Philip! – from the taxi-driver, and like as not—"

"You mean ...?"

"I mean Jeff *walked* home late that night, to save his money, *and* to sober up a bit, or to sober up a lot."

I was utterly stunned. "You mean it *wasn't ... Jeff Lloyd who was driving the Rolls?*"

Morse nodded. "I mean just that, Philip."

Once more Morse had been six furlongs ahead of the field, and quite assuredly, unlike on several future occasions, running on the correct racecourse. I felt compelled to find an answer to that final question.

"I'm quite sure you know what I'm going to ask you now, Pagan."

"You'd be right for a change, Philip."

Nevertheless I asked it: "*Who was it then who was driving the Rolls?*"

"You know perfectly well yourself. Christmas is the occasion for the giving and receiving of presents, is it not? The Magi started all that stuff, although there's considerable doubt in higher theological circles whether there ever *were* any Wise Men. But even I was willing to join in all that goodwill. I'd bought *my* Christmas present for Sally, remember? And somebody else had decided to deliver *his* Christmas present personally to his pal, Jeff Lloyd – somebody who was quite incapable of passing anyone he found fiddling underneath the bonnet of a broken-down car without stopping to sort out the trouble; someone who, like Jeff himself, probably couldn't keep his job if he got run in by the rozzers for drunk-driving – an offence of which he was most undoubtedly and totally guilty. *And he'd been at the Garage party.*" It was my turn now to nod as Morse continued:

"Helen drove him home to Kidlington that night. He's a wonderful chap and she was glad to be able to help him."

"You sound as if you know him."

"Not really. But I did go to see him yesterday. In fact he didn't seem to recognize me from the night before. Huh! He's fully recovered from his fictional flu, though, and he tells me he'll be back at work tomorrow, with a plaster across his forehead. He's going to say that his missus had hit him across the head with a roasting-tin. She's a lovely woman, by the way. Wouldn't hurt a hair on his head."

"And you mean Jeff Lloyd agreed to all this just to save Tom What's-his-name his job, his reputation, and all that?"

"Don't you remember me telling you what a good fellow Jeff was, too?"

Yes, I did remember.

Morse was right.

And very soon he was gone, and I sat alone in my room for ten minutes or so, taking in everything, and deciding to go out for a stroll to clear my head.

Helen Lloyd was prodding a garden-fork into the hydrangea patch as I walked out. "Can I ask you a question, Mrs Lloyd?"

"Try me!"

"Why was Pagan so anxious to keep the number-plate?"

"Perhaps there's a chance that Sally will write to him again? A chance her mother may die soon, perhaps?"

"Don't know," I muttered.

She smiled openly: "I suppose there's a much more obvious reason, though. It had cost him an awful lot of money, and he said he'd probably try to sell it back to the dealer."

She looked up at me, still smiling. "Always a bit on the tight side where money's concerned, isn't he?"

I turned to leave, but had one last question: "Why was it you turned to Pagan first of all when you needed help? Why *him*?"

"That's the easiest question I've been asked this whole wretched holiday, Philip. You see, I fell in love with him."

"And did he ... does he ...?"

"Reciprocate?"

Her smile had suddenly saddened, and slowly she shook her head.

Morse completed Mods, with, it was rumoured, the second highest marks of the year, but decided thereafter to discontinue his Classics Degree with Greats. He spent two years at the Patent Office in London before joining the Thames Valley Police. The rest is history. The Lloyds emigrated to Canada in 1978, but there has been no news of them since. Grove Street Garage is now a block of flats, but of the Rolls I have discovered nothing. For nostalgic reasons I walked along Daventry Road a week after my return to Oxford, and (mirabile dictu) watched awhile as the current owner of "The Firs" was creosoting a sturdy looking garden-fence. Should any reader reprimand me gently for forgetting my promise to the Lloyds, it should be noted that they are no longer "still around", and in fact seem wholly forgotten. But no, not wholly, since not infrequently there drift back into my mind some memories of one of them.

When I returned to College after the Christmas vac of the year in which Morse had left Lonsdale, awaiting me in the Porters' Lodge was a brown-papered parcel containing a Christmas present. It was the rather tattered paperbacked Homeric

Dictionary, inscribed in which I found the words: "Hunc librum Philippo, amico suo fideli, dedit Paganus". *It is the most precious book in my whole library.*

Philip Day (Lonsdale College, Oxford) 2008

GHOSTS

John Harvey

IT WAS MID-MORNING, and Kiley was in his office two floors above a charity shop in Tufnell Park, stranded between his second cup of coffee and his third. *Investigations*, read the ad in the local press, *Private and Confidential. All kinds of security work undertaken. Ex-Metropolitan Police.* The absence of carpet made it easier to hear footsteps on the stairs. A pause and then a knock.

She was late-thirties, dressed ten years younger, and looked all of forty-five, with the eyes of someone who woke up every day expecting to be disappointed and was rarely, if ever, disabused.

"Jack Kiley? Rita Barnes."

Her hand was all cheap rings and bone.

Kiley knew the name and a moment later he knew why.

"Bradford Barnes, he was my son."

The flowers had spread across the pavement close to the spot less than a hundred metres away where he'd been killed; tiny candles had burned through the night. Photographs and messages taped to the wall. *Always remembered. A tragic waste.* Bradford had been on the way home from a party, not late, a little after twelve, and had inadvertently brushed the shoulder of a young woman heading the other way. When he'd stopped to apologise, one of the men with her had raised his voice and then his fist. Punches flew and then a knife. When the group sauntered off laughing they left Bradford where he lay. A still-warm statistic, choking on his own blood. The twenty-second young person to have been stabbed to death in the capital that year and still months to go. Gang stuff, drug deals gone sour; the wrong look, the wrong word, the wrong place at the wrong time. Disrespect.

"A year ago next week he was killed," Rita Barnes said, "three days short of his birthday, an' the police still in't got a bloody clue."

The flowers had long since faded and been swept away; the photographs torn down.

She took an envelope from her bag and counted the notes out on his desk. "There's two hundred and fifty. I'll get more. Find the bastard as did it, okay?"

What was he supposed to say? It was a waste of his time and her money?

Well, he had the time.

When she'd gone he put in a call to a DI he knew at the local nick. Jackie Ferris met him in the back room of The Assembly House, its dark wood panelling and ornamented windows harking back to palmier days.

"Not got a clue, that's what she says?" Still on duty, Ferris was drinking lemon and lime.

"She's wrong?"

"We've had more than a clue since day one. Jason Means. It was his girlfriend Barnes bumped into. He's got form and a mouth to go with it, but forensics didn't give us shit and, surprise, surprise, no one's talking. Least, not to us." Ferris raised her glass. "You might have more luck."

Rachel Sams lived on the seventh floor of an eight-floor block close to the closed-down swimming pool on Prince of Wales Road. Three of the flats on her level were boarded up and padlocked fast. The first two occasions Kiley called she refused to open the door and then, when she did, it was only to slam it in his face. It took a fierce squall of rain – Rachel hunched against the wind as she manoeuvred a buggy laden with supermarket carrier bags and containing a wailing two-year-old – for Kiley to open negotiations.

"Here, let me help."

"Piss off!"

But she stood back while, after freeing the bags and handing them to her, he lifted the buggy and led the way.

Kiley followed her into the flat and, when she didn't complain, closed the door behind him. The interior was dominated by a wide-screen plasma TV, the furniture, most of it, third- or fourth-hand. Toys were scattered, here and there, across the floor. While Rachel changed the child's nappy, Kiley found a jar of instant coffee in the kitchen.

They sat at either end of the sagging settee while the boy piled wooden bricks on top of one another, knocked them down with a loud whoop and started again.

"Darren, for Christ's sake."

"He's Jason Means' boy?" Kiley said.

"What of it?"

"Jason see him much?"

"When he can be bothered."

"Bradford Barnes' mother came to see me, a week or so back."

"So?"

"She wants to know what happened to her son."

"She buried him, didn't she? What else she wanna know?"

"She wants to know who killed him. Wants some kind of – I don't know – justice, I suppose."

"Yeah, well, she ain't gonna find it here."

Kiley held her gaze until she looked away.

After that he called round every week or so, sometimes bringing a small present for the boy.

"Listen," Rachel said, "if you reckon this is gonna get you into my knickers ..."

But, stuck up there on the seventh floor, she didn't seem overburdened with friends and now, as soon as he arrived, Darren scrambled up into his lap and happily pulled his hair. Kiley hadn't mentioned Bradford Barnes again.

Ten days short of Christmas, the sky a low, flat unpromising grey, he got round to the flat to find Rachel hurling bits and pieces over the balcony, tears streaming down her face.

"That bastard! That lousy bastard!"

Kiley tried to calm her down and she lashed out, drawing blood from his lip. When he finally got her back inside, she was still shaking; Darren cowering in the corner afraid.

"One of my mates rung an' told me, he's only gettin' married, i'n it? To that skanky whore from down Stockwell. Saw it in Facebook or somethin'." Picking up a half-empty mug, she hurled it against the wall. "Well, he's gonna learn he can't treat me like that, i'n it? He's gonna pay, yeah? Pay."

Kiley listened while she told him what had happened that night, how Jason Means had stabbed Bradford Barnes three times, once in the neck and twice in the chest, and then walked off laughing. He phoned Jackie Ferris and listened while Rachel told her story again, then promised to look after Darren while the two of them went to the station so that Rachel could make a statement.

Three days later, Jason Means was arrested.

Rita Barnes had tears in her eyes when she came to thank him and ask what more she owed him and Kiley said to forget it, it was fine. He would have given the two-fifty back if it hadn't been for a little matter of paying the rent.

"You're sure?"

"Sure."

She kissed him on the cheek.

That night, Kiley walked past the spot where Bradford Barnes had been killed. If you looked closely, you could just make out the marks where the photos had been taped, a young man smiling out, his life ahead of him, ghosts on the wall.

THE BLOOD PEARL

Barry Maitland

"EVENING, BEN. THE usual?"

"Please, Sam." I sank with a groan of relief on to my usual stool at the end of the bar.

"Hard day?"

"Aren't they all?"

Sam passed over the double Scotch, and as I sipped thankfully he said, "Lady was in earlier, asking for you."

"Oh no." Even here I wasn't safe from them. It wasn't enough that I was with them all day long, grinding through the exercises, slaving over the tricky vowels and fricatives, lurching around the unpredictable pitfalls of the English language. It wasn't that they weren't keen – quite the opposite. They had strong family and money pressures from back home to make them want to gobble it all up, as fast as I could feed it to them. They dogged my steps, imploring my undivided attention to their painful efforts and demanding my contact details so they could phone or e-mail me at any time of the day or night to check some point. "But please Ben, what is difference between *there, their, they're*?" "Dear Ben, do I say *cough* like *plough* or *tough*?"

I didn't know they'd stalked me to the pub, but I wasn't surprised. It was only a matter of time. I contemplated moving on to some other watering hole, but what was the point?

"Ben. Finally tracked you down."

I spun around in my seat, slopping my Scotch, startled by the familiar voice. "Paula ..."

We hadn't met in maybe two years and I could see straight away that they had taken their toll. She looked older, tired, and I saw she was thinking much the same about me. Mind you, she was still the same beautiful woman beneath the weary frown, and my heart quickened to see her there.

"Let me get you a drink," I said, and from the look that crossed her face I guessed she was assuming that was my answer to all of life's problems, which was pretty much the case.

We went and sat at a quiet corner table. "Cheers," I said. "And how's Jack doing?"

"I buried him two months ago, Ben."

"Oh no." That did knock me back. "I'm so sorry, Paula. I had no idea."

"I tried to let you know, but you were hard to find."

"I'm so sorry," I repeated. "Was it sudden?"

"One evening he said he was going out with the dog. An hour later I heard the dog scratching at the back door and no sign of Jack. I went outside and heard the car engine running in the garage. There was a hose from the exhaust to the window, him inside."

I groaned.

"But no, it wasn't sudden, really. He'd been getting more and more depressed. When I found him I knew that this was just the last stage of what began three years ago, when everything fell apart." She sounded very bitter.

"Jeez, that's terrible, Paula. Must have been shocking for you."

"What happened has been hard on us all. Terry had his heart attack, leaving Alice with all those kids, you and Vicky split up ..."

"We're a sad lot, that's for sure."

Three couples, six good friends, happily making our way in the world, our lives trashed by one ruthless man. It was Jack who'd introduced us to Derek Mankey, Jack who should have known better, being himself an accountant.

"I'm tired of being sad, Ben," she said. "I want my life back."

"Yeah." I nodded, avoiding her eyes. Of course she did. We all did, but it wasn't so easy.

Maybe it should have been. People are ruined financially every day and they get over it – bushfires, floods, bankruptcies – they pick up the pieces and start again. But the way it happened to us was particularly insidious. Derek Mankey had offered us a vision of an irresistible future, for ourselves and our kids, and we had jumped at it. We weren't stupid – between us we had a fair bit of business experience. But Derek was very clever, very plausible and very dangerous. He revealed his plans to us one step at a time, drawing us in, until we had committed everything we owned and could borrow. And while our eyes were fixed on the golden promise ahead, he slipped away with everything, leaving us to face the creditors, the auditors, the banks and the Tax Office. Worst of all, he'd arranged things so that it was we who faced the accusations of fraud, whose names and pictures appeared in the newspapers, whose reputations were destroyed. It turned us against each other and ourselves, and in the end I had to get out just to keep my sanity.

I reached for my glass, but it was empty.

"I mean it, Ben," Paula said. "And I think I know a way to get back some of what we lost. I've found him."

"What?"

"Derek Mankey. I know where he is."

I just stared at her, and she got to her feet. "Here," she said, "let me get you another drink."

I watched her go to the bar and felt a little cold shiver of dread. The mere mention of Derek Mankey's name had brought back a flood of painful memories. In the mess that followed his disappearance, Terry had died of a heart attack leaving his wife Alice penniless with five small children, then my marriage had broken down, and now Jack had killed himself.

Paula returned with my whisky. I needed it, and thanked her and took a gulp. I noticed she was sticking to mineral water.

"I'm not sure I want to hear this, Paula," I said. "Frankly, I never want to hear that bloke's name again."

"Ben, it's time we faced up to things." She leaned forward, speaking with a quiet intensity, and there was a light in her eyes I remembered fondly. She had always been the most vital, the most exciting of the six of us. "Jack's death shook me."

"Of course ..."

"I realized I'd spent the last three years in a kind of daze," she said, "a half-life, just coping from day to day. Derek didn't just steal our money, he stole our lives, our futures, our confidence in ourselves. We thought we could turn to the authorities to fix things, but instead they accused us of being responsible for his frauds and dragged us further down into the dirt. When I found Jack dead that day, I realized that the only way we were ever going to be free was to put things right ourselves, with Derek Mankey."

She paused. I had the glass of whisky half-raised to my mouth, and she stared at it. I followed her gaze and saw the shake in my hand, which grew worse as the silence lengthened. I put the glass back down on the table with a thump and she reached out her hand to mine and gave it a squeeze.

"I think you know what I'm saying is true, Ben. We can't run away from this any more."

I took a deep breath. "Go on then. Where is he?"

"Western Australia."

That made sense – I'd heard people who want to disappear tend to head out west. "How did you find out?"

She hesitated, and then began the story she'd rehearsed. "Pure chance. After Jack died I was a mess, and by the time of his funeral I was just about washed up. Then one day, out of the blue, I got a phone call offering a bargain holiday in Broome, five nights accommodation at a resort, plus a camel ride on the beach and return flights, all for just two hundred bucks. I felt I needed to get away, and this was too good to turn down, so I thought, what the hell, and agreed. And it turned out to be exactly what I needed. Have you ever been there?"

I shook my head.

"It was a complete change, somewhere quite different. There was a restaurant overlooking Cable Beach where I'd go of an evening to watch the sun set over the ocean, and there was this nice young guy working behind the bar I'd chat to. One evening I had a long talk to him."

I felt a twinge of jealousy, quite unreasonably of course, imagining Paula engrossed in conversation with some handsome bronzed youth. "So?"

"His name was Justin. He told me about his previous job, working on a pearl oyster farm up north, in the waters off the Kimberley coast. It was hard work, he said, but he enjoyed it, he'd learned a lot about the industry, and it had paid well. But he'd got on the wrong side of his boss, the owner of the lease, an arrogant bastard, Justin said, a bully given to bouts of bad temper. 'Cranky, we used to call him,' he said, "cos his name was Mankey. That wasn't the only thing we called him behind his back.' I just stared at him while he told me that this Mankey had kicked him off the boat without giving him the pay he was due, or the bonus he'd been promised. Justin said he'd give a lot to get even with him.

"Mankey's an unusual name, but there must be others around, so I said, 'I used to know a Mankey. He was a bastard too – Derek Mankey.' And Justin said, 'Derek, that's right. Came from out east. Stocky little guy, not much hair, bright blue eyes. Smooth as butter one minute, vicious as a cut snake the next.'"

"That's him," I agreed. "But where does that get us?"

"Since Mankey kicked him out, Justin had had plenty of time to dream up ways to get even, and he'd come up with an idea that he said was foolproof. All he needed was a couple of partners to help, and a bit of money to hire a boat, and he could make us a million dollars without Derek Mankey even knowing he'd lost it. That's a million dollars each."

I stared at her.

"That's less than he took us for, Ben," Paula said, "but it would sure help me to move on."

"A million dollars each?" I repeated, staring at Paula in disbelief. "And Mankey won't even know it's happened? Paula, one thing I've learned from this whole sorry mess is that if a scheme sounds too good to be true then it *is* too good to be true! How gullible does this Justin think we are?"

"Yes, I know, Ben, that's what I thought at first. But just hear me out."

I looked at my empty glass. "I'm going to need another drink to swallow this load of baloney. You?" She shook her head and I lurched off to the bar. I was annoyed that Paula had fallen for whatever bullshit this young Casanova had come up with, but I was interested all the same. There's nothing like a good tale of larceny to stimulate the imagination.

"All right, let's hear it."

"It seems Derek must have used the money he fleeced from us to buy an oyster farm lease in the ocean off the Kimberley. Justin says it's huge, with thousands of oysters, way out in the middle of nowhere. At harvesting time, Mankey takes a special ship and crew up there from Broome, and they work the field, extracting pearls from the oysters, and implanting the beads of mussel shell that will form the core of new pearls. Of course Mankey doesn't do any of the work himself – it's hard and very skilful. But he goes to keep an eye on the crew and make sure they don't get up to any tricks."

I was trying to form a mental picture of the scene. "Don't they have sharks up there?" I asked.

"Yes, and worse, salt water crocodiles. They're really vicious. Anyway, the thing is that Mankey relies on the crew to keep the operation on track. Each oyster can produce three or four pearls in a lifetime, each bigger than the last, so you've got oysters at various stages of development, some surviving and others not."

"So?"

"The point is, no one really knows at any point how many oysters there are in the farm. At harvest time they just work up and down the lines, operating on what they find. So if someone hired a boat and went up there immediately before the harvest, they could remove oyster racks in a random pattern, and no one would know. Of course you would need the inside knowledge of someone who's worked the farm, and who knows what they're doing. That's Justin. We would put up the cash to hire a boat, and then act as labourers with him. Within a week we should be able to gather several thousand pearls, and be away before Mankey and his ship arrive, none the wiser. We'd take them to Hong Kong, and sell them on the open market there, no questions asked."

I laughed. "Paula, that is the craziest thing I've ever heard! We're middle-aged lounge lizards ..."

"Speak for yourself."

"Well, we're certainly not in the blush of youth, ready to fight sharks and crocodiles for the treasures of the deep!" I guffawed some more, but she didn't smile.

When I calmed down, she said. "Yes, it won't be easy, and maybe you're not up to it. In fact, seeing you here knocking back the Scotch I'm sure you're not. You'd just be a liability, actually. But I'm thinking of Alice too. Since Terry had his heart attack she's been struggling harder than any of us, trying to bring up those five little kids. Derek Mankey did that to her, and it makes me very, very angry. Angry enough to want to do something about it."

Her eyes were blazing, and I felt ashamed. Ashamed, and also excited. She was right, it did feel as if I'd been sleepwalking for the past three years. She wanted to shake me awake. A small part of me wanted her to succeed. The rest was absolutely terrified.

There wasn't a snowflake's chance in hell that we'd ever do it, I reassured myself, but I thought I'd better look as if I was prepared to consider the mad scheme seriously. "Okay, let's go over it again." I made a show of taking a notebook and pen out of my briefcase and she launched into it, this time in more detail. When she came to an end I asked, "And the timing of this, Paula? When would it have to be done?"

"Now," she said. "Right now."

I was still telling myself that this was ludicrous as our plane dipped down towards the blazing red earth of Broome. To the west the ocean stretched blue to the horizon, and the notion of taking a boat out across that expanse and up to the Kimberley to help ourselves to several million dollars worth of Derek Mankey's pearls, just sounded like something out of a boys' own adventure comic. But Paula was adamant that we should at least go over to speak to Justin, the former member of Mankey's crew who had come up with the crazy idea.

He was waiting for us at the terminal, and he looked pretty much what I'd expected, a loose-limbed, long-haired, bronzed young man with a lazy smile. I thought Paula responded a little too eagerly to his welcome, and I acted gruff and reserved as he swung our bags into the back of a small 4WD and took us to the motel he'd booked us into on the edge of Chinatown. The light was dazzling, the temperature pleasantly warm after the chill we'd left at home, and we changed into lighter clothes before heading out for an orientation tour. Justin took us first to the long jetty at the south end of town, to point out a large boat, or small ship (I'm a little vague on maritime matters), anchored a hundred metres out in the bay. It was Derek Mankey's apparently, a cross between a factory ship and a laboratory the way Justin described it, purpose designed for the large-scale impregnation and harvesting of pearl oysters.

"A crew of ten for the harvest," he said softly. He was wearing large mirrored sunglasses and a cap, and I had the impression that even at this distance he was nervous of being spotted by anyone on board. "They're waiting for the ocean temperatures to stabilize, when the oysters can be safely operated on. But we won't be operating on them, just harvesting, so we can go now."

"How long before they leave?" I asked sceptically.

"Should be about ten days, I reckon. This is the ideal time for us to go."

"On what?"

"I'll show you." We set off again, to the mangroves that grew further up the shore. He slowed at a small bay with a golden sandy beach, and pointed to a boat lying half-tilted on the low tide mud beyond. "*Starry Night*, an eight-metre Conquest. Available for charter for the next two weeks."

I looked at it, trying to imagine the three of us sharing that grubby little thing, bobbing about in a crocodile-infested ocean. "It's very small, Justin."

"Only thing suitable that's available, mate. I've made a provisional booking, but we gotta confirm and pay by the end of the day."

He told us how much, and I blanched.

"Okay," Paula said calmly.

"Hang on," I protested. "We need to talk about this."

We returned to the motel, stopping on the way for beer at a bottle shop at Paula's suggestion. She was probably hoping to sweeten me up, and I wasn't objecting. I thought it'd take a bit more than that to convince me to go along with this madness.

But as we sat around the small table in Paula's room, poring over Justin's charts and listening to his plans, I became increasingly impressed by his professionalism. I'd been misled by his youthful looks, but it turned out he had a Skipper grade three mariner's certificate, and was obviously a very experienced sailor and pearl farmer. He also had a steady, commonsense attitude that I felt instinctively I could trust, and after a while I began to believe that it might indeed be almost possible. It was wildly beyond anything I'd done before of course, and it was unabashed theft, but I opened another can of beer and listened quietly to Paula's impassioned pitch about how we had right on our side, and a duty to help the poor fatherless children of Alice, widowed, like Paula herself, by the heartless Derek Mankey, and at the end I surprised both them and myself by saying, "Okay then. Let's do it."

The fact that, of the original three couples who'd invested in Mankey's schemes, I was the only male left alive, didn't bother me as much as perhaps it should.

Once I'd made the decision, I felt an overwhelming sense of liberation and optimism, as if I were throwing aside all the failures that had weighed upon me over the past years. We were suddenly a great team, laughing and shaking each other's hands, the three musketeers setting off on a grand adventure. Paula hugged me, and whispered her thanks, and tears came into my eyes. Silly, of course, but what Mankey had done to us three years before had cast such a shadow over our lives that it was perhaps understandable.

There was much to be done. Justin had prepared detailed lists of the things we'd need – extra drums of fuel for the long trip, food, tools and many other supplies, for there were none where we were heading, on that long wilderness coastline of north-west Australia. But first we had to confirm our charter of the *Starry Night*. We set off from the motel for the owners' offices in the commercial area of Broome's Chinatown.

Justin led us down one of the narrow laneways that runs off Carnarvon Street, packed with little tourist souvenir shops, cafés and real estate offices, and we had just emerged on to Dampier Terrace when he came to a sudden stop, and pushed us back into the shadows of a shop veranda hung with bright fabrics. We followed his gaze across the street, where two men were walking along the pavement. I recognized Derek Mankey straight away behind the dark glasses, skipping along on his short legs to keep up with his companion.

"You little bastard," I growled.

He looked full of himself, head back, puffed up like a little cockerel in a scarlet shirt and black pants. I didn't know the man he was with, a good thirty centimetres taller than Mankey, and physically much more formidable. His shaved skull was deeply suntanned, tattooed biceps and pecs bulging beneath his black T-shirt, and a mean expression on his moustached face.

"Who's the other guy?" I said softly to Justin.

"Name's Chay Gatt, works for Mankey."

"Chay?" I said.

"Short for chainsaw, supposedly. A hard man. Always at Mankey's side."

"Really?" I wondered what Mankey was into these days. When he'd ripped us off he'd only needed his smooth forked tongue.

We watched them go into the showroom of one of the big pearl retailers on that stretch of Dampier Terrace, then Justin led us off in the other direction to the marine charter office. An hour later we emerged, our credit cards severely depleted, and hurried away to start organizing supplies. By evening we had most things in hand, and Justin took us back to the motel. He was nervous about us being spotted out on the street, and we decided to have takeaway in my room. Justin said he'd fetch it, then at the last minute asked Paula to go with him to help choose. They were away a long time, and when they returned I could sense that something had happened. Paula was tense, and she and Justin wouldn't meet each other's eyes when they spoke. I drew her aside and asked her what was wrong, but she just said, "Nothing." I asked, "Has Justin been bothering you?" but she shook her head and turned away. I put it down to last-minute nerves.

Early the next morning we went out to float the *Starry Night* off on the high tide, and Justin took her to a more convenient mooring he'd arranged further down the shore. There we ferried our supplies and loaded them on board. By mid-morning we were ready to leave. With heart in mouth I followed Justin's instructions to cast off, and we moved out in a wide arc across Roebuck Bay, keeping well away from Mankey's pearl ship anchored by the jetty on Entrance Point. Once out in open seas we swung north to run parallel to the long stretch of Cable Beach. Through binoculars I could see tourists riding a chain of camels across the sand. How innocent and safe they looked, and I was filled with a sudden desire to be with them. We were setting off in a tiny tub on a 1,400-kilometre round trip to the far northern point of the Kimberley, to steal pearls out of crocodile- and shark-infested waters, from a man whose closest companion was named after a chainsaw. How had I allowed myself to be talked into this?

Despite my initial cold feet, the journey up the coast began to settle me down. The ocean was calm, the sun was shining, and our mood became cheerful. Justin set a moderate speed, wanting to conserve fuel and not overtax the outboard, and when we stopped at lunchtime for a sandwich we threw lines over the side and managed to catch a couple of reasonable golden snappers. The coastline was rugged orange sandstone topped by low scrub, with the occasional grove of palms nestling in the hollows. After the first couple of hours we saw no other boats, nor signs of habitation on the shore, and gradually adjusted to the idea that we were alone in a vast wilderness. All around us we saw evidence of a dense and turbulent life beneath us in the ocean: a sea snake skimmed off across the surface as we passed; small fish flew into the air; the fins of sharks or dolphins surfaced and disappeared; and on a sandy beach we saw a long dark log, which lurched into movement at the sound of our engine and began to slither towards the water.

"A salty," Justin said. They were much more dangerous than their fresh-water cousins, he told us, being the largest reptiles on the planet and capable of hunting far offshore.

Justin was a competent and knowledgeable skipper, with a calm air that I was coming to trust, despite my initial doubts. At dusk he took us into the lee of a small island in the Buccaneer Archipelago, where we anchored for the night. We had come half way to our destination, and he was satisfied. Paula cooked up the fish for us on the stove in the little galley, and we relaxed with a couple of bottles of wine beneath a vast canopy of stars. At one point, Justin caught me watching Paula as she worked at the galley, and murmured, "Good looking lady, Ben. I reckon you two hit it off, yeah?"

I felt myself colouring. "Just friends, Justin. Good friends." Then I felt I had to add, "She's just buried her old man."

He gave me a raffish grin and I looked away, feeling a bit stupid that I'd had suspicions about him and Paula.

The next morning we eased out of our little bunks at first light and stood to stretch and watch the sun catch the rim of the fractured cliff beneath which we were anchored. The water looked inviting, placid and warm, but Justin wouldn't hear of us taking a dip. He wouldn't even let us put a hand into the sea to wash our dinner plates.

"Too risky, mate," he said. "You don't know what's lurking beneath you."

He pointed out an osprey's nest nearby, a dishevelled stack of sticks on top of a rocky outcrop, and we watched the owner stretch its wings in the morning sun while we gulped down coffee and toast and prepared to move on.

I took turns with Justin at the helm as we threaded our way on a northeasterly course through the Coronation Islands and around Bigge Island. We rounded Cape Voltaire in the early afternoon, and I sensed an increased alertness in Justin as he took over and changed our course to easterly, heading in to the Osborn Islands. I was dozing after a light lunch when I heard the engines throttling back and sat up with a start. We were in the middle of a sheltered stretch of water between the mainland and a long island. The sea was covered with round white floats in regimented lines, thousands of them, disappearing into the distance. I got to my feet and tried to take it in. The floats were set a couple of metres apart along each of the lines, which were spaced far enough apart to allow a boat to pass between them. There were hundreds of lines, thousands of floats, spread as far as the eye could see.

"Beneath the floats and longlines," Justin explained, "are suspended netting panels carrying the oysters, *Pinctada Maxima*, the biggest pearl-bearing oyster in the world. The guys come up here regularly throughout the year to clean them of grunge – weed, coral, barnacles – then in August for the big operation of harvesting and seeding. I have a pretty good idea where the most mature oysters are, six years old, with the biggest pearls. That's what we'll be looking for. We'll start tonight."

"Tonight?"

"Yeah, we'll do it in the dark. Customs and Immigration fly constant patrols along this coast, and we don't want word getting back to Broome that a small boat has been spotted working the field. We'll head around to the far side of that island now and get a bit of grub and rest, and come back after dusk." He looked hard at me. "No booze tonight, mate."

"Right," I agreed, although it seemed to me that was exactly what I'd need to brace me for the prospect of groping about in a dark ocean seething with tiger sharks and crocodiles.

Once night fell we returned to the oyster beds, the water shimmering beneath a half moon by whose pale light we could make out the rows of thousands of floats on the long lines from which the panels of oysters were suspended in the nurturing ocean currents.

Justin steered the boat up a long avenue between the lines, heading for one of the areas in which he knew that the oldest oysters were located, and from which the largest and most valuable pearls might be expected. I felt very tense, an intruder in this alien landscape, conscious of the creatures lurking beneath us, the tiger sharks and savage saltwater crocs, into whose domain we were trespassing. Paula sensed my anxiety, and stretched out her hand to mine. I took it gratefully and squeezed it.

"All right." Justin throttled back, bringing the boat to a halt between two lines. Paula took his place at the wheel, and he came to my side at the stern, carrying a long gaff. We were both wearing life-jackets and protective gloves. He had already explained how we should work, him snagging the rope below a float and the two of us hauling the metal-framed oyster panel to the surface and on to the boat, but as we began I discovered that it wasn't as easy as it had sounded. I stumbled and slipped, and caused the boat to tilt violently before we finally manhandled the first panel aboard. I sat there gasping as Justin opened it and removed two of the six molluscs, each as big as a man's widespread hand, dropping them into a plastic tub. Then we heaved the panel with the remaining oysters back over the side, and Paula took the boat slowly forward until Justin told her to stop again. In this way we moved about the oyster beds, without apparent pattern, removing small numbers as we went, so that the harvesters due the following week wouldn't detect our theft. I began to develop some rhythm and expertise, but after a while this began to deteriorate as fatigue set in. At midnight Justin called a halt.

"We've had a long day," he said. "This'll do for tonight."

I was grateful, my hands and arms aching from the work. We had collected two big tubs full of oysters, maybe a hundred, and I still hadn't seen a pearl.

That changed the next morning. After a restless sleep in our confined quarters, I woke again at dawn, and watched the island we were anchored by take shape. It had a fine looking sandy beach, beyond which low scrub covered a hillside surmounted by a rocky outcrop. The other two woke after a while, and Justin suggested we grill some oyster meat for breakfast. He took a shell from one of the tubs, and attacked it with a special tool he had, levering it open.

Paula and I huddled closer to see what was inside, the shining opal-escent mother-of-pearl inner lining of the shell, a blob of pale flesh, and at its heart a large white pearl. Paula gasped, and Justin picked it out, put it in his mouth to clean it, then held it up for us to see.

"Not bad," he said. "Fifteen millimetre, good shape, fine lustre."

He explained the qualities we were looking for, the best colours, the different shapes, and began opening other shells. It was like a lottery, you simply couldn't tell from the outside what you were going to find within. In some cases there was nothing at all, in others the seeded pearl was accompanied by other naturally formed pearls, or keshi. There were the gnarled baroque shapes, ovals and pure spheres, and a range of colours, gold and pink and white. When we were finished, the oyster shells and surplus meat thrown over the side, Justin spread the pearls out on the table and sorted them into categories, excellent, fair and rubbish. There were only four excellent ones, perfect large spheres with a golden lustre, which Justin put into a small bag. I was devas-tated – all that hard work for only four gems.

"The fair ones are worth keeping too," he said, and scooped up the so-called "rubbish" and threw them over the side.

That night we went back again, working for most of the hours of darkness, before returning exhausted to the island, boat laden with shells. The next night we repeated the process, and the next, and when we returned the following dawn, on the sixth day of our trip, our collection of pearls had grown into a substantial hoard.

Towards midday on that sixth day out of Broome, I woke to the sound of Paula and Justin talking. There was something odd about their voices, low and tense, as if they didn't want to be overheard, which wasn't easy on that little boat. I assumed they didn't want to disturb my sleep, and I yawned and eased myself out of the bunk, and immediately they fell silent. They were working together on our haul from the previous night, opening the big *Pinctada Maxima* shells and retrieving whatever pearls they found inside.

"Morning, guys," I mumbled, and sat down beside Paula, blinking in the bright sunlight. Absently I took up an oyster from the tub and used Justin's tool to prise it open. For a moment I thought the sun dazzle had distorted my vision, for the large pearl nestling in the white flesh was red. I blinked, but there it still was, a startling deep crimson. "Hey," I said, "look at this."

Justin glanced over, and his mouth opened as he took it from my hand. "Oh mate ..."

"What is it?" Paula asked.

Justin continued staring at it for a long while, then whispered, "A blood pearl. I've heard of them, but never seen one. I thought it was just a myth."

"Is it valuable?" Paula laughed.

Justin stared at her. "More than all the rest put together," he said.

I took it back from him, staring at the lustrous colour, then said, "Well, I found it, and I'm going to give it to you, Paula, because we wouldn't be here if you hadn't been so bloody stubborn." I handed it to her with a grin.

We got back to work with renewed enthusiasm, hoping to find another, but without any luck.

When we finished Paula made us a meal, and then suggested that we explore the island. I was keen, but Justin said that he'd better stay on board to look after things.

Paula said, "Maybe we should watch out he doesn't take off with the pearls, Ben, and leave us marooned here."

She was joking, but Justin seemed to take it seriously, and proposed he divide up the best quality pearls into three equal shares that we'd each carry from now on. It seemed unnecessary to me, but he insisted that it was the right thing to do. We watched as he made up three small bags. Paula slipped the blood pearl into hers, and then Justin took the boat as close into the shore as he could, worried as always about us being in the dangerous waters. We appreciated his concern when we got on to the beach, and saw a long sinuous track leading across the sand.

"Turtle?" I said hopefully, but I knew it was too big, made by the sweeping tail of a large croc.

We hadn't stood on dry land for six days and I found it strangely disorienting. I stumbled, and absurdly began to feel seasick. Maybe all that oyster meat had upset me too, or the heat of the sun, but as we trudged up into the scrub my gut began to feel queasy.

Paula said, "There's something I need to talk to you about, Ben." Then she stared at me. "You all right? You look a bit pale."

I said, "Feel a bit crook, actually. I'm going to have to go into the bushes for a bit of private business, Paula."

"Okay. Do you want me to take the bag?"

I said yes, and handed her the backpack that contained the binoculars and both our bags of pearls.

I had a bottle of water with me, and after resting in a small grove of palms for a while I began to feel better, and got to my feet and set off after Paula towards the rocky outcrop that crowned the small island. There were wide overhanging rock shelves at its base, and I came across aboriginal paintings on the sheltered surfaces. There were kangaroo, snakes and the biggest of all was one I recognized as a Wandjina figure, which I knew was a guardian spirit of the Kimberley, with huge black discs for eyes, a halo and no mouth.

I continued, climbing up over the rocks, and came out on to the crown of the hill. There was no sign of Paula. From up there I could get a panoramic view over the surrounding ocean, to the mainland on one side, the Osborn Islands on the other, and the waters of the pearl farm in between. And there my eyes locked on the figure of a white ship.

I recognized it straight away, the pearl farming vessel which Derek Mankey and his crew used to harvest and reseed their pearls, and despite the warm afternoon a shiver went through me. He wasn't supposed to arrive for several more days. If he discovered us here, and knowing all three of us, he would immediately guess what we were up to. Even now, I realized in a kind of panic, he might be watching me through his binoculars, wondering if his eyes were playing tricks.

Filled with panic, I began to clamber back down the rocky hilltop, then scrambled through the scrubby grassland that led down to the beach. I found myself in a dense thicket of trees and paused for a moment, wondering which direction to take, when suddenly I heard Justin's voice, quite close by, call out, "Paula? I'm right here."

"Oh, thank goodness," I heard her reply. They were on the other side of a thick patch of tall grass, and quite close by.

"Where's Ben?"

"I don't know. He was feeling unwell and we separated."

I was about to call out to them when Justin said, "The ship's arrived."

I was surprised. Surely he could only be referring to Derek Mankey's ship, yet he didn't sound in the least worried.

Then Paula said, "Oh damn, I just hope Ben doesn't see it. We'd better find him."

They both began to call my name, while I tried to make sense of the fact that they obviously weren't surprised by Mankey's arrival and seemed to have been expecting it.

"Damn," Paula's voice said. "Where the hell is he?"

"Have you got the pearls?"

"Yes, I've got both lots, here."

"Good."

A horrible chill had formed in my gut. I didn't really know Justin, but Paula? I'd known her for years. Surely she would never double-cross me? But then I thought of how hard her husband's suicide must have hit her. Maybe I didn't know her any more.

I heard the crackle of a radio, then Justin's voice, "Hello? Justin here."

"Justin, old fellar. How are you?" I recognized Derek Mankey's oily tones, filtered through the radio static. "Where are you?"

"We're on the small island, mate. You'll see our boat at the beach."

"We're on our way. Everything go according to plan?"

"Perfect, boss."

The radio noise was cut off, and then Paula said, "What about Ben?"

"We'll just have to play it by ear. He's probably waiting for us down at the beach. You go on down. I'll have one last look around here."

I crept to the edge of my cover and watched them separate. Justin was now carrying the backpack, and once Paula was out of sight, he took out the two bags of pearls, mine and Paula's, and buried them beneath a rock at the foot of the tallest palm tree around. Then he too set off for the beach. I felt sick. Everything I'd assumed, taken on trust, was false.

I let them get ahead, then followed until I came to the edge of the high dune that stood at the head of the beach. Lying down in the tall grasses, I crawled forward until I could see what was happening. There was another small boat coming in to the shore now, a tender from the pearl ship with two people on board. I recognized Mankey, and the taller figure of his scary bodyguard, Chay Gatt.

Mankey paddled ashore and went straight up to the pair waiting on the beach and shook Justin's hand, nodded at Paula. Behind him Gatt tethered the boat's anchor rope and joined them. A rifle was slung from his shoulder. I was too far away to hear what they were saying, but after a moment they began looking and pointing up the beach, talking, I assumed, about me. Gatt began scanning the slopes with binoculars, and I crouched lower into the grass. Mankey began waving his arms, and at one point I thought he might have slapped Paula, but I wasn't sure. However, when Paula and Justin turned away and began heading towards me, I scrambled back and ran, crouching, into the scrub.

What should I do? I had no idea what was going on, but it was clear to me that I couldn't trust any of them. I could only think of one way in which I might gain some leverage, and I ran towards the tall palm beneath which Justin had hidden our pearls. I grabbed both bags and continued running to the nearby boulders where I'd found the Wandjina rock painting. Scrambling up on to the ledge below its broad overhang, I realized that there was a very low cave stretching back into the rock, in which I thought I might hide the bags. But then I heard Justin's voice, very close. I knew they would find me at any moment, and I squeezed myself into the cave, scraping my arms and knees as I wriggled back into the shadow.

"Where the hell has he gone?" Justin's voice sounded almost by my ear.

"I'm worried," Paula said. "If Chay sees him he'll likely take a shot at him."

"Well, at least we've got his pearls."

"You'll give them to Derek?"

"Of course, we'll trade. Don't worry, I'll look after you."

They moved away, and I lay frozen in miserable immobility in my narrow space like a tomb.

I was devastated to think that Paula had betrayed me. It made me realize, too late, how fond I'd grown of her, how trusting. They continued searching for me all afternoon, but they didn't find me, although at one point Chay Gatt appeared outside and stared directly into my hiding place, yet didn't see me. It was almost as if the aboriginal Wandjina figure painted on the rock above me was protecting me, making me invisible.

At last, when the light began to fade from the sky, the voices died away. I heard the putter of two outboards and I realized that I was alone on the island.

I woke the next morning after an uneasy night beneath the stars, and finished the last dribble of water from the bottle I had. It wasn't long before I heard the sound of a boat, and their search for me resumed. I returned to my hiding place in the Wandjina cave and waited. After an hour I heard Paula and Justin's voices. They were arguing about something. Then Derek Mankey called to them and they abruptly stopped.

They must have moved to within metres of my hiding place and I could hear them clearly as Mankey spoke, panting with exertion. "All right, Chay's gone back to the boat. Gimme the pearls."

Justin said cautiously, "There's a problem, boss. We left them under that palm tree there, and they've gone."

Mankey exploded, accusing them of cheating him and threatening to have Gatt deal with them.

"It's true, Derek," Paula's voice cut in. "Ben must have taken them."

There were more curses and threats before they moved off.

Later Mankey and Gatt came by, and I heard the bodyguard say, "If he's tried to swim to the mainland he's a dead man anyway. Even if the crocs didn't take him, there's no one over there to help him. There's no water here on the island. If he's hiding somewhere he'll be dead in a day or two. We've wasted enough time. We need to fly the crew up here and get on with the harvest."

There were a couple of things about this conversation that puzzled me. First, Chay wasn't talking like Mankey's employee, more like his boss. Second, it sounded as if he and Mankey had brought the pearl ship up here by themselves, without the crew, and I wondered why. But he was dead right about the water. I was already parched, and the heat was building.

By dusk I was very aware of how precarious my situation was. I made my way to the rim of the shrubs overlooking the beach and made sure that there were no boats there, then I staggered round to a rocky point that faced the broad expanse of sea in which the pearl farm lay. I felt weak and dizzy, my throat parched as I slumped against a boulder. Mankey's ship lay anchored about 200 metres offshore, and our boat, the *Starry Night*, lay nearby. There was no one on the *Starry Night*, but the line of portholes along the side of the pearl ship were illuminated.

As I sat there, wondering in despair if my voice would reach that far if I called for help, a terrible scream ripped through the still evening air. It must have lasted for three or four seconds before it abruptly cut off, and the pitch, neither male not female, but of pure animal terror, made the hairs rise on the back of my neck.

I waited, straining every nerve, and a couple of minutes later another sound echoed over the sea, again like an animal, but this time an enraged roar.

Then silence.

I think I must have fallen into a kind of daze, almost a trance, as darkness closed in around me. I don't know how long I sat there before a cool breeze roused me. What choices did I have? To die slowly of thirst tomorrow or the day after? Or to face my fate head on, out there across the water?

I got stiffly to my feet and stepped down across the rocks to the water's edge. I tried not to think of the sharks and salt water crocs that teemed in these waters as I slipped off my T-shirt and sandals, made sure the bags of pearls were safe in my pockets, and slid down into the cool briny deep.

Once in the water I struck out hard for the ship on the most terrifying swim of my life, expecting at any moment to be dragged down by a crocodile or shark. At one point I became disoriented, not sure where I was heading and beginning to panic, but then the ship's lights bobbed up above the swell and I turned towards them.

When I reached the stern, I paused, hearing voices, Mankey and Gatt arguing. They were on the open top deck, and Mankey sounded drunk and scared, almost pleading with the other man. I clambered out of the water and slipped into the shadows. I was beside a steel door leading into the main deck of the ship, whose lights I had seen from the shore. The door was open a crack, and I pushed it gently, hearing no sound from within. I peered through into a large, brightly lit space, all stainless steel and white, like a laboratory or operating theatre, where the work would be done on seeding the pearl oysters. There were fixed steel stools ranged down both sides of a broad central table, and sinks and cupboards along the walls. Something was lying on the table. No, some*one*. I saw a foot, a strap. Drawn by the sight, I eased the door a little wider and crept inside.

Justin was spread out on the table, ankles and wrists strapped down, his shirt pulled over his head, trousers down at his knees, and his stomach a bloody mess of entrails. I gagged, and I think I would have thrown up if I hadn't been so dehydrated. Then I saw something so bizarre I couldn't quite believe it – nestling in a scarlet fold of his gut was the silvery glint of a large pearl.

Oh jeez, I thought, *he swallowed the bloody things!*

There was a thump from the deck above, and the sound of feet coming down steel steps. I hurried to a door at the far end of the room, stopping on the way to quickly stuff the pearl bags behind a stack of boxes. Beyond the door I stepped on to a small landing. The only way forward was down a steep flight of stairs. At the foot I found myself in a corridor lined with doors, presumably cabins. Heart pounding, I tried one, a small bare room with bunk and cupboard, deserted. The next was the same, and the next. Then I heard a sound, like a whimper. It seemed to come from a door opposite. I opened it and found myself facing Paula.

She was sitting on the edge of the bunk, her wrist handcuffed to the post that supported it. Her face was shockingly battered, swollen and purple, and her lip was bleeding.

"Ben," she gasped, a mix of hope and terror in her eyes.

I closed the door and went and crouched beside her. "Paula, what have they done to you?"

She shook her head, tears streaming down her cheek. "It's all gone horribly wrong," she sobbed.

"Tell me, quickly, before they come." I wiped the tears gently from her face.

She spoke in a rush. "Mankey found out what we were doing. One night, while you were asleep, I heard Justin on the radio, talking to him. He was telling Mankey where we were. When I challenged him he said he'd had to do it, but it would be all right, we'd do a deal with Mankey and he'd look after us. He begged me not to tell you, because he was afraid you'd do something rash, and then Mankey would go crazy and hurt us all. I agreed, but I wanted to tell you, only Justin never left us alone on the boat. I was going to tell you when we got on the island yesterday, only we got separated."

I wanted to believe her, but I still wasn't sure. "What happened to Justin, Paula?"

"Oh, Ben, it was terrible ..." She began sobbing again. Finally she told me. "Justin knew they'd search us for pearls when they found us, and he tried to cheat them by swallowing his best pearls in plastic sachets. But Chay was suspicious and hurt him until he admitted what he'd done. So they cut him open ... It was so awful, Ben. He was alive. They made me watch."

I felt sick and turned away, the blood roaring in my ears. Then I heard a sound behind me.

"Nice of you to drop in, Ben."

I turned and saw Mankey standing there in the doorway. Behind him was Chay Gatt, a bloody carving knife in his hand.

I couldn't drag my eyes away from the knife in Gatt's hand, its long blade and the whole of his right arm stained in Justin's blood. Beside me Paula sobbed.

"Good to see you again, Ben," Mankey said cheerfully. "Didn't swim out here, did you? Crazy thing to do in these waters. But I'm afraid that's where you're going to end up."

I tried to frame some sort of reply, but he ignored me and spoke over his shoulder to Gatt. "Lock him up across the way, mate, then get rid of Justin. There's a few things I need to ask Paula. Maybe she'll talk to me now."

I didn't struggle as Gatt shoved me into the cabin across the corridor and locked the door. I sat on the bunk and tried desperately to think. What Paula had told me didn't make sense. Why had Justin betrayed us, and how had he hoped to save us? In fact the whole bizarre story seemed to make less and less sense, from it's beginning with Paula's accidental meeting with Justin onwards. I began to wonder if we'd got the whole thing wrong. We'd thought we'd been cheating Mankey, but maybe it hadn't been like that at all.

The handle turned and Mankey stepped in, shutting the door behind him.

"One last chance, Ben, for you and Paula. Tell me where the pearls are."

"On our boat ..."

He shook his head impatiently. "Not that rubbish. I want the good stuff that you set aside – your share and Paula's. You've probably gathered that we've already found Justin's share."

"That's all there was," I said.

He leaned forward and said softly, "I know better. Where have you hidden them?"

I thought I understood now, and decided to take a gamble. "No, I won't tell you, Derek. I'll tell Gatt."

His eyes narrowed, then he got to his feet, opened the cabin door and said a few words. Gatt came in, big silent brutal bloodstained Gatt, and hauled me to my feet. Mankey said, "Time for your operation, Ben."

I tried to speak, but my throat was dry. "Haven't ..."

"What's that, Ben?"

"Haven't swallowed any pearls."

Mankey smiled. "That's what Justin said too. I'll leave you to Chay's tender mercies. He knows not to listen to a dying man's ramblings. For myself, I don't think I can take any more graphic violence tonight."

Gatt pushed me down the corridor, then dragged me up the stair to the next deck, where the operating room of the pearl ship was set out. Justin's body was gone from the large, bloodstained table, and Gatt pushed me towards it. I tried to summon up some last vestige of effort.

"I haven't swallowed any pearls, Chay," I said desperately, "but I know where they are, my share and Paula's, of the best pearls we set aside, more than I could ever swallow. I'm the only one who knows. Paula doesn't. I moved them when I was alone on the island. You kill me and they're gone forever."

He hesitated just a fraction and I ploughed on. "And I know more than that. Things your syndicate will want to hear. Do yourself a favour, just listen. Mankey wants the three of us dead – Justin, me and then Paula. You should know why."

He hauled me around, and stared at me, his cruel face twisted in a frown. Finally he spoke. "What's to know?"

When I'd finished telling him, trying not to sound hysterical in my panic to make him believe me, he stared at me in silence a bit longer, then raised the bloody knife. I gulped as he pressed the point into the soft flesh beneath my chin.

"You're not going anywhere," he said, and turned abruptly and strode off.

I looked wildly around, but any tools or possible weapons were locked away. I ran to the door, down the stairs, then turned sharply into a doorway as I heard Mankey's voice, yelling loudly at Chay.

I found myself in the galley, and this did present more possibilities. I selected a heavy cleaver and then peeked out into the corridor again. They were between me and the cabin where they were holding Paula. I didn't want to grapple with Chay, even armed with a cleaver, and decided I'd have to go up and over the top. But before I took to the stairs I turned back and looked wildly around the galley for some inspiration. I noticed the gas rings on the stove, and turned them all on full, unlit, then hurried out. When I reached the top deck I raced forward to the prow. There were more stairs there, and I dropped down to the cabin level again, getting to Paula without having to pass Mankey and Chay, although their angry voices were very close. She looked up at me, then at the cleaver in my hand.

"Ben! I thought ... What are you going to do?"

I stared at her left wrist, trapped by the handcuffs, and she gave a little gasp. "Oh no."

The handcuffs were tempered steel, and I knew the cleaver couldn't cut through them. Paula saw the look in my eye and said again, voice tight, "What are you going to do, Ben?"

"I have to get you out of here, Paula," I whispered. "Turn your head away."

I raised the cleaver, then brought it down as hard as I could. She gave a little shriek as the blade bit into the aluminium tube stanchion to which she was handcuffed. It was hollow, the metal softer than steel, and it buckled under the blow. Another slash and it gave way. I threaded the handcuffs free and she fell into my arms.

"Come on," I hissed. "We have to get away."

I eased open the door and cautiously peered out. From the next cabin I could hear the growl of Gatt's voice, putting the questions that I had planted in his head, and then Mankey's reply, his usual smooth persuasiveness ruffled by panic. "I swear, Chay, there was nothing like that. You can't seriously believe anything he told you."

We slipped out into the corridor and retraced my route to the stern of the ship. Out in the dark water I heard a sound of thrashing disturbance, and guessed Justin's body, thrown overboard by Gatt, was attracting curious predators. There was no chance of us swimming, but the ship's tender was tied to the stern rail, and we hurriedly climbed down into it and cast off. Not wanting to risk the noise of starting the outboard motor, I used the oars stowed on board to pull us away, towards the dim form of the *Starry Night* anchored nearby. It seemed to take me an age to get us over there, expecting to be discovered at any moment, and a couple of times something in the water thumped against the boat. We reached the back of the Conquest and clambered aboard. I rushed to get the motor started, my fingers all thumbs, then abruptly froze as a blinding beam of light caught us, along with Gatt's angry roar.

"Don't move an inch, you fuggin mongrels," he bellowed, and the beam of light slid forward across the boat. As it moved off our faces I was able to make out his silhouette on the top deck of the pearl ship. With a chill I saw that he was holding his rifle in one hand, his other arm wrapped around a bundle of some kind. Then I realized that the bundle was moving, struggling. It was Derek Mankey.

Gatt gave another shout. "Your mate wants to join you. Here ..." He heaved Mankey forward over the rail, and with a yell, arms windmilling, he pitched down into the sea.

We stood transfixed as Mankey surfaced, spluttering, and then began splashing ineffectually towards us.

"You'll have to go quicker than that, you little slug," Gatt jeered, and raised the rifle to his shoulder. I saw the muzzle flash, heard a crack, and then a howl from Mankey.

He kept thrashing his arms, and Paula said, "He missed," but I knew better. Gatt didn't want to kill him; he wanted him to bleed.

Coughing, spluttering, flailing, Mankey continued moving slowly towards us. Then, very suddenly, he disappeared. After a moment he surfaced again, gave a horrible scream, then was jerked down once more. He didn't reappear.

A terrible silence settled over the scene.

Then at last Gatt called out to me. "You want that to happen to you and your girlfriend, Ben?" He raised his rifle menacingly.

Despite the terrifying circumstances, I felt an absurd pleasure that he should call Paula that. I put my arm around her. She was trembling, and I pulled her protectively close.

"No, Chay," I shouted back.

"Where are the pearls?"

"If I tell you, can we go free?"

"Sure mate. I guarantee it."

I hesitated, but what choice did I have? "They're on board the ship with you." I told him where I'd hidden them, and he said, "This better be right. Don't you move while I look."

We watched him climb down to the next deck, and I said to Paula, "It's going to be all right. That's all he wants."

After a moment he reappeared at the ship's rail. "Good on ya, mate."

"You've got what you want, Chay. There's one thing ..."

But he cut me off harshly. "Sad thing is, I can't let ya go."

"You promised ..."

"Doesn't work like that, mate."

He raised his rifle to his shoulder. Feeling numb, as helpless as a tethered calf, I watched Chay line us up in his sights, adjusting his aim to the roll of the swell. I saw the muzzle flash, felt the wind of the bullet pass my ear, then watched a blinding ball of light burst out, consuming first the dark figure of Chay, and then enveloping the whole of his ship. The shock wave blew us off our feet and our boat began rocking madly as pieces of metal and burning plastic showered around us.

While I'd been on board the pearl ship I'd turned on all the cooker taps in the galley, and now Chay's shot had ignited the gas-filled hold. I had been about to tell him about the gas when he'd cut me off to say he was going to have to kill us. How's that for dramatic irony.

We watched the fireball subside, leaving a flickering ruin where the ship had been, the surrounding waters scattered with small flames and a stinking pall of smoke hanging over it all. I made sure Paula was all right, then sent out a Mayday distress call on the radio. I hadn't had a drink of water in thirty-six hours, and thankfully gulped from a bottle in our little galley. Then I got the boat's toolbox and sat down with Paula and tried to unfasten her handcuffs while I explained what had happened.

Right from the beginning, things hadn't been as they'd seemed. Paula's apparently innocent cheap holiday offer to Broome had been engineered by Derek Mankey. He didn't own the pearl fields, but rather operated them for a syndicate of, I imagined, rather dangerous people. They employed Chay Gatt, not to protect Mankey, but to watch him, to make sure he didn't siphon off pearls for himself. Frustrated by this arrangement, Mankey had hit upon a scheme to defraud them, just as he had once defrauded Paula and me and our friends. He couldn't just send his sidekick Justin in a boat up to the pearl farm to steal pearls, because the constant aerial and satellite surveillance of those waters would have sent word back to Broome of an illegal operation. So when he'd heard of Paula's husband's suicide, he'd hit upon a nasty scheme to lure her, and me, into playing the role of the thieves. We, with Justin acting on Mankey's instructions, would raid the pearl farm, gather the pearls, then be betrayed by Justin and duly punished. But the pearls would not be discovered, and would be retrieved later by Mankey and Justin.

Things, of course, didn't work out that way. First I removed the pearls, causing distrust between Mankey and Justin, and then Chay began to suspect that something dodgy was going on. Justin had in fact decided to cheat them all, by swallowing the best of the most valuable pearls, and when Chay forced the truth out of him, he suffered that terrible fate on the ship's operating theatre.

We sat in silence in the dark, thinking over the whole extraordinary story, then Paula said, 'I owe you an apology, Ben. I thought you had become a useless drunk, and instead you turned out to be the hero."

"No," I said, "you were right, I had."

"And I had become a bitter and angry old bitch. Maybe this has changed us both.'

I took her hand and felt the pressure of her fingers.

"Shame about the pearls, though," she said.

"Yeah."

"How much were they worth, do you know?"

"Justin reckoned a couple of million."

I gave a little snort at the thought, and she giggled, and then we were both laughing, tears running down our faces, our laughter echoing out across the waters to the wilderness beyond.

When we finally settled down, I lit a lamp and then reached under my left armpit and with a wince ripped off the dressing strip I'd stuck there. I held my hand under the light and showed her what I had. She gasped as she recognized it – the blood pearl, its impossible deep lustrous colour glowing in the light.

I finally managed to get the handcuffs free just before the first helicopter arrived, and the questions began. We told the story we'd agreed upon, the innocent trip to the pearl farm at the invitation of Derek Mankey, the smell of gas in the ship's galley, the shocking explosion, the devastating loss of Mankey, Justin and Chay Gatt. We were given a medical check, then allowed to take our hired boat back down to Broome, where we were interviewed again, over several days. We enjoyed our enforced stay there, Paula and I, and as the days passed, we became closer.

A couple of months after we returned to the east coast, we had another holiday together, to Hong Kong. While we were there we visited the pearl market. Justin had told us that the blood pearl was worth more than all the rest put together, and our discreet inquiries with the merchants in Hong Kong confirmed it. They were astonished by it and eager to buy, but we decided to hang on to it. Paula wears it now, on special occasions, as she did recently on our wedding day.

THE COMMON ENEMY

Natasha Cooper

THE SCREAMING STARTED early that night, only a few minutes after "News at Ten" had started, instead of nearer midnight. Sue Chalmers swore.

"Don't let it get to you," Dan said, chucking the *Evening Standard* on the floor by his chair. "Block it out."

"How can I? Night after bloody night. They have to yell like that to make it sound as if they're having fun, when they're really feeling sick as dogs from all the booze and just as unsure and lonely and wondering why they don't enjoy the stuff everyone else does as we were when we were in our teens. I'd like to ram their stupid little heads against the nearest wall and bash some sense into them."

Dan pulled his long body out of his chair, brushing his hand casually against her hair as he passed on his way out. She was so tense the pressure on her scalp seemed like an assault instead of the comfort she knew it was supposed to be.

"I know," she said through her teeth. "They're only young. And you hate it when I'm so vehement. But it gets to me."

"Tea?"

"Why not?" She leaned back and turned her head so she could smile over the back of the chair. "Sorry."

The newsreader was talking about the Middle East and Sue hated herself for getting so wound up about a bit of irritating noise when there were people out there living in hell. Dying, too. A dose of that kind of reality would sort out the shrieking, drunken teenagers and make them see what really mattered.

When silence fell five minutes later, it was like warmed oil oozing into an aching ear. Sue felt able to concentrate on the news again. Dan came back with the tea. This time, his hand on her head felt right, kind. She leaned closer to him.

Ten minutes after that footsteps sounded on the narrow pavement outside. They were even more familiar than the partying teenagers' screeches: Maggie Tulloch from three houses down was on her way home from another long stint in the probation office. Tonight her feet were dragging more than usual. She must have had a frustrating day. Sue liked her, and admired the way she went on and on trying to make her clients behave like human beings instead of filthy, thieving thugs.

Maggie heard Sue's television as she walked past the windows of number twenty-three, knowing she had only a minute and a half more of freedom. You shouldn't use your job as an excuse to stay out late, she thought, then took some reassurance from the knowledge that her work mattered.

If only one of the miserable, infuriating, self-indulgent, drug-addled ex-cons she had to deal with refrained from hurting someone else because of her efforts, then her addiction to work would be justified. The trouble was, none of them had refrained yet, and she'd been doing the job for thirteen years.

She stopped on her own front door step and had to force herself to get out her key and stuff it in the keyhole. The television was on in her house too, but unlikely to be showing anything as real or useful as the news. Leaning sideways to listen, she caught Celia Johnson's clipped and tragic voice, saying: "It can't last. This misery can't last."

Oh can't it? Maggie crunched her key in the lock and turned it.

"Hi, Mum!" she said aloud as she dumped her briefcase by the cold radiator and swung off her thin linen jacket to hang it over the end of the bannisters.

"You're late, darling."

I wish you wouldn't call me darling, she thought, when everything else you say shows how much you hate me.

"Your supper's probably ruined, although I did turn the oven down a couple of hours ago. It's chicken."

"No worries." Maggie walked towards the kitchen, repeating Celia Johnson's thought: it can't last; this misery can't last.

How sensible it had seemed when her father had died only months after her husband had decided that married life and a toddler were not for him after all. She'd needed help; her mother, pension-less, work-less and utterly lost, had needed somewhere to live and something to do. Thirteen years ago.

The toddler was now fifteen, nearly sixteen. And Maggie's mother was not lost or uncertain any longer. Absolutely certain, in fact, about everything that was wrong with her daughter and the way she was bringing up Gemma, and not at all surprised Michael had decided to leave because who could possibly want to spend his life with someone who wouldn't eat what she was given, who dressed so badly, who swore so much, who was so work-obsessed she was the most boring person on earth, who was so ...

Don't do it, Maggie said to herself. Don't let her get to you. These are old battles and they can only be fought by two people. Refuse to fight back and she'll stop. One day she'll stop.

She listened again, then felt her neck muscles relaxing. For once there wasn't any thudding angry music from Gemma's room, distracting her from the work she had to do if she was to get anywhere near a decent university. Maggie looked at the kitchen clock. Ten fifteen. That meant fifteen minutes to eat whatever was edible from the oven and calm down, then nip up to talk to Gemma and make sure she was feeling okay about tomorrow's exam, then a long hot bath and bed.

An open bottle of Australian Shiraz stood by the cooker. She slopped some into a huge old rummer. It had been one of the few wedding presents Michael hadn't taken with him. Then she took herself to task, found a second rummer, polished it carefully, filled it with wine and carried both through to the sitting room.

"Oh, darling, is that for me?" Her mother glanced away from the screen for a second. "Isn't it rather a lot?"

"You don't need to drink it all if it's too much," Maggie said, lowering herself on to the sofa and letting her eyes close for a second. She took a deep swallow. "Mmm. My drug of choice!"

"Don't be like that, darling. You're nowhere near addicted, even if you do drink ra-ather more than you should."

"Thanks, Mum." Maggie looked at Celia Johnson being intensely unhappy on the screen and wondered whether the choice of film was meant as a reproach. She knew her mother was lonely, and maybe it wasn't her fault that she wouldn't even try to make friends or find herself any kind of occupation except watching DVDs of old films. "How was your day?"

"Tiresome." She flashed a long-suffering smile at Maggie, who smiled back and felt her jaw muscles crack. "You know the gas man was supposed to deal with the boiler."

"I remember. Didn't he come?"

"Of course not, and then there weren't any pomegranates left in the supermarket, so I couldn't do Gemma's favourite dish, which I'd promised her as a pre-exam treat."

"She'll understand." Maggie drank again. "And you've obviously managed her brilliantly tonight, getting her to work without that awful music taking half her attention away from her books."

"Oh, she's not in tonight, darling. She needed a treat to relax her before tomorrow, so I gave her a little something to augment your mingy allowance and said she could go and see that friend of hers, who lives so near. Gillie, isn't it?"

Maggie put down her glass as though she didn't trust herself not to throw its contents all over her mother.

"You did what? On the night before an exam? Mum, how could you? You know how hard it's been to make Gemma take her work seriously. For God's sake!"

And then her mother laughed, with a pitying, condescending kind of amusement that turned all kinds of ancient levers in Maggie's brain.

"Funny how things change, darling. I can see you now, standing with your arms akimbo, thirty years ago, explaining to me precisely why I was the cruellest woman in the world when I forbade you to see your best friend on a school night."

Maggie turned on her heel and headed for the kitchen. Even dried-out charred chicken would help stifle all the words she couldn't say, musn't say.

I'm not a cruel woman, she told herself. Anyone would find this hard. It can't last.

She switched off the oven, opened the door and looked at the blackened stumpy chicken legs. There were four, which meant

Gemma hadn't eaten before she left. The ration was always one drumstick and one thigh each. Her teeth were more than sharp enough to rip the hardened flesh from the bones of two of the joints, then she ran the cold tap until the water was icy, washing first her hands and then her face.

When she went back to the sitting room, she was calm enough to say: "I know I was a tiresome adolescent, but you can't hold it against me forever. You know why I want Gemma to stay here on school nights. Encouraging her to rebel may give you satisfaction, but it's damaging all her chances."

"Don't make such a fuss, darling. She'll be back any minute now. She promised to leave Gillie's by ten."

"*What?*" Maggie reached for the phone, feeling the ground lurch beneath her feet. She knew the number as well as she knew her own, but for a few awful seconds she couldn't make her fingers work. At last she heard the ringing, on and on, then the voicemail cut in:

"Hi, it's Gemma," came the light cheery voice. "I'm having much too good a time to answer, so leave a message and I'll ring you back. Bye."

"Gemma, it's Mum. Phone me." It was at least three years since Gemma had last addressed her as Mum, but she wasn't going to call herself Maggie to her own daughter.

She found the number of Gillie's house and rang it. Diana, Gillie's mother, answered almost at once.

"It's Maggie," she said, without any kind of greeting. "Is Gemma there? I need to talk to her."

"Oh, hi, Mags. No, she isn't. She left, what? Must be at least twenty minutes ago. She'd promised your mother she'd be home by ten. Isn't she back yet?"

"No." The floor wasn't moving any more, but waves of heat and cold were washing through Maggie and she felt more unsafe than ever. "It shouldn't have taken her more than six minutes at the very most. Did she leave on her own?"

"Of course, not. I wouldn't have let her. Jed was with her. You know, Jed Springthorpe, the most responsible boy in the whole school. She'll be all right with him. Honestly, Maggie. Don't fret. They've probably just stopped off for an illicit drink. Or a fag or two. I know they're not supposed to smoke, but I bet they do."

Maggie muttered something vaguely polite, then cut the connection to phone Gemma's mobile again. Again she got the jaunty message.

"I'm going to look for her."

"I'll come with you."

"Mum, don't be silly. With your knees, I'll be quicker on my own. And someone needs to be here in case she gets back."

Maggie thought there was no point bothering with a jacket. The air was warm enough. Even the pavements still held some of the day's heat. Thank God it was light still. Somehow this would seem even worse in the dark. And Gemma was nearly sixteen. Lots of people started work at sixteen. In her day, people of that age were travelling the world on their own. Maybe they still were. This panic was absurd.

But she couldn't keep it down. Something had happened. Gemma never turned off her phone. And she never left it to ring so long the voicemail cut in. She was far, far too keen to have any kind of contact with anyone.

She and Jed could have chosen any of four different routes from Gillie's house on the other side of the main road. The most direct would have taken them past the local supermarket, but there were no enticing attractions to make them linger there. It shut early on Mondays, so they wouldn't even have been tempted to drop in to buy drink. But two of the other streets had pubs, and the third an expensive wine bar. Normally that would have been out of their reach financially, but tonight they had the money Maggie's mother had handed over.

Maggie pushed open the door of the first pub to be assaulted by heavy, pounding music, and excited yelling conversations. She almost fainted with relief when she saw the bright blonde straight hair of a tall slim girl by the bar.

"Gemma!" she shouted across the shrieky crowd. "Gemma!"

Three girls looked round. None of them was her daughter. The girl at the bar turned her head lazily, perhaps wondering at the unexpectedly adult voice, and revealed herself to be a total stranger.

Maggie was out again an instant later, running now towards the other pub. She had no more luck there. Outside again, she sent Gemma a text:

"RUOK? Pls phone."

Then she waited, leaning against the wall outside the pub, among a bunch of curious smokers, staring down at the small screen, begging for an answer. Nothing came. She phoned again. Again she heard the message.

"Jed," she said aloud, trying to think of the quickest way of getting his number. Her mind wasn't working properly. Gillie, obviously. But she hadn't brought that number with her either.

She began to run again, heading for home by the most direct route, needing to get to her address book as fast as possible. Her useless feet caught in every loose paving stone, until she gave up and kicked off her shoes, bending down to scoop them under one arm. As she righted herself, she pressed the speed dial for Gemma's number, and ran on, her shoeless feet keeping a much better grip on the paving stones.

Her tights ripped in moments, but that didn't matter, and once her right foot hit something soft, disgusting. Even that didn't make her pause. She ran on until a stitch savaged her midriff and forced her to stop just at the entrance to the supermarket carpark.

She'd forgotten the disabling pain; it was so long since she'd moved faster than a brisk walk. Gasping, fighting to get past the spasm, hugging herself, she looked at the long low buildings of the supermarket and thought how odd they seemed with no lights on and no cars lined up in front. Rubbish was strewn all round the recycling bins and the lid of the paper and cardboard one was propped open.

A ringing sound forced itself into her mind, and she looked down at the little phone she was carrying, sticky now from the sweat on her hand. The sound wasn't coming from there; all she could hear as she held it was a faint buzz, but the rhythm of buzz and ring was the same.

When she put her finger on the off button the ringing stopped, along with the buzz. She pressed the speed dial button for Gemma's phone again and the ringing started up. The sound was coming from somewhere near the recycling bins.

"She dropped her phone," Maggie said, holding her right hand over her heart, as though to hold down its leaping and banging. "That's all that's happened. She's not answering because she lost her phone. She's probably safe home by now and they're laughing at my neuroses again."

Miraculously the stitch had gone, and the breathlessness with it. She felt fit and well and marginally more sensible.

She followed the ringing sound as she searched for the phone. If she could restore it to Gemma, it might help their continuing war, show how she understood that endless phoning was important, and texting and friends and doing everything except revision.

Another sound punctuated the ringing. A tiny gasping voice. "Mum. Mum. Mum. Mum. Please. Oh, please. Mum."

Maggie felt as if something had gone wrong with time, as though it was stretching out towards eternity. Her thoughts were racing, but each step took aeons to achieve.

Each recycling-bin lid she lifted seemed to weigh several tons. That agonizing voice went on and on and the phone kept ringing. She reached the glass recycling-bin and fought with the lid.

"Mum. Mum. Mum. Please come. Please. Mum."

This was the one. The voice was louder here.

"Gemma, darling, I'm here. Don't worry. I'm here."

The light was much dimmer now. It must have been nearly eleven. But Maggie could see down into the blackness of the bin, to where her daughter was lying in a foetal curl.

Gemma's head was a mass of dark-red stickness, the laboriously straightened, gleaming blonde hair matted now with blood. Light from the street lamps caught edges of broken glass and showed cuts all up and down the bent bare legs.

Maggie leaned down to touch her daughter's skin, but her arms were too short to reach deep enough into the bin. She punched 999 into her phone, all the time saying Gemma's name, pouring out words of reassurance that meant absolutely nothing, because there was no reassurance to be had here.

"Police," she said into the phone when they answered. "Police and ambulance."

"What's your address?"

She told them where she was and what she'd found, not saying it was her own daughter.

A patrol car drew up only two minutes later, and two uniformed officers got out, putting on their caps as they strolled towards her.

Maggie couldn't speak now, just gestured towards the bin and stood back to let them see.

"Christ!" said one, pulling at his phone.

"I've already asked for an ambulance," Maggie said, surprised to find that her voice still worked. "Thanks for coming so quickly."

She couldn't understand why the two officers looked at each other in such a weird way.

"We'll hurry up the ambulance," said the woman. "Come and sit in the car and tell me how you found this girl."

"What?" Maggie stared at the officer's pleasant pink ignorant face. "What d'you mean, sit in the car? I'm not leaving her."

Later, hours and hours later in the hospital, she was sitting down, waiting. She'd told the police everything she knew. She'd phoned her mother to report and spent what felt like hours reassuring her. No, no, of course it wasn't your fault. Of course you were doing what you thought was right. It was generous of you to give her money.

And then she'd come back here to wait, sitting on the edge of the hard plastic chair, not even noticing it was cutting off the blood supply in her legs until the pins and needles started actively to hurt.

A white-coated girl, woman, was walking towards Maggie now. The stethoscope banged her chest lightly with every step. Her expression was serious. Maggie ground the nails of one hand into the palm of the other, and waited again.

"She hasn't been raped," said the doctor. "That's one thing."

"And the rest? How bad is it?"

"All head injuries are serious. She's taken quite a kicking. I'd say there were at least two of them. Scans show she's been bleeding into the brain, but we don't yet know the full extent of any damage."

"And the prognosis?"

The doctor's face froze into blank, stubborn politeness, and something inside Maggie – some last vestige of hope – died.

"Darling! Darling, wake up!"

Maggie opened her gummy eyes. Moving her neck was agony. She'd fallen asleep with her head at an atrocious angle against the wall.

"I've brought you some coffee. Come on. It's a new day. You need to be strong now."

"Have they said anything?"

Her mother bit her lip. "Not yet. I got here about an hour ago, and they said they wouldn't know anything for a while. But the police are coming. They're going to want to talk to you, and I thought you'd like a chance to have some coffee, and maybe a wash even."

Maggie was picking hard crunchy grits out of the corners of her eyes. She took her fingers away and looked at her mother, whose own eyes were covered with a film of tears.

"Come on, Maggie darling. There's a cloakroom at the end of the passage. Shall I take you?"

A tiny smile was all she could produce, but she could see it registering, which made it easier to speak without snapping.

"I can probably manage. But thank you, Mum."

Her mother's hand encircled her wrist for a second, then let her go. "I'll be here with the coffee," she said. "And I brought a sandwich too in case you're hungry, but it doesn't matter if you're not. You don't have to eat it."

Tears were pouring down Maggie's face as she headed for the loos.

The police officer who was waiting beside her mother looked much more senior than the two who'd come last night. He was wearing a suit made of some thinnish grey material and a white shirt, with a dark-blue tie.

"Mrs Tulloch?" he said, shaking her hand. "I'm very sorry about what's happened to your daughter. Do you feel up to talking?"

"If it'll help," said Maggie.

Her throat felt as though someone had stuffed it with wire wool they'd then pulled slowly up and down all night. And all her joints were stiff and painful.

"Didn't anyone see anything?" she said. "Or hear it? I know the supermarket shuts early on Mondays, but there are usually people in the streets at that time. And there are houses all round. You can't be kicked like that and make no noise. Someone must have heard something. The marks on her body make the doctors think there were two of them at it."

Which means it wasn't Jed, she suddenly thought, with real gratitude. Jed. Why didn't I think of him before?

"Has anyone found the boy?" she said aloud.

"Boy?" said the inspector. "What boy?"

And so she told him about Jed, who was supposed to have been so responsibly escorting Gemma home by ten o'clock.

"Have you got a phone number?"

"No. But I can get it for you."

"Or a surname?"

Her brain had shut down again as guilt poured through it. What if Jed had been in one of the other bins, bleeding all night, bleeding out maybe? Dying? And she hadn't said anything.

"Gerald Springthorpe," said her mother.

"Was he – I mean, *is* he Gemma's boyfriend?"

"No. Just a friend. They're all at school together, so he's probably sitting in the exam room now."

Maggie noticed that her mother was talking absolutely normally, sensibly, without any carping or martyring herself. She was in charge, and in some weird way it helped.

"We'll talk to him later. Can you tell me ...?"

His voice seemed to be coming from further and further away. Maggie's temperature control had gone again. Shivering, boiling, she felt the floor tilting upwards and then nothing.

They'd found Jed by the time Gemma was pronounced dead three hours later, and one of the DI's juniors was relaying his story to Maggie. Listening to it helped to hold her in the present, but it couldn't stop the tears that came out of her eyes in great gouts. More fluid than she'd ever have believed a body could hold. She didn't even try to stop them, or dry her face.

"He says they were together all the way to the Bull, then a mate of his called out and wanted them to come in for a drink," the police officer told her. "He says Gemma refused, said her nan would kill her if she was late home again. He said OK, he'd take her to the door, then come back to join his mate in the pub, but Gemma asked him if he thought she was a baby."

"So he let her go," Maggie said, thinking what tiny things had made this huge unalterable disaster: her own insistence on not being out late on school nights; Gemma's pride; Jed's friend hanging around the pub at just the wrong moment.

"It wasn't his fault, Mrs Tulloch. Really it wasn't."

"Didn't he hear anything?" Maggie said. "It was only a street way. She must have screamed."

Then she thought about the noise she'd heard in the pub. Jed had probably been inside then. If she'd known, if he'd recognized her, would there have been time to find and save Gemma?

Maggie bent over her knees, fighting to keep the howl inside her body.

"With all that music no one could've heard anything from outside," the officer said, then echoed her thoughts: "You'd know that I expect. I mean, you were in there yourself. We've got you on the CCTV, calling her name. Jed and his mate were there, too. The film proves his story."

"So no one knows who did it?"

"Not yet. I'm sorry, Mrs Tulloch. We're doing everything we can. We've taken every possible kind of sample. The labs will ..."

Maggie stopped listening. What did it matter anyway? Gemma was dead. It could've been anyone – one of her own clients, even, hanging about, bored, grabbing a passing girl to rob her of her phone and whatever pathetic little amount of money she had.

Had she fought back? Was that why they'd kicked her to death. Or were they crack-crazed thugs, getting off on her terror and their power?

"What about the secret cameras by the bins?" said her mother.

Maggie raised her sodden face and saw the officer looking sceptical.

"What secret cameras?" he said.

"The council put them there by the bins only a few weeks ago. One or two of the sluttier neighbours were flytipping nearly every day. Dumping their smelly rubbish in the recycling bins. So we got the council to put the cameras there. They should've had film in and been running. They must show what happened."

"It'll haunt me until I die," Sue Chalmers said to Dan that night. "They were only thin scraggy boys who did it. Twelve-year-olds. You and I could've fought them off, stopped them killing her, if we'd known. But how could we know?"

"It's not our fault. I phoned the cops when we heard the screaming but it took them more than half an hour to come."

"You did *what*?"

"Like you, I thought it was just kids making a racket, enjoying themselves, so I rang the local nick to complain, instead of 999. By the time they got round to investigating, poor Maggie Tulloch had already found Gemma. But at least they've got the boys now, and the evidence to prove it was them. They'll definitely go down for it."

"I don't suppose that'll help Maggie, though. D'you think I ought to go round and see her?"

"No. You'd be intruding on that awful grief. And she's got her mother with her, after all."

BLOODSPORT

Tom Cain

1

Looking through the sniper sight as the couple left their holiday home and walked down the path between the rhododendrons, down to the gate where a scrum of photographers, reporters and TV crews were waiting, it was the wife Carver felt sorry for. He had nothing against her. Quite liked her, in fact, as much as you can like anyone you've never met or even spoken to. From everything he'd seen, she seemed sensible and down-to-earth. She looked like she was doing her level best to show that there was at least one sane person in the country who still thought her husband was up to the job. Carver thought she was wrong, but he admired her loyalty in trying.

So the fact that this perfectly pleasant woman would soon be wiping blood off her simple, unpretentious summer dress – chosen, he supposed, in the hope of pleasing all the bitchy columnists who'd accuse her of dowdiness if she looked too plain, or vulgarity if she went for anything too expensive in these recessionary times – well, that bothered him.

Not enough to call the whole thing off: but it bothered him nonetheless.

Her husband, though – the Prime Minister of the United Kingdom of Great Britain and Northern Ireland, and First Lord of the Treasury – he was a different matter. Carver had a bone to pick with him.

After all the politicians' lies, the corruption, the greed, the mountainous debts, the obsessive control freakery and the rampant incompetence, it had taken the death of a single soldier in Afghanistan to shift Carver out of the general herd of pissed-off, moaning but essentially inert citizens, into a group of one: the man who was going to do something about it.

The soldier's name was Mike Swift. In the newspapers, he'd been described as a Major in the Royal Marines. The reports said he'd been attached to the British forces' headquarters staff in Helmand province. They said he'd died in a helicopter accident.

The newspaper reports were bullshit.

Carver didn't need anyone to tell him that Swift, though his original commission was indeed in the Marines, had actually served as an officer in the Special Forces. He'd arrived in the SBS as a first lieutenant, newly elevated from one elite force into an even more exclusive group of fighting men during Carver's last couple of years in uniform. Carver remembered Swift well: tough despite his youth and inexperience, resourceful, respected by his men and blessed with a thoughtful, reflective side to his nature that always conveyed a sense that he saw the bigger picture. Even as a junior officer, Swift had clearly been destined for bigger things. Now he was lying in a coffin, awaiting his last flight back to RAF Lyneham.

It took a call to another former SBS man, Bobby Faulkner, to tell Carver what had really happened. By "accident" the Ministry of Defence did not mean that a helicopter had crashed. The truth was, it had never turned up at all. When Swift had called in, requesting immediate extraction from a job up-country that had just turned critical, he'd been out of luck. The British Army had been forced to act like a third-rate radiocab company on a busy Saturday night. There weren't any aircraft available. They were all busy. Those that weren't already being used were out of service: "Sorry, sir, have you tried the Americans?"

The Taleban made sure that Swift's body was found, just as they'd done with his redcoated predecessors, back in 1841. There's something about a body with the skin flayed off its limbs, the entrails neatly piled upon a slit-open stomach and a crudely-carved, gaping wound where the genitalia should be that sends a powerful message.

The general public had not heard the message. Great trouble had been taken to ensure they never would. But Carver had inside channels unavailable to the average punter. He'd heard the message all right. And the moment he did, he decided to act upon it.

Very publicly.
With force.

2

Carver was high up an oak tree. He'd been there for three days,
remaining as motionless as humanly possible, rendered invisible by
the combination of thick summer foliage and a shaggy, camouflaged ghillie suit that broke up his outline and blended him into his
surroundings.

The oak grew beside a lake in Cumbria. Carver had his back to
the water. In front of him was an open expanse of grass, which ran
as far as a road that ran north–south, parallel to the eastern shore of
the lake. For the past thirty minutes there had been no traffic along
the road, nor would there be for another thirty to come. Manned
police barriers, approximately 200 yards apart, both clearly visible
to Carver, had made sure of that.

Directly opposite Carver's position there was a turning off the
road, which formed a semi-circle of tarmac, ringed by the high brick
walls of a large property. This semi-circle was where the media were
massed. Their assorted cars, vans and trucks, now parked along the
road on either side of the semi-circle, and the police cars that had
accompanied them, had been the last vehicles allowed past the
barriers.

The walls were lined with trees and shrubs and bisected, right in
the middle of their arc, by a gate. Behind it a tarmac drive led up to
the Victorian villa that had been rented for the Prime Minister's
holiday accommodation. Carver was watching the PM and his wife
walk down that drive towards the gate, the waiting media and,
though they did not know it, to him.

The official schedule for the next few minutes had been very tightly
scripted. Every move that the prime ministerial couple would make,
and every word they would say had been accounted for. They'd walk
up to the gates, apparently engrossed in happy conversation and
pleasurable contemplation of the property's well-manicured grounds
and delightful lake views. The gates would open. The couple would
walk through them and pose with the gestures of enforced normality
that distinguish pictures of politicians, regardless of race or ideology,

attempting to look like normal human beings. Carver felt reasonably certain that this would involve the Prime Minister pointing off towards the middle distance while the missus followed his finger with a look of adoring fascination plastered on her face. He had never seen any normal human beings do this, but somehow it was expected of our leaders and their spouses.

A few bland questions would be asked, avoiding any reference to contentious political issues and concentrating instead on the general desirability of a family holiday amidst the glories of the British countryside. The Prime Minister would assure his people, with a cheery smile, that he was enjoying himself enormously.

More pictures would be taken and then proceedings would draw to a close and the loving couple would walk back through the now-closing gate and up the drive again.

Whoever had scripted the whole charade had cast the stars, brought in the extras and even found a delightful set. The one thing they had not counted upon was the special effects. Samuel Carver would be providing them.

Or would he?

Now that the time was drawing near, he suddenly felt afflicted by doubts and misgivings. The whole thing had been almost too easy up to this point. Carver had contacts from his old days in the forces scattered throughout Whitehall, the private security industry and even the media – nothing said "credible defence analyst" like actual combat experience. They had managed to find out everything he'd needed to know. He had been careful not to tell them exactly what he had in mind, if only to save them from any legal retribution later. But his general intentions had been clear enough. Yet between them they gave him everything he needed: schedules, locations, security protocols, shift patterns (because the most vulnerable moment for any security operation is the handover between one shift and another), even the precise gap between the couple and the rope holding back the photographers. And then, when he'd asked for one, last personal favour, every one of them had willingly complied. Perhaps he shouldn't have been surprised. Feelings were running high.

So he had emerged from the lake at 4 a.m., three nights earlier, taken up his position and begun his long wait. And all the while a thought had been growing in the back of his mind, a niggling seed of doubt that had steadily expanded until now it seemed to fill his whole consciousness. For whatever he had done and how many sins he had committed Carver believed himself to be, if not a good man – there were too many deaths on his conscience for that – certainly a man of honour and integrity. Many years ago he had sworn to serve his Queen and country, and he still felt bound by that obligation.

He was certainly not a psychopath. He had a conscience and a profound sense of right and wrong. And so, as he lay in that oak tree, he kept asking himself, "Can I really go through with this?"

3

The US Army regards the Heckler and Koch 416 assault rifle, a development of the standard M4 carbine, to be the best gun of its kind in the world. Its elite Delta Force actually helped develop the 416's design. So Uncle Sam is happy to pay up to $1,425 a unit to provide his top troops with such an outstanding weapon. Samuel Carver, like the men of Delta Force, was armed with an M4 variant. It was called the RAP T68 Avenger, and in the custom specification he required it had cost him just over $4,000, roughly three times as much as a 416. It really was a very, very special piece of kit.

The T68 was much quieter than a conventional weapon. It emitted no muzzle flash, making it much harder for any opponent to spot. Its rounds were of a much larger calibre than standard ammunition, exploded on impact and were virtually guaranteed to take out anyone they hit. The T68 was a game-changer.

For every ladder, however, there must be a snake, and the slithery reptile in this particular case was that the maximum range of the T68 was just 300 ft. For anyone interested in marksmanship – anyone, for example, intending to take out a target with a headshot – the effective range was reduced to a mere 150 ft. Carver was aiming for the body, but even so, he had a lot further than 150 ft to cover. And it wasn't an easy shot given the downward angle at which he was shooting, the breeze off the lake and the mass of men and women, armed with cameras and microphones, who were standing directly between him and his target. Carver was no great fan of the journalist classes. But he didn't want to hit one of them.

Overhead, a police helicopter was sweeping the area. It would be gone by the time the couple reached the gate of the property: no one wanted the noise of a chopper to interfere with the audio quality of the Prime Minister's interview. But its presence provided a welcome distraction for Carver. It made him forget his moral qualms and worry about a practical issue: the degree to which he was shielded from any thermal imaging equipment the helicopter or the officers aboard it might be carrying. It was a warm day, with bright sunshine. He was counting on them trusting their own eyes to do the job.

The helicopter made one last pass over the scene of the photocall and the surrounding area then clattered away across the lake. The air fell silent. Now Carver had nothing to take his mind off his self-appointed mission.

He nestled the butt of his rifle against his shoulder and went into the standard routine of slow, deep breaths, preparing to shoot after he had exhaled, at the calmest point of the cycle. He visualized the process: the smooth, easy trigger action; the repetition as he went for his second and third shots.

Through the T68's Super Sniper 3-12 × 50 Scope, he could see every line on the Prime Minister's face.

The green crosshairs moved downwards, past the open collar of the PM's shirt to a point directly between the narrowest parts of the lapels of his casual, holiday jacket, smack in the middle of his chest.

Carver kept the sight there as his target – a man, he reflected, who had done him no personal harm: who could not even raise his taxes, since Carver had long lived in a flat in Geneva – proceeded through the gates of his rented lakeside villa, and up to the mark where he and his wife would stand for the photocall. The mark, Carver knew, was 247ft from where he lay, at one corner of a right-angled triangle. The ground formed the long, horizontal side. The tree formed the short, vertical side. The line of fire was the hypotenuse. Basic geometry.

The Prime Minister reached his mark.

Carver could not shoot.

For the first time in his life, his will, or maybe his nerve had deserted him. He had sabotaged planes and helicopters and condemned their inhabitants to terrible, screaming deaths. He had sent cars spinning across motorways into the paths on oncoming trucks. He had set houses alight, along with everyone in them. He had shot, stabbed and strangled. But this, for some reason, he suddenly could not do.

He gave a single sharp shake of the head, as if physically trying to dislodge his uncertainty.

Carver settled back into his routine: slow, deep breaths; mental images of smooth, easy trigger-pulls; preparation for subsequent shots.

The Prime Minister was posing for pictures. He was smiling at his wife. He was, as Carver had predicted, pointing at something across the lake. His wife appeared to find this utterly fascinating. The green crosshairs were still pointing directly at his chest: the fourth button down of his shirt, to be precise.

Still Carver did not shoot.

Now the Prime Minister was taking a question. It seemed to be a very entertaining question, since he was smiling and even chuckling as he answered.

Carver knew the schedule. There would be three questions. At the end of those questions, the PM and his wife would turn around and walk back the way they came. His chance would be gone.

There was a second question, a second smiling answer.

No shot.

Then the third question was asked. The Prime Minister nodded thoughtfully and brought his hands up in front of him to emphasize a point he was making.

Carver fired.

He shot three times, and they all hit.

Three crimson explosions burst upon the Prime Minister's chest. He staggered backwards, stunned by the force of the blows. Blood erupted over his body, his hands and the shocked woman standing beside him. As her husband fell backwards to the ground, she began to scream as she saw that the blood was on her too. So much blood, spattering over her pretty summer dress.

The media onlookers were split between those too horrified by what they were witnessing to be able to function and those hardier, more experienced souls who kept their cameras running, tightened the focus, grabbed every second of footage that would now be flashing around the world as a small, domestic photocall became a global phenomenon.

All the policemen, MI5 agents and counter-terrorism specialists, in and out of uniform, were shouting at one another, looking round to try to find the origin of the shots, desperately calling for medical attention. They were giving in to the momentary loss of control that grips even the best-trained operatives when the unthinkable occurs.

So it took a few seconds for people to notice that the Prime Minister was slowly getting back to his feet, rubbing the back of his head where it had hit the tarmac. He was drenched in blood, but he was, as he tried to assure his poor wife, completely fine.

The cameras kept clicking and rolling. The news-reporters changed the tone of their coverage from horror at a death to bafflement at an amazing resurrection. And at that precise moment an e-mail arrived at the Press Association in Vauxhall Bridge Road, London, copied to the BBC News headquarters at Broadcasting House and CNN's European headquarters in Great Marlborough Street. It was signed by a number of former officers in Her Majesty's armed forces and it revealed that they had donated the blood with which the Prime Minister had just been covered. He now, they observed, really did have the blood of British soldiers on his hands.

Carver, meanwhile, had taken advantage of the total confusion at the scene of the hit to slip out of his ghillie suit, scramble down the tree and slide into the water of the lake. He swam away under water, using a standard Special Forces rebreather system.

He left his gun behind in the tree, carefully wiped down to remove any fingerprints or DNA traces.

The RAP T68 Avenger bills itself as the finest paintball weapon in the world.

THE RAT IN THE ATTIC

Brian McGilloway

"SHE'S NOT WISE, Inspector," Artie Moran said, squinting against the glare of the winter sunlight reflected off the snow blanketing his garden. He raised his hand above his eyes to reduce the glare and nodded towards the Transit van parked in the driveway, the snow an inch thick on the windscreen. "I've not been out all night. Who'd drive in that weather?"

"You've no idea what happened to her cat?"

"None: *I* didn't kill it."

I had called out to see Moran's immediate neighbour, Mary Hannigan, that morning. The thickening snow meant it took me almost twenty-five minutes to drive the ten miles to the estate of semi-detached houses where they lived, the car wheels spinning beneath me on corners. All for a bloody cat.

Mary, now well into her eighties, had spent her working life as a primary-school teacher. Despite this (or indeed perhaps because of it), she had never had any children of her own and had, seemingly, grown increasingly eccentric over the latter years of her widowhood following the death of her husband, Robert. For a few years now, someone from the station called her each morning at 9 a.m. While initially the call had been an alarm call for Mary, increasingly we saw it as a way of checking that she was okay. It had been my turn to call her that morning and, when I did, she had begun crying on the phone.

She'd answered her door wearing a woollen hat and a heavy man's overcoat that hung down almost to her furred boots, gesturing me into her house without comment, then shutting the door behind me.

"To keep in the heat," she explained.

I stood to one side in her hallway, pressing the backs of my legs against the storage heater, but the metal casing provided little warmth.

"Would you not be better turning the heating up, Mary?" I asked, my breath misting before me.

"I can't afford it," she snapped. "My electric bill's gone through the roof. I called the electric company but they're thieves the lot of them. I haven't the money to run the heating high."

"You took your time," she muttered as she shuffled down the hallway. "It could just have easily been me that was murdered."

"Murdered?"

"It's Tammy," she said, turning towards me, her features sharp with anger. "That thug, Moran, next door killed her."

"Who's Tammy?"

She gestured with one crooked finger that I should follow her into the kitchen. In the corner, in a small plastic bed, lay the stiffened body of a cat.

Mary looked at the bed askance, then rifled up her coat sleeve and produced a tissue which she held against her nose in preparation for further tears.

"I didn't know you had a cat, Mary?" I said. In truth, despite calling her a number of times from the station, I had never been in Mary's house before. I wondered was it always so cold.

"She weren't mine," Mary said. "She was Robert's. We've had her nine years. Then that animal killed her. He hit her with his van."

"Did you see this happen?"

She shook her head, her mouth a tight white line. "No need. He drives in and out of here at all times of the day and night. I came out for her this morning and she was lying dead on the road. He just left her there." Her eyes, red and rheumy, began to weep. "Left her lying," she repeated.

I squatted down to the animal. Despite her claim, it bore no injuries on either side of the body.

"Tammy wouldn't have died of natural causes, Mary?" I asked. "I don't see any sign of injury to her. Maybe it was her time."

"Was her time?" Mary snorted, her eyes glinting fiercely. "He did it. You ask him."

"I'm not sure, Mary," I said, trying to be placatory.

"Ask him," she snapped, folding her arms.

"She's not wise," Artie Moran concluded as we stood in his doorway. "You can see from the snow that I wasn't driving last night."

I nodded agreement. "She's just upset," I said. "She's on her own in there."

He rifled through his pocket, produced a fifty-euro note. "That'll buy her a new cat," he explained.

"That's not necessary, Mr Moran," I said. "I know you're not responsible. To be honest, I'm only checking to keep her happy."

He waved away my comment. "Give it to her anyway. I feel kind of sorry for the old woman."

Mary Hannigan watched from the old wooden-framed kitchen window as I struggled to pierce the frozen ground of her garden to bury the cat. I'd been hacking with the old shovel she'd given me for a few minutes with little success though the effort at least allowed me to generate some warmth. Taking a breather, mid-burial, I stood among the snow swirls and lit a cigarette. Leaning on the shovel, I regarded the backs of the houses and tried to ignore Mary's look of annoyance. Something struck me as unusual about her block. Despite the lack of heating in her house, I noticed that the roofs of both her and Moran's houses were free of snow while all the other pairs of houses along the street retained a thick covering of snow on their roofs.

With the burial completed to her satisfaction, Mary made me a cup of tea. She huddled in her seat, her hands clamped around her hot cup.

"That'll warm you up, son," she said, blowing across the surface of the drink before sipping tentatively at it.

"Speaking of which, I think you need your attic insulated, Mary," I said. "Any heat in the house must be escaping through the roof."

She tutted, her jaw set flintily. "It is insulated. Robert insulated it himself a few years before he passed away."

Treading carefully, I ventured, "But you've no snow on your roof."

"I'm telling you he did it. Check if you don't believe me."

"I believe you," I said, my hands raised in surrender.

"You believe nothing," she snapped. "Go up and see for yourself."

Cursing softly to myself for having ever brought the subject up, I climbed up on one of her rickety kitchen chairs to reach the trapdoor, hoping the thing would bear my weight long enough to get me up and down again. Mary stood below me, her arms folded tightly across her chest.

"Watch out for the rat," she said as I reached up.

"What?" I looked down at her pinched face.

"There's a rat up there; I hear it at night moving around."

"Just when you need a cat ..." I muttered, pressing the palm of my hand against the trapdoor to push against the magnetic lock and open it. The wood of the door felt unusually warm, particularly in contrast with the cold of Mary's house.

I pushed. The trapdoor swung open in a waft of humidity and I stared up into the blazing glare of heat-lamps. Pulling down the stepladder, I climbed up jutting my head up into the roof space.

The room was heavy with heat and the scent of greenery. The whole length of the loft was lined with row upon row of cannabis plants, the dark green spikes of their leaves reaching towards the lights hung from the rafters.

Glancing up, I noticed that the lamp's cables ran down the length of the rafters and were patched into Mary's attic light socket. At once, I understood why her electric bill was so expensive.

I stepped up into the attic. Looking across I saw that Artie Moran had broken through the wall separating his attic from Mary Hannigan's in order to increase the space available to him in which to cultivate his plants. He stood now on his own side, open-mouthed, pausing in the middle of stashing blocks of fifty-euro notes into a black bin bag.

He glanced around him, as if to gauge the likelihood of escape. The bag in his hands was clearly heavy and I knew that, to run, he would have to let it go. In the event, he could not.

As I approached him, I put my hand in my pocket and pulled out the fifty he had given me for Mary Hannigan.

"You felt sorry for the old woman?"

Moran swallowed heavily, his body slumping slightly where he stood as I pulled out my phone and called for backup.

Over the course of the next five hours, we removed 200 plants, and over 50,000 euros from the attic in six black bin bags. This cache did not include the two blocks of fifties I had removed from the bag before my colleagues had arrived, which I had hidden in Mary Hannigan's kitchen.

A week later I stood in that same kitchen watching as the plumbers fitted the central heating. I had arranged for Mary to be booked into a hotel until the work was completed. The glazier approached me to announce that he'd finished installing the double-glazing.

He glanced around at the various workmen moving around the house, raising his voice to be heard above the cacophony of hammer blows and electric drilling.

"How the hell does an old doll afford all this at her age?" he asked.

I looked at him levelly. "Drugs money," I said.

Had I not been wearing my Garda uniform, he might even have believed me.

ENOUGH OF THIS SHIT ALREADY

Tony Black

S HOPPING IS, LIKE, my way of getting over Steve ... until the meds kick in anyway.

Been to Wal-Mart buying stuff I don't need or want – picked up my fourth pair of Ugg boots for Chrissakes – got them under my arm as Brad Johnson squeezes beside me in the elevator to math class, starts his shit again.

"Been trappin'?" he says, leaning in close enough to let me know he'd sprung for a second chilli-dog at lunch.

"*Excuse me.*"

"What Dad calls it when my mom comes back all bagged up like a fur trapper," a laugh on his last word, like, for *no* reason. This jock shit has me weirded out, but I've got good cause.

The elevator jolts and Brad rocks forward on the heels of his Nike Airs, I get a feel of his semi and I'm thinking, *whoa* ... that stuff about me putting out is such fiction already. But my heart's racing. Pounding and pounding because this is my first day back after ... The Incident. Brad and I haven't even spoken about The Incident.

"This is my floor!" I say, edging away real fast. I'm sweating, shit, this is too full on.

"Your floor, my floor ... I don't mind one bit!"

That's not even funny. Six weeks past, at Trish Jacob's party, Steve caught Brad on top of me, doing stuff. I was way out of it, can't remember a Goddamn thing, but Steve and me are so over now. And Brad, I just feel way too strange around him. Real strange.

I'm shaking as I turn to push the button and he smiles at me, moves in close, all slimy-like. In the polished elevator door I see him eyeing my ass, pursing his lips and flicking out his tongue like a snake or a lizard or something. It's all for his jock buddies, they high-five, and I want to hurl. No shit, I want to throw chunks here and now.

Brad's hot hands grab my hips, pull me back. His semi feels more like a hard-on now. I can't move, I want to say something but I'm too choked, what a wimp-out!

"You remember this, Alana?" he says, smiling, laughing.

My heart goes from flat-out to stopped in a second. I feel chills all over me. But I remember nothing.

Ding! The elevator stops; feel a judder.

I shake off Brad's hands and run out.

I'm in such a rush I nearly drop my new Ugg boots.

"Hey, someone's been to the stores, let's see," says Louisa. She comes running over and takes my bag with the boots. "Oh my God, Alana, these are so awesome!"

I'm too pissed to respond, my heart is, like, racing as I think of Brad and his buddies laughing at me. What the hell were they saying?

"What the fuck is this?" cries out Louisa, she holds up a little white box I took from the pharmacy. I mean took, I never stole before, but I couldn't bring myself to buy it. I'm acting real strange since The Incident.

I snatch back the box, tuck it away. "It's ... you know, a test." I whisper on the last word.

Louisa's eyes widen, she drops her voice lower than mine, mouths the shape of the word, "*Pregnancy?*"

I nod.

Louisa rolls her eyes, "But, you and Steve ... I thought you never did it!" I can take hearing his name from Louisa, she's my friend, she makes me laugh, but I still don't like it.

"We never."

Louisa sticks her tongue in her cheek, rolls up her eyes again, "*Oh.*"

I don't think she understands.

Shit, I don't think I do.

* * *

I sit through math but I don't think I'm learning a frickin' thing. My head is full of Steve and how I'd promised he'd be my first and the way his face looked when he said about catching me with Brad. He roared and cried and said I was like all the other dumb chicks jumping in the sack with an asshole just because he gets his daddy's Porsche on weekends.

I cry, too, when I see the little white stick go blue. I cry and it hurts because I don't know why I'm crying. Is it because that's my life, like, over already? Or is it because I've done one more thing to hurt Steve? I don't know anything anymore.

"Alana, you dumb bitch," I say. I've been sitting in the girls' john for an hour; took me so long to build up the courage to pee on the little white stick but now I have the answer I wish I didn't. I wish I was never born, Christ, how did this ever happen?

I pull up my panties and take Mom's gun from the strap thing on my leg. Mom loves this little gun; she saw it in a movie once and Dad bought it for her, strap thing and all. She laughed and laughed that day. That was a long time ago. All the happy days seem a long time ago now. I look at the gun, it's small, says Beretta on the side but Mom calls it her Bobcat, like, why? I dunno. I don't know anything. I don't even want to think about anything.

I put the gun in my mouth and close my eyes but I can't pull the trigger. All I see is, like, my mom and dad and Grandpaw crying and crying and crying and the tears are just too much. I don't want to cause anymore tears. I didn't want to cause any tears, ever.

"Hey, Alana ... how 'bout a replay?" shouts Brad to me.

Am I, like, underwater or something? My mind feels all fuggy, could be the tears but I feel changed. My thinking just doesn't work. Dr Morgan said I'd feel different when the medication kicked in, but I don't think this is what he meant.

"Are you talking to me?" I shout back.

Brad's jock buddies slap him on the back, there's white teeth lighting up the whole corridor as all the queen bitches stop to stare and you could hear a fuckin' pin drop, like they always say.

"That night at Trish Jacob's place was, ehm, y'know ..."

I sure as hell don't know.

"Was what?"

More back slapping, one of the goofballs gets so excited he drops a folder, papers swirl about when the door to the schoolyard opens and the breeze takes them.

Brad puts his hands out. "What, you don't remember?"

I shake my head. I'm just so glad Steve's moved to Lincoln High and can't see any of this.

"Well, how about I give you a re-run tonight?"

This is, like, tennis or something, eyes flitting up and down the hallway to catch what I'm gonna say next. I don't even know, only, I've said it before I realize.

"Okay, sure."

The silence breaks into uproar.

"Woop-woop-woop," carries down the hall and Brad's buddies try to lift him up. The noise brings out Mr Martinez from the history department and he smacks his hands together to get everyone to shut the hell up.

Soon all I hear is the queen bitches slipping past me and muttering, "slut" over and over.

Like I give a fuck, now.

The black Porsche 911 is sat outside our front porch for, like, maybe a minute before Brad's hitting the horn and yelling.

"Who *is* that?" asks Mom.

"No one," I say.

"Don't you lie to me, missy!" She goes to the window, pulls back the drapes, "What in the name ... who do you know drives a car like that, Alana?"

"No one!" I'm pulling on my Ugg boots and then I'm running for the door when Mom starts to flap.

"Now, just you hold on a minute my girl ... I know you've been a little out of sorts but remember what Dr Morgan said about taking things easy!"

"Mom ..."

The horn again.

"Alana, I don't think running about all over town is the way to get your head together."

"I'm not running about, Mom ... I'm just ..."

"Alana, I never ... I didn't mean that." She looks concerned, starts to undo her apron strings at her back, then moves towards me with her hands reaching for my face.

"Mom, please."

She clasps her hands round my face, her eyes are all misty as she speaks, "You're such a pretty, pretty girl my darling ... You could have anything you want, anything in the whole world."

I want to say, "Anything?" Like it's a real choice or something, but I know it's not. I can't have Steve.

I pull away and run for the door.

I can hear Mom yelling after me as I get into the Porsche.

We drive, like, forever. Brad talks and talks about a whole heap of crap, what the Dodgers need to do next, how his daddy knows President Bush, his vacation in France and England and wherever. Eventually, we're parked out by the flats. They have crags and rocks out here and they say some serial killer used a scope-gun to shoot kids who were making out way back. I dunno if that's true, but it's what they say. I think about that a little as Brad turns off the engine and swivels round to face me. He has that shit-eating grin of his on. I never noticed before now but the grin's crooked, too.

"So, here we are," he says.

"Yeah."

He's sat on the edge of his seat with his crotch facing me, like maybe that serial killer's scope-gun once looked.

He touches his lips, sways a bit. Goes on and on. Says Steve's name, like three, maybe four times, I lose count. I'm, like, hearing Steve,

Steve,

Steve,

Steve, and I'm thinking, why? Why's he keep on him?

Enough. Enough already.

All the while I just look into him and want to hear this is all, like, a nightmare or something. That my life's a bad dream I'm soon gonna wake from. But I don't hear it. Nothing like it.

"Hey, c'mon, you know I wanna fuck you again, Alana, and I know you ain't getting none from old loverboy Steve, so I'm guessing you could do with the action."

This is the best he can do?

I'm tuned in to what he's saying and I'm, like, is that it? We done? You had your say already?

He reaches out and tries to pull me towards him but I pull away.

"Oh, I get it."

"You do?"

"Yeah, you want some stuff."

"*Stuff?*"

Brad goes into his jacket and pulls out a baggie, I can see a little white powder in the corner. He takes a few pinches and lays out a line on the dash and offers it to me.

"Go on, it's what you want."

I shake my head.

"Go on, go on."

"I don't do drugs, Brad."

Now he does the eye-roll thing, looks through me. "Oh, yeah."

"What do you mean, *oh yeah*?"

He starts to tie a knot in the baggie, tucks it back in his pocket.

I ask him again, "What do you mean, *oh yeah*?"

"Nothing, I mean, well ... you were pretty out of it back at Trish's place."

I feel my heart beat fast again.

"Yeah?"

"Hell, yeah."

He leans in again. I feel him start to breathe close to my neck. He starts to kiss me, then his hands move over me.

"Where did you get the coke, Brad?"

A laugh, then, "Connections."

I feel his tongue come out, it runs up and down my neck, onto my chest. He starts to unbuckle his belt. It seems to take him, like, forever to draw down his zipper, but when I look up at his face I see he's grinning and trying to tease me or something, yeah, like he was some strip-joint dream boy, I don't think.

"Your connections, they can get you anything you want?"

He's on top of me now, pops it out, starts grinding, pulling at my panties. "They can get me anything I want."

He's grinning and acting like some frat boy who's just got the town slut in the back-seat of his daddy's Buick.

I lay there feeling my head pushed against the door and my ass jammed against the stick shift and I want to scream but my voice is so weak I can hardly get the words I have to say out. "Like Rohypnol?"

He puts his hand on my ass, says, "You know, Steve ain't coming back, Alana, why don't you relax?"

He moves fast, now. There's no, like, struggling with buttons or straps or whatever, he's ripping at me.

"Stop!" I tell him.

"*What?*" He looks pissed with me. "I can't stop now!"

His hands move fast but mine move faster as I slip the Beretta out of the leg strap and point it at his crotch. As he feels the cold metal touch his balls his face looks white as death, but that might just be the moonlight. He's sure as hell stock-still ... until I pull the trigger.

Blood splatters the window behind him instantly. I move the gun about and I'm firing and firing until there's smoke everywhere, so much I can taste it.

For a moment, I lie there.

I can feel the gun smoke burning my throat.

My lungs fill up and I start to cough.

Brad's mouth isn't crooked any more. It flops open and his lips spill blood on me. I'm like, *yeuch*. He's a dead weight on top of me as I slide out from under him. I wonder, does he know why?

Oh yeah, like I'd care if he did.

HOGMANAY HOMICIDE

Edward Marston

New Year's Eve, 1906

FROM THE MOMENT the Frenchman crossed his threshold, Crippen was suspicious of Landru. The newcomer unsettled him. What annoyed him more than anything else was that his wife, Cora, liked the man so much. Her predilection for the opposite sex was something to which he'd grown wearily accustomed. Now that they slept apart, Cora was able to entertain male friends at will in her own room, forcing Crippen into a half-hearted complaisance. While he was ready to turn a blind eye to some of her conquests, however, he was determined to prevent her from adding the name of Henri Desiré Landru to her list.

"What exactly is the fellow *doing* here?" he demanded.

"He's our guest," replied Cora, adjusting her hair in the mirror.

"I thought we agreed to stop taking guests."

"We could hardly turn him away. Besides, he came on Mr Richards' recommendation. When he met Henri in Paris, Mr Richards assured him that we'd offer him accommodation." Reaching for the glass, she downed the last of her gin. "You remember Mr Richards, surely?"

Crippen remembered him only too well. Richards had been one of a number of boarders at 39 Hilldrop Crescent and, like the others, had been a source of irritation and resentment to him. Because his wife refused to engage a servant, they had to do all the chores, cooking meals, changing beds and – the job Crippen found most demeaning – cleaning the dirty boots of their guests every morning. Relieved when they stopped taking in lodgers, he was suddenly thrust back into the role of a landlord.

"I don't want Landru here," he said, petulantly.

"Show some hospitality on New Year's Eve," said Cora, shooting him a look of reproof. "Henri is delightful. I know his English is poor but I like having him around. It's the same with Mr Rennie. Angus was always one of my favourites. When he needed somewhere to stay for a few days, I welcomed him with open arms."

"Mr Rennie, I can accept but I find Landru so *shifty*."

"Gee, Hawley, can't you try to enjoy yourself for once?"

"Not while that Frenchman is here."

"You've gotten so dull and boring lately."

The rebuke silenced Crippen. It was horribly true. He was no longer able to arouse his wife's interest let alone her affection. When he first met her in New York, he'd been entranced by the beauty and effervescence of a seventeen-year-old girl. He hadn't minded that her voice was so strident. She, in turn, had been attracted by his politeness, his diffidence and his status as a doctor. Cora wasn't daunted by the age gap between them of over a decade or by the fact that Crippen was a short, slight, bespectacled man with thinning hair. Beside him, she could shine and he bathed in her glow. But that glow had now been removed to a spare bedroom and was reserved for interlopers like Landru. It was humiliating.

Cora rose to her feet. "How do I look?" she asked, turning full circle then striking a pose. "Am I ready to see in the New Year?"

"Yes, my dear," he said, dutifully.

"You're not even looking at me."

"I don't need to, Cora. You *always* look swell."

"I've made a special effort for tonight. It's the first time we've celebrated Hogmanay with a real Scotsman. I don't want to let Angus down. Now take a *proper* look at me," she ordered. "What do you see?"

What he saw was the bird of paradise he'd married after the death of his first wife. Cora was an attractive, raven-haired woman in her thirties with an unquenchable vivacity. Russian and Polish blood coursed through her veins. She had put on a little weight over the years but could still turn heads. From her colourful wardrobe, she'd chosen an evening dress of blue silk with a tight, boned bodice, lace motifs, velvet ribbons and short puff sleeves. A silver necklace, silver earrings and large silver bracelet lent an additional glitter. Crippen's eye fell on an elaborate silver brooch.

"I've never seen that before," he said.

"It was a present from an admirer," she replied, airily. "There was a time when *you* gave me presents, Hawley. Now I have to rely on others." She spread her arms wide. "Well?"

Crippen heaved a sigh. "You'll be the belle of the ball, my dear. In fact," he went on, venturing a rare pun, "you'll be the Belle Elmore of the ball."

Cora laughed. When she appeared in music hall, Belle Elmore was her stage name. Her ambitions to be an opera singer may have foundered but she could still win applause in the world of variety. Applause and alcohol were her twin necessities.

"Cheer up," she urged, taking him by the shoulders to shake him. "Hogmanay is a time for celebration. We'll have some real fun for a change. This is going to be a truly *amazing* night."

"Yes, my dear," he said through gritted teeth.

There were five guests in all. Angus Rennie, staying again at the house where he'd once been a lodger, was a thin, angular, hairy man in his thirties with a jocular manner. Otto Helsing, Master of Magic, was a music hall artiste, tall, portly, ever-smiling and carrying his sixty years with extraordinary lightness. Dorothy Quinn, his assistant, was, like all of her predecessors, young, petite and excessively pretty. Mabel Roy was another of Cora's music hall friends, a handsome woman in her late thirties with the grace of a dancer and an exquisite dress of red velvet accentuating her figure. Then there was Landru, also in his thirties, short, frail, well-mannered and with dark eyes that smouldered quietly in the presence of a woman. He stroked his thick red beard like the fur of a much-loved cat.

All of them, Crippen noted, had been invited by his wife. He disliked Helsing intensely. The magician had called on Cora recently and might well have been the admirer who gave her the silver brooch. Crippen was certain that the Master of Magic had earlier bestowed the bracelet on her, a clear sign that she'd succumbed to his oily charms. Dorothy Quinn had a bloom and innocence that suggested she hadn't yet been seduced by her employer. She reminded

Crippen of Ethel le Neve, the bookkeeper and secretary at the firm he managed. Both women had an elfin loveliness. For Mabel Roy, he had some respect. She was the least obnoxious of Cora's theatrical friends, most of whom competed shamelessly for attention. Mabel, by contrast, an excellent dancer, singer and pianist, had poise and restraint. Her beloved husband, another Scot, had died in tragic circumstances the previous year and Crippen had been impressed by the bravery with which she bore his loss.

Landru was the odd one out. In fact, it was his oddness that worried Crippen. The Frenchman seemed furtive, ill at ease and rather sinister. There was a sense of suppressed power in his small frame. He was as dapper as his host but not as much of a dandy. The difference was that none of the women there even looked at Crippen whereas they all showed considerable interest in Landru. Cora was characteristically over-familiar with him, Mabel was friendly and Dorothy, who spoke a little French, conversed haltingly with him in his native language. While the rest of them drank, laughed and made merry, Crippen stood on the sidelines, plucking at his moustache and watching Landru.

Questions burned in his mind. Why had the fellow turned up on their doorstep unannounced? Didn't he have a family and friends with whom to see in the New Year? What made him keep looking over his shoulder? How long was he staying? Who *was* he?

"Music!" shouted Cora, clapping her hands. "We must have some music. Play for us, Mabel."

"Very well," said Mabel, putting her drink aside and moving to the piano. "Give us a song, Cora."

"Yes," encouraged Rennie, patting Cora on the back. "Let's hear one of Marie Lloyd's songs."

Cora was offended. "You'll hear one of Belle Elmore's songs," she said with indignation. "They have more taste."

With her friend at the piano, she launched into an aria from a Puccini opera, singing with well-rehearsed emotion and using a series of dramatic gestures to enhance her performance. She acknowledged the generous applause with a curtsy. Crippen noticed that Landru clapped with more enthusiasm than anybody, his eyes roving over Cora's body with undisguised hunger.

"Now it's your turn, Mabel," said Cora.

"I can sing," boasted Rennie. "Let me go first."

"You can wait, Angus."

"This is Hogmanay. Scotland takes priority. Mrs Roy knows that because she was married to a Scot." He put an arm around Mabel's shoulder. "Play something from bonnie Scotland."

Cora tried to intervene but Rennie was too drunk to brook any refusal. Wearing the tartan of his clan, he banged the top of the piano with a fist. In order to placate him, Mabel played a Scottish air and Rennie got through one verse before he completely forgot the lines. He was outraged when some of them laughed at him and vented his spleen on Landru.

"What are *you* grinning at, you frog-faced, bloody Frenchman?" he shouted. "This is Hogmanay. We don't need foreign turds like you here." After gulping down some whiskey, he beat his chest. "I'm going to show you a Highland dance."

"Later on, perhaps," said Crippen, taking him by the arm. "I think you need to sit down for a while."

Rennie shrugged him off. "Go away."

"Try to calm down."

"Who wants to calm down on Hogmanay? It's the greatest night of the year for a Scot. Get a wee dram inside you, Dr Crippen, and enjoy the party. You've a face like a smacked arse."

"There's no need for vulgarity, Mr Rennie."

"If you won't touch whiskey, drink some of that quack medicine you palm off on people. Maybe that'll cheer you up."

Crippen was hurt. "I'm not a quack," he asserted, "I'm a qualified doctor. It just so happens that my qualifications aren't recognized in England. Now please do us all a favour and sit down."

"Let him alone, Hawley," chided Cora. "Angus is entitled to show us how he can dance."

"Yes," said Helsing, dryly. "We need some amusement."

While the Scotsman moved to the centre of the room, the others drew back to the walls. Crippen moved two chairs out of the way and Cora shifted an aspidistra to safety. A small, cluttered parlour was hardly the ideal dance floor but Rennie was undeterred. While Mabel supplied the stirring music on the piano, he danced a Highland fling by the flickering light of the gas lamps. Rennie showed surprising nimbleness at first, dancing on his toes and holding an arm aloft. At the height of his performance, however, he suddenly lost his balance and tumbled to the floor amid mocking jeers. Hauling himself angrily to his feet, Rennie turned on Helsing this time.

"All right," he challenged, "let's see *you* dance, Mr Magic."

"I wouldn't be so foolish as to try," replied Helsing.

"Then what *can* you do?"

"I can hold my whiskey a lot better than you, my friend."

Rennie bristled. "Are you saying that I'm drunk?"

"Otto is saying nothing of the kind," explained Cora, taking Rennie by the elbow. "Now you come and sit over here with me while Otto shows us one of his tricks."

"They're not tricks," corrected Helsing. "They're pure magic."

"There's no such thing," sneered Rennie.

"Wait and see, my friend."

Helsing moved them all to one end of the room and took up a position near the door. Dorothy, meanwhile, had run out into the hall to retrieve the Master of Magic's voluminous cloak from its peg. When she handed it to him, Helsing whisked it through the air, making the gaslight dance crazily.

"What I'm going to do," he announced, "is to make Dotty disappear before your eyes."

Rennie cackled. "I could make her disappear as well," he claimed. "She can disappear up to my room any time she wishes."

"Please be quiet," said Crippen, mildly.

"The same offer goes to you, Mabel. I know you like Scotsmen because you married one. Did he have a kilt like mine?"

"Sit still and watch," said Mabel, hiding her annoyance behind an indulgent smile. "Otto really is a master of his craft."

Taking his cue, Helsing held his cloak out so that its hem touched the floor. After a little curtsy, Dorothy stepped out of sight behind the cloak. Seconds later, Helsing flicked it aside to show that his assistant had apparently vanished into thin air. Cora, Mabel and Landru clapped in appreciation. Rennie glowered. Crippen wondered how it was done. Helsing gave them no time to work out the secret. With another twirl of his cloak, he held it out for a few seconds then dropped it to the floor. Dorothy had reappeared again, spreading her arms to take the applause.

"That's not magic!" yelled Rennie. "It's a cheat."

"*Merveilleux!*" said Landru, still clapping. "*C'est un miracle.*"

"Speak English, you snail-eating bastard."

"Don't be so rude, Angus," said Cora, reproachfully. "Henri is a guest here. Show him some respect."

"I don't want Hogmanay spoiled by a Frenchie."

"You'll do as you're told."

Crippen spoke surreptitiously to Helsing. "Is there any way you could make Mr Rennie disappear?" he asked.

"I can think of the *perfect* way," murmured the magician.

"Why don't we all have another drink?" said Mabel, taking charge of the situation. "Then we can play a few games."

Rennie cackled. "And I know just the games to play!"

Crippen had to spring into action. Whenever Cora's friends descended on him, he was given the task of passing refreshments around and pouring the drinks. He always felt strangely excluded as if he were a hired waiter rather than the master of the house. It was the same tonight. Alone in the kitchen, he replenished the glasses. His wife was drinking gin while Helsing and Rennie preferred malt whiskey. Mabel, Dorothy and Landru opted for wine. Crippen himself, never a committed tippler, was happy to nurse a glass of stout all evening. He could never understand how the others could drink so much. As he handed the glasses out, he got no sign of gratitude from Rennie and Cora berated him for taking so long.

When the games started, Crippen joined in reluctantly. The noise got louder, the laughter wilder and Angus Rennie progressively more out of control. As the hours rolled by, the Scotsman managed to insult or upset everyone, reserving his real venom for Landru and making the Frenchman's dark eyes blaze with fury. Mabel was caught between them. On learning that she was a wealthy widow, Landru began to court her and even suggested that she might visit Paris with him. Having his own designs on Mabel, Rennie was enraged. He did everything but throw a punch at Landru.

During a lull in the festivities, Crippen took Dorothy aside.

"I wonder if I could ask you a favour, Miss Quinn?" he said.

She was guarded. "What sort of favour, Dr Crippen?"

"I noticed that you have some command of French."

"Oh, I speak it very badly," she said with a self-deprecating smile. "Monsieur Landru was very patient with me."

"What do you make of the fellow?"

"He's very shy but that's understandable. I like him."

"Could you spare me a few minutes?" he asked, escorting her out of the parlour. "There's something I want you to translate."

"My French is not *that* good, Dr Crippen."

He guided her upstairs and along the landing until they came to Landru's room. Letting her in, he turned up the gas so that light flooded the whole area. Landru was travelling light. All that he'd brought with him was a small valise. Crippen opened it and extracted a newspaper. Dorothy was alarmed.

"Should we be doing this?" she said. "It's private property."

Crippen stiffened. "Landru is under my roof, Miss Quinn. That gives me certain rights, I feel." He opened the newspaper. "There," he said, pointing to an item. "Translate that for me, please."

"I'm not sure that I can."

"This edition is four days' old. There has to be a good reason why Landru has kept it. Tell me what that reason is."

Dorothy studied the item carefully and Crippen was struck afresh at how closely she resembled Ethel le Neve, an employee he'd come increasingly to admire. He controlled a powerful urge to touch her and contented himself with inhaling her delicate perfume. Dorothy was nervous. Fearing that they might be disturbed by the Frenchman, she was anxious to get out of the room quickly. She shook her head.

"I don't know some of the words," she confessed.

"But the police are mentioned, aren't they?" he said.

"Yes – and so is Monsieur Landru. This is the word that I can't translate," she went on, indicating it. "*Escroquerie.*"

"What does it mean?"

"I'm not certain, Dr Crippen."

"You must have *some* idea."

"All I can do is to hazard a guess."

"Go on."

"I think it's something to do with fraud."

"I *knew* it," said Crippen. "We're harbouring a criminal."

* * *

After replacing the newspaper and turning down the light, Crippen
led the way out. He sent Dorothy back downstairs alone. Standing in
the shadows, he weighed the significance of what he'd just discovered.
Landru was on the run. That accounted for his unheralded arrival on
their doorstep. He was a swindler. It was Crippen's duty to inform
the police at once and he moved off to do so. Then he checked
himself. There was no need to rush things. Cora would never forgive
him for wrecking the Hogmanay celebrations by having one of their
guests arrested. Besides, Crippen wasn't sure that the British police
would have any jurisdiction over Landru. He agonized for several
minutes about what he should do and decided that he'd simply bide
his time. The important thing was that the Frenchman had been identified as a criminal. Crippen resolved to keep a close eye on him.

When he went downstairs, he heard a noise from the kitchen and
went to investigate. Mabel Roy was looking in a cupboard.

"What are you doing in here?" he asked.

"I was searching for some cake," she replied. "Part of the
Hogmanay tradition is to give oatmeal cake to children. That's why
its other name is Cake-Day."

"We don't have any oatmeal cake."

"Any kind of cake will do. Since we don't have a child either,
we'll have to make do with Miss Quinn. She's the youngest here."

"Let's forget about the cake, shall we?" said Crippen, closing the
cupboard door. "If Mr Rennie is an example of how Scotsmen
behave on Hogmanay, I don't think we need to be too faithful to
tradition. I've never seen him so drunk. The man's conduct has been
abominable."

"It's only because he's very unhappy."

"Oh?"

Crippen's first impulse had been to get her out of the kitchen as
swiftly as possible because it was so embarrassingly dirty. Cora
didn't believe in cleaning the stove or stacking the utensils in any
kind of order. Unwashed crockery stood in the sink and every
surface was covered by piles of tins and bottles of alcohol. The only
consolation was that the subdued light hid most of the grime.
Crippen didn't try to usher her out because Mabel Roy was a shrewd
woman. She might have some insight into Rennie's unpardonable
antics and he wanted to hear what it was.

"This is only an opinion, mark you," she warned.

"I trust your judgment."

"Well, according to Belle – to Cora, that is – Angus Rennie was a pleasant man when he lodged here. She spoke fondly of him."

"Mr Rennie was tolerable enough," conceded Crippen.

"I think he's been badly wounded in an affair of the heart. That's why he has that air of desperation about him. Your wife knows him, of course, and is ready to let him take a few liberties but he was very forward with me and more or less pursued poor Miss Quinn into the basement during one of the games." She smiled sadly. "I feel sorry for the man. I know what the loss of a loved one can do to you."

Crippen was about to point out that a blighted romance didn't entitle Rennie to behave so aggressively but Cora swept into the room.

"Is this true, Mabel?" she demanded. "I've just been speaking to Otto and he tells me there's every possibility of a strike."

"I'd say that it was more of a probability," replied Mabel.

"If we go on strike, we earn no money."

"That's not the way to look at it, Cora. At the moment, we're at the mercy of the managers. Our contracts usually oblige us to perform one matinée a week. But they now want us to add three or four matinées without any extra payment. I call that sheer exploitation."

"I don't care what you call it," said Cora, truculently. "Nobody will make me go on strike."

"If the Variety Artistes Federation makes the decision, you'll have to obey it. We must stick together."

"My place is on a stage and nobody will shift me from it."

"Need we have this discussion in here?" bleated Crippen.

Cora was dismissive. "Oh, be quiet, Hawley!"

"Go into the parlour where we have a fire."

"I'm glad you mentioned the fire," she said. "It's dying. Make yourself useful for a change and fetch some coal." Crippen hesitated. "Off you go, man. We want a good blaze at midnight."

Smarting at her brusque treatment of him, Crippen went into the parlour to retrieve the coal scuttle. Dorothy was at the piano, tapping out a ditty with one finger.

"Where are the others?" asked Crippen.

"There was nobody here when I came downstairs," she said, "though I heard Mr Helsing talking to your wife in the dining room."

"What about Landru?"

"I've not seen him for ages, Dr Crippen."

"Say nothing of what we found out about him."

"I won't breathe a word," she promised. "In any case, we don't *know* that he's a criminal. Just because the French police want him, it doesn't mean that he's done anything wrong. He seems such a kind and attentive gentleman. I can't believe he'd commit a crime."

"Then why is he *here*? Why did Landru flee abroad?"

"People leave their countries for all sorts of reasons. Mr Helsing left Germany thirty years ago because he was invited here. He's now as English as I am. You and Mrs Crippen left America because you felt you could better yourselves here."

Crippen groaned inwardly. "Let's not talk about why my wife and I emigrated," he said. "What I can assure you is that we were not in flight from a police warrant."

Picking up the coal scuttle, he excused himself and went off to the cellar. Before he descended the stairs, he picked up an oil lamp to light his way. It was cold and dank in the cellar. Shivering his way down the steps, he told himself that there were far better ways to spend New Year's Eve than being at his wife's beck and call in a house filled with her friends. Mabel and Dorothy were acceptable company. For the others, he had nothing but contempt. Of Landru, he had a positive loathing. When he reached the bottom of the stairs, he put the coal scuttle aside so that he could open the door with a free hand then he raised the lamp to illumine the scene. What he saw made him step backwards and let out a gasp of horror. Face down on a heap of coal was a man whose head had been smashed open. It was Angus Rennie.

Crippen stayed long enough to make sure that the Scotsman was dead then he closed the door and put his back against it. As he considered what to do, his heart was pounding. Somewhere upstairs was a killer, someone who'd been provoked beyond measure by Rennie and turned on him. Landru was the obvious suspect but

Helsing had also clashed with the man. Nor could the women be discounted. All three of them had been harassed at some stage of the evening by Rennie. Crippen reeled as a thought struck him. Had Cora struck the fatal blow? Was he married to a murderer? Having regained his composure, he opened the door to take a closer look at the victim. Blood surrounded the scalp wound. There were no other marks upon the Scotsman.

Crippen used the lamp to guide himself to the top of the stairs. As he entered the parlour, he found Cora still expressing disapproval of the projected strike. Mabel, who was on the committee of the Variety Artistes Federation, was strongly in favour of it. Helsing supported her. Dorothy took no part in the argument.

"We have to stand up to the managers," insisted Helsing.

"It's all very well for you to say that, Otto," retorted Cora. "You're famous and in constant demand. I'm neither of those things. If I go on strike, managers will never employ me again."

"Yes, they will," said Mabel, earnestly. "If we take united action, we can close every music hall in the land. We'll only go back to work on our terms – and that means getting paid for every matinée."

"Excuse me," said Crippen, walking over to them.

"Don't interrupt us now," snarled Cora. "This is important."

"It's not as important as what I have to say, my dear."

She turned on him. "Where's the coal? Can't you even manage to fill a scuttle on your own?"

"Mr Rennie is dead."

"What are you talking about?" she snapped.

"Angus Rennie is in the coal cellar. He's been murdered."

The others looked stunned but Cora was furious.

"Is this some kind of a joke?" she said.

"If you don't believe me, go and see for yourself."

"I'll do that," said Helsing, seriously. "Your husband is not in the habit of making jokes, Cora. I'm inclined to believe him."

As the magician left the room, the three women felt the full impact of what they'd just heard. Dorothy emitted a cry, Mabel put a hand to her heart and sank into a chair while Cora glared at her husband as if blaming him for the sudden interruption to their celebrations. It was not long before Helsing returned.

"It's the truth," he acknowledged. "Rennie is dead."

"*How?*" cried Cora.

"Who could have done such a thing?" asked Mabel in a daze. "We must call the police immediately."

"No," decided Crippen, feeling empowered for once. "I want to uncover the truth first. I want to unmask the killer myself."

"Well, don't look at me," said Cora, huffily. "I liked Angus."

"I detested the fellow," admitted Helsing, "but that doesn't mean I'd bludgeon him like that."

"Is that how it happened?" asked Dorothy, tremulously.

"Someone hit him with a lump of coal."

"What on earth was he doing down there?"

"We must put that question to Landru," said Crippen.

It was at that precise second that the Frenchman walked back into the room. He was startled when they all turned to look at him so intently. He ran a finger around the inside of his collar.

"Something, there is wrong?" he asked.

"Where have you been, Monsieur?" said Crippen.

"I go out for the fresh air."

"It must be freezing cold out there."

"I not like to be indoors all the time," explained Landru. "I take the little walk."

"And did that little walk include a visit to the coal cellar?"

The Frenchman shrugged. "But no – why should it?"

"Because that's where Mr Rennie was killed," said Helsing, looming over him. "That's where someone battered him to death."

"Is not me," pleaded Landru, eyes darting.

"You didn't like Mr Rennie, did you?"

"No, sir, is true. I no like him."

"He baited you time and again."

"What is this 'baited' you say?"

"He provoked you," said Crippen. "He insulted you. He called you names. You were bound to be upset."

"I no touch the man."

"You wanted revenge."

"Is not true – I *swear* it."

"I believe him," said Cora, stoutly. "You only have to look into his eyes. Henri takes after my husband. He's too gentle by nature to commit a murder."

"Even the gentlest of men will strike out if pushed to extremes," said Crippen, grimly. "Let me suggest two things to you, Monsieur. The first is this. I put it to you that the reason you hate to be cooped up inside a house is that you served a prison sentence. You can't stand being locked away." Landru gulped and brought both hands up to his face. "I had a feeling I might be right on that score."

Cora blenched. "A prison sentence – whatever was his crime?"

"He's a swindler, my dear."

"Is a lie," howled Landru. "I not guilty."

"Listen to my second suggestion," said Crippen. "You fled to England because the French police were after you for another crime."

"Is a mistake, Dr Crippen."

"We don't need to hear any more of this," said Helsing, grabbing Landru's wrist. "He needs to be arrested for murder. I'll detain him here while someone calls the police."

Crippen headed for the door. "Leave that to me."

Hilldrop Crescent was a leafy thoroughfare off the Camden Road. When Crippen came out of the house, he saw a clutch of revellers waiting to greet the approaching New Year with flagons of beer in their hands. He spoke to one of them and the man eventually agreed to run to the nearest police station. Returning to the house, Crippen first went into his dispensary. When he found what he was after, he slipped it into his pocket. A loud scream from the parlour alerted him. Rushing into the hall, he collided with Landru who knocked him flying before fleeing through the front door. Crippen got up and went into the parlour where he saw Otto Helsing sprawled on the floor with blood dribbling from his nose. Dorothy was crying and Mabel was bending solicitously over the magician. As if by reflex, Cora identified her husband as the culprit.

"This is *your* fault, Hawley," she said, bitterly. "You should have stayed here to hold him. He punched Otto and ran away."

"That *proves* he was the killer," declared Helsing, rising to his feet and dabbing at his nose with a handkerchief. "So much for him being too gentle, Cora – the man's a violent criminal."

"He may be a criminal," said Crippen, calmly, "but he didn't murder Angus Rennie. I'm certain of it."

"Don't be so obtuse, man. Use your eyes."

"My ears proved to be more useful, Otto. When I went into the street just now, there were several people who'd been out there for the past hour. One of them told me he saw a strange man come out of this house and walk up and down for at least fifteen minutes. Fifteen *minutes*," he emphasized. "It was during that time that someone took Mr Rennie's life in the coal cellar. Whoever killed him, therefore, it couldn't possibly have been Henri Landru."

Cora was aghast. "Are you saying that it must be one of us?"

"You're not a suspect, my dear," said Crippen, "and neither is Miss Quinn. She and I were in Landru's room, searching for evidence, when the murder took place." He looked from Helsing to Mabel then back again. "That leaves only two possibilities."

"Don't you dare accuse me," blustered Helsing. "I never went near the man. Dotty will vouch for that."

"I can only speak for the time we were together," said Dorothy, quailing under his glare. "We were separated during that last game then Dr Crippen and I went off to look at a French newspaper."

"Stand by me, Dotty."

"I must tell the truth."

"The truth is that I never got close to the fellow."

"You didn't *appear* to go near the victim," said Crippen, "but then you're a master of illusion. You know how to do one thing while seeming to do something quite different. A magician who can make his assistant disappear before our very eyes could easily contrive to kill someone without apparently getting close to him."

Helsing folded his arms defiantly. "I won't say another word."

"You won't have to, Otto, because I know you're innocent. I go down the cellar every day," Crippen went on, "so I know how dirty your hands can get when you pick up a piece of coal. You need to wash them thoroughly and the obvious place to do that is in the kitchen." His eyes flicked to Mabel. "That's where I found you, pretending to look for oatmeal bread."

Mabel gave a hollow laugh. "You surely don't think that *I* had anything to do with this?" she said. "Angus was a strong man. How could I possibly have got the better of someone like that?"

"With a little assistance, I suspect." Crippen took a small box from his pocket. "This used to contain a dozen grains of hyacin. It's now empty. You knew where I kept my drugs, Mabel. You also knew the properties of hydrobromide of hyacin. It's what they use at Royal Bethlehem Hospital to subdue restless patients. It was administered to your own husband before he passed away there."

"Stop it!" she begged, burying her face in her hands.

"I watched Angus Rennie badgering you all evening. He knew that your husband had died in an asylum because I was there when Cora told him. He felt that you were fair game," continued Crippen. "He hounded you, Mabel. He molested you at some point so you stole the hyacin to slip into his whiskey."

"I only meant to calm him down," she wailed.

"A couple of grains would have done that. You deliberately gave him a fatal dose, one that would make him delirious at first then very drowsy. You lured him down the cellar," said Crippen, levelly, "and hit a defenceless man on the head so that it looked as if he'd been battered to death. In fact, it would simply have left him with a very bad headache because you didn't have the strength to crack his skull." He held the box high. "*This* is what killed him, isn't it? And the beauty of it was that you had an obvious scapegoat in Landru."

Cora was staggered by her husband's skill in working out what had happened. She was also shocked to realize that her close friend had committed a murder and wished that she'd never agreed to have Hogmanay celebrations in the house. She looked at Mabel with a mixture of fear and disgust. Helsing and Dorothy had already backed away from the killer. There was a long silence. It was broken by the rapping of the door knocker. Crippen went out into the hall.

At the very moment he opened the door, bells rang out in the distance and delighted revellers in the street began to sing a welcome to 1907. The policeman beamed at Crippen.

"Happy New Year, sir," he said. "What's this about a murder?"

FRUITS

Steve Mosby

CAROLINE.

This place is very different to the home we shared. My small cell is made of bare sandstone. The walls make the floor dusty: I think the breeze from the single, barred window is gradually eroding the surfaces, so that when I pace, my bare feet swipe the slabs, sounding like a broom across dry floorboards. If I shout through the window, my voice disappears across the field and into the trees, sounding like nothing.

I have a dirty mattress for a bed, and a hole in the floor for a toilet. The door is at the far side. I've never seen it open, but every day I wake up to find the man has somehow placed a tray just inside. He brings me a pitcher of water, several thin curls of ham, a chunk of bread, a wedge of cheese, and two bright green apples.

I focus on the apples. I don't know why, but I do.

Today, he left me this pencil and scrap of paper too, presumably because he knows I used to be a writer. I think he expects me to write to him.

Instead, I'm writing to you. For you. Because I always did.

If I can, I'll write more tomorrow.

John.

Do you remember the evening I signed the contract, when we had champagne together? I think about that a lot: a pointless tatter of memory. It's like studying a treasure map for a land I can't visit anymore. But it keeps me occupied.

You'd always had faith in my fiction, through all the penniless years, and you forced us to mark the occasion. I wanted sparkling wine; you insisted on champagne. As we drank, I imagined its history: the transformation from the grapes on the sun-drenched vines into the liquid in the bottle before us, fizzing with a different kind of life. I thought about the things that had died to enable our celebration, and I felt guilty. But you were so proud of me, and I couldn't tell you. Not then.

I know you'll never read this, but I want you to know:

I'm sorry for what I did; we never had a reason to celebrate that night.

And I miss you more than I can ever say.

I had a revelation this morning. I focus on the apples he feeds me because I know they're not poisoned.

My window faces out onto a patchy field. Over to the right, there's a small rose garden, the blood-red flowers nodding lazily in the breeze, and at the far end, before the woods begin, there is a large apple tree. I've seen the man down there. He's fat and pink and simple-faced, like a pig in overalls. I've called out to him, but he keeps his back to me and never replies. The only sounds I hear are the birds and the steady, delicate click as he clips apples from the lower branches.

So I know where they come from. I can turn them over, and check that the skin is clear and unbroken, that the fruit sealed inside is safe to eat.

But something must be poisoning me. Because how else does he get the tray in without disturbing me? Also, I remember … words. Things he must have said. We're all made of stardust. Or perhaps I sleep too long and dream too much.

No, he has said that, I'm sure.

And also: Nothing dies.

But he knows that's not true, doesn't he?

Another memory.

I'm in a small tearoom. There are flowers on the wallpaper, wooden beams overhead and tassels on the curtains, and I keep hearing the elegant chink of teaspoons on china. A journalist is sitting opposite me, older and more austere than I'd been expecting. (Many of them were prettier than I told you). But this is Whitrow, Jane Ellis' hometown, and I have no right to expect a warm welcome. Her name is almost sacred here.

"Why did you use the roses?" she says.

Jane Ellis' body was never found, but a rose was delivered to her husband the year after her disappearance, with a note that said, "She lives forever". The families of his other victims had similar deliveries.

This is only one of the details I stole.

"I found it moving," I say. "Poignant. It felt true."

"Did you ever worry you were exploiting the victims?"

I think of those grapes again. Arrogantly, I think of the champagne that was made from them.

"I don't see it that way," I tell her. "Something terrible happened to those girls, and I wanted to tell their stories." I spread my hands. "Carefully. Delicately, even. I hope I did them justice."

She looks at me. I suppose she can see through that thin screen of noble intentions to the sales and nationwide tour behind. The expression on her face reminds me of the one you had, although yours was worse because of what it replaced.

She changes tack. "Nobody was ever caught. Does that concern you?"

It takes me a second, and then I almost smile. Am I frightened? It's nothing to do with me. I've touched it from a safe distance, skimming the surface so gently my fingers came away clean.

The idea is absurd, and yet I don't say I'm not.

The truth is, I almost like the idea of danger as long as I'm safe.

She will live forever.

Last night, I opened my eyes and everything was still pitch-black. I didn't know what had woken me ... then I heard it again and my heart caught. A woman – out in the corridor. Sobbing and begging, although the words were incoherent. He had brought someone back and was dragging her past my cell.

Something thumped against the wall. She screamed.

The next thing I knew, I was hammering on the door, shouting out your name. Slurring it. Even after they'd moved away, I was still punching the wall. This morning, I came to my senses and found myself hugging my knees in the far corner of the room, the mattress overturned and flung aside.

On the ground by the door: my apples, my paper.

I've no idea how he got them in here but you can see that this time, at the top, he's written something himself.

The controversy fed the attendance at the readings on my tour. I suppose he'll have been in the audience at one of them. It's possible he was just curious then, but perhaps he'd already felt a kinship. That seems most likely – that I was part of this from the moment I heard Jane Ellis' name and noted it down in my pad.

We're brothers.

My body juddered passively, strapped in the back seat of his truck. My mind was swirling, drifting. What had happened? Had someone drugged me? Attacked me? I could remember being in the bar, then outside smoking, then ... then the fear arrived quickly – absurdly – like I'd fallen into icy water.

We're the same. You understand.

He's told me those other things since, while I've been half-dreaming. Nothing ever dies. He means it just becomes something else, like grapes become wine, and I think that's why he killed those girls: to change them somehow. That's why, in his mind, we're the same: because I did something similar to them with my writing.

I hope I did them justice.

I've not heard the girl again.

She will live forever.

I saw him kill her. I heard the commotion outside, then watched through the bars. I didn't want to, but it's what I do, isn't it?

The man dragged her across the field to the rose garden. Then he squatted awkwardly above her, reached round ... and his elbow started sawing the air. I couldn't see, but I could hear: her sobbing became a horrific, gargling cough for a few seconds, and then she fell shockingly silent. The man stood up and walked away. Her body was still for a moment, then rolled slowly onto its back, and a hand began lazily brushing at a flower. She died in her own time. I watched her blood soaking slowly into the earth beneath the roses, and I thought:

The next petals will be made of her stardust.

So she will live forever.

And then ... all I could do immediately after what happened next was sit and stare at the apple in my hand. Finally, I understood. I'm eating it now, even though I realize every one of them was poisoned. The fruit sealed inside was exactly the problem. But it's mine.

This is what happened.

An hour later, I saw the man return. I watched him pick up the body carefully and delicately. I watched him take it down to the bottom of the garden. And then I watched him bury it, with all the others, in the ground beneath the apple tree.

A PLACE FOR VIOLENCE

Kevin Wignall

D AN WAS MESMERIZED by the young guy in the pool. He was in his late teens or early twenties and looked about as graceful and athletic in the water as anyone he'd ever seen.

Of course, he probably wouldn't have been mesmerized if it hadn't been for the wheelchair. It had been there when Dan came out, against the metal railing of the steps with a towel on its seat. The kid was the only one in the pool but it had still been a few minutes before Dan had accepted the chair had to be his.

That's how long it had taken him to notice that his legs weren't doing any of the work, that they were thin and undeveloped against the kid's swimmer's torso. Even so, he produced the impression of someone who left the handicap on the poolside.

When the pool boy brought his drink Dan turned his attention to his book, looking up every few minutes, a glance at the kid's steady soothing progress up and down the pool, a glance to the hotel.

He'd taken a lounger by the side of the pool. The ones in front of the hotel faced across the pool to the beach and the ocean but he wanted to see the hotel. It wasn't a bad view anyway, the double-storey main building, the single-storey annex, both with their high thatched roofs. And the pool was fringed on all four sides by gardens and tall palms.

He'd almost finished his drink when the view deteriorated dramatically. He heard the pool boy first, a cheery, "Good morning, Mr Tully."

Mr Tully either didn't think so or didn't see why he had to share the sentiment with a pool boy. The guy was in his late thirties, probably only a few years older than Dan but he looked like he'd been living dog years. He was balding, fat, too tanned, yet held himself with a proprietary, walk-on-water confidence. He sullied the place.

His wife had a conversation with the pool boy, so quiet that Dan didn't pick out a single word. She was slim in a tired way, blonde, with body language that was desperate to be decorative and inoffensive to her husband – Dan could see it was killing her.

The two kids were the same. Maybe it wasn't killing them yet, but it would. They were blonde, a boy and a girl, their builds teetering on the brink, showing they could yet take after either parent. The girl was maybe eight, the boy a year or two older and they both moved with the timid attentiveness of kids who were terrified of their father. Whenever possible, they chose to stand behind their mother.

Tully had taken his shirt and sunglasses off now and looked about fifteen months pregnant. He walked across to the steps and clicked his fingers at the pool boy. He pointed at the wheelchair.

"Get this piece of junk out of here." There was a hint of something in his accent, Boston maybe. "My kids trip and hurt themselves, there'll be hell to pay."

His kids had each arranged themselves on a lounger next to their mother and were showing no childlike desire to get in the water. The pool boy approached and took hold of the wheelchair handles but spoke quietly to Tully, gesturing to the swimmer.

Tully was having none of it, and said, "So he's a cripple, that doesn't give him the right to endanger other people. Move it."

Dan wondered if this was possibly the crassest person on the planet.

The pool boy bowed and pushed the chair along the poolside, reluctant to disobey one guest or to inconvenience another. But as if sensing the discomfort of the pool boy, and perhaps having heard some of the exchange, the kid turned on to his back and called, "It's okay, I'm done." He was American too.

He turned in the water and glided over to the side where the pool boy was waiting with the chair. He heaved himself out at the same time as Tully crashed into the water at the other end, not even using the steps after causing such a scene about his access to them.

The pool boy held the wheelchair steady and the kid pulled himself up. He'd lost all his aquatic grace now, but he didn't do a bad job of getting into the chair and Dan reckoned there was a residue of movement or sensation in his legs. He knew the kid wouldn't have thanked him for it, but he couldn't help thinking to himself, "too bad".

The kid didn't hang around once he was in the chair. He folded the towel over his lap, put another around his shoulders and wheeled back along to the hotel, as cool about it as a kid on a skateboard.

Tully had been swimming furiously, throwing up a lot of spray, but he stopped to look as the kid wheeled away. He looked smug, but with that victory under his belt, he turned to his family and called out, "Pete, get yourself in here. You too, sugar."

The two kids stirred and Dan took that as his cue to leave. Tully saw him getting up and looked over, as if wanting to stare him down or ask what his problem was. Dan ignored him, but as he passed Mrs Tully and the kids he smiled and said, "How's it going?" They smiled back uncertainly, but didn't speak.

Later in the afternoon, Dan found the kid sitting in the terrace bar. He was reading and apart from an elderly couple in the far corner he was there on his own. Dan ordered a Tiger Beer from the bar and strolled over.

"Hey, mind if I join you?" He saw what the kid was reading, *The Stranger* by Camus, and wondered if befriending him was a mistake.

But the kid smiled and said, "Sure – I'm struggling with this book anyway."

Dan held up his Murakami doorstop as he sat down and said, "Me too." He put out his hand and said, "Dan Borowski."

They shook hands.

"Luke Williams."

The waiter came with Dan's beer but once they were on their own again, he said, "So what brings you here, Luke?"

"Just a vacation, you know." Dan swigged from the beer and nodded. Luke laughed then and said, "I'm going to college next year, Harvard ..."

"Good on ya."

"Thanks. Anyway, I wanted to get away on my own, you know, like travelling, but I've never done it before so this is my first big adventure."

"Enjoying it?"

Luke smiled and said, "Not really. The spa treatments are good."

He shrugged and said, "What about you, why are you here?"

"Mate, I'm Australian, Bali's where we come to relax." He watched a trickle of condensation making a run down the side of the beer bottle, then said, "Truth is, I was meant to meet an ex-girlfriend out here but she had to cancel at the last minute. Thought I might as well come anyway."

That was half true, at least. He was meeting Juliet the following week, but in Sydney, and she was an old girlfriend, not an ex – an important difference when it came to reunions. There was no need for Luke to know all that, nor that he lived in London and was probably the only Australian who'd never been to Bali before.

Luke didn't seem to know how to respond and said, "What do you do?"

"Security analyst." That killed that line of conversation. "How d'you end up in the chair?"

Luke shrugged and said, "Three years ago, riding home from a friend's house, some guy doing around sixty knocked me off my bike. They didn't think I'd pull through, then they said my legs were finished, but I got a little bit back. I can walk a little way with a frame."

He reeled it all off with the speed of someone who knew it like a mantra – Dan guessed the question always got asked sooner or later.

"The guy go to prison?"

There had been no bitterness in the description of the accident or the injury, but the wound was still raw when it came to the guy who'd done it.

Luke sipped at his drink and Dan noticed the muscle under his left eye twitching as he said, "The dick had been drinking hard, but him and his wife swapped seats. She claimed I'd come speeding off the sidewalk and into their path. I knew what I saw, but there were no other witnesses. The pair of them walked. I still see the guy around, still drives like a jerk."

"That can't be easy, seeing him all the time, knowing he got off with it."

"You have to live with it, I guess. I mean, what can you do about it?"

"You could kill him." Dan waited a beat to let the shock sink in, then laughed and said, "The world's full of jerks. Look at that guy this morning out by the pool."

"Brian Tully," said Luke with a mixture of contempt and grudging respect.

Dan looked askance and said, "You know the guy?"

"Give it a couple days, you'll know him too. He's the kind of guy who makes himself known. I heard him telling someone in the restaurant the other night, he's like a mobster from Vegas."

So Tully really was a jerk. Probably liked to act the tough guy but it was undoubtedly nine parts swagger, one part bullying.

"Luke, I'll guarantee he's from Vegas, but any guy who brags about being a mobster has gotta be way down the pecking order." He swigged at his beer and added, "Probably still not a guy you'd wanna cross."

Luke nodded, but Dan could see he had a lot of pluck, that the presence of Tully and his insults was a big part of why he wasn't enjoying this vacation, and that he'd give anything to be able to get out of his chair and give the guy a smack. It was almost certainly better for him that he couldn't.

Luke visibly let the thought go and became brighter as he said, "What are you doing for dinner tonight?"

"I reckon we could eat here in the hotel, maybe eight o'clock, pick up some girls, steal a boat – how about it?"

Luke laughed and said, "I could manage the dinner part of it."

"Yeah, you're right. It's a long time since I stole a boat." He smiled and swigged from his beer.

Dan would rather hire a boat nowadays anyway, and he didn't chase girls when he was working, but they stuck with the plan for dinner. Dan got down there a little early, had a drink at the bar and looked out across the restaurant. It was less than half full but Tully's presence made it seem overcrowded.

The guy was loud, talking like there were twenty extrovert people at his table, not three timid ones. He knew a couple of people on neighbouring tables, too, and called lame jokes and comments across at them, getting polite, almost subservient laughs in response.

Dan glanced out at the intense blackness beyond the restaurant lights. The hotel prided itself on its ecological credentials, so the lights that were scattered around the grounds were low-key, providing just enough illumination to ensure no one on a late-night walk would trip and sue.

There were no cameras, either, he'd already noticed that. And the staff were good at keeping out of the way. It was ironic, given the philosophy that underpinned both the hotel and its spa, that this place was ideally designed and situated for violence.

"You tell that to the gooks," shouted Tully, following up his own bizarre punchline with a raucous laugh.

Dan looked at where Luke would enter the room, looked at the tables that were free, calculated how Luke would get to each of them. He crossed the room then and sat down. When the waiter came, Dan asked for two menus and asked him to take the chair away.

"Mr Luke?"

"Mr Luke," said Dan. The waiter nodded and whisked the chair away.

A minute later, Luke wheeled into the room and looked across to where Dan was sitting. He looked for a path to reach the table, but turned away from the obvious one and started looking for another.

Dan got up and waved him back toward the obvious path, the one that went past Tully's table. He walked over then and tapped Tully on the shoulder, saying, "Mate, do you mind moving a mo just to let my friend through?"

Tully looked down at his own shoulder, a theatrical indication of how dangerous it was that anyone should touch him without permission, then looked up at Dan, trying to figure him out. He didn't look at Luke but said, "There's plenty of room to get past."

"No, see, there isn't – he's in a wheelchair."

Luke looked alarmed and impressed, but the hint of a smile disappeared as Tully said, "So what, everyone has to move around the cripple, is that what you're saying?"

Dan put his hand on Tully's shoulder, this time exerting just enough pressure to let him know how things stood, and when Tully looked up Dan fixed his stare, saying, "Mate, I'm asking you to move because I can see you're the kind of guy who does the right thing when it matters."

Tully stared back for a second or two, his eyes twitching, giving away his entire decision-making process, then said, "I didn't catch your name."

"Dan Borowski."

Dan held out his hand and Tully shook it, saying, "Brian Tully." He turned and looked at Luke and said, "Just messing with you, kid, don't take it so serious." He got out of his chair and pushed it under the table.

"Thanks," said Luke as he wheeled through the gap.

"Decent of you, Brian, thanks very much."

Tully nodded like someone convinced he'd just been scammed but unable to see what had been taken or how. And throughout the meal, Dan noticed him glancing over with a confused meanness. Tully knew he'd been humiliated in some way or other and was weighing up how he could get back at Dan or more likely at the kid.

He didn't get any quieter, but he never directed his comments at Dan and Luke. They were only a few yards away but he was rattled enough by his first encounter with Dan that he didn't want to risk another exchange just yet.

Luke didn't mention what had happened at first, but as Tully shouted for about his tenth beer since they'd sat down, his eyes lit up and he said, "I get it – I've been wondering why you confronted the guy, and now I know. You did it on purpose."

"Luke, I don't know what you mean."

But Luke was having none of it, laughing now as he said, "You chose this table on purpose, knowing I'd have to pass him to get here."

"Busted," said Dan, laughing. He was impressed that Luke had worked it out, but then the kid was going to Harvard so it shouldn't have been that much of a stretch. "You know, there's a place in India where the workers in the fields kept getting eaten by tigers. Then a tiger expert comes in, and makes masks for them, but tells them to wear them on the back of their heads while they're working – see, the tiger likes to attack from behind, so the mask makes it think it's looking at someone's face and that rattles it. Tiger attacks stopped overnight."

"Is that true?" Dan nodded and Luke said, "Cool. I still don't see what it has to do with you picking a fight with Tully."

"I wasn't picking a fight. Sometimes you just have to show your face, make people understand they're not the only predator in the jungle."

By the time they finished dinner, Tully's family had left and the man himself was at the bar. Dan looked at his watch and said, "Think I'll turn in – it's been a long day and I'm diving in the morning."

Luke looked envious and said, "I wanted to dive out here, but the guy who runs it says they can't take me, something about the hotel's insurance."

"You've gotta be kidding me." Luke shook his head. "You been diving before?"

"No, but I will, someday."

Dan nodded and said, "Tell you what, I'll have a word with the guy tomorrow, see if we can sort something out."

"Thanks," said Luke, but he smiled as he pushed himself away from the table. "You won't get anywhere, but thanks anyway."

Dan got up, and he knew Luke was talking from experience, that the kid would have tried every angle to get on that dive boat. They chatted as they made their way out of the restaurant, but Tully didn't turn to look at them. He was pretty drunk by now and Dan guessed he probably hadn't even noticed them.

When Dan got to his room he kept the lights off and walked out on to the balcony. He needed to get everything done in the next couple of days and was thinking through his options when he noticed the unmistakable figure of Tully swaying along in the half-light by the pool.

It took a second longer to see that there was a girl with him, one of the small local girls, her figure obscured by Tully's bulk as she led him by the hand along the side of the pool. At the far end, they made their way down on to the beach.

Curious, Dan left his room and followed them as far as the gardens that formed the divide between pool and beach. He didn't need to go any further – the compliant moans and Tully's breathy running commentary were bad enough without seeing it. And how typical of Tully that he should even talk himself up during bought sex.

Dan took a couple of steps back and found a small path that cut through the gardens to the side of the pool. It was paved so he could wait there without leaving footprints, not that he really believed anyone would care.

What really intrigued him was whether this was a regular thing, and what other solo jaunts Tully took. He was still thinking about that when he heard footsteps. It was definitely Tully because he was mumbling to himself as well, drunker than Dan had realized.

He saw him walk past and glanced out to see if the girl was with him – she wasn't. It was a risk, because she could still be lurking back there, but occasionally, instinct just demanded that the time was right. This was one of those occasions and Dan was happy to take serendipity over professionalism any day.

He stepped forward, eased up behind Tully and pushed him into the pool. Tully managed to spit out the word "bitch" before he hit the water with a dull thud of a splash. Dan stepped back a moment, looking around to see if the noise had attracted the girl – unlikely, given that Tully seemed to be blaming her for the push – or any of the hotel staff.

Tully was struggling and sputtering back to the poolside and now that Dan was certain no one was coming he stepped forward and said, "What happened, mate?"

"Bitch pushed me," said Tully as he reached up to take Dan's offer of a hand, too drunk to be suspicious of his presence.

It was quick then. Dan grabbed the hand, used it to flip Tully over onto his back as he pulled him up out of the water, then used his free hand to crack the back of Tully's head down on to the poolside. It was so quick, Tully didn't even get chance to cry out.

As he slid him back into the water he turned him on his front again. The guy was unconscious and bleeding badly from the gash to his head, but it was best not to take any more chances. As things stood, a drunk had slipped after sex on the beach, cracked his head on the poolside and drowned – they'd probably name a cocktail after him.

For Dan, it had ended up being about as easy as he could have hoped, so easy he hadn't even had time to get an adrenaline buzz off it. But that was job done, and he really was going diving in the morning, so he went straight to bed now, and the following day he made no attempt to find out what had happened and none of the hotel staff mentioned it to him.

When he got back to his room around lunchtime he showered and dressed and was ready to head out again when there was a knock on his door. He opened it to the worn face of Stephanie Tully.

"Hi, what can I do for you?"

His breezy tone put her on the back foot, but she said, "I'm not sure, at least, I hope you are who I ..."

"You shouldn't have come here," said Dan. "Don't speak to me again."

She nodded with an eager obedience that Dan almost wanted to shake out of her, then said, "Thank you, anyway."

"You're welcome. And I hope you realize I don't usually do domestics – it's only because you know Lo Bello."

"I know. And I appreciate that. Did you get the money?"

He smiled and said, "Lady, I wouldn't be here if I hadn't. Don't get me wrong, I'd have happily done him for nothing, but I try to limit pro bono work to about once a year."

She smiled back, still uncertain, but he could see now the relief that was creeping into her. And it had been an accident, just as requested, ensuring none of Tully's colleagues would come after her – Dan found it hard to believe they'd have cared that much anyway.

He found Luke in the bar and it was he who was first to officially break the news about what had happened to Tully. The pool was closed for the day, but Luke made it clear that was the only reason he was sorry. He didn't appear to suspect anything.

Dan made the right noises, then, as if remembering the really big news of the day, he said, "Oh, tomorrow morning, hope you don't have plans – we're going diving."

Luke laughed in disbelief and said, "How? How did you manage that?"

"It wasn't so hard. You know, on the whole, people wanna do the right thing – you just gotta help them see a way." He swigged from his beer as Luke thanked him a couple of times.

They talked diving for a while, but as soon as the moment allowed, Dan swigged from his beer and said, "Anyway, I was thinking – tell me a little more about the guy who put you in the chair ..."

FOUR HUNDRED RABBITS

Simon Levack

THE DANCE OF the Four Hundred Rabbits was a part of the midwinter festival of the Raising of Banners, a time when we Aztecs honoured our war god, Huitztilopochtli, the Hummingbird of the South. While warrior captives were having their hearts torn out in front of the war god's temple at the top of the Great Pyramid, a more genial ritual was being enacted nearby, in honour of the gods of sacred wine.

The priest named Two Rabbit presided over the temple of the god whose name he bore. He called together dancers, young men from the Houses of Tears, the priests' training schools. Each dancer represented one of the four hundred lesser gods of sacred wine, the Four Hundred Rabbits.

The task of organizing the proceedings fell to Two Rabbit's deputy, Patecatl. It was his job to set up the jars of sacred wine that were at the heart of the ceremony and to lay out drinking straws ready for the dancers at the end of their performance. For the climax of the dance was the moment when their graceful, sinuous movements broke up and they fell greedily upon the jars and the drinking straws, every man jabbing his neighbour with knee and elbow and fist in his eagerness to be first.

There were four hundred dancers and fifty-two jars. But there were only two hundred and sixty straws, and of those, only one was bored through. Among the four hundred young men who had been picked for this ceremony, one alone would stand with a hollow reed at a jar of sacred wine, happily drinking his fill.

It was a game of chance, but also a ritual, watched closely by Two Rabbit and Patecatl for clues to the will of the gods. Two hundred and sixty was the number of days in our sacred calendar, and fifty-two, the number of years between the ceremonial kindling of one new fire and the next. To see which young man seized the right straw and which jar he drank from might give the priests a clue to what lay in the future for our people.

Unless somebody tried to shorten the odds.

"Move yourself, Slave!"

I scrambled to my feet, narrowly avoiding the kick my master's steward had casually aimed at me while I bolted what was left of my warm tortilla. The sweet girl from the palace kitchen who had passed it to me fresh from the griddle backed away into a corner, her eyes wide with sudden fear, but the big bully did not berate her for wasting bread on me. Nor did he demand to know what I was doing or hurl some witless insult at me, which was unusual. Instead, with a curt "Come with me!" he turned and stalked away.

"Thanks a lot, Huitztic," I grumbled. I glanced over my shoulder but the girl had fled. "We were getting along nicely there, too ..."

I hung back, preparing to dodge the kick that a remark like would normally provoke, but all the response I got was, "This is no time for jokes. His Lordship has something to show you."

That was restrained by the steward's standards. Intrigued, I caught him up, and noticed that he was sweating. It was a cold, clear morning, when the frost lay late on the earth and the sky above the city of Mexico-Tenochtitlan was a blue so bright it hurt the eyes, yet his brow was beaded with moisture, glittering in the sunshine.

"In here." He led me into a courtyard. "Your slave Yaotl, my Lord!" he announced in a loud whisper.

The enclosure was dark, surrounded by high walls the Sun had yet to clear, and the only warmth and light in it came from a squat brazier at its centre. I paused, squinting into corners while my eyes adjusted and I tried to make out what it was I was meant to see.

The feeble glow of the coals set off my master's features perfectly, picking out every line and wrinkle in his gnarled old face, but making his bright, ferocious eyes shine. Lord Feathered in Black, the Chief Minister, Chief Justice and Chief Priest of the Aztecs, the second most powerful man in Mexico-Tenochtitlan and perhaps the most dangerous, did not trouble to greet me. Instead he leaned forward in the high-backed wicker chair that was an emblem of his rank, clutching his jaguar skin mantle around him, and snarled: "Look at the boy – the rabbit, here. Tell me what happened to him."

I followed his gaze and saw for the first time that there was a young man sprawled against the courtyard wall. His legs were splayed like an infant's. In the poor light his skin looked sallow and unhealthy, and a trickle of saliva glittered like silver leaf on his chin. His eyes were open, but as I looked more closely I realized he saw nothing through them. Their pupils were huge black disks that stayed fixed on something far away when I passed a hand in front of them. His breath had a sour reek that I knew well. He had been drinking sacred wine. Perhaps he had been celebrating: I noticed that he was missing the single lock of hair that boys grew at the napes of their necks, and this was a sign that he had taken his first captive in battle, and could call himself a warrior.

Why had my master called him "the Rabbit"?

I felt a moment of panic as I struggled to answer his Lordship's question. The old man was not renowned for his patience.

It was the steward who saved me, unwittingly. With a sudden nervous giggle he called out: "Come on, Yaotl. What's he taken? You're the expert!"

I stiffened indignantly at the taunt. Huitztic knew my past: how I had sold myself into Lord Feathered in Black's service, trading my freedom for the sum of twenty large cloaks, enough to keep me in drink when I had nothing left but the breechcloth wrapped around my loins. He knew also what had first driven me to seek refuge in a gourd of sacred wine: the despair and humiliation of being expelled from the priesthood, years before. As a priest I had learned and experienced the use of every kind of leaf, herb, seed and root, everything a man could put into his body to turn him into a slobbering imbecile. The steward's comment was a deliberate jibe, and it stung, but even as I bit back my retort I realized the oaf had given me the clue I needed.

My master responded before I could. "Be quiet, you idiot," he snapped. "You're in enough trouble over this already! Yaotl, I want your answer before I have both of you strangled!"

"He's been drinking," I said hastily. "That's obvious, I can smell it. But it's not just that. Sacred wine wouldn't leave him like this. He'd just have been violently sick and then fallen asleep, and by now he'd have a sore head and a tongue like tree bark. Anyway, you didn't send for me to tell you he's got a hangover. He's had something else – mushrooms, perhaps: the Food of the Gods. But I don't understand ..." I hesitated before turning to look at the grim-faced old man in the chair. "What's he to you, my Lord? Why do you need to know what happened?"

"Isn't it enough that some prankster chose to break up the Dance of the Four Hundred Rabbits – a religious ceremony, and me the Chief Priest? But it just so happens that this young fool is my great-nephew. So I take what happened rather personally."

The Dance of the Four Hundred Rabbits! In the years since I had left the priesthood I had all but forgotten about it, but it came back to me now. And the young man had reeked of sacred wine, which could mean only one thing. "Your great-nephew won the contest?"

The Chief Minister's deathly features twisted into something resembling a smile. "His prize turned out to be more than he expected – as you have confirmed for me. Now you'll find out the rest – how it happened, and who was responsible." He cast a sideways glance at his steward, who squirmed grotesquely. "You and Huitztic will look into this together."

I had to repress a groan. Being made to investigate what sounded like a childish trick would be bad enough without having that vicious buffoon of a steward for company.

"I will not be made a fool of." I noticed with a thrill of dread that my master's voice had dropped to a whisper, a sign of his rage. "I will not have my family made fools of. Somebody did this to young Heron here to spite me. After you've brought me his name, I'll have him cursing the gods for ever letting him be born!"

"What are you in trouble for?"

We were barely out of earshot of Lord Feathered in Black. The moment we were dismissed, Huitztic strode on ahead as before with barely a backward glance. I hung back until I judged I was out of range of his fists before I dared mention the thing that had most intrigued me about the interview we had just had: the steward's obvious fear and our master's equally evident anger with him.

I had miscalculated. The man spun on his heel and his long, powerful legs brought him back to me in two steps. Before I could react he had the knot of my cloak in his fist and was twisting it, tightening the rough cloth around my neck until I could feel my skin burning under it and was struggling to breathe.

"Let's get one thing clear, you little worm." Spittle flew into my face as he dragged it closer to his. "I am not the one in trouble. I only did what he told me to. It was Patecatl who let him down, not me, and I'm not going to let you talk the old man into believing otherwise. I'll cut your tongue out if I catch you even thinking about it!"

"Patecatl?" I managed to gasp. "You mean the priest?"

"He's already in prison. That's where we're going now – to see if they've sweated the truth out of him yet. Maybe you can think of some clever way of tricking him into giving it to us. If you can't then you'd better just keep your mouth shut. Old Black Feathers may have told me I had to have you trailing around after me like a lost dog, but I don't have to like it!" He let go with a snarl, thrusting me away from him so hard that I fell over backwards, my legs buckling under me.

"The priest's in prison?" I repeated, as I got up. I had to run to keep pace with him as he made off into the street outside our master's palace. "What for, though? You may as well tell me what you think he did."

Huitztic ignored my suggestion until he was brought up short by one of the city's countless canals. As he looked right and left for a boat that could take us to the prison, he apparently had second thoughts. Wrinkling his nose as though he had caught a whiff of the green water at his feet, he muttered: "All right. I may as well since we've got to see him together. But you remember what I said. I only did what I was told!"

"So how do you think Heron managed to win the contest?" the steward asked, as he flopped angrily into the stern of the boat.

"It wasn't just luck, then?" I had already guessed that if the gods had willed the outcome, they had had some human help to arrange it.

"Only if having one of the most powerful men in the World for your great-uncle counts as luck. Actually old Black Feathers can't stand the young toad, but he dotes on his niece – the boy's mother – and she wants to see her son get to the top."

"And winning a contest like this won't do the lad's career any harm." To be marked with the gods' favour counted for almost as much as taking a captive in war. "So our master ordered you to give him a helping hand, is that it?"

Huitztic gripped the boat's sides so hard his knuckles turned white. "Me and the priest both. Young Heron had the only hollow drinking-tube sewn into the hem of his cloak, after I'd been to get it from Patecatl. Only I reckon it had more than a hole in it. How hard would it have been for him to prime it before he gave it to me?"

I thought about it. "Not hard. Mushrooms, you could dry them, grind them into powder, and as long as you didn't pack them in too tight I suppose the young man could have sucked it up with the sacred wine without noticing – at least until it started to work. Did anyone look at the tube afterwards?"

"Sure. Heron was still clutching it when he was brought here. But the poison was all gone by then, of course."

"It would have been a lot simpler to put the stuff in the jar, wouldn't it?"

Huitztic sniggered. "You're not so clever after all, are you? Which jar would you put it in, then?"

I grasped his meaning: how could the poisoner have known which of the fifty-two vessels to dope? "All of them?"

"No. Lord Feathered in Black let some of his serfs drink the rest of the jars dry. You missed an opportunity there! They could barely stand up afterwards, of course, but it was nothing like what happened to Heron."

I frowned. "The rest of the jars?"

"Heron had polished off the jar he was drinking out of before the stuff started taking effect. So we can't tell what may have been in it."

I was still puzzled. Cheating the gods was a fearful thing to do, but at least their vengeance was uncertain, and might be a long way off. I could not understand why a priest who had agreed to do that would go on to risk the immediate and all-too-certain consequences of angering Lord Feathered in Black.

Perhaps I was about to find out; for the long stone wall of the prison now loomed above us.

I knew the prison. I had been confined here once, awaiting punishment after my arrest for drunkenness. I had to halt on the threshold for a moment, clutching the doorway and shutting my eyes as the sights, sounds and smells came back to me in a rush: the lines of cramped wooden cages stretching away into the gloom; the stench of piss and fear and starvation; the shouting. At almost any time of the day or night, as I remembered, somebody would be raving, protesting his innocence or hurling abuse at the guards or calling for his mother, and when he fell silent others would take up the cry, screaming or crying and rattling the wooden bars of their cages hopelessly.

Somebody was shouting now. The words seemed to run into one another as they echoed through the long hall, so that I could not make them all out.

Huitztic shoved me from behind. "Get a move on, before I have them lock you up too!"

I stumbled forward, almost colliding with the guard who had come to find out what we wanted. When we had told him he said: "Good thing you're here. Maybe you can make him shut up."

My master's steward laughed harshly. "Just bash him over the head! That ought to do it."

The guard, a stolid-looking man in a veteran warrior's long cloak and embroidered breechcloth, hefted his cudgel and gave us a lopsided grin. "I don't think so. I don't want to have to explain to my chief why I laid out Two Rabbit."

I frowned. "I thought it was his deputy you had in here."

"It is. But the prisoner's chief came to pay him a visit. And he's the one shouting."

We hurried past the rows of cages, ignored or tracked obsessively by the wretches who squatted in them. At our approach the shouting seemed to reach a crescendo, before dying out abruptly as the tall, slender figure standing in front of one of the cages swung his gaunt face towards us.

If he had not been making so much noise I might have missed him altogether. As a priest he was draped in black, and had stained his face and limbs with pitch, so that in the gloom there was little to see of him but his eyes, which were wide and startlingly pale.

The guard stepped forward. "Now, Two Rabbit," he urged, "there's no need for this. You'll start them all off, and that'll bring my chief running, and I'll never hear the end of it."

The priest turned back to the cage and kicked it hard enough to make the bars rattle. There was a rustle of movement in response, but with Two Rabbit between us I could not clearly see the occupant.

"Hey!" the guard yelled. "Be careful, that's government property!"

"Do you know what this creature did?" the priest rasped. The words burst between his tightly compressed lips like steam from a green log thrown on a fire.

Huitztic pushed himself forward. "We know exactly what he did!" he cried eagerly. "And my master's going to see him punished for it!"

"Your master?" The pale eyes narrowed. "But you're lord Feathered in Black's steward, aren't you?"

"That's right, and the Chief Minister will ..."

We never found what the Chief Minister was going to do, because his steward's words were drowned by the other man's outraged howl. "Lord Feathered in Black! He's as guilty as this vermin here. He ought to be in that cage with him!"

"Now, steady on," the guard said anxiously. "That's dangerous talk."

"As dangerous as mocking the gods? As dangerous as making a laughing stock of their priests?" With a last, baleful glance at the cage, he moved, pushing past us before stalking out of the hall. "He won't get away with it! Tell him that from me!"

Huitztic said nothing. It was the man in the cage who spoke next.

"Yaotl? Is that you?"

Everybody appeared to be staring at me: Huitztic, the prison guard, even the desperate, hollow-eyed prisoners in the shadows around us. They all seemed to be saying: you know this person? And the tone in which they seemed to be saying it was not friendly.

"You must remember me, Yaotl. We trained together." With Two Rabbit gone, I could see his former deputy clearly now. Patecatl had pushed his hand between the bars of the cage in an imploring gesture.

At first I could only gaze at him while I tried to work out where he might have seen me before. When the answer came to me I could only whisper: "Fire Snake?"

"Yes!" the man cried eagerly, straining against the wooden bars until they creaked. "Fire Snake, that's right! Your old pal. Listen, you've got to get me out of here."

Fire Snake: a name from my childhood, from the House of Tears, the harsh school for boys who would be priests. We had not known each other well or liked each other much, but if I had been where he was, I too might have looked upon any familiar face as a long-lost friend's.

Huitztic interrupted before I had a chance to reply. "'Get you out of here'?" He took a step towards the cage and swung his foot at it, making the prisoner leap backwards as the wooden bars rattled for a second time.

"Will you leave my bloody cage alone?" the guard yelled.

Ignoring him, the steward went on ranting at the prisoner. "This slave isn't going to get you out of anything! All he's here for is to listen to you telling us how you poisoned Heron. Go on, how did you do it? How did those mushrooms get into that tube?"

"I don't know what you're talking about!" the man in the cage protested. "Anyway, I'm not telling you anything. It's your fault I'm in here. You set me up!"

"You'll talk, or I'll ... I'll ..." Huitztic lunged at the cage, grasping the bars and shaking them impotently. "Let me at him! It's time we got him out of there and knocked the truth out of him!"

"You keep away," the guard warned. "Nobody touches my prisoners without orders."

"This is ridiculous!" Huitztic spluttered. "Don't you know I work for the Chief Minister?"

"So do I," the guard pointed out.

Just then Fire Snake spoke up. "I'll talk to Yaotl. No one else."

"Who asked you?" the steward snapped. "We'll make you talk!"

"How are you going to do that?" I enquired. "The guard won't let you torture him."

The steward turned on the guard resentfully. "What kind of a prison are you running here, anyway?"

"We usually just starve them," the other man offered. "A few days without food loosens their tongues, and it's much less messy than mutilation."

"We haven't got a few days!"

"I'll talk to Yaotl," the man in the cage offered quietly.

"Why don't you leave him to me?" I suggested. "Lord Feathered in Black told me to investigate this business, didn't he? So let me do it."

"This man's a friend of yours!" the steward objected. "You just want to get him off and put me in that cage instead!"

It was a tempting thought, but all I said was: "Then leave the guard here. He'll tell you if we start hatching any conspiracies."

"This had better be good," I told the man crouching on the other side of the bars, "otherwise Huitztic's likely to talk the old man into having me move in there with you."

The steward had stormed off, declaring that he was going to see what the Chief Minister had to say about this, and that he would be back.

Fire Snake peered up at me miserably. "But he's the man who set this thing up! You've got to help me, Yaotl!"

I glanced uneasily at the guard, who was pacing about the hall, snarling at his other charges as if it would help him keep them in order. I suspected he was wondering whether it would not after all have been wiser to have looked the other way while Huitztic beat a confession out of his prisoner.

"Old Black Feathers sent me here for a reason," I replied, speaking half to myself. "If he wanted you roasted over a slow fire for what happened to his great-nephew, then you'd be cooking already. I think I'm here because he doesn't know what happened himself and he doesn't believe what he's been told about it."

"So you think I've got a chance?" he demanded eagerly, his hands gripping the bars.

"Only if you tell me the truth. I can't convince the old man otherwise. Did you put the poison in that straw?"

"No!"

"How did it get there then?"

"Huitztic must have done it!"

"You're going to have to do better than that," I said a little testily. "It's just your word against his. Who's the Chief Minister going to believe, you or his own steward?" And more to the point, I thought, what would the steward do to me if I accused him without evidence?

Fire Snake looked at the floor. "I don't know what happened," he admitted. "That straw was clean when I gave it to the steward. I remember holding it up to the light, to check it had been bored right through. There was nothing there."

"Why did you agree to help Heron cheat? Two Rabbit was right – you were making a mockery of the ceremony. Did you expect the gods to be happy about that?"

"Lord Feathered in Black isn't afraid of the gods," he muttered. "His steward made it pretty clear what would happen to me and my family if I didn't co-operate. He even had the cheek to suggest I make whatever sacrifices were needed to assuage the gods' anger afterwards!" The bitterness in his voice was unmistakable, and for the first time I felt a pang of sympathy for him.

"I know what it looks like," he added wretchedly. "I was there when they tested all those jars, right up until the last slave started snoring and they took me away. If any of the sacred wine was poisoned it was only the jar Heron drank out of, and how could anyone have known which one that would be? It has to have been the tube, but I wasn't the one who put the stuff in it."

"There's no way he could have taken the stuff before the dance? Or during it?"

"No chance. Someone would have noticed him munching on mushrooms between dance movements, and if he'd had them before it started he wouldn't have been standing up by the end."

"Then somebody must have poisoned the sacred wine," I said. I had been stooping over the cage. Now I stood up briskly. "It has to have been one or the other, doesn't it? The straw or the pot. Did you see anybody else doing anything to the pot Heron drank from?"

"No, but there were so many of them clambering over each other and pushing each other out of the way it was hard to see anything clearly."

I imagined the climax of the ceremony: fifty-two clay pots in the middle of a violent, heaving mass of eager young men. Even if one of them had been able to guess which jar Heron would drink out of, how had he managed to slip the poison into it without anyone noticing?

Out of the corner of my eye I saw the guard moving purposefully towards us. Our conversation was almost over. As I turned to leave, however, one last thought struck me. "Could Heron have told anyone about the edge you and Huitztic had given him? Someone with a motive to interfere?"

Fire Snake uttered a gasp of laughter. "I can think of three hundred and ninety-nine men who had a motive!" he said. "Four hundred if you count Two Rabbit."

"Why him?"

"You heard him just now. He thinks the gods have been mocked and he's been made a fool of. And he blames me. He's never liked me, says I'm too ambitious."

"Heron's hardly likely to have told Two Rabbit what he was planning, though, is he?"

Fire Snake scowled for a moment, as if in disappointment. "I suppose not. He could have boasted about it to someone else, though."

"Who would that be – one of the other young men? One of his rivals in the competition? I don't think so. Is there anyone else?"

"I don't know ... I think he has a girl. But I don't know where you'd find her."

A cough at my shoulder told me it was time to move on.

I crept furtively about my master's palace, peering cautiously in before I would look into a room, keeping to the shadows as I skirted the edges of the courtyards, taking cover when I needed to behind acacia bushes, yucca plants from the lowlands and other greenery. I did not want the steward to see me until I had reported to the Chief Minister, and I would not be ready to do that until after I had spoken to Heron. I assumed he was still at the palace, since I suspected that even if he had recovered consciousness, he was unlikely to be in a fit state to go wandering off for a while yet. I wondered whether he would co-operate if I asked him who he had told about the trick. If he did not, then I had no idea what I would do. I did not seem to have learned anything useful from Fire Snake.

I wondered about the girl the priest had mentioned. A young man like Heron, with his noble connections and fresh from his first triumph on the battlefield, might have his pick of the girls from the pleasure houses. From what I had heard, though, it sounded as though he had a more settled arrangement than that. If she knew about the young man's attempt to cheat the gods, I had to find out; and then I would need to know whom she might have told the secret to.

I was padding as silently as I could along a dark colonnade when a sudden sound stopped me my tracks: a loud groan, a cry of pain.

The noise appeared to be coming from a nearby courtyard. As I crept towards it, I heard it again, but this time it was shut off abruptly, and replaced by something quite different: a woman's voice, hissing furiously: "It's no use moaning and expecting me to feel sorry for you. What happened was your own fault!"

"How do you make that out? I didn't put mushroom powder in that jar myself, did I?"

I grinned. It seemed as though I need look no further for Heron or his girl.

"If you hadn't tried to cheat it wouldn't have happened!"

"How was I supposed to win if I didn't cheat? And please don't shout, Precious Flower."

The girl had not raised her voice above a whisper, but clearly the sacred wine and the mushrooms had not quite worn off, so it probably sounded to Heron as though a Master of Youths were shouting orders into his ear. I peeped around the corner to watch them. He lay stretched out on a stone bench with a cloth over his head. The girl, a tall, slim beauty in a fine cotton blouse and skirt, stood over him with her arms folded. Her hair was loose, like a pleasure girl's, but there was no red stain around her mouth and no sign of the yellow ochre that pleasure girls wore to lighten their skins.

Heron raised his head a little, thought better of it and let it drop again. Hastily Precious Flower stooped to put her hand under it to stop it striking the bare stone.

"Anyway," he mumbled ungratefully, "how did they find out what I was going to do? You must have told them!"

She stepped away from him, probably wishing she had let the hard limestone knock some sense into his skull after all. "It would serve you right if I did!" she cried indignantly. "You would keep boasting about having an edge over the others!"

Heron squirmed, either in pain or anger, but did not get up. Instead he turned his head to glare at the girl. "I knew it!" he snapped. "Who did you tell, you bitch? Was it Firstborn Son or Owl?"

I watched shock and hurt cross the girl's features, making her blink in time to the young man's words. "No, I ..."

I decided I had heard enough. Strolling into the courtyard I said, deliberately loudly: "You're absolutely sure it wasn't the steward who poisoned you, then?"

The girl squealed and darted to one side. Heron gasped, squirmed again, and fell on to the floor in a tangle of limbs and soiled cloth.

I smiled at the girl. "I'm Yaotl. His great-uncle told me to find out what had happened."

She stared at me through big, moist eyes. "I don't understand."

"Did you tell anyone about the trick with the tube?"

"She must have done!" the young man protested, heaving himself back on to his seat. "How else did they know to put the mushrooms in that jar?"

"Oh, shut up," I told him. I looked at the girl.

She did not lower her eyes. "No," she replied firmly. "I didn't, and I will eat earth." She bowed down and touched the ground with a fingertip, then put it to her mouth, in the gesture that was an Aztec's most sacred oath.

The young man was sitting up now, with his knees slightly apart, and seemed to be watching something fascinating on the ground between them. "It can't have been Huitztic," he said indistinctly. "He's my pal. Keeps my great-uncle off my back – covers up for me when I'm out late. When the old man's gone and I get my share of his lands, there'll be something in it for old Huitztic – he knows that."

"So he expects to profit from your advancement?"

"That's it," the youngster said eagerly. He looked up. "The old man told me you were a priest, so you know what winning that contest would mean, especially now that I've taken my first captive."

I wondered whether that had been arranged for him too. "Why would Huitztic want to screw it up for both of us?"

It made sense, I realized. I realized something else, too: my master was too shrewd not to know what was going on between his steward and his great-nephew. That was why I had been told to look into it with Huitztic. Old Black Feathers had not been able to think of any explanation for what had happened that did not implicate the steward, but he had not been able to work out what Huitztic's motive for humiliating his great-nephew might have been either.

"So who else did you tell, apart from Precious Flower here?"

"I didn't! And I'll eat earth too, if you want!"

"Don't bother. Just tell me about those two you mentioned – Owl and Firstborn Son. Who are they, young toughs like you?"

"That's right. Thought they were my friends, too, but Owl in particular ..." He shot a venomous look at the girl.

"What was I supposed to do?" she cried out, colouring. "He asked for me. I'm a pleasure girl, Heron, I'm not allowed to save myself for you, you know that!" And then, suddenly, she burst into tears. "It wasn't me, really it wasn't. I wouldn't tell anyone, even though I was angry with you. And I was only angry because you kept boasting about what you were going to do!"

As she went to embrace him, and he allowed her to, I decided it was time to withdraw. I had learned all I was going to here, and I had seen enough of Heron's smirking, winking face.

I decided it was time I paid a visit to the temple of the god of sacred wine.

To my surprise, the temple was deserted. As I approached its precinct I had to shoulder my way through the city's usual evening crowd – traders taking unsold goods back from the marketplaces, youngsters going home from the Houses of Youth, labourers returning from the fields – but as soon as I was within the walls, all the bustle and noise was gone, replaced by a strange, echoing silence. The sudden change gave the place a forlorn air, which was added to by the way it had been left. Normally the flagstones would have been carefully swept, but not today. It did not appear to have been touched since the chaotic events of the previous afternoon. The large pottery jars stood where they had been put out for the dancers, mostly empty now but still filling the air around them with a stale, sour smell. On the ground around them were scattered the reeds, apparently lying where they had been dropped. Some were slightly flattened, probably squashed by the young men as they squabbled over them. Here and there a scrap of torn cloth or a severed sandal-strap showed where a fight had broken out.

I had been hoping to find the head priest, Two Rabbit, here, but he was clearly not coming back today. I noticed that the brazier in front of the temple, which ought to have been permanently lit, had gone out. I wondered whether after what had happened, the priest was afraid that the gods might have withdrawn their favour. Maybe he thought the place was now unlucky. I remembered that Lord Feathered in Black had sent his serfs to taste the sacred wine that had been left in the pots, but presumably he did not care what curses he might bring down on their heads.

I shivered. I felt suddenly sick, not with fear but from the smell of all that sacred wine. Some of the old craving had returned, and I was glad the pots were empty, because my body had started telling me that what I needed at that moment was a drink.

"I'm wasting my time," I muttered, kicking at the straws scattered at my feet. "I got nothing out of Heron and his girl, and there's nothing here either. I still don't even know how they managed to get the poison into that jar, never mind who did it." For a few moments I pretended to look for clues, although I had no idea what I hoped to find: something that looked like powdered mushrooms, perhaps. I soon gave up in disgust.

"Nothing here," I repeated. "Just fifty-two empty pots and two hundred and sixty straws no one could drink with." I thought about that. "No, two hundred and fifty-nine, of course."

Then I thought about it again.

I looked at the straws scattered around me, now looking as pale as bones in the gathering dusk. I whispered a curse, and then set to gathering them, scooping them up in handfuls and carrying them to a corner.

After I had taken a last look around to ensure that none had rolled away unnoticed, I began to count them.

* * *

By the time I had finished my task, sorting the reeds into thirteen neat piles, the light in the plaza was too poor to see by, and I was working by touch, stooping to put the last few straws in place. I finished the job in haste. Night and the things that haunted it frightened me less than they did most Aztecs – my priest's training helped with that – but there was something about this place that unnerved me, making me feel as though I were being watched. I wanted to be done as soon as I could.

By the time I had finished, however, I knew how the Chief Minister's great-nephew had been poisoned, and I could make a good guess at who might have done it. I had to smile as I thought about the trick: it was clever and somehow fitting.

I could feel my smile fading as I contemplated the report I would have to give my master. I remembered the vain young man I had seen arguing with the pleasure girl, Precious Flower, and wondered whether the person who had decided to teach him a lesson truly deserved whatever brutal punishment Lord Feathered in Black had in mind. But I could not see what I could do to prevent it without bringing the old man's wrath down on my own head.

There was no sound in the courtyard that I could hear. Nonetheless the sensation that I was not alone would not go away. I could feel it as a tingling at the nape of my neck and a coldness beyond the chill of the evening air.

I turned to go, expecting to feel my way out of the Plaza. However, I had not taken three steps before I bumped into something large and hard.

"Hey ...!"

The thing moved. Suddenly I was lifted off my feet, the breath squeezed out of me in a bear hug. I heard a man's voice, very low but clear: "So the priest told you, did he?"

I struggled, lashing out with my feet but kicking only empty air. I wanted to shout but had no breath to do it with.

"Where is it?" the man holding me hissed. "You found it, didn't you? What have you done with it?"

All I could manage by way of reply was a strangled gasp. My assailant's grip slackened a little when he realized that I could not answer his questions unless he stopped trying to suffocate me.

I thought quickly. "It's all right," I croaked, using up the little air he allowed me. "I know what happened. It was Huitztic, the steward! He put the poison in – I've got the proof!"

It did not work. The powerful arms gripped me tighter than ever. I felt dizzy. Coloured lights began to dance before my eyes.

Then another man spoke, from somewhere in the shadows. I knew the voice instantly.

"Who's that? Yaotl? What's going on?"

The man holding me dropped me on the ground.

As I fell, crashing backwards on to the flagstones, my lungs filled up and I was able to yell: "Huitztic, stop him!"

The steward did not understand. "There you are!" he bellowed triumphantly. "I know your game. You thought you'd hide from me until you'd made up a pack of lies to tell to Lord Feathered in Black. I'll see you dead before you pin this thing on me!"

I groaned aloud. "No – you idiot! – quick, stop that bastard before he runs away!"

A foot flew out of the night and slammed into my shoulder. I gasped in pain. I drew breath to call out again but then I heard the sound of running feet, moving away.

Huitztic yelled: "Got you, you miserable slave – wait, who are you?"

His words turned into a cry of pain as the young man who had assaulted me hit him.

After that there was a long silence, broken only by the steward's painful whimpering.

"So which one was that?" I wondered out loud, while I nursed my bruised throat. "Was it Owl or Firstborn Son, do you think?"

There was no answer.

"I think we'd better go and see old Black Feathers now," I continued, "and if you don't say anything about how both you and that young fool tried to silence me, then I won't."

My master, seated in his favourite place, under the magnolia on the roof of his palace received me alone. We left the steward in the courtyard below to fret and pace about nervously. He still thought I was going to accuse him, but I knew that would not do for the old man. He wanted proof.

I showed him what I had brought from the temple. It was, I had guessed, the thing the young man who had attacked me had been after: the one reed out of the two hundred and sixty I had found that had seemed lighter than the rest. As he held it up to peer at the Moon through it, I told him what had happened.

"There were four hundred dancers, two hundred and sixty straws and fifty two jars," I began.

"Yes, yes, I know," he replied absently, still squinting through the tube.

What I said next got his full attention, however. "Wrong! There were two hundred and sixty-one straws – and two of them were bored through. The one your great nephew had, and this one."

"No, that doesn't make sense. If two of them had cheated, one of the others would have become intoxicated – or worse, if he'd drunk from the same jar as Heron."

"He was at the same jar as Heron, my Lord. He didn't drink, though. He must have smuggled that tube in just as Heron did, but he never intended to suck through it. He blew."

My master's sharp eyes glittered as he stared at me.

"That ceremony always turns into a riot. There's no time for anyone to check whether the tube they've got is hollow or not, if they're lucky enough to be able to lay hands on one at all. So you'll always get several young men sucking away at each jar, most of them due to be disappointed. The one who poisoned your great nephew knew that and took advantage of it. He stuck close to Heron with a hollow reed full of powdered mushrooms, knowing nobody would think anything of it if he dipped his reed in the same jar. He blew the poison in just as Heron was slurping the stuff up."

Lord Feathered in Black looked at the tube with distaste. "Clever," he conceded. "But if what you say is right, then how do we know which of them it was?"

"I don't think we ever will," I replied carefully. I was sure it had been either Owl or Firstborn Son who had attacked me, but I did not blame him. He must have been terrified when he found out how hard the Chief Minister had taken his prank.

"Well, at least we know where he got the straw from," the Chief Minister said.

"We do?"

"Two Rabbit. He vanished yesterday, just after you saw him at the prison. Collected a few things from his lodging at the temple and hasn't been seen since. I don't suppose he ever will be again, at least not in Mexico."

I found Fire Snake looking none the worse for his brief stay in the prison.

"You did it! Well done, Yaotl – thank you, old friend, thank you! I shan't forget this ..."

"I wish you would," I said shortly.

"If there's ever anything I can do ..."

I looked at his eager face, the grin white against the pitch he used to stain it, and felt disgusted. The gods had been affronted, but all that mattered to Fire Snake was that he had got away with it. "Just tell me something," I said quietly. "How did Two Rabbit know what you and Heron had done?"

The effusion of words abruptly halted. He hesitated before saying: "But we talked about that. Didn't he learn it from someone Heron had been bragging to? What about that girl?"

"Precious Flower didn't talk. I've met them both. She didn't like what Heron had done but there's no way she'd betray him. That young fool doesn't deserve her."

"Well, then ..."

"In fact," I went on, "It seems to me there's only one person who could or would have told him, expecting him to do exactly what he did. His assistant, the one he thought was too ambitious. You knew how this was likely to turn out, didn't you? When that young man attacked me – I still don't know who it was, by the way, and I don't want to – he said he thought the priest had told me what happened. At first I thought he meant you, but he was talking about Two Rabbit. Your chief gave one of Heron's rivals a tube full of sacred mushrooms, but he only did it because he knew what Heron was going to do. And he can only have learned of that from you."

"That's absurd!" Fire Snake protested, but I could hear the tremor in his voice.

"No, I think it's quite clever. You didn't actually poison young Heron but you found a way to bring it about. The possibility of implicating poor old Two Rabbit must have made it even sweeter for you. Of course it went a bit wrong when you were arrested – you didn't expect that, I'd guess – but it all turned out well in the end, didn't it? Will they make you chief priest now, I wonder?"

He clutched anxiously at the hem of my cloak as I turned away from him, but I did not want to hear any more claims on an old friendship that had never existed.

As I walked out, though, I called over my shoulder: "But don't worry. I won't tell old Black Feathers. I don't really care who made a fool of his great-nephew, or why. It probably served him right."

HISTORY!

Toby Litt

THEY MET IN the thickest part of the woods; also, the furthest from the edge. To get there, they had to hack through thick brambles, use compasses, check their synchronized watches and remember the routes of their country girlhoods. Radio silence was maintained, however. It was twilight, clement because late summer. This den within a copse had been their place of recourse, when the adults had made it plain they were becoming too alive to be tolerated – too alive meaning too fast, too loud, too vivid in thought and question.

All of them, all three, had had both original parents to respond to; since then, all three had lost one or the other. Later, it was speculated that this might have had something to do with their actions. Information was initially hard to come by, and what there was seemed contradictory.

First to arrive at the meeting point was Margaret – her usual distinguishing feature, an aureole of chestnut ringlets, now squashed beneath a black balaclava. Her eyes, if one had been able to see them, were underlined with brown semi-circles. Margaret had given birth five years previously to triplet boys, two of whom were hyperactive; the third was given to feigning death behind the sofa for no apparent reason. Margaret, who of course herself dies before the night is out, left behind a written statement saying she did what she did for them. The consensus among the villagers was, she was a bad mother, knew it, and took the coward's way out.

"Hello," said a low voice from the cover immediately behind Margaret. "I wondered whether I'd be able to sneak up on you."

Margaret had at first given a real jump; the voice interrupted thoughts of whether she could trust the teenage babysitter with John, Jack and James. Her husband had funny business at the Lodge.

"Well, then, you succeeded," said Margaret.

Out from behind the thick trunk of a tree stepped Beatrice, known as Bee, who also dies. "It doesn't matter," she said, "No one else is going to be out here."

"This isn't a game."

"To be entirely serious is to play into their hands," said Bee, who was theoretically minded in her opposition. "I am maintaining an element of joy."

Margaret smiled a sad smile, almost as if she knew they were going to die. "It's good to see you," she said, and the two women hugged. Both were aware of the crackling sounds of the woods around them – were they being crept up on?

"How are the boys?" asked Bee.

"They are very well," said Margaret, willing herself not to cry. "It's still all battles in our house, though. War-war-war."

"Any sign of Liz?"

"Not yet," replied Margaret.

The two women sat on the loamy earth of the woods. It was nice for once not to have to worry about dirt – tonight was a time for being deliberately dirty. "She's late," said Bee, who had turned thirty the week before.

"She'll be here," said Margaret.

"What if she doesn't come?"

"She'll come."

There was a moment.

"I like your hair like that," said Margaret.

"Thank you," said Bee.

Bee's hair was usually done in a neat black bob, but she had shaved this off earlier in the evening – down to a number one. Some have taken this as a sign that she was all along intending martyrdom. She had been anorexic for years, which was also taken as an explanation – hatred of the self and of the world. But although she probably did not know it, at the time of her death she was three weeks' pregnant. Despite DNA testing, the father has to this day not been found.

"Do we go ahead anyway, if she doesn't come?" Bee asked.

"I think I hear her now," said Margaret. If she heard something, it wasn't Liz; perhaps a fox or a badger. After this, though, they waited in a listening silence.

Eventually, a quarter of an hour later, Liz crashed out of the undergrowth and fell against them. It took her two minutes to regain her breath – during which time both the others wanted to tell her to keep quiet but didn't feel it possible.

"I was followed," was the first thing she said that they understood.

"Calm down," said Margaret, who wasn't the leader – they didn't have a leader; hierarchies being part of what they wanted to destroy – but who often was first to introduce ideas into their circle: she had suggested tonight; the others had not been slow to agree. "Tell us whenever you're ready."

Liz – who dies – sat with her head between her legs, gasping less and less. At twenty-nine, she was the youngest of them. (Margaret was thirty-one, Bee – as mentioned before – thirty.) "I'm sorry I'm late," she said.

"We have plenty of time," said Margaret, but checked her watch anyway.

"Who followed you?" asked Bee.

"A policeman," Liz said, her breath a little more even. "He was dressed in civilian clothes, but I could still tell he was a policeman."

"How?" asked Margaret.

"Because I hated him so much," Liz said, then sniggered. "And he walked as if he'd been taught how to march – you know what I mean."

"Do you think they know anything?" Bee asked.

"No," said Margaret. "How could they?"

"I'm not so sure," said Liz. "He seemed to want to follow me – for no reason."

"You managed to lose him, didn't you?" asked Margaret.

"Of course," said Liz, sitting up straight. "Or else I wouldn't be here."

"How?" asked Bee.

"Well ..." said Liz, and took a long breath.

It turned out she had gone to the house of a sympathetic female friend, knocked on the door, been invited inside and then, after a brief explanation (seedy man loitering, fear of rape), had climbed over the back fence and into the concreted area behind the cricket pavilion. From here, she had been able to make her way to the woods without breaking cover more than once – to cross the main road near the stables.

All three women kept horses there, and this was later the cause of much speculation. Perhaps it was a sign of sexual frustration – unhappiness in marriage. The husbands of Margaret and Liz denied this as libel. Singleton Bee was discovered (by the tabloids) to have been gratifyingly promiscuous. In the end, more than seven men came forward to testify to her total lack of frigidity. "She was very intense," one of them said. "Almost too intense. I didn't like it." Nymphomania became the favoured diagnosis.

Margaret coughed quietly. "All set?" she asked.

"Yes," said Liz.

"Ready," said Bee.

They started walking, in single file. All of them were quite fit – Bee did yoga, Margaret did Pilates and Liz did a weekly salsa class – so they made very rapid progress. It took them half an hour to reach their destination: a gamekeeper's cottage in a small clearing, surrounded by a neatly kept garden – lawn, rockery, fruit trees. By this time, it was starting to get dark. The lights were on inside the cottage, the now infamous "Bower of Bliss"; the flowery curtains of the sitting room had not been drawn. A Mercedes saloon and a Renault Clio were parked on the drive, which had long-ago been done in crazy paving.

The three women made a quick check of their equipment, particularly their radios. These were small and made of black plastic; across the top of them, the words *Action Man* were written in bright orange.

"Fine," said Margaret. "We follow the plan."

She and Bee proceeded to the front door. Liz, keeping low, made her way to the kitchen door – around the other side. She could hear the sound of the television. It was the theme tune to the "Antiques Roadshow". They were bang on eight o'clock.

From her rucksack, Liz took out two rolls of camouflage-patterned tape and a chunky pair of childsafe scissors.

Bee radioed to check Liz was in position.

"All present and correct," said Liz, a phrase of her father's.

Margaret pushed the front doorbell with the middle finger of her left hand; in her right was a toy gun belonging to one of her sons. It was very realistic, as long as one didn't get too good a look – which was why she had chosen to use it.

A man answered the door – fifty-eight, fat, dressed in a green tweedy suit but with leather slippers on. This was Colin Richardson, the Mayor of the village, publican of the Queen's Head, left-arm orthodox spin.

"Margaret," he said. "What can I do for you?"

She pointed the toy gun close up to his forehead, where it would be out of focus.

"Do exactly what we say," she replied.

"Is that real?" Colin asked.

"Yes," she said. "And if you don't get inside, I will demonstrate how real."

Colin turned and walked back into the house.

"Hold your hands up where I can see them," said Margaret. "I know you keep a shotgun."

"Not any more, alas," said Colin. "I had to hand it in – sop to the council lefties."

"I think you're lying," said Margaret, as they passed out of the hall and into the TV-loud living room.

"Numfon," said Colin. "Be calm. There's nothing to worry about."

A Thai woman in her mid-thirties was sitting on the left of the sofa, holding a glass of Australian Riesling in her hand. The glass was made of cut crystal. Her fingernails were long and had paste jewels on them.

"Sit down," said Margaret. "Not next to her."

"Hello, Numfon," said Bee.

"Bee," said Numfon.

"Please come with me, quickly, and fetch Roger," said Bee.

The two of them went off through an adjoining door. The name ROGER was spelt out on it with a rhino, an ostrich, a giraffe, an emu and another rhino.

"What's this about?" asked Colin. "It's clearly not the usual parish council business. Is it planning permission?"

"It's about everything," said Margaret. "You'll find out soon enough. Now, please be quiet."

She radioed Liz.

"Building secured. You may enter."

Liz tried the back door. It was unlocked. A moment later, she had joined Margaret in the living room.

"You, too?" asked Colin.

"Oh, yes," said Liz.

On the television, they were valuing a wig that was said to have belonged to Samuel Johnson.

Numfon reentered the room, carrying Roger, a five-year-old boy, half-Caucasian, half-Asian. He was still groggy.

"Sit down," said Margaret. "If you can keep him quiet, we won't need to gag him."

"Margaret," said Colin, "the nearest house is half a mile a way – half a mile of thick woodland. You could shoot the lot of us, and no one would hear."

"Yes," said Margaret. "We could. I just don't want to have any whining bloody kids around. I get enough of that at home."

"So, what can I do for you?" asked Colin.

"You can call the police," said Margaret. "Tell them you've been taken hostage. Tell them we're serious. And that, when they get here, we can discuss terms."

"Anything you say, Margaret."

Margaret slapped Colin's face, with her non-gun hand.

"Don't be such a smarmy cunt, Colin. You can die painlessly or very painfully indeed."

"Yes," he said, his hair disarranged.

"Dial 999," said Margaret. "Tell them to get here as soon as they can. Tell them we'd like a helicopter."

"What, to escape with?"

"No, just to fly around overhead, so we feel important."

Colin picked up the receiver and dialled.

It took him five minutes to get through to the right person.

"Yes, they're very serious indeed, it seems," Colin said. "No, I don't know what they want."

"Tell them we'll only speak to an officer specially trained in hostage situations."

"Did you hear that?" Colin asked the policeman. Then, to Margaret, "He heard. He said, that might take some time to arrange."

"Tell him we will shoot your wife in one hour," said Margaret.

Colin soberly repeated the words.

"Now give me the phone," she said.

Colin obeyed.

Margaret took the receiver from him. "You can be quick when you want to be," she said into it, then hung up.

"Back in there," Margaret said, and shoved Colin into the living room. She was really enjoying this – more than she had expected.

On the sofa, Numfon was cowering and Roger was crying.

"Gag them," she said. "The police are on their way."

Colin slumped into the armchair and sent a brave smile towards Numfon. "Don't worry, darling," he said. "We'll be alright."

"No, you won't," said Bee. "You'll never be alright."

"You deserve this," said Margaret.

Liz handed over one of the rolls of tape to Bee, who started on Numfon. "Lift your hair out of the way," Bee said.

"What does that matter?" Liz asked.

"Don't hurt my mummy," wailed Roger, just before Liz sealed his mouth. Snot immediately began to run down the slick surface of the tape. Roger's eyes were no longer those of a five-year-old.

Bee taped up Numfon's hands and feet. Liz left Roger's hands free, so that he could put them round his mother.

Then Margaret taped Colin's feet together, and his hands behind his back. His mouth, she left alone.

"Tea, anyone?" asked Liz.

"Yes, please," said Margaret. "And see if you can find some biscuits. I'm sure they keep some nice ones."

On television, they were valuing a Queen Anne table with very fine cabriolet legs.

Margaret sat down on the sofa with the toy gun in her lap. Bee took the armchair on the left hand side, after removing the antimacassar. She crumpled it up and threw it into the fireplace, where imitation coals sat ready to be gassed.

Apart from Roger's sniffles, everyone was quiet until Liz returned with the tea. There were mugs for the three hostage-takers, nothing for the family.

"So, Colin," said Bee, "why did you call your son 'Roger'? It's such a stupid name."

"We like it," said Colin.

"Which only proves how stupid it is," said Margaret. "Almost as bad as Colin. Who wants to be five and be called 'Roger'?"

Bee turned to the boy. "Let's ask Roger. Roger, do you like your name?"

Roger looked at his mother.

Margaret leaned across and pulled the tape off Roger's mouth.

"Do you like your name?" asked Liz, with a gentle tone.

Roger shook his head.

"Does that mean you like it or you don't like it?" asked Margaret.

"Don't like it," the boy said.

The three hostage-takers all laughed.

"You see," said Bee. "Even he hates it."

"So," asked Liz, "what would you like to be called?"

Roger looked down into his chest.

"Optimus Prime," he said.

"Right," said Margaret. "From now on, you're Optimus Prime. Which is going to sound pretty silly in twenty years' time – but I don't think there's much reason to worry about that."

"Would you like some juice, Optimus Prime?" asked Liz.

He said, "Yes, please."

"Very polite," said Margaret. "That's good."

Liz went and got him a beaker full of orange. He drank it very quickly.

"Do you still wear a nappy, Optimus Prime?" Margaret asked.

"No," he said. "I'm a big boy."

"Then you must tell us if you need to go wee-wee," said Margaret. "Do you understand?"

"Okay," said Optimus Prime.

"Look," said Colin. "What is it exactly that you want? Perhaps we can sort it all out before the police get here?"

"What we want," said Margaret, "is for the police to get here. Now, please, don't speak again."

They watched the television for a while.

"Do you like this programme, Optimus Prime?" asked Margaret.

"No," he said, becoming more confident. "It's boring."

"What would you like?" Bee asked.

"Cartoons," he said.

Margaret passed him the remote, which had been sitting on Colin's arm of the sofa.

"Choose something," she said.

Optimus Prime skipped through the channels until he came to a programme called "Robotboy".

"Ah, yes," said Margaret.

They watched it for ten minutes. Then Bee said, "Optimus Prime, do you have any guns?"

Optimus nodded.

"If we undo your legs, will you go with me and fetch them?"

"Yes," he said.

Liz came across and cut through the tape with the chunky scissors.

Bee took Optimus' hand and led him into the bedroom.

A few minutes later, they came back, arms full of imitation pistols, lasers and machine guns.

"Which is your favourite?" asked Margaret.

Optimus picked out a red and black laser.

"You keep that one, then."

"And I'll have this one," said Liz, choosing an old-fashioned looking revolver. It had cowboys on the handle and a wagon train running along the barrel.

"And can I have this one?" asked Bee, picking up a business-like automatic in black plastic.

"Yes," said Optimus. "As long as I can have them back."

"Of course you can have them back," said Margaret.

They sat down to watch the TV – all much happier, now they were armed.

Colin had been looking at Margaret's gun. "That one's not real either, is it? You came in here and held us up with a toy!"

"Shut up or we tape your mouth up," Margaret said. "What do you think about that, Optimus Prime?"

The boy looked surly.

"Then he won't be able to tell you to go to bed," said Liz.

"Or tell you to do anything at all," said Bee.

Optimus Prime said, "I do anything I want all the time."

"I bet you do," said Margaret, and laughed. "But, shall we tape up your daddy's mouth? Just for a game."

"Okay," said Optimus Prime, with a sideways glance to see the effect of his words.

"Roger!" Colin shouted.

He struggled as Liz and Bee wound the camouflaged tape around his head. His face was pink by the time they finished. It became even more pink when Bee pinched his nostrils for half a minute, to check his mouth really *was* sealed. When she let go, he snorted raggedly.

"I need a wee," said Optimus Prime.

The hostage-takers looked at one another.

"I'll take him," said Margaret. She went and picked him up from the sofa. He put his arms around her neck. Colin flinched at this.

Margaret carried Optimus Prime through the kitchen and into the toilet; she knew where it was. She pulled the boy's pyjama bottoms down until they were around his knees, then lifted him on to the seat.

He put his finger on his willy, to point it down, then peed almost immediately. They both listened to the small gush until it went quiet.

"Finished?" asked Margaret.

Optimus Prime nodded.

"You don't want a poo?"

"No," the boy said.

"Come on, then."

Margaret dried Optimus Prime's willy with a sheet of toilet paper, then hiked his pyjamas up.

"All done," she said, carrying him back into the living room.

Just then, sirens came into earshot. They became louder quite gradually. And then blue lights flashed across the stripy wallpaper.

"At last," said Margaret.

But it took another ten minutes before the phone rang.

Bee picked it up.

"We are surrounded," she said, relaying the words to the other hostage-takers. "We can talk about this calmly. Whatever issues we have can be addressed. We can come outside with our hands above our heads. No, we're not going to do that," she said. "Where's our helicopter?" She listened. "That's not good enough. We wanted a helicopter. Half an hour? Okay, I want you to make helicopter noises. Yes, you heard me. Make helicopter noises, or we shoot the woman."

She held up the phone so the others could hear the chunka-chunka-chunka sound.

"Very good," said Bee. "But we want the real thing."

She put the phone down, then picked it up when it rang.

"What else do we want?"

Margaret and Liz nodded at her. The plan.

"We will exchange the woman for a policewoman. A straight swap. You have five minutes to decide."

She put the phone down.

It rang again two minutes later.

"We can have a policewoman," she said, after listening for a few seconds. "But they want the boy as well. No," she said, "that's not the deal. One for one." A pause. "Alright. They'll come out the front door."

Bee replaced the receiver.

Liz cut the tape off Numfon's ankles.

"Don't try to run," she said. "Not until the policewoman's inside."

Margaret took her into the hall, then slowly opened the door. She was disappointed to see so few police cars – only three.

A WPC was standing beside the open passenger door of the nearest, her hands in the air.

"Come towards me," shouted Margaret, who could feel herself tickled by the sights of real guns.

The policewoman walked steadily forwards, until she was halfway.

"I want you here," said Margaret, pointing to the paving stones with the gun-barrel.

The WPC started moving again.

When she was close enough, Margaret pushed Numfon away and grabbed the WPC by the neck.

Numfon stood on the spot.

"Run, you silly cow," said the WPC.

Numfon looked back, then started to walk away. She was bawling.

Margaret pulled the WPC inside.

"What's your name?" she asked, leading her through into the living room.

"Jane McDowell," said the young woman.

"Would you like a cup of tea?" asked Liz.

"No, thank you," said the WPC, assessing the situation.

What she saw, on the floor, was a pile of toy guns. Then she looked at the guns the hostage takers were holding. First Bee's, then Liz's and, finally, turning her head round as far as it would go, at Margaret's.

"Is this some kind of sick joke?" she said.

"Gag her," said Margaret.

"We can talk," said the WPC.

"Now, why would we want to do that?" asked Bee, before placing a strip of tape across Jane McDowell's mouth.

The phone rang, was answered.

"They want to know what else we want," said Bee.

"Tell them 'World Peace'," said Margaret.

"We want World Peace."

Bee listened.

"He says, 'Don't we all?'"

"No, we don't," said Liz. "That's the whole point."

"World Peace, now!" shouted Bee, into the receiver. "Stop the violence."

She clattered it back on to the phone.

"So, Optimus Prime," began Margaret. "What should we do with the policewoman?"

Optimus Prime looked at the dark uniform.

"She hasn't got a gun," he said.

"No," said Bee. "But we do."

"Is she a real policeman?"

"I don't know," said Liz. "What do you think?"

"I think she's not a real policeman because a real policeman wouldn't just surrender and come in like that. They would fight and stop you."

"I think you're right, Optimus Prime," said Margaret. "I think she's just pretending to be a policeman."

"That's a very naughty thing to do, isn't it?" said Bee. "Really bad."

The WPC looked about in panic.

"Go on," said Bee. "Shoot her with your laser."

Optimus Prime hesitated.

"She deserves it," said Liz.

The boy stood up and pointed the laser at the WPC's face. Then, making a shoom-shoom sound, he fired off two zaps straight between the eyes. A red light glowed faintly on Janet McDowell's forehead; the thing's batteries were going.

"Good boy," said the hostage-takers. "Well done. Fantastic."

Optimus Prime smiled a sideways smile. He did not look towards his father.

"Into the kitchen," said Margaret.

She and Liz bundled the WPC through the door and slammed it shut.

Two minutes later, Liz re-emerged, a smudge of blood on her left forehead. She was holding a carving knife.

"Margaret says you can finish her off, if you like."

Colin looked through the doorway, and saw the black-stockinged legs of Janet McDowell lying on the wood-effect lino of the kitchen floor. They twitched, once, twice.

Bee took the knife and went into the kitchen, leaving Liz to watch Colin and Optimus Prime. The father was trying to say something, making an anguished humming sound. He had known Janet McDowell since she was a baby. He had several times slept with her mother.

"Did you kill the woman?" asked Optimus Prime.

"Yes," said Liz.

"Why did you kill the woman?"

"Because there was no other way."

This didn't satisfy Optimus Prime, but he had no more questions.

Liz, holding her toy gun, went across to the window and gazed out. Then she began to turn her head towards Colin, so the first shot ripped her left ear off. The second, coming almost immediately, took away the top half of the head to which the ear had been attached.

In the kitchen, Margaret and Bee only had time to look up from the WPC's blood-wet body before the window shattered and Bee's left temple exploded.

Margaret dived to the ground, pushed the kitchen door open and crawled through into the living room.

She could hear the back door collapse as the police battering ram smashed through it.

Optimus Prime was curled foetal on the sofa; Colin had managed to stand up, intending to hop across to his son.

Margaret stood in the middle of the room, legs apart, pointing the toy gun defiantly at the doorway.

The first policeman through took her out with a shot to the chest, then finished her with three to the head.

"It's alright, son," he said to Optimus Prime, who had been spattered. "You're safe now."

THE MASQUERADE

Sarah Rayne

I SELDOM ATTEND parties unless I think they might be of use in my career, so it was all the more remarkable to find myself attending this one. This reticence is not due to shyness, you understand, nor to a lack of self-confidence – I value myself and my attainments rather highly. But I have always shunned larger gatherings – the chattering, lovely-to-see-you, how-are-you-my-dear, type of event. Loud music, brittle conversation, ladies air-kissing one another and then shredding each other's reputations in corners. Not for me. My wife, however, has always enjoyed all and any parties with shrieking glee, telling people I am an old sobersides, and saying with a laugh that she makes up for my quietness.

But here I was, approaching the door of this house whose owners I did not know, and whose reasons for giving this party I could not, for the moment, recall.

It was rather a grand-looking house – there was an air of quiet elegance about it which pleased me. One is not a snob, but there are certain standards. I admit that my own house, bought a few years ago, is – well – modest, but I named it "Lodge House" which I always felt conveyed an air of subdued grandeur. The edge of a former baronial estate, perhaps? That kind of thing, anyway. My wife, of course, never saw the point, and insisted on telling people that it was Number 78, halfway down the street, with a tube station just round the corner. I promise you, many is the time I have *winced* at hearing her say that.

This house did not appear to have a name or a number, or to need one. There was even a doorman who beckoned me in; he seemed so delighted to see me I felt it would be discourteous to retreat.

"Dear me," I said, pausing on the threshold. I do not swear, and I do not approve of the modern habit of swearing, with teenagers effing and blinding as if it were a nervous tic, and even television programme-makers not deeming it always necessary to use the censoring bleep. So I said, "Dear me, I hadn't realized this was a fancy-dress party. I am not really dressed for it—" You might think, you who read this, that someone could have mentioned that aspect to me, but no one had.

"Oh, the costume isn't important," said the doorman at once. "People come as they are. You'll do very nicely."

He was right, of course. Dressed as I was, I should have done very nicely anywhere. I am fastidious about my appearance although my wife says I am pernickety. Downright vain, she says: everyone laughs at you for your old-fashioned finicking. I was wearing evening clothes – one of the modern dress shirts the young men affect, with one of those narrow bow ties that give a rather 1920s look, and I was pleased with my appearance. Even the slightly thin patch on the top of my head would not be noticeable in this light.

Once inside, the house was far bigger than I had realized; huge rooms opened one out of another and the concept put me in mind of something, although I could not quite pin down the memory. Some literary allusion, perhaps? It would be nice to think I had some arcane poet or philosopher in mind, but actually I believe I was thinking of Dr Who's *Tardis*. (Pretentious, that's what you are, my wife always says. We all have a good laugh at your pretensions behind your back.)

There were drinks and a buffet, all excellent, and the service – Well! You have perhaps been to those exclusive, expensive restaurants in your time? Or to one of the palatial gentlemen's clubs that can still be found in London if one knows where to look? Then you will have encountered that discreet deference. Food seemed almost to materialize at one's hand. I was given a glass of wine and a plate of smoked salmon sandwiches straight away and I retired with them to a corner, in order to observe the guests, hoping to see someone I knew.

The term "fancy-dress" was not quite accurate after all, although a more bizarre collection of outfits would be hard to find anywhere. There was every imaginable garb, and every creed, colour, race, ethnic mix – every walk of society, every profession and calling. Try as I might I could see no familiar faces, and this may have been why, at that stage, I was diffident about approaching anyone. It was not due to my inherent reticence, you understand: in the right surroundings I can be as convivial as the next man. This was more a feeling of exclusion. In the end, I moved to a bay window to observe, and to drink my wine – it was a vintage I should not have minded having in my own cellars. Well, I say *cellars*, but actually it's an under-stairs cupboard containing several wine-racks bought at our local DIY centre. It is not necessary to tell people this, however, and I always remonstrated with my wife when she did.

By an odd coincidence, the wine seemed to be the one I had poured for my wife quite recently, although I have to say good wine was always a bit of a waste on her because she never had any discrimination; she enjoys sugary pink concoctions with paper umbrellas and frosted rims to the glass. Actually, she once even attended some sort of all-female party dressed as a Piña Colada: the memory of that still makes me shudder and I shall refrain from describing the outfit. (But I found out afterwards that Piña Colada translates, near enough, as strained pineapple, which seems to me very appropriate.)

But on that evening we had been preparing to depart for my office Christmas dinner, so I was hoping there would be no jazzily-coloured skirts or ridiculous head-dresses. It's a black tie affair, the office Christmas dinner, but when my wife came downstairs I was sorry to see that although she was more or less conventionally dressed, her outfit was cut extremely low and showed up the extra pounds she had accumulated. To be truthful, I would have preferred to go to the dinner without her, because she would drink too much and then *flaunt* herself at my colleagues all evening; they would leer and nudge one another and I should be curdled with anger and embarrassment. Those of you who have never actually walked through a big office and heard people whispering, "He's the one with the slutty wife", can have no idea of the humiliation I have suffered. I remember attending a small cocktail party for the cele-bration of a colleague's retirement. Forty-three years he had been with the firm and I had been asked to make the presentation. A silver serving dish had been bought for him – I had chosen it myself and it was really a very nice thing indeed and a change from the usual clock. I had written a few words, touching on the man's long and honourable service, drawing subtle attention to my own involvement in his department.

You will perhaps understand my feelings when, on reaching the hotel, my wife removed her coat to display a scarlet dress that made her look – this is no exaggeration – like a Piccadilly tart. I was mortified, but there was nothing to be done other than make the best of things.

After my speech, I lost sight of her for a couple of hours, and when I next saw her, she was fawning (there is no other word for it) on the Chairman, her eyes glazed, her conversation gin-slurred. When she thanked him for the hospitality she had to make three attempts to pronounce the word, and by way of finale she recounted to four of the directors a joke in which the words *cock* and *tail* figured as part of the punchline.

The really infuriating thing is that until that night I had known – absolutely and surely *known*! – that I was in line to step up into the shoes of my retiring colleague. I had been passed over quite a number of times in the past (I make this statement without the least shred of resentment, but people in offices can be very manipulative and the place was as full of intrigue as a Tudor court), but this time the word had definitely gone out that I was in line for his job. Departmental head, no less!

And what happened? After my wife's shameless display at the retirement cocktail party they announced the vacancy was to be given to a jumped-up young upstart, a pipsqueak of a boy barely out of his twenties! I think I am entitled to have been upset about it. I think anyone would have been upset. *Upset*, did I say? Dammit, I was wracked with fury and a black and bitter bile scalded through my entire body. I thought – you lost that promotion for me, you bitch, but one day, my fine madam, one day ...

Nevertheless, I still looked forward to that year's Christmas party. I had always counted the evening as something of a special event, so before we left, I poured two glasses of the claret I kept for our modest festivities, setting hers down on the low table by her chair. She did not drink it at once – that was unusual in itself and it should have alerted me, but it did not. I remember she got up to find my woollen scarf at my request, and then, having brought it for me, asked me to go upstairs for her evening bag. She knows I hate entering her over-scented, pink-flounced bedroom, but she sometimes tries to tempt me into it. I have learned to foil her over the years: the room makes my skin crawl and her physical importunities on those occasions make me feel positively ill. It was not always so, you understand. I fancy I have been as gallant as any man in my time.

So, the evening bag collected as hastily as possible, I sat down with my wine although it was not as good as it should be. There was a slight bitter taste – it reminded me of the almond icing on the Christmas cake in its tin – and I remember thinking I must certainly complain to the wine shop. I set down the glass, and then there was confusion – a dreadful wrenching pain and the feeling of plummeting down in a fast-moving lift ... Bright lights and a long tunnel ...

And then, you see, I found myself here, outside the big elegant mansion with the doorman inviting me in ...

It was instantly obvious what had happened. The sly bitch had switched the glasses while I was getting her evening bag. She realized what I was doing – perhaps she saw me stir the prussic acid into her glass while she pretended to find my scarf, or perhaps she had simply decided to be rid of me anyway. But whichever it was, I drank from her glass and I died instead. The cheating, double-faced vixen actually killed me!

It seems this house is some sort of judgment place, for the doorman came back into the room a few moments ago and said, "Murderers' judgments" very loudly, exactly as if he was the lift-man at a department store saying, "Ladies' underwear".

Are these oddly-assorted people all murderers then? That saintly-looking old gentleman in the good suit, that kitten-faced girl who might have posed for a pre-Raphaelite painting? That middle-aged female who looks as if she would not have an interest beyond baking and knitting patterns ...?

Having listened to fragments of their talk, I fear they are.

"... and, do you know, if it had not been for the wretched office junior coming in at just that moment, I would have got away with it ... But the stupid girl must go screaming off to Mr Bunstable in Accounts, and I ended in being convicted on the evidence of a seventeen-year-old child and the bought-ledger clerk ... Twenty years I was given ..."

"Twenty years is nothing, old chap. I got Life – and that was in the days when Life meant Life …"

"… *entirely* the auditor's own fault to my way of thinking – if he hadn't pried into that *very* small discrepancy in the clients' account, I shouldn't have needed to put the rat poison in his afternoon tea to shut him up …"

"… I always made it a rule to use good old-fashioned Lysol or Jeyes' Fluid to get all the blood off the knitting needle and they never got me, never even suspected … But that man over there by the door, he very stupidly cut costs: a cheap, supermarket-brand cleaner was what he used, and of course it simply wasn't thorough enough and he ended his days in Wandsworth …"

"… my dear, you should *never* have used your own kitchen knife, they were bound to trace it back to you … An axe, that's what I always used, on the premise that you can put the killing down to a passing homicidal maniac – what? Oh, nonsense, there's always a homicidal maniac somewhere – I've counted six of them here tonight as it happens – matter of fact I've just had a glass of wine with a couple of them … Charming fellows …"

Well, whatever they may be, these people, charming or not, *I'm* not one of them. *I'm* not a murderer. This is all a colossal mistake, and I have absolutely no business being here because I did *not* kill my wife. I suppose a purist might argue that I had the *intention* to kill her, but as far as I know, no one has yet been punished for that, although I believe the Roman Catholic Church regards the intention as almost tantamount to the actual deed—

And that's another grievance! I may not actually have attended church service absolutely every Sunday, but I never missed Easter or Christmas. As a matter of fact, I rather enjoy the music one gets in a church. (Once I said this to my wife – hoping it might promote an interesting discussion, you know – but she only shrieked with laughter, asked if I was taking to religion, and recounted a coarse story about a vicar.)

But I have been a lifelong member of the Church of England and I should have thought as such I would have been taken to a more select division. However, there may be a chance to point this out later. Presumably there will be some kind of overseer here.

It's unfortunate that for the moment I seem to be shut up with these people – with whom I have absolutely nothing in common. And all the while that bitch is alive in the world, flaunting her body, drinking sickly pink rubbish from champagne flutes. Taking lovers by the dozen, I shouldn't wonder, and living high on the hog from the insurance policies ... Yes, that last one's a very painful thorn in the flesh, although I hadn't better use that expression when they come to talk to me, since any mention of thorns in the flesh may be considered something of a *bêtise* here. They'll have long memories, I daresay.

But I shall explain it all presently, of course. There's bound to be some kind of procedure for mistakes. I shall stand no nonsense from anyone, either. I did not kill my wife, and I'm damned if I'm going to be branded as a murderer.

I'm *damned* if I am ...

TAKE DEATH EASY

Peter Turnbull

Monday

In which in the sultry month of August in the golden Vale of York, a loathsome man with a loathsome machine makes a loathsome find, and a woman fulfilled becomes a woman haunted.

HIS NEW TOY, she thought, said it all. And it said the end, after ten years it was the end, as, eventually, she knew it would be. No more hiding from it, or from him. It astounded Sandra Schofield that it had taken her ten years to "see" her husband, to see that she had been worshipping a myth. They had met at university, both students of English literature. She had immersed herself in her course, entered into the spirit of it, and had obtained a great enrichment from it and had been awarded a lower second. She could have got a 2:1 her tutor said, but her old problem of tending to write unfinished sentences had been her downfall, so a 2:2 it had to be. Gary Schofield who liked being called "Gaz" as he had been in primary school, also on the same course, had been awarded a First. She assumed that he had had the same attitude to the course as she, and whilst she had taken a modest 2:2, he on the other hand had taken an impressive First and you don't get better than that. She could only respect him. She respected him further when with his First he went to teach in an inner city school, while she had gone to teach in a traditional genteel girls' grammar school where the pupils want to learn and school discipline is not an issue. The truth emerged slowly, and two children and ten years later it was inescapable. It emerged because of a comment here, an attitude there, and its emergence was hindered by her initial refusal to believe what she was hearing. It was for example his boast, *his boast*, that their second year Shakespeare paper consisted of questions on either King Lear or Julius Caesar, and that Lear being a minefield when it came to examinations, and Caesar being a simple play by comparison, he had gone in knowing nothing at all about Lear, had not even read Lear that year, but had depended solely on his knowledge of Caesar, of which he knew so much. She on the other hand had familiarized herself with both plays, read both, read all the critics on both. She had taken the lesser degree. And that's how he had done it; examination technique, not as she had thought, academic brilliance. Not cheating by any means, but there was something cynical and exploitative about it. When she realized that, Sandra Schofield realized that after all her husband just would not thrill to three words, or even three lines of Shakespeare. And the throwaway remark by which she learned why he had taken a job in the inner city school: inner city schools are not expected to produce good results anyway, so there's less pressure on the teaching staff. So while she stayed up until midnight marking the homework of her pupils who were going to become doctors and lawyers, he spent the evening in front of the television or in the pub in the village because inner city children don't do homework. Set as much homework as you like, it won't get done. After ten years to settle in the harsh North of England out of devotion to her new husband who would not leave Yorkshire, she realized that her husband was a lazy, cynical, self-centred, emotionally immature individual. She grew to find him loathsome. And his new toy said it all.

A metal detector.

She had always found such devices loathsome. Men walking across fields, sweeping the thing from side to side before them; scavenging. If they were birds, they'd be vultures. And here he was still wanting to be called "Gaz" as he had been when six years old, tearing off the wrapping of his new toy, with six weeks of uninterrupted school holidays to play with it in. And while his wife and children wanted attention, and despite his complaining about the tightness of the household budget, he'd flashed his credit card and had indulged himself. It was then that Sandra Schofield "saw" her

husband, and when she did, her home in Dorset beckoned, and
beckoned warmly.

Gary "Gaz" Schofield, insensitive to his wife's coldness, to her
ever-increasing emotional distance, not even noticing that she was
rummaging in the cupboard where their suitcases were kept,
announced that he was going out for the day, but he'd be back for
dinner. Without waiting for her reply, he left the house, metal
detector, instruction manual and small spade in hand, and walked
to where his gleaming car stood in the driveway.

He drove to the countryside east of York, to the area of Roman
roads and ancient settlements. It was a hot day, flat field of golden
corn or yellow oil seed lay about him, a distant horizon, a vast blue
sky. He drove off the main road onto a "B" road, and from the "B"
road he turned up an unmarked track on which he parked the car.
From the track he walked up a path to a small wood, one of many
small woods which serve to break up the landscape in the Vale of
York. As he approached the wood, detector in hand, he saw a sign
nailed to a tree at the edge of the wood "Private Wood – Keep Out".
He smiled. That sign he thought would serve to keep many people
out and so with luck, he'd be the first metal detector owner to use
his device in this location.

He stepped into the shade of the wood, in which many flies
swarmed, and saw that the wood with its smooth mossy floor leant
itself well to detecting. He put on the headphones, switched on the
machine and began to criss-cross the wood, sweeping the machine
widely before him. At first he found nothing, but he kept on sweeping
because like all who pursue the hobby, he knew that the next sweep
could bring about the earthenware pot of coins that had been buried
in order to prevent the Romans from looting them, or another such
similar discovery: such discoveries being made from time to time in
the soil of England.

Then his headphones buzzed. He took them off and laid down the
detector, and began to dig with the small spade. About a foot down
he came across a metal torch, about twenty years old. He went
down further and came across a rucksack also of a design which he
recalled being popular about twenty years ago, an aluminium frame
on a Terylene sack, still red in colour. Digging further, he struck a

hard object, but not metal. He scraped the soil away. He saw it was a skull.

A human skull.

Harriet Cooper was a tortured woman. A haunted, tortured woman, and she knew the torture now would be endless. She would take it to her grave. If she was by herself she would have gone to the police and confessed, but she had a husband to consider, a man of standing, the scandal would ruin him and he knew nothing of what had happened all those years earlier, before they had met. And she had teenage children, both settled in school, both wanting to become doctors like their father.

The memory, when it returned, came in pieces. It came suddenly, the first bit, sewing a patch on her son's jeans: the night in the wood, the hole, the smell of freshly turned soil, the scent of summer vegetation, sharpened because of the recent shower of rain ... then all she could do was sit there, wondering whether she had remembered a dream. Two days later she had accepted that it was no dream, but that she really had once helped to bury a body.

And the body was that of Norbert Parkes. Poor Norbert, little Norbert, university life for him was not a good experience, just another rejection in a life which had been a series of rejections ... then two days later, the memory of the murder itself. Miles swinging the pick axe handle down on Norbert's head from behind ... and the sound of a woman screaming, then realizing that she had been the only woman present. And what was it that Miles had said as he looked down on the body ... what was it? Oh, yes, "Take death easy, Norbert, take death easy".

Then at the moment if either she or Cameron had picked up the phone, called the police, it would have been alright, not for Norbert, not for Miles, but for them, she and Cameron, because they had no idea what Miles was going to do, even Miles didn't seem to premeditate it. That's what it seemed like. Miles just couldn't contain his contempt for Norbert any longer, and then Norbert's head sticking up above the back of the chair, Miles just happened to be walking past with a pick axe handle in his hand ... everything conspired at one to make Norbert's head an irresistible target.

But Miles had a way of controlling people and before she knew what she was doing, she was helping Miles and Cameron bundle Norbert's little body into the back of Cameron's old Land Rover to carry it to where Miles knew was a private wood. And there they buried him, possessions and all, cheap, inexpensive possessions. Then they had returned to Miles' parents house and collected the rest of Norbert's possessions, his bus ticket, his cheap sleeping bag, the small pile of coins on the bedside cabinet. And when they had finished, Norbert Parkes had never been in the house.

The very next day Miles' parents had returned from their holiday in Jamaica and thanked Miles and his two university friends for "sitting" the house for them, and hoped that the "three of you" had had a pleasant two weeks in "our house". After lunch that day, she and Cameron had driven back to York in total silence. At York Station she had gotten out of the Land Rover without a word being spoken or without a backward glance. And that had been the last she had seen of Cameron McKay or Miles Trewlawney.

She and Miles and Cameron were all now in their early forties. She, until she recovered the memory, had been a fulfilled and privileged woman, and all three had remained in the vale. McKay Electronics was Cameron's contribution to the micro technology boom, and Trewlawney, Wells and Isles was a feared firm of solicitors, and had acted for one of her husband's patients when he had tried, unsuccessfully, to sue for medical negligence. The headed notepaper described Miles Trewlawney as one of the "senior partners".

She began to return to the wood. When they had left the wood that day dawn had broken and they had sat, the three of them side by side in a stunned silence, in Cameron's Land Rover. She remembered the journey back to the Trewlawney house, white painted, standing in its own grounds, and so twenty years later, she had little difficulty retracing the route to the vicinity of the wood. The next step was to visit each small wood and copse in the location until she found one marked "Private Wood – Keep Out" which she found with ease. In the wood she located the spot where Norbert had been buried. She began to re-visit the wood, near twice weekly, drawn by some horrific fascination, drawn as she had read all murderers are to the scene of their crime, over and over again. But that Monday, blisteringly hot, the first Monday in August, the wood was different.

Not standing in isolation as usual with no activity about it, it had now become a focus of much activity.

Police activity.

Harriet Cooper drove on but she knew from that moment her life was effectively over.

In which Chief Inspector Hennessey takes charge.

George Hennessey woke with the sun as he found he often did, early rising in the summer, rising on time but with difficulty in the deep mid-winter. He dressed, went downstairs, breakfasted, let Oscar romp in the rear garden of his house. He propped the main back door open but locked the grill with its dog flap so that Oscar could come and go as he pleased during the day. He drove from Thirsk across flat country to York, to Micklegate Bar Police Station and was at his desk by 8.30 a.m. He had then driven to Northallerton and the H.Q. of the North Yorkshire Police to attend the monthly "Chief Inspector Meeting". He returned to York for lunch to be informed that Sergeant Yellich required his attendance at a location to the east of the city. "Body discovered, sir," the uniformed officer said. "Shallow grave job, I believe." Hennessey decided to forego lunch.

"Gentleman here found it, skipper." Yellich indicated to Schofield who stood with his metal detector looking pleased with himself. "Or rather his metal detector did."

Hennessey glanced at the screen which encircled a small area of the wood. "Who's here?"

"Dr D'Acre, skipper."

Hennessey nodded and walked to the screen, opened the flap and stepped inside. Louise D'Acre, slender, short hair, slightly greying, knelt over the body in the shallow grave, by now completely uncovered. She glanced up at Hennessey and then she looked down at the body again. "Young male," she said, "early twenties, short and slight of build, distinctive red hair, there's a few strands remaining. He sustained a massive blow to the back of the head. That would have killed him, if he hadn't been already dead."

"Already dead?"

"Well, we can't rule out the possibility that he was poisoned or strangled or suffocated, and the blow on the head was just to make sure or if he had been suffocated and his body dropped head first from a high place to make it look as though he fell to his death, but I doubt that will be the case." She stood and peeled off her latex gloves. "No point in burying him then is there?"

"Point taken."

"There were some possessions buried with him."

"Were there indeed?"

"Beyond the screen."

Hennessey stepped out from the screen to where Yellich stood. "Items found with the body?"

"Here, skipper." Yellich bent down and picked up a production bag, one rucksack, pockets contained a few things, one of which ... he delved into the bag and brought out a small clearer bag of cellophane, which contained an I.D. card. "Norbert Parkes, a member of the National Union of Students, least he was twenty years ago. University of York." He handed the cellophane sachet to Hennessey who pondered the photograph. A thin-faced youth with striking red hair, the I.D. card clearly having been preserved by the thick plastic wallet it was held in, and the Terylene of the rucksack, and several feet of soil to keep out the sun's rays and the frost's damage.

"Get on to the university please Yellich, have an address of one of their students of twenty years hence ... you know the name."

"He's in a meeting."

"Tell him it's personal and urgent." The phone line clicked and the Blue Danube Waltz was played, reached the end of the tune then started again.

"McKay!" The voice was angry, ill-tempered.

"It's Harriet Cooper."

"I don't know a Harriet Cooper. I'm in an important meeting, I have to get back to it."

"Harriet ... 'Hat' ... 'Hat' Sewell."

A pause.

"Hat ..."

"Cameron, they've found Norbert's body."

A sigh. A longer pause.

"Cameron ..."

"Yes, I'm still here. We've got to meet."

"Yes."

"I'll phone Miles."

"Are you still in touch with him?"

"No. Not since that day."

"I only recently remembered doing it."

"I never forgot it, not a single day goes by ... but ... When is a good time to phone?"

"Mid afternoon but not at weekends. My husband's a doctor, this will ruin him. I've got two children at school."

"I've got a business worth three million pounds which will sink if I don't stay at the helm. And three children. And a wife."

"What are we going to do? But we owe Norbert. We owe his family."

"Nothing. Do nothing. If in doubt, do nothing. I'll phone you at home. You'd better let me have your number."

The University Registrar provided the police with Norbert Parkes' address as recorded by them. It was in Bridlington. Hennessey and Yellich drove there. The address proved to be in small hotel land, near the beach, tall, thin terraced houses with names like "Seaview", "Holmlea" and "Morevilla". Many had "no vacancies" signs in the window, attesting to the busy August period, when the coal mines and steelworks in the industrial north close for two or three weeks, the "stop weeks" for maintenance when the steel workers and miners take their families to "Brid" for a fortnight and stay at "Seaview" or "Holmlea" or "Morevilla": bed, breakfast and evening meal.

The address provided by the university specifically was 147, Cannaby Terrace. Hennessey and Yellich parked their car as close as they could and then walked to 147, along the terrace, savouring the sea air, the smell of fish and the glimpse of the blue North Sea upon which, a long way out, a white ship sailed northwards. Number 147 was called "Sandene" and had cockleshells cemented to the stone gateposts and also a "no vacancies" sign in the window. Hennessey and Yellich stepped up to the front door and rang the bell. Half an hour later the worst was over.

"They wouldn't sell the hotel in case Norbert returned." Thomas Parkes, a heavily jowled man, remained to speak to Hennessey and Yellich after Mrs Parkes had left the house tearfully to go to their church to light a candle, and Mr Parkes had excused himself to be by himself for a while. "They retired about ten years ago. Their living room is in the basement, their bedroom is in the attic, the middle bit of the house was the guests area, all gone a bit musty now as you see."

"What did you know of your brother's last movements?"

"Movements or moments?"

"Movements."

"Pleased you said that," Thomas Parkes forced a smile, "because of his last moments I know nothing. I don't want to know anything. But at least now the waiting is over. Now we bury him. Say goodbye properly. Last time I saw Norbert he was off to visit some university friends. He'd just graduated, not a good class of degree, but he could use it and said that he'd been invited to help sit a house."

"Sit a house?"

"As in babysitting. Live in a house while the occupants are away so as to keep the property occupied to deter burglars."

"I see. You don't know were that was or whose house?"

"I don't. Norbert only had one friend at university. It wasn't a good experience for him. He was out of his depth, intellectually and socially. Didn't get acceptance, always a bit of a hanger-on."

"You saw that?"

"No … just things he said. Messages he gave out. When he visited home he always caught the last train back. Sometimes he managed to miss that and had an extra night at home … messages like that. I went to teacher training college, less taxing, not as pukka … I got on better for that. Norbert would have been better going to a teacher training college, more his level. Less of a bad experience for him. He came away using an expression … 'take life easy' … which irritated me."

"It would irritate me too." Hennessey glanced out of the grimy window which looked out to the rear of the house and to the backs of the houses which lined the next street.

"He had no confidence. Ask him what he was going to do with his degree and he'd say he was going to 'take life easy for a while'. He allowed it to enter his thinking and was an excuse for doing nothing. He was like a hippy from the 1960s but without the culture; 'laid back' all by himself but it was a reaction to a lack of confidence. So the body, it's definitely Norbert?"

"More than likely. Your description fits the description given by the pathologist Dr D'Acre of the appearance of the body as it would be in life. The NUS ID card was found in the rucksack."

"I remember his rucksack, a red one."

"Sounds like it is him. The dental check will confirm it. You'll be able to let us have the name of Norbert's dentist?"

"Mr Vere, Station Terrace, Bridlington."

Yellich wrote the name and address in his notebook.

"And Norbert's friend?"

"Fella called Joe, Joe Patterson. I have Norbert's address book upstairs, if that would help you."

"Ideal," Hennessey smiled. "Ideal."

In which a man of the cloth provides three names and the police decide to rattle a cage or two.

By virtue of the address book, the only "Joe" in the book was deemed to be Joseph Patterson. The phone number beside the name was twenty years old but was rung nonetheless. It proved to be the number of "Joe's" mother, who provided the police with "dear Joseph's" present address, in Harrogate. One hour later Hennessey and Yellich knocked on his door.

"Oh, Norbert." Joe Patterson had invited the police officers through the pleasant chaos of his house, wife, children, dog, cat, hamsters, to the sanctity and the tranquillity of his study. "He didn't have an easy time of it. It's difficult to be accepted if you're not particularly bright, don't have a perceptible personality, don't come from the middle classes."

"Which was Norbert Parkes?"

"As you say." Patterson sat back, wearing his clerical collar and smooth front, buttonless shirt. "He had nothing to offer, basically that was his problem, no image, no academic skills, no interest outside the course that he could talk about or that would give himself an aspect to himself. He wanted to belong, as we all do, but had nothing to offer as a means of gaining acceptance. So he became a bit of a hanger-on."

"Do you remember your social circle at the university?"

"Oh, like yesterday. Let me see. I suppose the leader of the group was Miles Trewlawney, came from a well established legal family in the Vale of York. He had a real down on Norbert, gave him a hard time, resented people like Norbert attending the university. He was a real snob. I didn't take to him, but I did like 'Hat' Sewell, Harriet to give her her full name, and a Scots lad called Cameron McKay. I was accepted by them and Norbert latched on to me. And we socialized together throughout the three years of the course, with Norbert 'taking life easy' all the time."

"That's an expression we've heard before today."

"It was Norbert's catch phrase. His excuse for not applying himself. He'd 'dropped out' without ever really having 'dropped in'. I don't know the full extent of his home circumstances, his background, his growing up, but he wasn't equipped for life. The over-indulged younger son perhaps? I don't know. But university was a shock when he found he wasn't the centre of attention and that he was expected to work for his grades. A bit 'disabled' in a sense. I suppose that's why I allowed him to latch on to me."

"The last time you saw him?"

"After graduation. The last time I heard of him though was when I was invited to help Miles housesit his parent's house. He phoned me up and added with a snigger that 'Norbert will be there'. I declined. I knew Miles Trewlawney, I knew his invitation to Norbert was only so as to show Norbert what he was missing in terms of quality of lifestyle and to have him there as the butt of all jokes and patronizing comments. And I also thought I'd done enough for Norbert. That was the summer after graduation, twenty years ago. How time flies."

Driving back to York Hennessey asked Yellich to prepare a press release, stating that the body discarded in the wood in the Vale of York "is believed to be that of Norbert Parkes who disappeared, aged twenty-one years, twenty years ago".

"That," said Hennessey, "ought to rattle a cage."

"Or two," added Yellich, keeping his eyes on the road.

Tuesday

In which three well-set, middle-class felons learn the meaning of Dame Agatha Christie's observation that "the past casts long shadows".

Harriet Cooper noted with distaste how overweight Miles Trewlawney had grown and was impressed how, despite his wealth, how
youthful and slender Cameron McKay had remained. They had
arranged the meeting at short notice, a rapid ringing round, a
meeting place had been agreed as being the car park behind the
Rising Sun, a pub they used to drive out to in their student days.
The three had arrived within five minutes of each other. She had the
modest Ford, her family's second car, Cameron McKay had a
Mercedes Benz, and Miles, of course, had a Rolls Royce. They
approached each other, nodding sheepishly. This was not the sort of
joyful, hugging, hand-shaking reunion that they might have
envisaged having when in their youth.

"It was on the mid-evening news last night," Harriet Cooper
said.

"I heard it too," Cameron McKay nodded. "Believed to be
Norbert Parkes. It's only a matter of time before they confirm
identity. I read they can match dental records because teeth don't
decay, well not like flesh. I mean that ..."

"We know what you mean." Miles Trewlawney cut him off.

"We've got to go to the police." Harriet Cooper was urgent,
agitated. "Make a clean breast of it."

"No." Trewlawney avoided eye contact. "There'll be no police."

"Thought you might say that, Miles." Cameron McKay glanced
coldly at him. "You've more to lose than we have. And further
from grace to fall, not only your position, but your family's hard
earned reputation in the Vale. What are you, third generation in
the firm?"

"Fifth actually. Well fifth in the family. Third since we
amalgamated with Wells and Isles and Co."

"Don't get off the point," Harriet Cooper snapped. "You're
looking at life, Cameron and I ... much, much less ... perverting the
course of justice ..."

"Accessory to murder." Trewlawney raised his eyebrows. "We're
all looking at serious time."

"Accessory ..." Cameron McKay's voice trailed off. "Are you
sure?"

"I am a solicitor."

"You're also motivated to frighten us into silence."

"There's nothing to link us to the murder." Trewlawney spoke slowly. "Nothing. The police investigation will peter out. It has to, they're thinly stretched. In a few days time there'll be another murder, much fresher and the file on Norbert will be put in a drawer to gather dust. We're all about halfway through our life expectancy, we've kept quiet for twenty years, if we can keep quiet for another forty, we'll have got away with it."

"You see, that's the point, Miles." Harriet Cooper spoke in the way she only wished she could have spoken to Miles Trewlawney at the time. "I don't know whether I want to get away with it."

"Ah …" Trewlawney pulled his shoulders back. "Don't go soft on me, Harriet. Not after all this time."

"Actually, it's not after all this time, it's only a month ago in a sense. I buried the memory, you see. It's very fresh for me. It belongs to yesterday."

"And your husband? And your children?"

"Don't you think I haven't thought of them? But what about Norbert's family? They have a right to know what happened to their son."

The conversation fell away into a silence as a young man walked past them to his car. Then Cameron McKay asked, "Did anyone know where Norbert was? Who else knows he was at the house at the time?"

"Well, he couldn't have told his parents because he didn't know the address."

"That's right," Cameron McKay said softly. "I remember I picked him up at York Station in my Land Rover. The 'Great Green Land Crab' I called it."

There was a lull in the conversation then Harriet Cooper said, "Joe Patterson, he knew. He phoned me and asked me if I was going to Miles' parents house for a few days? I said I was. He said he was undecided but he probably wouldn't because he was tired of protecting Norbert."

"You've got a good memory," Trewlawney sneered.

"Like I said, for me it's like it happened yesterday."

"But it means Joe Patterson can put Norbert at Miles' house at the time he disappeared. It's all they need."

"No, that and a confession, perhaps. But that alone won't be enough to convict." Trewlawney glared at Harriet Cooper. "So we stay silent. Understood?"

But driving home Harriet Cooper thought Miles Trewlawney had intimidated her for far too long. And he hadn't seen the look of shock, horror and betrayal that had flashed across Norbert's eyes the instant that the pickaxe handle had struck the back of his head. She had. Nor had Miles Trewlawney seen the look of sneering contempt on his own face as he put every ounce of strength he could muster into delivering the blow. She had. She had seen that too.

And finally, in which a woman reminds her children of Captain Laurence Oates, George Hennessey tells his wife about his lover, and a man thinks a smug thought about his wife.

The woman pondered whether to wait for her husband to come home but she decided against it, the wrench would, she felt, be too much to bear. But she made an excellent lunch for her two delighted children and then went to speak to the daily help. She explained to the help that she had to go out, and asked her, in return for extra money, if she could wait in the house until her husband returned at about six p.m. so as to ensure the children were supervised by a responsible adult at all times, as the law requires. She then returned to the dining room and said, "I'm going out now. I may be some time."

To which Jonathan, eleven, her eldest, said, "You sound like Captain Oates." The woman smiled, and said, "Mrs January will stay in the house until Daddy gets home."

She took the bus into York. She indulged herself with a visit to the Minster where she lit a candle, and walked the walls, savouring the city. Finally she fetched up at Micklegate Bar where once the head of Harry Hotspur had been impaled as a deterrent to any who would betray the Crown. At Micklegate Bar she saw the police station. She walked into the building and at the enquiry desk she said. "My name is Harriet Cooper, I'd like to give information about the murder of Norbert Parkes."

George Hennessey stood in the rear garden of his house, sipping a mug of tea, enjoying the late evening. The garden had been laid according to his wife's design when she had been pregnant with their first and only child. Three months after he was born she had died, suddenly, and her ashes had been scattered in "her" garden. He felt that she was still there, and he came out to say hello to her, to Jennifer, each day.

"So with her statement we wrapped it up." An observer would see a middle-aged man talking to himself. "We picked up the other two. Trewlawney held out but when we showed him Harriet Cooper's statement and Cameron McKay's statement, he too confessed. For twenty years the secret had remained buried, then along came a bloke with a metal detector and it all crumbled, or fell into place, whichever way you look at it, inside forty-eight hours." He sipped his tea. "Jen, I'm going out tonight, staying out. We've found each other. It doesn't mean my feelings for you are diminished. But we both have our needs. I want you to be happy for us." When he said that he felt a warmth close about him that could not be explained by the last of the day's sunrays alone.

He packed an overnight bag and drove to the village of Skelton, north of York, a wealthy village, with a tenth-century church. He went to a half-timbered house. He rang the doorbell. Louise D'Acre opened it and smiled, hooking a hand round the back of his neck. "Come in, the children have gone up."

"That's her, that's her all over, all the time." Garry "Gaz" Schofield sat in the armchair getting hungry and he thought that that was her. Her old bugbear, unfinished sentences. He read the note "I've taken the children". Of course she's taken the children, he could see that, did she think he was simple? But where had she taken them? The Railway Museum? The Coast? And when will they be back? He sat and watched the sun kiss the distant skyline. He thought it could be worse, some men have to put up with much worse. Sandra's inability to finish a sentence ... when all was said and done, that could be lived with for the sake of peace. He switched on the television and waited for his wife and children to come home, wondering what excuse she'd offer for making him wait so long for his dinner.

THE PARSON AND THE HIGHWAYMAN

Judith Cutler

WILLIAM SCROGGINS, RAGGED, emaciated, balding and bandy-legged, had very little in common with the heroic figure my sister Georgiana always wished would hold up the family coach. She regularly beguiled the long hours on the road from my father's country seat in Derbyshire to our London house by imagining just such an adventure.

The moonlight glinting on his pistols and his pearly teeth, his eyes a-twinkle through the slits in the mask, a romantic figure on a jet black horse would appear before us, ready to seize the strong box. One sight of dearest Georgiana, however, would smite his heart. Begging her to do him the honour of descending from the coach, he would fend off the heavily armed postilions and outriders, swing her across his saddle bow and gallop off into the night.

Presumably at this point Georgiana's imagination transformed him from a thieving wretch into the handsome scion of one of the best families in the land, deprived by a cunning relative of his inheritance but not of his sense of propriety. Now he was ready to win and woo her like a Hyde Park beau, whereupon she would help him regain his title.

So what Georgiana would have made of a real highwayman, stinking from his incarceration in Warwick Gaol, and so far from heroic as to be weeping as he knelt in chains at my feet, I do not know.

While the rest of the country gossiped over the declaration that poor King George was to be replaced by his son as Regent, I had come to offer poor William the consolations of the next world, since he had so little time left in this. Indeed, he was to be hanged within the hour. The prison chaplain had already read the service to all the condemned men, but since William was one of my parishioners, and had, moreover, actually attended a few services, I wished to be there to offer my support and friendship.

"I've done some bad things, Parson Campion," he said. "And no doubt I deserve to hang. I've poached all my life, stolen a sheep or two, scrumped apples and I don't know what besides. Three times the Justice has let me off transportation with a warning." I nodded – I knew the soft heart of that particular Justice of the Peace. "And three times I've let him down. And now I've come before the Assizes ..." He wiped a tear with the back of his hand. "But I tell you straight, Parson, as God is my Witness, I never took that there bauble. Here, let me lay my hand on that Good Book and swear it." He suited the deed to the word.

I believed him. But I said very sadly, "Alas, Lady Grenfell swore to the court that you did, William. And you admitted that you were after rabbits in the area when the coach was robbed – and at gunpoint, too."

He snorted. "Can you imagine me touting a pistol? How would I afford one of they things? Taking game's one thing, Parson, but sending a fellow being to his death, that's a different thing – in my book at least."

It was in mine, too.

"What would I do with a diamond necklace, tell me that! I couldn't eat it. I wouldn't know where to sell it. I wouldn't even have hidden it where no one'd find it! What would be the point? And tell me this, Parson, how could she have recognized me when I'm supposed to have had a scarf pulled over my face and hat over my eyes?"

I did not know. Taking his hand, I declared, "William, I will make one more appeal—"

He shook his head. "Nay, Parson. Even if you did, for sure they'd transport me. Look at me – do you see me lasting out the voyage to Australia? Well, I'd rather have a swift death and a burial in good English earth than a lingering one and a watery grave. That'd be the worst thing ... But if you could spare a corner of the churchyard in Moreton St Jude's I'd be mighty grateful. I should like to feel close to everyone I know. And – one last thing – swear you won't let those anatomists or whatever they're called take up my corpse. Else how can I be there for the Last Judgment?"

"No one but Dr Hansard shall touch your body," I declared.

And with that he had to be satisfied. The bodies of felons were not permitted the dignity of being buried whole. Dr Hansard, not just the kindly Justice of the Peace who had been merciful to William in the past but also the best doctor in the neighbourhood, was in fact the first to argue that advances in medical knowledge depended on surgeons dissecting their corpses. On this occasion, however, he had begged the courts for the right to examine William himself. Poor William had a growth Hansard was privately sure would soon have proved fatal, and he wished to examine its origins.

There was a jangle of keys and the gaoler was upon us. It was time for the solemn journey to the scaffold, accompanied by the far from solemn jeers of the crowd. As we walked we said together the prayer Our Lord taught us, and he died on the words, "Deliver us from evil."

I buried William the next day, bidding him farewell with a solemn knot of villagers who remembered his better days.

As the grave was filled, Dr Hansard took my arm and led me off. "Time for a glass of Madeira, Tobias. Now, dear Maria tells me that our cook has made your favourite soup, and that if you do not come to sup with us at Langley Park she will be deeply offended."

"I fear I will not be good company."

"What are friends for, but to support you in times of solemn reflection? And I must tell you, Tobias, that poor William could not have survived long." As he propelled me towards his gig, he explained what had ailed him.

"All the same, Edmund," I protested, "a man is entitled to die in his bed, not have life snuffed out on someone's false accusation!"

"Such men as poor William do not have the luxury of a four-poster or a half-tester!" he snorted. "And he would have soon been in such pain that even my skills could not have prevented the most extreme suffering."

"So we are to thank Lady Grenfell for her part in what you see as an act of euthanasia?" I demanded bitterly.

"Indeed no! In fact, Tobias, one of the things we shall talk about tonight is how we will right this patent injustice."

There were some who put it about that I was estranged from my family, but that was not the case. My father had certainly not wanted his youngest son to turn his back on success in this world and become a mere country parson; he spoke many harsh words. But they were not unforgiving – or unforgivable – words. Through the good offices of my dear mama, my family at last welcomed me back to its bosom – if not exactly as the prodigal son, because I in no wise repented my new life. Indeed, for the first visit or two, we had tiptoed round each other, as if performing a complicated cotillion, with the steps of which no one was totally familiar. The sigh with which they bade me farewell was certainly one of regret, but I was not sure that it was not also one of relief.

However, if I was to keep my promise to poor William, it was to my family's milieu that I must return. The Grenfells were – like my family – part of the *ton*, the upper ten thousand families who controlled, for better and often worse, the lives of the rest. Lady Grenfell, whom even her fellow aristocrats considered decidedly high in the instep, would certainly not receive as a caller a humble country parson, but if I were staying in my father's London house, in Berkeley Square and my mother were to accompany me, I might be positively welcome. Lady Grenfell might see it as an indication that I was at last in the marriage mart, and if my memory served me she had no fewer than five ill-favoured daughters to dispose of. My heart was by no means engaged elsewhere, I told my mother as I handed her from her carriage, but unless there had been divine intervention, I would not be seeking the hand of any one of them.

"But it would be a charitable act, my dear," Mama declared with a twinkle – she was the only one of my family who dared tease me about my calling.

"I do not think the Almighty demands my martyrdom," I responded. "Or if he did, I hope he would ask it in somewhere other than Mayfair. The very least I would hope for is to be boiled alive in Africa."

"But are you going to flirt with one of Almeria's girls?"

"I shall not mislead them – not a single heart will be even chipped, let alone broken, if I can help it. But if the only way I can speak to Lady Grenfell is when she is chaperoning her daughters, then so be it."

Lady Grenfell had enjoyed ill-health for as long as I had known her. Fading behind voluminous trailing shawls, without a wisp of energy to pick up something six inches from her hand, she ruled her household with a rod of iron, thinly disguised as the vinaigrette vital to deal with her palpitations. When she had her own way, of course, there was no sign of ill-health that Dr Hansard would surely have diagnosed as chronic boredom and acute selfishness.

This morning there was no sign of the offending diamond necklace, nor should there have been, for neither Lady Grenfell nor my mama would have had any hesitation in stigmatizing diamonds as vulgar if worn during the hours of daylight. There were daughters a-plenty, however, all plain and simpering, apart from Miss Honoria, the next to youngest. She was quiet to the point of surliness, and in other circumstances I would have devoted myself to drawing her out, and perhaps even making her smile. But that would have been construed as flirting, and if I were to flirt with anyone it must be with someone whose heart I believed incapable of pain. The pallor of Miss Honoria's cheeks, emphasized by the dress of vicious mustard yellow she had for some reason chosen to wear, suggested feelings deeper than anything her invalidish mother had ever known.

As is the custom, we exchanged nothingnesses for precisely half an hour, at which point, correctly declining refreshment, we prepared to depart. But something was arousing Lady Grenfell from her fluttering inertia: we were the recipients of an invitation to an evening party.

"Nothing formal. Perhaps cards, perhaps three or four couples standing up to dance. You would be so welcome—" she murmured.

We bowed our acceptance and went on our way.

"Did you ever see such surprise as was on the faces of those pasty-faced dowds?" my mother demanded. "And poor Honoria in that hand-me-down that would have disgraced a nursery-maid."

"I fancy all was not well with her," I mused, handing my mother into the carriage and looking significantly at the footman. My mother and others of her class enjoyed the sublime belief that persons from the lower classes were deaf, dumb, blind and stupid. My work had shown me that the reverse was true. "Do we have any other calls to pay?"

"To Hatchard's in Piccadilly, if you will. I have lent my copy of *The Lady of the Lake* to your aunt, and find I cannot survive without it another instant ..."

I was too much in demand as a dancer to have a chance of speaking to Lady Grenfell at her soirée, or I might have commented on the diamonds sparkling like new about her surprisingly unlined neck. The promised three or four couples had metamorphosed into twenty or thirty, though females in the form of her five daughters heavily predominated. Even Stourton, her son, whose debts were rumoured to outstrip his father's, graced the room for a whole ten minutes, though he did no more than lean against the wall, in what he no doubt conceived to be a Byronesque way. Naturally I could not slight the poor wallflowers, and it was thus left to my mother, kindly gracing an occasion that held absolutely no charm for her, to sit in the ranks of the dowagers and chaperones and whisper behind her fan to her hostess. From the way my partners' eyes lit up at the sight, it was clear that they believed our joint futures were being discussed – each daughter smiled as voraciously as a hyena each time she caught my eye. Each except Miss Honoria, whose smile was at very best perfunctory.

The ballroom was no place to solicit confidences, so I addressed mere commonplaces to her as to the others, agreeing truthfully that the refreshments were excellent and lying about the quality of the champagne. Of bigger issues, of the poor King's health, for instance, or wars overseas, there was no mention.

It was not until my mother summoned me to her boudoir and dismissed her dresser that I asked what her conversation had uncovered.

"*Uncovered*, Tobias? What an agricultural term! I heard a great deal about Sarah Grenfell's hideous ordeals, including the hideous strain of having to depose to the Warwick Assizes that her necklace had been veritably torn from her neck by a most vicious highwayman, clearly the William Scroggins who stood before her in the dock."

"*Torn from her neck?* She stated it was removed from the jewel case she concealed beneath the carriage cushions. And what were her servants, her postilions, her outriders doing the while? Do not tell me that they were too terrified by poor William's fearsome demeanour to protest! Why, the man would have been blown over by a good yell!"

"With a gun pointed inches from your employer's bosom, perhaps even a yell is too great a risk," she said dryly.

"On the contrary, it would have been very good value, in my book," I retorted. "And what other *on-dits* were you privy to, Mama?"

"Would it bring you to the blush to learn that Lady Grenfell considers you most eligible?"

"I hope that you disabused her. But, mama, you joke with me. Your eyes are twinkling like her diamond necklace. Did you hear anything to arouse your suspicions?"

"Only what I have told you – that Lady Grenfell has you in her sights, my love. For, I gather, one or other of the girls must marry soon. It is clear that Grenfell is expecting the duns any moment."

I reflected on the cost of the champagne, however inferior. "And they waste all that money on entertainment! And on a new diamond necklace."

"On *investment*, my love – for you must know that a hostess must present her best looks to a prospective son-in-law."

"Son-in-law!"

"News of an engagement would certainly stave off Grenfell's creditors."

I hung my head. "It was altogether wrong of me—"

"Nonsense! You do no more than pay a morning call and you become the property of one of her dreadful daughters? Leave them on the shelf where they have been gathering dust this age, my love."

"But what of Miss Honoria? Why is she so melancholy? She is not old enough to have been too long on the marriage mart."

Although the room was empty, Mama looked about her with the air of a conspirator. "There is a rumour – but not circulated by Sally Grenfell, I do assure you—"

"By one of the other tabbies you were talking to?"

"Tabbies! I am bosom-beaux with some of them! But not with Lady Cotteridge, who declared, almost unasked, that Honoria had entered into a most unsuitable *liaison* – with a gamester to whom her brother, that young scape-grace Stourton, introduced her. He even acted as go between, would you believe?"

"He is far more than a scape-grace, Mama – well on the way to being a rake, by all accounts. And who was the man in the case? Did you discover that?"

"A Frenchman. The Comte de Valliers. Oh, he is no more a count than I am, Tobias, but a charming gamester. Beware of accepting one of *his* invitations to play at White's, I beg you!"

"Mama, a country parson plays with no one at White's, let alone an ivory turner. Now, I must bid you goodnight."

She held me at arm's length as I bent to kiss her. "Nay, these are country hours indeed, Tobias – and if you want to understand Miss Honoria's plight, should you not speak to the villain in the piece himself? Here." She reached into a drawer in her dressing table. "You will not find this *Comte* at White's, of course – such a club is far too respectable. I understand from Lady Cotteridge that he is to be found at a discreet little hell in St James'."

"Populated by card sharps with loaded dice!"

"Indeed. But you must know," she said so serenely that I wondered what my elder brother had had in his youth to confess, "that the first time a young man presents himself they let him win for quite some time before they begin to cheat." She pressed a heavy purse into my hand.

"So that he is lulled—"

"Just so. Promise me just one thing! Quit the table the instant you lose so much as a penny. For that purse holds a goodly part of my pin money, and I should not like to have to apply to your father for more, not, at any rate, with a truthful explanation of how it disappeared."

The *soi-disant* Edmund Hansard – I had not only borrowed my mother's money, I had assumed my best friend's name – presented himself at a discreet door, naming my father as a guarantor. Papa would have been apoplectic had he known any of the night's doings, but perhaps most of all at this appropriation of his good name. I stammered that I was but a distant cousin of his lordship, but that he had encouraged me to taste the delights of the town before I returned to my village.

My card skills had never been more than third-rate, even when I played regularly, but I was not surprised to see a steady stream of guineas coming my way. I was being gulled, softened up. With what I hoped was a suitably rustic grin, I called for a bumper for all those playing, even covering with bravado my wince as I understood the cost.

I soon found young Stourton at my elbow. There was an inner room, kept for a select few, he whispered, evincing no surprise that a man seen but two hours ago leading his sister into the dance should now be indulging in ludicrously high play. But he had dipped too deep to make rational judgments about anything. He did not even demur when I pumped him full of the expensive but throat-burning brandy I was now persuaded to buy.

Despising myself, I turned the conversation to his sisters. Like a man seeing a far distant shore with but a thin spar before him, he seized my arm and began to extol their virtues, displaying an imagination quite creditable in one so far gone.

"But Miss Honoria—" I shamelessly interrupted a disquisition on the eldest. "Tell me about her."

He raised his eyes to the heavens. "Damn me if she isn't quite in the basket." He belched. "Shouldn't have said that. Forget it."

"Of course. Do you mean that she has behaved without discretion?"

"Fine discretion getting yourself in the family way!"

I did not have to feign my shock and horror. Such a lapse is not uncommon amongst country lads and lasses, though I have tried most strongly to discourage such behaviour. But for a gentlewoman to betray herself – truly, I was appalled.

"And the man in question—?" I prompted, as if he were one of my flock.

"Would marry her, but for one thing." He rubbed his fingers to suggest a fat dowry.

"But does her mother – her father—?"

"No, no! Of course not."

"Her condition will manifest itself ere long," I pointed out.

"And that's the devil of it. Antoine has slipped out of the country – things were getting a bit hot for him when they discovered how he loaded the dice. When he returns, I make no doubt that he will make an honest woman of her – egad, I shall call him to account if he does not – even if I have to buy the marriage licence myself!" he concluded, with an air of positive generosity, which he rather spoilt with another belch.

"So you need to win tonight," I said, "and win well."

He shook his head. "I've cash in hand, never fret. If only I can run Antoine to earth."

"I'd heard that you were about to be hauled into a debtors' prison," I said.

"Aye, so I was – this far from the Marshalsea." He held his fingers a hair's breadth apart. "Or following Antoine to Geneva. But I had a plan. And damn me if it didn't work rather well."

"And what was the plan?"

He peered at me hazily. "Tell you what, if you're ever dunned, I'll tell you then. Until then, mum's the word." And that was the last I got from him.

To my amazement and horror, it was soon all about town that I was dangling after Miss Honoria. Since I had spoken to the young lady no more than one could achieve in a country dance and also knew her true position, I suspected that the origin of these rumours was none other than Lady Grenfell herself.

"I take it that you do not find these rumours likely to entice you into her family?" Mama asked, as I squired her to the Royal Academy.

"On the contrary, they raise horrible suspicions."

She narrowed her eyes. "Against whom?"

I flushed. I had not revealed even to her that Miss Honoria might be *enceinte*. "About Lady Grenfell's truthfulness," I answered at last.

"You mean in the matter of the diamond necklace?"

"Exactly. I simply cannot believe that a family up to its eyes in debt buys a diamond necklace. Champagne, yes, a necklace, no. And Lady Grenfell's shone like new, did it not?"

She nodded.

"Mama, which jeweller does her ladyship patronize?"

When I indicated to John Bridge, of Messrs Rundell and Bridge, that I wished to speak with him on a matter of some delicacy, he glanced with amazement at my clerical garb, worn for the first time in London, but swiftly returned to his usual calm and pleasant demeanour, inviting me into his private office.

"In fact, it is not a matter of *some* delicacy," I corrected myself, "but of the *utmost* delicacy – secrecy, indeed."

He bowed. "You have my word, my lord—"

"Parson Campion," I corrected him. "I am not here on family business. I am here to enquire about the purchase of a diamond necklace."

"You know that I may not betray secrets," he demurred.

"I do indeed. Neither may I, in my calling, though the two are somewhat different. But I believe that someone has been punished for a crime he did not commit. May I ask you if anyone has recently bought a diamond necklace to replace a lost one?"

He responded to my smile, with a courteous one of his own. "It is – I am pleased to say – an all too regular occurrence. But I do keep records: perhaps if you gave me a definite name I might check? But please do not ask me to do more than confirm an absolute truth. I dare not point you in anyone's direction!"

I held his gaze. "Mr Bridge, did Lady Grenfell purchase a copy of her stolen diamond necklace?"

"Sir, she did not."

My mother heard the news with interest. "But Almeria was certainly wearing a necklace remarkably similar to the lost one. Indeed," she added reflectively, "it positively glistered."

"And *all that glisters is not gold*!" I quoted the proverb with gusto. More soberly I added, "I fear I have to ask a few questions – nay, not of Lady Grenfell herself. Not yet. Now, Mama, if you had to have a copy of a necklace made, to which discreet jeweller would you go?"

"To the one to which you have already been – to Rundell and Bridge, of course."

My mother had kindly invited Dr Hansard and his wife to join us in Berkeley Square, engaging to show Mrs Hansard the sights of the town and introduce her to her milliner and her *modiste* while Edmund and I conferred about our next move. Our dispositions were somewhat hampered by the continued presence in the capital of Miss Honoria, looking more and more unwell.

"If only her wretched lover would return and remove her from the country for good! It cannot be good for a lady in her condition to be embroiled in the scandal that is about to ensue," I said.

Dr Hansard raised an eyebrow. "Women are a great deal tougher than is widely believed," he declared. "But her very situation must be distressing, and a wedding band, put in place by no matter how shady a gamester, might be perceived as preferable to prolonged rustication and separation from her bastard babe, which is usually the price such unfortunate girls must pay to be rehabilitated into society."

"We have no alternative but to seek out Stourton again. He must have some idea of the young man's whereabouts. He might even be prevailed on to escort his sister to whichever city he has descended upon," I added slowly.

But such an idea found no favour with Stourton. He had no particular reason not to go, but mentioned an engagement with friends, a horse to see to – all facile excuses that made my knuckles itch.

"It would be the deed of a generous brother," I urged

"When was I ever generous?" he asked with an unpleasing sincerity.

Lady Grenfell was equally unhelpful. Without suggesting outright that Miss Honoria had lost her virtue, we hinted as best we could the reason for her illness. Either her ladyship was indeed ignorant, or whether she was so stupid not to understand our insinuations I know not. But she averred without hesitation that her daughter was not at home, but had just stepped out to a lending library.

At last I could restrain myself no longer. "Lady Grenfell, may I speak to you about the diamond necklace you wore to your ball?"

How did I expect her to react? With a blush of guilt? One of her famous spasms?

Certainly not with an indulgent beam.

"Dear Stourton knew how upset I was when that monster stole it from around my very neck! He had a run of luck at cards or on the horses … What a sweet boy, to purchase a replacement for me."

"Sweet indeed," I echoed.

"So what is your latest theory?" Mama asked me indulgently, as we ate an exquisite luncheon. "Do you believe that young Stourton has such a generous spirit as to buy such a gift for a woman with whom he has scarcely been on speaking terms this last five years?"

"No," Edmund replied on my behalf. "On the contrary, I believe she suspected him of stealing it – hence her lies under oath to the court. To 'prove' his innocence, he came up with a replacement. Which may not be a replacement at all, but paste."

"Since it glisters," Mama agreed, nodding to me. "So you need to see the necklace again, but more closely. We will invite the family to dine before joining us in our box for the opera. No woman worth her salt would fail to wear her diamonds for such an event. Now what is it, Tobias?" I might have been an importunate seven-year-old tugging at her skirt.

"Would not such an invitation lend credence to this ridiculous rumour about my attachment to Miss Honoria?" I asked stiffly.

"It might indeed. Or it might shock her into confessing that she is … betrothed … to someone else."

Hansard smiled. "I see only one problem, my lady. How do we get a sufficiently close look at this necklace? It cannot be such an event as you would invite Mr Rundell or Mr Bridge!"

"That does not mean that they cannot give an opinion," I declared. "Mr Bridge will only answer direct questions, not volunteer information. Last time I asked the wrong question. This time I must ask the correct one."

The party never reached the opera, but a fine drama was enacted before our eyes.

It was Miss Honoria – or rather her absence, with a trifling indisposition, according to her mama, her eyes spitting fire – who provoked what threatened to become an unseemly altercation.

Stourton looked from one cool face to the next, finished his champagne in one gulp, a mistake, as he was already well into his cups when he arrived.

"We have such hope of you two lovers," she announced, with a hard titter and a smile in my direction. "Do we not, Stourton?"

"I am sure Stourton has no such thing," I declared, incensed. "Stourton knows that Miss Honoria's feelings are engaged elsewhere, and he is in fact about to take his sister to her intended."

"Am I, old chap? I think not."

"I think so indeed," I persevered. "You have a great deal of money at your disposal, have you not? And you might as well spend it on someone who – if not precisely deserving – is in need of it. And once you have reached Geneva—"

"Geneva!" he snorted. "I learned today that he has fled to Canada! Catch me going there!"

"Well, you will escort your sister there instead. I suggest that you stay there. In fact, if you ever return to this country, you will almost certainly hang."

As we had arranged, Hansard was carefully watching not me or Stourton, but Lady Grenfell. In a moment he was at her side, producing smelling salts and pressing her back into her chair. "Nay, your ladyship – please remain seated. I cannot answer for your health otherwise." As he plied the vinaigrette, he most deftly unfastened her necklace.

"Hang? Why should a gentleman hang?" Stourton asked insolently, but with a pallor that suggested he knew exactly why.

"For sending an innocent man to the gallows. That poor wretch whom you identified in court, ma'am, was entirely innocent, as I am sure you know. You recognized your son as he robbed you. What words you exchanged subsequently I can only imagine. But I suspect that you demanded the return of your property as the price of your silence – a reasonable request, after all. What mother would want her son to swing? Accordingly, your necklace was returned. As a gesture of remorse, your son had even had it cleaned. It looked very fine. But in fact, Lady Grenfell, your son reneged on the deal. He had the necklace copied." So much had Mr Bridge confirmed. "Indeed, these are but trumpery beads!" Hansard concluded, casting them at her feet.

"Do you now object to Stourton's journey abroad?" I asked. "I cannot think so, because he will of course be escorting you, ma'am. You may have had no hand in the robbery, but you committed perjury of the very worst sort. You sent an innocent man to a hideous death. You deserve – you *both* deserve – to be handed over to the law this very evening. But we will be generous where you were not. We will give you till tomorrow night to quit these shores forever, with a written undertaking that you will never return – and, of course, why. Go now. I fear our dinner engagement must be cancelled."

"At least poor Honoria will have her mother beside her when she marries," Mama declared sentimentally. "And when she delivers her child."

"I think not, ma'am," Hansard said, staring down at the fire. "You tell me that she has long cried wolf in the matter of her health. So I fear that no one will take any notice at her next spasm or the next but one. But I can tell you that her pulse indicates the most serious of heart conditions. She will not reach Canada if the crossing is rough."

"She would be buried at sea?" I asked slowly.

"In all probability."

"Then truly God moves in mysterious ways. I thought that we had let the pair off lightly. But now it seems that poor William is truly avenged after all."

SPECIAL DELIVERY

Adrian Magson

NUMBER 184, CEDAR Point Road stood in about two isolated acres on a narrow, winding road leading into the hills of North Carolina's southern Appalachians. Out front was a mailbox on a pole, the kind with a little flag so you can see if anything has been delivered. The box had been drilled with an ominous-looking hole.

I thumbed the entry-phone on one of the stone pillars and waited while the insects and heat and silence settled around me like an itchy blanket.

"Yeah?" A reedy voice came from the entry-phone.

"Jake Crompton to see Mr Krasky," I announced, and wondered if they had a fishpond I could throw myself into for a day or two.

"Who?"

"Jake Crompton—"

"No. Who're you after?" The voice sounded testy, as if I'd spoiled an afternoon nap with my damn-fool question.

"Mr Krasky. Gus Krasky?"

"Oh. *Gus.* Why didn't you say so? Are you the guy from England?"

"Yes."

"C'mon in." There was a buzz and the gates began to trundle open on their tracks.

I drove up a curving drive and stopped in front of an impressive plantation-style house with a clapboard front. Twin pillars stood either side of a gleaming black door mounted with a scroll-shaped brass knocker. The windows of the house were blanked off by heavy curtains, lending the place a deserted, even desolate air.

As I stepped out of the car a man appeared at the side of the house. He was carrying a pair of shears and wore leather gardening gloves. Under his weathered baseball cap he was burned a deep tan and looked about ninety.

"Hey-up, young fella," he greeted me, and beckoned me to follow him. "Gus said you was comin'." His voice was as reedy in the flesh as it had been over the entry-phone. "He's out seein' some people 'n said to wait. I'm Frank."

I told him that was fine, and on the way round the side of the house asked him about the mailbox with a hole in it.

"Bullet hole," he replied shortly. "Dumb kids with a squirrel gun." He gave me a knowing look. "I'm guessin' that don't happen much where you come from."

"No," I told him. "Our kids use Semtex."

We arrived on a terrace bordering a fifty-foot swimming pool. It was overlooked by a double set of french doors beneath a large balcony. It looked like the set of "High Society", where Grace fenced with Frank before opting for Bing.

Upholstered loungers were scattered around the terrace, and off to one side was a barbecue bay big enough to roast a small elephant. In the background, the garden extended into a thick carpet of trees which ran up a slope for half a mile before meeting the sky.

"There's drink 'n stuff over there," said Frank, indicating a table in the shade. "You fancy a swim, go right ahead – there's towels there, too. Won't cost you nuthin'." He smiled genially, his face creasing up like old, soft leather. "Don't go in the house, though, y'hear?"

This last sounded like he meant it, so I nodded. He pottered away, leaving me with the hum of the pool pump and the trickle of a small fountain at the end of the terrace.

I dropped my bag by the table and poured some chilled orange juice. I slugged it back, feeling the coldness seeping outwards as it went down. It felt so good I topped it up and went for a stroll around the pool.

Out in the open the sun bounced off the water's surface like liquid fire. I hadn't brought a costume, but suddenly it seemed too good an opportunity to waste. I stripped off and fell into the water, feeling the freshness soaking right into my pores. I hadn't been skinny-dipping since I was ten years old.

I kicked my way to the far end, counting tiles on the bottom. It had been a while since I'd done any swimming, too, and I had to stop for the occasional cough when I breathed in at the wrong moment. After a couple of lengths I rolled on my back, squinting against the sun. When I looked towards the house, to check I hadn't gathered an audience of old ladies from the local church harmony group, my heart bounced off my rib cage.

My clothes had disappeared. Along with my bag.

The bag contained the envelope from Alvin Culzac. It was my sole reason for being here. Without it, I might as well consign myself to a life-long exile somewhere so remote even God wouldn't find me.

I came out of the pool like a floundering walrus. When I rubbed the water from my eyes, I saw my bag over by the table.

"For a second, there, I thought I was going to have to come in and rescue you."

The voice was soft and languid and came from the shadows near the table. I squinted through the glare of the sun and saw a long, bare leg swinging back and forth, a stylish sandal hanging from five elegantly-painted toes.

The owner of the voice appeared, holding my shirt. As she shook out the creases, a faint jangling came from a clutch of bracelets on her wrist.

That's when I remembered I was naked. Before I had to choose between going back in the pool or sucking in my stomach and smiling bravely, she handed me my shirt and turned away.

"I moved your things to save them getting creased," she said, her voice a slow, Bacall-type drawl. "Down here everything wilts in the humidity, y'know?" She glanced back with a raised eyebrow and the barest hint of a smile.

"I'm sorry." I retrieved my trousers and grabbed a large towel. "The gardener – Frank? – said it was okay to take a dip. I didn't have a costume ..."

"*Costume*? Oh, you mean swim-shorts. You're from England, aren't you?"

While she obligingly turned her gaze away I towelled myself dry, studying her profile. She was tall and slim, with auburn-tinted, glossy hair. I'd already seen clear, dark eyes that seemed full of humour and a mouth that curled at the edges, and one eyebrow was slightly cocked as though she found the world permanently puzzling. She wore a thin cotton sundress with brown polka-dots on a cream background, which set off her tanned skin to perfection. I put her age at somewhere in the late thirties.

She stepped closer, bringing with her a delicate trace of lemons. She tilted her head sideways. "I'm Lilly-Mae Breadon. How 'bout we go for a walk? Gus'll be along soon." As she walked away round the end of the pool, I couldn't help but admire the movement of muscle down the back of her thighs under the sundress. Well, it would have been impolite not to.

"In case you're wondering," she said conversationally, "I work for Gus." She turned her head and gave me a grave look, and I realized she'd dropped the country drawl. "No more, no less. Other people think otherwise, but I don't care." The smile had gone, signifying she probably cared more than she pretended. "So, how about you, Jake? What do you do?"

"I carry things," I explained.

"Things?"

"Small packages mostly – usually documents but increasingly electronic storage devices. To anyone, anywhere." It sounded lame but it pays well and suits my way of life. A lot of my work comes from the agency run by Culzac.

"Is it legal?"

It's a question I've often asked myself, but I live with the thought that it's best not to know. Before I could reply, a car roared up to the front of the house, followed by doors slamming and the sound of footsteps. Lilly-Mae looked past me and muttered, "Shoot." Then her face assumed a welcoming smile and she waved her fingers in greeting. "Hi, Gus, darlin'… guess who I've got here?" The drawl, I noticed, was back in place.

"I know who you've got there, Lil," a harsh voice replied sourly. "Just where'n hell were you taking him, is what I want to know."

The muscles in my back flinched at the accusation in the man's voice. I turned to see a bear of a figure standing by the pool. Gus Krasky was dressed in work jeans and a check shirt, and two other large men hovered behind him, both wearing suits and look-alike faces. Their stance gave them the look of a wrestling tag team, but they were nowhere near as worrying as their boss.

He was holding a rifle pointed right at my chest.

* * *

Krasky wore the aura of a bad-tempered construction foreman, as if the entire world was there solely to annoy him. His hair was cut in a military-style brush-cut, and I guessed his age at fifty-plus but it was hard to tell. I knew we weren't going to become best buddies even without the cold look he gave Lilly-Mae, as if we'd been caught red-handed in the bushes.

He looked pointedly at my feet. I'd forgotten to put my shoes back on. "You some kinda nature freak?" he muttered. Then he turned and went inside, leaving me to follow. The wrestler twins watched me go, their dull expressions no doubt the result of too much in-breeding.

Inside, Krasky jerked his head at Lilly-Mae, who went round opening the curtains and revealing a scattering of armchairs and coffee tables and, in one corner, a desk bearing a telephone, a small lamp and a laptop computer. When she was finished he said, "You got things you gotta be doing." It wasn't a question. She flushed slightly, then walked to the door, a faint frown on her face.

"Nice to meet you," she drawled in that low voice, "Mr Crompton."

"Umm … you, too," I said neutrally.

Krasky scowled and put the rifle down by the desk. I dropped the envelope in front of him and made for the door. I could do without the alpha male stuff.

"Where are you going?" he snapped.

"Package delivered," I said. "I'm booked on a flight from Charlotte."

"Uh-uh. Take a seat." He pointed at a chair across the desk.

"Pardon?"

"Relax," he growled. "I have a delivery for you. It's what you do, isn't it – deliveries?"

"Yes. But I work for Mr Culzac."

"I know that. I already checked with him, and he said it was okay. Now, you want to earn some easy money or just go back to London with what you've got?"

Actually, I was in no hurry to get back just yet, but I had no idea what Krasky wanted me to do for him. And why didn't he use his own people, of whom at least three were within snarling distance?

"All right," I said. "But no drugs."

He gave me a hard look. "What is it with you Brits? You think everyone over here's a crack-dealer?" He reached in one of the desk drawers and pulled out a bulky envelope, which he tossed across to me. "Your fee. In advance. I got an envelope to go to Palm Springs. It'll be ready for you in the morning, with an address. And no, I can't spare any of my own people. Any questions?"

"Only one. Is there a hotel near here?"

He nodded. "Ask Frank on the way out."

I found Frank waiting for me, idly ripping the heads off some flowers. He looked sour but gave me directions to the hotel. As I drove back down the drive, I looked back and noticed Lilly-Mae at an upstairs window. She was still frowning.

By eight next morning I was back at the Krasky gates leaning on the bell. It was probably earlier than planned, but I was hoping it would get me away from here sooner rather than later. While waiting I stepped over to the wounded mailbox for a closer look. The flap hung open like a drunk's mouth and I poked my forefinger through the hole and felt the sharp edges on the inside. On the other side of the box was an identical hole. Some squirrel gun.

I went back and pressed the entry button again, then noticed the iron gates were already off the latch. I pushed them back and drove up to the house.

The door-knocker brought reverberations inside the house but no response. After a few heartbeats I walked around the side of the house towards the pool.

That's where I found Frank. Only he wasn't doing any gardening.

He was floating in the shallow end, head down as if he was searching for something on the bottom. A widening ribbon of red was coming from a large hole in his back.

I stared at him for a few seconds, as if he might suddenly flip over and ask me if I wanted some juice and by the way, why not take a swim while you're waiting? Then reaction kicked in. I ran and grabbed a long-poled skimmer for collecting debris from the surface of the water. I slid it under his body, taking care not to let him sink. I dragged him to the side; the last thing I needed was to have to go in and fish him off the bottom. As he bumped against the side, he turned with a slow-motion roll and stared up at me with a look of surprise on his weathered face.

Have you seen those films where the hero finds a floater in the pool and drags it out single-handed for mouth-to-mouth resuscitation? Hah. One tug at Frank's body told me there was no way I could lift him out. Dry and alive, he was lightweight; dead and wet, it was like lifting a small family car. And he was leaking.

I decided to leave him where he was.

Using the buoyancy of the water I flipped him over again and studied the hole in his back. There were scorch marks around the wound. No wonder he looked surprised.

Since he wasn't going anywhere, I let him drift away, then went over to the house. I tried the french doors, but they were locked. Same with the windows. I eventually arrived at the front door and tried the handle.

It's the one thing cinema audiences always expect the hero to do, but he rarely does. Mainly because it's more fun to take out a gun and blow holes in the woodwork. All very useful if you have a large gun to hand. I didn't.

As I touched it, the door swung open, emitting a wave of cool air.

"Hello?" I called out politely, feeling desperately English. If I were Hugh Grant I'd be holding a tennis racket and wearing flannels and pumps. What should I do next – announce the bad news about how they'd got a dead gardener floating in the pool? I just hoped his replacement could tell a camellia from a giant redwood.

Across a large foyer was the living room where I'd had my chat with Krasky. It looked the same, even down to the laptop, its power light winking at me.

The kitchen was empty and clean. No notes, no open drawers, no ransacking. I was halfway up the stairs when a little voice of caution kicked me in the ear and shouted at me. *What the hell are you doing? Frank didn't commit suicide – the killer could be up here waiting to blow your stupid head off!"*

In rapid succession I found two bathrooms, a dressing room and four bedrooms, all yielding a deserted, opulent – if slightly garish – interior and no signs of anyone with a grudge against inept gardeners. One of the front bedrooms held a familiar lemony aroma and an array of clothing scattered carelessly across the bed. No bodies in the bathroom, just a whole load of jars and bottles. That Lilly-Mae was a messy bird.

Whoever had shot Frank hadn't come inside and gunned down the rest of the household, but where were they? Then another thought occurred; what if Frank's assailant had come *from* the house rather than to it? Had Gus finally got fed up with Frank's attempts at horticulture and taken up his gun in a fit of rage? Had Lilly-Mae—?

Ridiculous. That kind of thing doesn't happen. I should call the police. What was the number Americans dialled in the movies? 555 or 911? On the other hand, what would I tell them? That I'd come to pick up a package to take to Palm Springs – and no, officer, I had no idea what was in it nor who it was for – and found Frank the gardener trying to drink the pool dry? I'd seen programmes about how gun-toting law officers in LA dealt with suspects – even innocent ones. They beat the crap out of them.

I ran down the stairs and was about to open the front door when I saw a dark, broken line on the tiles leading through to the kitchen. Somehow I'd missed it on my way in.

A line of blood.

I stopped, breathing heavily. This was getting worse. I stepped over to the front door and pulled it open ... and found myself face to face with a gawky youth in jeans and a T-shirt bearing a company logo. Behind him was a bright red van with the same logo down the side.

"Hi," he greeted me with a cheery wave. "Should I just go on round back?"

No! The inner voice screamed, and I managed to shake my head, quickly pulling the door to behind me so he couldn't see the blood on the floor. Somehow I didn't think blood and bodies were what pool cleaners usually found when doing their job.

He looked at me. "Is there a problem?"

"Sorry," I gabbled. "Heavy night last night. Can you come back later?"

He grinned in understanding. There's nothing another man can relate to more than an obvious hangover and the need for absolute silence. "Hey – sure thing," he chuckled. "I got plenty of other stuff to do."

I nodded and waved a hand to avoid the need to talk further. He probably wouldn't recognize my accent but I didn't want to risk it. With my luck he'd studied at Oxford for three years and could spot a UK regional accent at a hundred paces.

I closed the door and leaned against it, breathing slowly to lower my pounding heart rate. That had been way too close. I waited until he'd gone, counted to fifty, then stepped outside and closed the door after me.

The gates were still open. I paused at the road, about to drive away, when something caught my eye. It was the mailbox; balanced carefully on top was a small, brown envelope.

I jumped out and picked it up. It was one of those with a padded interior. Through the padding I could feel a familiar outline. Attached to the front of the envelope was a sticky note bearing the words: *D. Selecca – Hyatt Regency Palm Springs. Leave at front desk*.

It must be the package Gus had wanted me to deliver. But why wasn't he here to give it to me himself? And where were his two goons, the inbred Twins? And Lilly-Mae?

Two minutes later I had my answer. A short drive along the road I spotted a small, dark Toyota. Standing by the door was Lilly-Mae.

As I pulled over she detached herself from the car and walked on shaky legs towards me. She looked sick, like all the buzz of yesterday had been sucked out of her.

"Are you okay to drive?" I said. She nodded dumbly. "Okay, follow me." I wasn't sure where to go, but anywhere away from here seemed a good idea. Once I was sure she was following, I headed towards Charlotte and civilization. On the way I prayed we didn't meet a testosterone-charged SWAT team coming the other way. Somehow *"English tourist dies in police shoot-out on lonely mountain road"* wasn't quite the obituary I'd been planning.

At the first shopping mall I pulled in and Lilly-Mae followed. We found a fast-food joint with two bored waitresses and no customers. I ordered coffees and sat her down across from me. She looked worse up close.

"What the hell happened back there?" I asked. Call me Mr Delicate, but I hate puzzles.

"Did you find Frank?" Her voice was barely a whisper.

I felt a chill down my back. I'd been hoping she hadn't seen that much. "Yes. You?"

She nodded. "I knew something had happened, but not what, exactly. It was all a blur, y'know." She shivered and sipped her coffee, dribbling a little down the side of the cup. By the way her hands were shaking, events of the last few hours were catching up with her.

"So what happened?" I asked softly. Uncle Jake the psychologist. A problem shared is a problem pushed on to someone else, according to my mother.

"Ab ... about two this morning, I heard Gus and Frank shouting at each other downstairs. Frank sounded really mad. He was accusing Gus of being a snake and saying how he'd get us all killed. I thought I heard your name mentioned and the police. Gus told him to watch his mouth or he'd regret it. There was a lot more shouting then a shot, followed by a splash from out back. I figured someone fell in the pool but I couldn't see because my room's at the front. Next thing, Gus yells up to say I should grab my things and get out."

"What about the twins?"

"Jesse and Dino? I didn't see them."

"Where is Gus now?"

She shrugged, her eyes filling up. "I don't know. When I got downstairs he was gone. There was some ... blood on the floor. It looked real bad. I couldn't see him anywhere."

"You went looking?"

"Sure ... why not? I didn't think he'd do me any harm. I wasn't thinking straight. That's when I saw Frank in the water." She sniffed and wiped her nose on a paper napkin. "I didn't know what to do. He was dead, so I figured I'd best get away from there. I didn't know who to trust, so I drove to a quiet spot I know and slept in the car. Then this morning I rang your hotel but you'd already checked out. I came back to see if you were here. Or if Gus was."

"To do what?"

She looked totally lost. "I don't know. Something. To make sure it wasn't a bad dream, I guess. It's my home, too ... sort of. I also wanted to stop you getting caught up in ... whatever it was." She stared back at me. "You seemed a nice guy. Besides, I thought you might be able to help me."

"Had they ever argued before?"

"A few times. Quite a lot recently. Frank was a real straight-talking guy, even though he worked for Gus. He openly disapproved of Gus's business deals, but I never figured it would come to this." She shook her head. "Gus has been acting strange for weeks. He can be such an asshole sometimes."

She was right; it takes an asshole to shoot an employee. Yet there had to be more to it than a simple divergence of views. "What kind of business is he in?"

She gave me an odd look. "You don't know?"

"Why should I?"

She sighed and pulled a face. "He's supposed to be in construction – he has a site just outside Charlotte. That's the work I do for him, although it's not much. But that's just a sideline now. You want something that doesn't come from Wal-Mart, Gus can get it."

"You mean stolen goods?"

"I guess," she said quietly. "He sells weapons."

"What – pistols? Rifles?" I figured somebody had to.

She winced at the tone in my voice. "Bigger."

"Machine guns? Mortars?" I was actually joking, but Lilly-Mae jumped in her seat.

"Mortars." She stabbed the air with a decisive finger. "I've heard him say mortars once. And rocket launchers."

Holy Moses. Mortars and rocket launchers were used in theatres of war. No wonder Frank hadn't liked it. Suddenly I was squarely in the frame with an arms dealer. I pulled the envelope out of my pocket and studied the sticky note.

"What about this D. Selecca?" I asked. No doubt he'd be into aircraft carriers and intergalactic star ships. I wasn't far wrong.

"The same," confirmed Lilly-Mae. "Only bigger." She shivered as if someone had walked over her grave. "I met him once. He gave me the creeps. He calls himself Dwight, but Gus said his real name is Diego. He pretends he's American, but he comes from down south. Colombia, I think."

Colombia. Colombia meant coffee. And drugs.

"What are you going to do with that?" she continued.

I fingered the envelope again. We needed to get away from here. But I needed to do the job I'd been paid for.

"D'you have to?" said Lilly-Mae, reading my thoughts. "I don't think anyone would hold you to it."

She was right, of course. But maybe I'm old-fashioned. I stood up. "Let's go to the airport."

We took a shuttle flight to Palm Springs. I hadn't got a definite plan, but was coasting on instinct to see where it led. All I knew was, I couldn't simply leave and go back to England without finding out what had happened. Don't ask.

When we cleared arrivals I rang the Krasky house. If anyone had found Frank by now, the place would be teaming with murder squad detectives bawling at each other to get results from the lab like yesterday and did anyone bring coffee and bagels? Well, that's how they do it on *Columbo*, anyway. There was no answer.

We took a cab into Palm Springs which, with its lush green lawns, broad, tidy streets and low-rise, stylish buildings, was slumped gracefully in the sun like a dozing salamander.

The Hyatt Regency was on North Palm Canyon Drive in the downtown area. I paid off the cab, and while Lilly-Mae found somewhere to wait nearby, I walked into the cool interior.

"May I help you, sir?" the receptionist turned away from chatting to a man in a suit and gave me a full-wattage smile.

"I've a delivery for Mr Selecca," I said.

To my surprise she passed the envelope to the man in the suit. He wore Clark Kent spectacles and had a build to match, and looked at me with a faint air of suspicion. The girl faded into the background.

"There's no name on it,' he said, taking the envelope and turning it over.

"There was," I replied. "Look, I have to go—"

But he stepped aside and gestured for me to go towards the stairs. "What's your hurry?"

There didn't seem any point in arguing, so I walked ahead of him until we reached the first floor. He indicated a door and led the way inside.

Sitting by the window was a neat, compact man in golf slacks and a sports shirt. He was wearing an unbelievably bad toupee. I wondered if he realized it looked like a piece of road-kill.

"Who's this?' he breathed harshly, staring at me with coal-black eyes and licking his lips like a lizard.

They say that in the presence of real danger you can feel a change in temperature, as if the spirits are warning the unworldly of impending doom. All I got was a click of metal. When I turned my head, Mr Muscles was holding a very large automatic pistol pointing vaguely in my direction, like he wanted to use it but was reluctant in case he made a mess of the carpet. With his free hand he handed Selecca the envelope.

"He brought this."

"Sorry about Paulie," said Selecca, flapping a vague hand. "He watches too many bad movies. You want a drink?"

After seeing the size of Paulie's cannon, what I needed was a pee. But I decided to go for a hasty withdrawal instead. "No, thanks," I said politely. "If I can see some ID, though, I'll be on my way."

"Oh. Okay." He looked mildly surprised, but reached into his back pocket and produced some credit cards all in the name of D. Selecca. One was an Amex.

"That will do nicely," I said. Before I could move, he had the envelope opened and slid a data stick into his palm. It was two inches long by half an inch wide. He turned it over a couple of times like he'd never seen one before. Then he peered into the envelope as if expecting to find something else. In the distance I heard the whoop-whoop of a police car. The atmosphere in the room was very still.

"What's this?" he asked, looking at me with those cold, dark eyes.

"It's what I was given to bring here," I said, "by Gus Krasky."

The police siren came closer, the noise beginning to overlay Selecca's breathing and the rustle of the envelope.

"Krasky? He said bring it here? To me? Why?"

"That's right," I replied carefully. "I don't know why."

Selecca flicked the stick to Paulie and pointed to a laptop on a side table. "Check it."

Paulie inserted the stick with his free hand and tapped the keys while keeping the gun pointed at me. "It's a bunch of letters,' he said finally. "Letters from you to Jean-Francois Aboullah."

Selecca's eyes bulged as if he'd swallowed snake bile. Then the phone jangled, making us all just jump. I hoped Paulie's finger wasn't curled too tightly around the trigger. Accidental discharges can kill you.

Selecca snatched up the phone. "Yeah?" He looked at me. "Sure – he's here. Who is this?" Then he handed me the phone with an irate snarl. "What's this – a family business? You got your sister keepin' tabs on you? We ain't finished, you and me." He flicked the torn envelope away from him and stomped across to the window.

I wondered if I was in a bad dream and any minute I'd wake up in bed at home, safe from all this. *I don't have a sister.*

"*Jake ... get out of there!*" It was Lilly-Mae. There was a background clutter of traffic noise and a man's voice issuing orders. "*You've got less than two minutes!*"

"Wha-who ...?" The phone went dead. Suddenly I didn't want to be here. Call me sensitive.

"My sister – Emma," I said, snatching for a name. "She's a worrier ... says we have to catch a flight out in the next hour. I'd better go." I started towards the door and found Paulie in my way, his gun at head height. Then a police siren gave a whoop right outside before being choked off in mid-stream. Instantly Paulie jumped towards the window and looked down. He cursed and looked at Selecca.

"There're cops everywhere!"

It was all the opportunity I was going to get. I was across to the door and through it before they could stop me, and running along the corridor towards the stairs. I had no idea what the police activity was about, but after Lilly-Mae's warning I didn't want to stay and find out.

Halfway down the corridor was an ice machine. I grabbed a plastic bucket and filled it with cubes just as the door at the end opened and two men in suits appeared. Behind them was a uniformed cop. They didn't even spare me a glance, but hurried by, the uniform holding the door for me. Whoever they were here for, it evidently didn't include guests bearing ice buckets.

Downstairs another cop was blocking the fire door to the outside. This one didn't look like he would let me go by so easily, so I veered towards the reception area and wandered through as casually as possible, keeping as far from the receptionist as possible. Then someone grabbed my arm, nearly upsetting my ice-bucket all over the floor.

It was Lilly-Mae.

"Keep walking," she hissed, and steered me towards the front door, chatting away excitedly about what a wonderful time we'd have on the aerial tramway and how we could take a hot-air balloon out over the desert or maybe drive out to the Indian Canyons. By the time we reached the outside and I ditched the ice-bucket, she almost had me believing we were newly-weds.

Five minutes later we were in a Mex-Tex restaurant a few blocks away, facing each other over margaritas with a good view of the street.

"We could head for the airport," I suggested. First rule of not being caught: run away quickly.

"Uh-uh." Lilly-Mae shook her head. She looked wonderful, as if she'd been relaxing on a beach all day instead of rescuing inept Englishmen from the clutches of Mafia-type gunmen. "We're safe enough."

"We are?"

"Sure. Selecca won't set the police on you ... he'll be too busy trying to worm his way out of trouble. With his record, that won't be easy."

"Having a man with a gun in his room won't help."

"That's Paulie."

It reminded me that she probably knew a lot about people like Selecca and Paulie. I felt depressed. Why couldn't I meet someone normal?

"You phoned just in time," I said. "Thanks."

She gave me a no-problem look. "What did Selecca say?"

"He wasn't expecting the package." I told her about his reaction to the contents of the data stick. "He was about to quiz me when you rang. Then the siren went off." I paused as a knowing smile spread across her face. "Was that you, too?"

"Yup. Lil' old me."

"And the police?"

She looked puzzled about that. "No. They were already on their way. But I guessed where they were going and was worried you'd get picked up with Selecca."

"Quick thinking."

"Thank you. After I spoke to you, I thought maybe I should start a diversion. I saw this police cruiser out back with nobody in it, so I let it whoop." She rolled her eyes and flapped her hand as if she had been shocked breathless. "Gosh, loud, huh?" I didn't ask how she knew where to find the siren button in a police car.

"Good job you did. I think Paulie was about to shoot me. You saved my life."

She made a face, dropping into a cornball drawl. "Aw shucks, really? Where I come from, that means I own you. Gee, I ain't never owned nobody before."

I couldn't help but laugh. There was something about Lilly-Mae that veered erratically from sophisticated and elegant to plain screwball. Whichever was real and which was the put-on I couldn't tell, but right now it didn't matter. Still, there was something bothering me about the envelope. "I'm still confused," I said, looking Lilly-Mae straight in the eye, "about the envelope being on the mailbox. It wasn't there when I arrived."

Lilly-Mae looked blank. "You didn't see anyone in the area?"

"Only the pool man. At least, that's what he said he was."

When I described him, Lilly-Mae nodded. "That's Billy. He's the pool man, all right."

"Well, someone must have dropped off the envelope after I'd gone to the house. But why leave it there? What if I'd taken one look at Frank and run for the airport and home?"

"Unless ..." She chewed her lip. "Unless you got there earlier than expected."

We let that one settle between us for a while. She was right: I had been hoping for an early departure. "So whoever left it there didn't know I was already inside, but counted on me seeing the envelope when I arrived and automatically bringing it to Palm Springs, because I'd know all about it, seeing as I'd already been paid."

Lilly-Mae's eyes went wide. "But that could have only been—"

I nodded. "Gus Krasky." I wondered if it was Gus who set the police on Selecca.

"If we could look at the computer," said Lilly-Mae, "we could see what was downloaded to the data stick. We could go back to the house tomorrow."

Great. This was turning into "Mission Impossible". "You're kidding." What had been exciting at first was wearing off like the coating on a cheap Singapore watch. Anyway, I already knew what was on the stick.

"But I have a key," Lilly-Mae insisted, before I could explain. "And I know a back way in through the woods."

See, this is what comes of raising girls on Nancy Drew mysteries. They forget quilting and want to conquer the world instead.

"Two things," I said. "First, the stick held copies of letters from Selecca. So we don't need to look any closer. Second, I want to try something." I led her over to a phone and dialled the number. While it rang, Lilly-Mae crowded in on me so she could listen. She smelled fresh and soapy, and I remembered what she had looked like in that backless sundress. Then someone picked up the phone.

I waited for them to speak, but all I could hear was wheezy breathing and the mouthpiece rasping against stubble. Definitely not a cleaning lady. Lilly-Mae pressed closer, eyes like dark liquid pools and her arm sliding round my waist.

"Gus?" I said finally.

"Who is this?" It was a man's voice. In the background came a burst of radio static. I felt the hairs move on the back of my neck. *Cops.* I put the phone down. I could see Lilly-Mae had reached the same conclusion. "They must have found Frank."

"And now they've got Selecca – and the data stick." Lilly-Mae chewed her lip.

Back at our table, I said, "Have you ever heard of a Jean-Francois Aboullah?"

She shook her head. "I don't think so. Why?"

"Because the letters on the stick were from Selecca to Aboullah. If it's the Jean-Francois Aboullah I'm thinking of, Selecca's been corresponding with a man who tops probably every Western government's list of people not to talk to. He's an African warlord."

"Oh, gosh," said Lilly-Mae, her voice tiny.

"What?"

"I know Gus wasn't happy with Selecca," she said. "They used to be really thick, always cooking up deals together. But a few days ago I heard Gus telling Frank about having evidence that would put Selecca out of the picture, if he needed it."

"What sort of evidence?"

Her eyes were like liquid pools. "Stuff about arms deals. He mentioned Africa, and something about a State Department blacklist. Is that serious?"

"If it's an official one, yes," I said. "And there's Gus."

"Huh?"

"Across the street." I pointed through the window to where the inbred Twins, Jesse and Dino, were lumbering by on the other side. They were followed at a discreet distance by a casual and surprisingly chipper-looking Gus Krasky.

I grabbed Lilly-Mae in time to stop her going after him. "Wait."

"But what's he doing here?"

"What else? He's come to make sure his plan goes right."

"Plan?"

"Think about it. He pays me to drop off a package for Selecca. The same night he has an argument with Frank about something that could 'get us all killed', and Frank mentions the police and me. Frank gets shot. Gus can't let me near the house, so he leaves the envelope at the gate, knowing I'll see it, knowing it will end up with Selecca, because that's what I do. I deliver stuff. And he wants Selecca out of the way."

"So it was him who called the police? But that could implicate him, too – especially if you'd been arrested."

"Not necessarily. The instructions were for me to leave the envelope at reception. It was just bad luck that Paulie was there when I arrived." I went over to the phone and re-dialled Gus' number. The same husky voice answered.

"In the main room," I said softly, "there's a desk with a laptop."

"What? Who is this?" The man sounded annoyed, like a cop with a headache.

"Just tell me and I'll explain. The laptop."

"Laptop? There's no laptop here."

"How about the blood in the hall?"

"Blood?" He sounded really irate now. "What blood? Look, fella, we had a call about an intruder, but the place is empty. And clean. Who are you?"

I cut him off and looked at Lilly-Mae. Gus had cleaned the place up. "There's no laptop and no blood. I bet there's no Frank in the pool, either." I stared up at the ceiling, thinking it through. If the letters were genuine – and I guessed they were – they were bad news for Selecca. He'd have a hard time explaining them to the Federal agencies. Somehow Krasky must have obtained copies. All he had to do was sit tight and feign ignorance, no matter what Selecca tried to throw at him in exchange for a deal. None of it could be traced back to Gus. As for me, I was a complete unknown, who'd happened to walk conveniently into the middle of a takeover bid. Clever.

Lilly-Mae looked sick. "He used us," she said, her voice faint. "He killed Frank, he lied and ran out on me, and he nearly got you shot or arrested with Selecca. And all for what?"

"It's called competition. Get rid of Selecca and he'd pick up all of the business going. It must have been worth his while. But risky, as Frank tried to tell him." Frank must have threatened him with the police and paid the price.

Thirty minutes later we were at the airport waiting for a flight out. Lilly-Mae had been very quiet since leaving Palm Springs. She turned to me. "Are you married?"

"Why?"

She shrugged. "Just making conversation. I was wondering if there was a Mrs Jake waiting at home, that's all."

"There was once," I said truthfully. "But she moved on. How about you?"

"Me, too. He was in the navy. It didn't work out."

"So how did you come to be with Gus?"

"Living in his house, you mean?" She stared absently across the lounge. "When my husband and I split up a year ago I was living on the coast and needed a job. Someone who knew Gus told me he was looking for help. He had contacts in the San Diego Navy yard and was buying ex-military stuff pre-public auction. He needed someone to deal with paperwork on the construction side, so I applied." I didn't say anything, and she looked at me with a hint of fire in her eye. "Gus was my boss, period. I lived at his place, but I had my own room."

"I know," I said smugly. "I've seen it." I explained about searching the house.

"So what are you going to do now?" she asked.

"Go home, I suppose. You?"

She shrugged. "Head back to the coast. Start again. I've done it before. I need to get my stuff from Gus' place, though."

The indicator board showed my flight number. There must be something about airports that appeals to the romantic in me. Either that or I need my bumps examining. "You mean clothes?"

She thought for a while, then shrugged again. "I guess. Mostly. But I can always buy more. And I could stay with Mom for a while." She gave a half smile and seemed to brighten up at the idea. "I've done that before, too."

I took out the envelope Gus had given me and looked inside. I was half-expecting it to be full of plain paper. But it wasn't. Whatever else Gus might be, he believed in paying well.

"Do you have your passport with you?"

"Sure," she said. "It was a habit Dad got me into. Why?"

"No reason," I said, my pulse beginning to beat a little faster, "I just wondered if you'd like to take a holiday. On Gus' account."

"With you?" She gave a flash of her old smile and looked at me as if I might suddenly pop and disappear. As the smile blossomed into an excited grin, I stood up and took her arm.

"Why don't we," I suggested, "go out and buy ourselves some swimming costumes, and look for somewhere hot and quiet to hide away for a while?"

She laughed in a way that made my spirits soar. "*Costumes*? Did you say *costumes*? That's *so* cute!'

"Tomayto, tomarto," I responded easily. "You'll get used to it ..."

A BLOW ON
THE HEAD

Peter Lovesey

ALMOST THERE. DONNA Culpepper looked ahead to her destination and her destiny, the top of Beachy Head, the great chalk headland that is the summit of the South Downs coast. She'd walked from where the taxi driver had left her. The stiff climb wasn't easy on this gusty August afternoon, but her mind was made up. She was thirty-nine, with no intention of being forty. She'd made a disastrous marriage to a man who had deserted her after six weeks, robbed her of her money, her confidence, her dreams. Trying to put it all behind her, as friends kept urging, had not worked. Two years on, she was unwilling to try any longer.

Other ways of ending it, like an overdose or cutting her wrists, were not right for Donna. Beachy Head was the place. As a child she'd stayed in Eastbourne with her Gran and they came here often, "for a blow on the head", as Gran put it, crunching the tiny grey shells of the path, her grey hair tugged by the wind, while jackdaws and herring-gulls swooped and soared, screaming in the clear air. From the top, five hundred feet up when you first saw the sea, you had a sudden sensation of height that made your spine tingle. There was just the rim of eroding turf and the hideous drop.

On a good day you could see the Isle of Wight, Gran had said. Donna couldn't see anything and stepped closer to the edge and Gran grabbed her and said it was dangerous. People came here to kill themselves.

This interested Donna. Gran gave reluctant answers to her questions.

"They jump off."

"Why?"

"I don't know, dear."

"Yes, you do. Tell me, Gran."

"Some people are unhappy."

"What makes them unhappy?"

"Lots of things."

"What things?"

"Never mind, dear."

"But I do mind. Tell me what made those people unhappy."

"Grown-up things."

"Like making babies?"

"No, no, no. Whoever put such ideas in your head?"

"What, then?"

"Sometimes they get unhappy because they lose the person they love."

"What's love?"

"Oh, dear. You've such a lot to learn. When you grow up you fall in love with someone and if you're lucky you marry them."

"Is that why they jump off the cliff?"

Gran laughed. "No, you daft ha'porth, it's the opposite, or I think it is. Let's change the subject."

The trouble with grown-ups is that they always change the subject before they get to the point. For some years after this Donna thought falling in love was a physical act involving gravity. She could see that falling off Beachy Head was dangerous and would only be attempted by desperate people. She expected it was possible to get in love by falling from more sensible heights. She tried jumping off her bed a few times, but nothing happened. The kitchen table, which she tried only once, was no use either.

She started getting sensuous dreams, though. She would leap off the cliff edge and float in the air like the skydivers she'd seen on television. If that was falling in love she could understand why there was so much talk about it.

Disillusion set in when she started school. Love turned out to be something else involving those gross, ungainly creatures, boys. After a few skirmishes with over-curious boys she decided love was not worth pursuing any longer. It didn't come up to her dreams. This was a pity because other girls of her age expected less and got a more gradual initiation into the mysteries of sex.

At seventeen the hormones would not be suppressed and Donna drank five vodkas and went to bed with a man of twenty-three. He said he was in love with her, but if that was love it was unsatisfactory. And in the several relationships she had in her twenties she never experienced anything to match those dreams of falling and flying. Most of her girlfriends found partners and moved in with them. Donna held off.

In her mid-to-late thirties she began to feel deprived. One day she saw the Meeting Place page in a national paper. Somewhere out there was her ideal partner. She decided to take active steps to find him. She had money. Her Gran had died and left her everything, ninety thousand pounds. In the ad she described herself as independent, sensitive and cultured.

And that was how she met Lionel Culpepper.

He was charming, good-looking and better at sex than anyone she'd met. She told him about her Gran and her walks on Beachy Head and her dreams of flying. He said he had a pilot's licence and offered to take her up in a small plane. She asked if he owned a plane and he said he would hire one. Thinking of her legacy she asked how much they cost and he thought he could buy a good one second-hand for ninety thousand pounds. They got married and opened a joint account. He went off one morning to look at a plane offered for sale in a magazine. That was the last she saw of her husband. When she checked the bank account it was empty. She had been married thirty-eight days.

For a long time she worried about Lionel, thinking he'd had an accident. She reported him missing. Then a letter arrived from a solicitor. Cruelly formal in its wording, it stated that her husband, Lionel Culpepper, wanted a divorce. She was devastated. She hated him then and knew him for what he was. He would not get his divorce that easily.

That was two years ago. Here she was, taking the route of so many who have sought to end their troubles by suicide. Some odd sense of completion, she supposed, was making her take those last steps to the highest point. Any part of the cliff edge would do.

She saw a phone box ahead. Oddly situated, you would think, on a cliff top. The Samaritans had arranged for the phone to be here just in case any tormented soul decided to call them and talk. Donna walked past. A short way beyond was a well-placed wooden bench and she was grateful for that. She needed a moment to compose herself.

She sat. It was just the usual seat you found in parks and along river banks all over the country. Not comfortable for long with its slatted seat and upright back, but welcome at the end of the stiff climb. And it did face the sea.

In a moment she would launch herself. She wasn't too scared. A small part of her still wanted the thrill of falling. For a few precious seconds she would be like those sky-divers appearing to fly. This was the way to go.

Revived and resolute, Donna stood and checked to make sure no one was about. Perfect. She had the whole headland to herself.

Well, then.

What it was that drew her attention back to the bench she couldn't say. At the edge of her vision she became aware of a small brass plaque screwed to the top rail. She read the inscription.

In memory of my beloved wife Donna Maria Culpepper, 1967–2004, who loved to walk here and enjoy this view.

A surreal moment. Donna swayed and had to reach out and clutch the bench. She sat again, rubbed her eyes, took a deep breath and looked a second time because she half wondered if her heightened state of mind had made her hallucinate.

The words were just as she'd first read them. Her name in full. She'd never met anyone with the same name. It would be extra-ordinary if some other Donna Maria Culpepper had walked here and loved this view. The year of birth was right as well.

Two things were definitely not Donna. She hadn't died in 2004 and the way her rat of a husband had treated her made the word "beloved" a sick joke.

Was it possible, she asked herself now, still staring at the weird plaque, that Lionel had paid for the bench and put it here? Could he have heard from some mistaken source that she had died? Had he done this in a fit of conscience?

No chance. Freed of that foolish infatuation she'd experienced when she met the man and married him, she knew him for what he was. Conscience didn't trouble Lionel. He'd had the gall to ask for a divorce – through a solicitor and after weeks of silence. He was cowardly and callous.

How could this bench be anything to do with Lionel, or with her?

It was a mystery.

Cold logic suggested there had been another Donna Maria Culpepper born in the same year who had died in 2004 and had this touching memorial placed here by her widowed husband, who was obviously more devoted and considerate than Lionel. And yet it required a series of coincidences for this to have happened: the same first names, surname, date of birth.

She took another look. In the bottom right corner of the plaque was a detail she hadn't noticed – the letters "L.C." – Lionel's initials. This, surely, clinched it. The odds against were huge.

She no longer felt suicidal. Anger had taken over. She was outraged by Lionel's conduct. He shouldn't have done this. She had come here in a wholly negative frame of mind. Now a new challenge galvanized her. She would get to the truth. She was recharged, determined to find an explanation.

First she had to find him. After their break-up she'd had minimal contact, and that was through solicitors' letters. She had no idea where he lived now.

She walked down the path towards the town.

The Parks and Recreations Department at Eastbourne Council said that about forty seats had been donated as memorials by members of the public. A helpful young woman showed her the records. The bench had been presented last spring. A man had come in with the plaque already inscribed. He'd particularly asked for a teak seat to be positioned at the top of Beachy Head. He'd paid in cash and left no name, though it was obvious he had to be a Mr Culpepper.

Donna asked if he'd left his address or phone number and was told he had not. She took a sharp, impatient breath and explained about the shock she'd had. The clerical assistant was sympathetic and said it could only be an unfortunate duplication of names.

While Donna was explaining why she thought it couldn't be coincidence, an assistant at the next desk asked if they were talking about the seat at the top of Beachy Head. She said a few months ago she'd had someone else in, a woman, asking about the same seat and the man who presented it.

"A woman? Did she say why?" Donna asked.

"No, but she left her business card. I put it in the folder, just in case we found out any more."

The card had slipped to the bottom of the folder. Donna was given a pencil and paper to make a note of the name and phone number. *Maggie Boswell-Jones, Starpart Film, TV and Theatrical Agency, Cecil Court, Off Charing Cross Road, London.* There were phone, fax and e-mail numbers.

Donna didn't have her mobile with her. She hadn't intended using it on this last day of her life. She used a public phone downstairs.

The conversation was all very bizarre.

"You're Lionel's wife? But you're dead," Maggie Boswell-Jones said. "You were killed in a flying accident."

"I promise you I wasn't," Donna said. "I'm who I say I am."

"How can you be? There's a seat on Beachy Head with your name on it. Lionel put it there in your memory."

"He ran out on me in the second month of our marriage. May I ask why you were looking for him?"

"Because he's my boyfriend, darling, and he's missing."

Donna felt as if she'd been kicked in the stomach. She knew Lionel was a rat. Now she knew he was a two-timing rat. He'd walked out on her and started up with this woman. She made an effort to save her fury for Lionel.

"How did you know about the seat?"

"He took me up there specially. He wanted me to know that you were dead. I made it very clear to him that I don't get involved with married guys. He spoke nicely of you."

"Look, can I come and see you?"

"Is that necessary?"

"I'm determined to find him. With your help I'm sure I can do it."

At the agency Donna recognized a man who stepped out of the lift. He was an actor she often saw in *Coronation Street*. In the waiting room upstairs there were framed movie posters. In a glass showcase were various awards, including what looked like an Oscar.

Maggie appeared high-powered with her black fringe, tinted glasses and purple suit, but she turned out to be charming. Coffee and biscuits were ready on a low table in her office. They sat together on a black leather sofa. "I've been trying to understand what's going on with Lionel ever since you phoned and I'm still at a loss," Maggie said. "He's such a bright guy. I can't think how he got to believe you'd passed away."

"He made it up," Donna said.

"Oh, I don't think so. He said the kindest things about you. I mean, why would he go to the trouble and expense of buying a seat for you?"

"To fool you into believing I was dead and he was free to have an affair. Can't you see that?"

Maggie took a lot of convincing. Clearly she was still under Lionel's spell. Just as Donna had believed him incapable of leaving her, so Maggie insisted he must have lost his memory in the flying accident.

"There was no flying accident," Donna said. "He talked about taking me in a plane, but it never happened. He took ninety thousand pounds from our account."

"Really? This shocks me." The colour had drained from Maggie's face. "I certainly need to find him because I lent him sixty grand to renovate a house he'd bought for us in the south of France."

"You'll never see that money again," Donna said. "He's a conman. He befriends women like you and me and fleeces them. If you don't mind me asking, how did you meet him? Was it through a newspaper?"

"What a skunk!" Maggie said, and Donna knew she'd got through to her at last.

That evening Maggie took Donna for a meal at a restaurant near the agency. "I'm not short of a bob or two," she said, "but let's admit it, I'm unattached and on the lookout. I meet plenty of hunky blokes in my job, but it doesn't do to mix work and pleasure, so I put my ad in the *Guardian*. Lionel was the best of the bunch who responded – or seemed to be."

"I wonder how many other women he's conned," Donna said. "It really upsets me that he went to all that trouble to make out I was dead and he was a free man. There must be some way of stopping him."

"We can't stop him if we can't find him."

"Couldn't we trace him through the newspaper?"

"I don't think so. They're very strict about box numbers. And they cover themselves by saying you indemnify the newspaper against all claims." Maggie thought for a while, and took a long sip of wine. "Right," she said finally. "What we do is this."

GORGEOUS Georgie, 38, own house, car, country cottage, WLTM Mr Charming 35–45 for days out and evenings in and possible LTR. Loves fast cars, first nights and five star restaurants.

"What's LTR?"

"Long term relationship. That should do it," Maggie said.

"It's a lot more pushy than mine," Donna said.

"How did you describe yourself?"

She blushed a little. "Independent, sensitive and cultured."

"Independent is good. He's thinking of your bank balance. But we can't use it a second time. This will pull in quite a few gold-diggers, I expect. We just have to listen carefully to the voice messages and make sure it's Lionel."

"I'll know his voice."

"So will I, sweetie."

"And who, exactly, is Gorgeous Georgie?"

"One of the best stuntmen in Britain."

"A *man*?"

"Ex-boxer and European weightlifting champion. He's been on my agency books for years. He'll deliver Lionel to us, and the money he stole from us. When Georgie has finished with the bastard he'll beg for mercy."

Maggie called ten days later. "He's fallen for it. A really unctuous voice message. Made me want to throw up. He says he's unattached—"

"That's a lie."

"Professional, caring and with a good sense of humour. He'll need that."

"So what's the plan?" Donna asked.

"It's already under way. I got my film rights director to call him back. She has the Roedean accent and very sexy it sounds. I told her to play the caution card. Said she needed to be certain Lionel isn't married. He jumped right in and said he's a widower and would welcome the opportunity to prove it. They're meeting for a walk on the Downs at Beachy Head followed by a meal at the pub."

"Your rights director?"

"No, silly. She was just the voice on the phone. He'll meet Georgie and get the shock of his life. All you and I have to do is be there to take care of the remains."

Donna caught her breath. "I can't be a party to murder."

"My sense of humour, darling. Georgie won't do anything permanent. He'll rough him up a bit and put the fear of God in him. Then we step up and get our money back."

Maggie drove them to Eastbourne on the day of the rendezvous. She took the zigzag from Holywell and parked in a lay-by with a good view of the grass rise. From here you wouldn't know there was a sheer drop. But if you ventured up the slope you'd see the Seven Sisters, the chalk cliffs reaching right away to Cuckmere Haven. It was late on a fine, gusty afternoon. Georgie and the hapless Lionel were expected to reach here about five-thirty.

"Coffee or champagne?"

"You *are* well prepared," Donna said. "Coffee, I think. I want a clear head when we meet up with him."

Maggie poured some from a flask. "We'll save the champers for later."

Donna smiled. "I just hope it stops him in his tracks. I don't want other women getting caught like we did. I felt so angry with myself for being taken in. I got very depressed. When I came up here I was on the point of suicide."

"That's no attitude. Don't ever let them grind you down."

"I'm not very experienced with men."

"Well, at least you persuaded the bastard to marry you, darling. You can't be a total amateur. Me, I was conned every which way. Slept with him, handed him my money, accepted his proposal."

"Proposal? He proposed to you? Actually promised to marry you?"

"The whole shebang. Down on one knee. We were engaged. He bought the ring, I'll say that for him. A large diamond and two sapphires. He knew he had to chip in something to get what he wanted. What did it cost him? – a couple of grand at most, compared to the sixty he got off me."

"I had no idea it got that far."

"He'd have married me if I hadn't caught him out. Bigamy wouldn't have troubled our Lionel."

Donna was increasingly concerned about what she was hearing. "But you *didn't* catch him out. When I first phoned, you called him your boyfriend. I had to persuade you that he was a conman."

"Don't kid yourself, ducky," Maggie said with a harder edge to her voice. "I knew all about Lionel before you showed up. I had him checked out. It's easy enough to get hold of a marriage certificate, and when he gave me the guff about the flying accident I checked for a death certificate as well, and there wasn't one, so I knew he was lying. He was stupid enough to tell me about the memorial bench before I even saw it. I went to the council and made sure it was bloody Lionel who paid to have it put there. He handed them the plaque and a wad of cash. What a con. He could go on using that seat as his calling card every time he started up with a new woman."

"If you knew all that, why didn't you act before? Why are you doing this with me?" Donna said.

"Do you really want to know?" Maggie said. She reached for the champagne bottle and turned it in her hands as if to demonstrate good faith. "It's because you would have found out. Some day his body is going to be washed up. The sea always gives up its dead. Then the police are going to come asking questions and you'll lead them straight to me."

"I don't know what you're talking about."

"Get with it, Donna dear. Lionel is history."

She felt the hairs rise on her neck. "You killed him?"

"The evening he brought me up here to look at the stupid bench. I waited till we got here and then told him what an arsehole he was. Do you know, he still tried to con me? He walked to the cliff edge and said he would throw himself off if I didn't believe him. I couldn't stand his hypocrisy, so I gave him a push. Simple as that."

Donna covered her mouth.

"The tide was in," Maggie said in a matter-of-fact way, "so I suppose the body was carried out to sea."

"This is dreadful," Donna said. She herself had felt hatred for Lionel and wanted revenge, but she had never dreamed of killing him. "What I can't understand is why we're here now – why you went through this charade of advertising for him, trying to find him – when you knew he was dead."

"If you were listening, sweetie, I just told you. You knew too much even before I gave you the full story. You're certain to shop me when the police come along."

It was getting dark in the car, but Donna noticed a movement of Maggie's right hand. She had gripped the champagne bottle by the neck.

Donna felt for the door handle and shoved it open. She half-fell, trying to get out. Maggie got out the other side and dashed round. Donna tried to run, but Maggie grabbed her coat. The last thing Donna saw was the bottle being swung at her head.

The impact was massive.

She fell against the car and slid to the ground. She'd lost all sensation. She couldn't even raise her arms to protect herself.

She acted dead, eyes closed, body limp. It wasn't difficult.

One of her eyes was jerked open by Maggie's finger. She had the presence to stare ahead.

Then she felt Maggie's hands under her back, lifting. She was hauled back into the car seat. The door slammed shut. She was too dazed to do anything.

Maggie was back at the wheel, closing the other door. The engine started up. The car bumped in ways it shouldn't have done. It was being driven across the turf, and she guessed what was happening. Maggie was driving her right up to the cliff edge to push her over.

The car stopped.

I can't let this happen, she told herself. I wanted to die once, but not any more.

She heard Maggie get out again. She opened her eyes. The key was in the ignition, but she hadn't the strength to move across and take the controls. She had to shut her eyes again and surrender to Maggie dragging her off the seat.

First her back thumped on the chalk at the cliff edge, then her head.

Flashes streaked across her retina. She took a deep breath of cold air, trying to hold on to consciousness.

She felt Maggie's hands take a grip under her armpits to force her over the edge.

With an effort born of desperation she turned and grabbed one of Maggie's ankles with both hands and held on. If she was going, then her killer would go with her.

Maggie shouted, "Bitch!" and kicked her repeatedly with the free leg. Donna knew she had to hold on.

Each kick was like a dagger-thrust in her kidneys.

I can't take this, she told herself.

The agony became unbearable. She let go.

The sudden removal of the clamp on Maggie's leg must have affected her balance. Donna felt the full force of Maggie's weight across her body followed by a scream, a long, despairing and diminishing scream.

Donna dragged herself away from the crumbling edge and then flopped on the turf again. Almost another half hour passed before she was able to stagger to the phone box and ask for help.

When she told her story to the police, she kept it simple. She wasn't capable of telling it all. She'd been brought here on the pretext of meeting someone and then attacked with a bottle and almost forced over the edge. Her attacker had tripped and gone over.

Even the next day, when she made a full statement for their records, she omitted some of the details. She decided not to tell them she'd been at the point of suicide when she discovered that bench. She let them believe she'd come on a sentimental journey to remember her childhood. It didn't affect their investigation.

Maggie's body was recovered the same day. Lionel, elusive to the end, was washed up at Hastings by a storm the following October.

He left only debts. Donna had expected nothing and was not discouraged. Since her escape she valued her life and looked forward.

And the bench? You won't find it at Beachy Head.

CHICAGO

Jon Courtenay Grimwood

IT TOOK JACK Cogan five days to hunt me down. I don't know why because I was where anyone with half a brain would expect me to be. In my office. At the back table in Finnegan's, drinking New York sours and watching some old film on the screen. You know the kind; girl meets boy, boy gets killed, girl saves every cent to bring him back to life, boy goes off with someone else ...

Finnegan had turned down the lights; instantly lowering the ceiling and sending the wall into shadow. The place smelt of cigar smoke, whisky and cologne. The way you would expect a Chicago speakeasy to smell.

The bar stools held memories of those who'd already left. Little Pete, who overflowed everything except a four-seater settee; a whore I knew from somewhere else; a couple of soldiers; and a man who spent half an hour watching me before glancing away when I caught his stare.

He left shortly afterwards.

Maybe he had another appointment, and maybe pulling back my jacket to reveal a Colt 45 in my belt made him decide to leave me alone. That's what I thought at the time. When Jack Cogan came blustering into Finnegan's with his shoulders rolling and his belly jutting proudly, I knew the watcher had been one of Jack's sneaks.

"Take a seat," I said.

"Yeah," said Cogan. "I just did."

Leaning forward, he let his jacket drop open.

"Sweet rig," I said, looking at his double holster "Where d'you get it. Wal-Mart?"

Jack Cogan scowled. "From Lucky himself."

That was Lucky Luciano XI, unless it was Lucky Luciano X. They had a high attrition rate in that family. Since gang positions became hereditary, we'd seen some weird shit in this godforsaken city; like thirteen-year-old *capos* running whole districts and a seven-year-old pimp managing a stable of hookers without knowing what the punters were buying.

"You're a hard man to find."

"Can't have been looking hard enough."

Jack was broad and barrel-chested, running to fat. At the moment his chest was larger than his gut, but it was only a matter of time. He tipped his head to one side, inviting me to explain.

"It's been a bad year. This is the only bar where I'm not banned." Glancing at the door, I noticed three plain-clothes officers. They weren't clients for sure. They owned all their own teeth, wore clean clothes and were sober. One of those was possible, two at a stretch ...

But all three?

"I'm touched," I said. "You brought backup."

Jack Cogan flushed.

You can probably tell, the police captain and I go way back. In fact, we go back so far that I can remember when he was thin and he can remember when I was rich, successful and kept the key that wound up his boss.

"Al ..." he said, and his use of my first name killed my grin faster than a gun ever could. "I need to know. Where were you between two and three o'clock this morning?"

"Can't remember."

"Listen to me ..."

"Mean it," I said. "Had my memory wipe this morning. Last three days. Shit, I guess. Must have been, or I wouldn't have bothered to wipe them." Pulling an envelope from my pocket, I pushed it across.

You would think it was poisonous from the way Jack Cogan hesitated to touch it. Although it might have been the colour, which was purple.

"Classy," he said.

A young woman I couldn't remember told me she didn't want to see me again. She told me this in childlike writing with tear splotches crinkling the page. So I guess we'd gone from romance to break up in fewer than three days. Impressive, even by my standards.

"You're in trouble." Jack Cogan was saying.

"Guess I am," I said. "If her brothers or father ever catch up with me."

"No," said Cogan. "I mean you're in real trouble."

"And you're bringing me in?"

"Yeah," he said. "Felt I owed you that." The captain nodded at my screen. "Watched any news recently?" His sigh answered his own question. "Guess not, or you wouldn't be sitting round here drinking those."

Without asking, he leant over and flicked channels.

My face stared back at me. Only it was me as I might have been; if I were sober and my hair was clean and I'd bothered to shave any time in the last week. This version of me wore a pin-stripped suit, with a fancy waistcoat and patent leather shoes. He was carrying a tommy gun, the traditional mark of a recognized gang boss. The gun looked old, but it wasn't. Not really. My grandfather had it made the day he moved up from *consigliere* to *capo*.

"You might want to turn up the sound."

I did as Jack suggested, and discovered what part of me already knew. The other Jonny Falcone XI had checked out with a shot to the head.

"Professional," said the presenter.

A thin woman came on to talk about Chicago traditions and that particular MO. She talked about stuff that hadn't happened as well. Gut shots, blindings, slashes to the throat, tongues ripped out, testicles removed and sewn into the mouth; nothing everybody hadn't heard three hundred times before.

Round here the bosses appointed the mayor, and they helped choose the governor, and the governor helps choose the president. It was the system that had been in place since the president realized only the bosses could make prohibition stick, because only they had a cast-iron gold-plated reason for wanting it to stick. It was what made them rich.

"So," said the presenter. "You're saying this is *capo a capo*, right?"

The woman hesitated. "It's what that particular MO would suggest, but there's another rumour ..."

"What's all this got to do with me?" I demanded.

Something like sympathy showed in Jack Cogan's eyes. "We need you down the station," he said.

"We've got your fingerprints," said the man. "Your DNA and your ugly face on tape. All you got to do is sign." Picking up a rubber hose, he slashed me across the lip and grinned when pain forced its way between my teeth.

He and his companion had me naked and tied to a chair, with blood filling my mouth and three of my teeth shining like cheap ivory on the cell floor. I'd already watched myself limp down a corridor onscreen, slowly open a door and slip through it. Exactly 180 seconds later came the sound of a shot, exactly fifteen seconds after that I limped back through the door, shut it quietly behind me and shuffled my way downstairs. I came out of the wipe with one knee broken. Don't know how it happened any more than anything else that happened in those three days.

"You listening?"

"Yeah," I said. "I'm listening."

He hit me again anyway; swung the hose with enthusiasm, to make me listen harder. I knew him from my old life. While the other enforcer looked like the kid of someone I used to know.

Probably was. As I said, all gang jobs are hereditary.

One point troubled me though. I'd expected Jack Cogan to do the dirty work and here I was with a couple of high-level enforcers doing it themselves. Made no sense. At least, not to me.

"Why not leave this to Jack?" I asked.

For a moment, I thought the two men were going to tell me *they asked the questions*. But the man with the rubber hose grabbed a chair, flipped it round and straddled it, pushing his face close to mine. "Only three people it can be," he said. "Freddy, Machine Gun or you. Now my boss knows it's not him. And Mickey's boss knows it's not him. So that just leaves you ..."

Digging into his pocket, he extracted a pair of pliers, a switch-blade, a lighter and something that looked like cotton thread, and laid the first three on the table. In the time it took me to realize the fourth was not cotton; he's wrapped it round my ear and tugged.

"Fuck ..."

Then he reached for my other ear. "Come on, Jonny," he said. It was a day for people calling me by my first name. "You know how it goes. We slice off your ears. We sever your fingers. We crush your toes and then we crush your balls. Assuming you're too stupid to have signed before then."

The other enforcer snorted.

"So," he said. "Agree to sign and we'll get you a doctor. It's late, we're all tired, and we all know you're going to confess eventually."

The judge had a face like a sucked lemon or maybe she was constipated. Either way, she twisted her lips and shuffled in her seat; every *moue* of distaste and twitch of discomfort captured on camera. And there were numerous cameras, journalists and members of the public. The demand for seats for my trial had been so great the city had been forced to hold a lottery.

Now, I am sure there are prosecution lawyers who are polite, intelligent, quietly spoken and understated. The small man who stalked out into the well of the court was not one of them. Glancing around him, Mr Dalkin stopped when his eyes reached the jury box and he gazed at each juror sympathetically. *I don't know why he didn't just confess*, his expression said. *I don't know why you're being put through this.* And then he turned to me.

"Tell me," he demanded. "Why you refused to take a lie detector test."

"I didn't."

Mr Dalkin rolled his eyes at the jury and turned to where I stood behind bulletproof glass. "Then why are the results of that test not entered with the court?"

I shrugged.

"You don't have an answer?"

"I took the test," I told him. "But the results prove nothing."

"How is that possible?" he said. "How can they not show anything?"

"Because I had a memory wipe the morning after the murder."

He grinned wolfishly and flicked his gaze towards the judge, to check that she was paying attention. She was, leaning slightly forward to catch his reply. "Are you telling me that's a coincidence?" he said. "That you just happened to have a memory wipe that morning?"

I nodded.

"The defendant will answer the question," the judge ordered.

"Yes," I said. "It's just coincidence."

"And when was the last occasion you had a memory wipe before this?" Miles Dawson demanded. He was smiling.

"Three weeks earlier."

That was true and the police had already checked. In the last five years I'd had seventy-three memory wipes. Jack Cogan made the bank double-check the figure, and when they told him it was correct, he went to the clinic himself to check it was true.

"But why?" He'd asked me.

"Because I get bored."

"And memory wipes stop you getting bored?"

"No," I said. "They stop me remembering what's bored me."

He'd sighed, offered me a coffee and muttered that he was sorry. We both knew what he meant. Jack Cogan was sorry he had to hand me over to the enforcers. He was sorry he couldn't fix the jury. He was sorry he couldn't have the machine-guns that would kill me loaded with blanks and give me an exploding vest.

It wouldn't be the first time that happened.

When Mr Dalkin kept pushing the memory wipe angle, I told him how many I'd had in the last five years and suggested he confirm this with the police. He decided to move on to other matters after that.

"What you're going to see," he told the jury, "is horrific. If I could spare you this, I would. If the man in the dock had any decency ..." The little man paused to glare at me. "He would spare you having to see this by pleading guilty. But then, if he had any decency he wouldn't have done what you're about to see."

The lights went down, the shutters were closed, and a screen on a side wall began to flicker and then clear as the clerk of the court played back the house security tape from that night. At first none of us could see anything. We were looking at the wrought-iron gates to a mansion and we were looking at them from inside. From a camera just above the front door to judge from the angle of the picture onscreen.

I hadn't seen this section of tape before. I'd seen shots of the body, close-ups of the bullet wound meant to make me confess out of horror for what I had done. But everything I'd seen began with the corridor outside the boss's study. This was outside the house itself, and at the moment the killer was a shadow outside the gate.

He limped up to the gate, slapped his hand on the lock and blinked as a flash of light read his palm and lit up his face. A hundred people, maybe 150 filled the court, and all of them turned to stare at me.

A click announced the gate had unlocked and a shuffle of gravel could be heard as the killer made his way towards the front steps. An automated machine-gun bolted to a gatepost followed him and a tiny gun satellite dropped into view, skimmed once around his head and then slipped away.

As the killer approached the front door, it clicked open for him. "Welcome," said the house AI.

The killer nodded absent-mindedly.

In the light from the hallway, his face could be seen more clearly than ever. It was my face. His hair was dirty and his face unshaven. A tatty overcoat hid a shoulder holster that became visible as he turned towards the stairs and his coat swung open slightly.

He checked his watch.

And the entire court glanced at my wrist. I wondered why the guards had given me back my Omega before letting me into court, and now I knew. The heavy black ring around the dial and the fat metal links of its strap were unmistakable.

He took the steps clumsily, obviously troubled by his bad leg. All the same, he knew where he was going and that, in itself, was significant. On the landing, he looked once into a mirror to adjust his hair slightly, brushing it out of his eyes. Then he pulled a Colt from its holster and dropped out the clip, skimmed his eye down the clip to check it was fully loaded and slipped it back into the gun, flicking the safety catch and jacking the slide.

After which, he extracted a silencer from his side pocket and began to screw it on to the muzzle of the gun. Something made him change his mind, because he shrugged, in exactly the way I shrug, unscrewed the silencer and dropped it back into his pocket. A few seconds later he was in the corridor and approaching the door.

As we watched the screen froze.

"What did you say to him?" demanded the defence attorney. "In those three minutes when he was staring death in the face. Did you mock him? Tell him he had it coming?"

"It wasn't me."

But I knew all the things I would have wanted to say.

In the old days when you talked to yourself it was inside your own head. These days …? One of me was dead, the other stood here. I had no idea who the third man was because I'd only ever had myself cloned once and look at the trouble that got me into.

At a nod from Mr Dalkin, the screen came back to life and I watched myself step out of the door and shut it behind me. I was smiling. It was a self-satisfied smile.

"Notice the complete lack of remorse," Mr Dalkin demanded, turning to the jury. Obediently, they did exactly as told. A bunch of sheep the lot of them, although I was the lamb to their slaughter.

Whatever glamour my defence attorney once had was reduced to a tired-looking flower in her buttonhole. The rest of her was a washed-out ghost in a cheap black dress. She was court appointed, which tells you all you need to know. And the entire court – including the judge – had decided that I was guilty as sin long before she even stood up to defend the indefensible.

When I smiled at her, she looked away.

I'd been wondering what defence she'd been planning to use. Insanity, drunkenness, unhappy childhood. We could have used any of those. But someone would have had to talk to me first to extract some facts and no one had bothered.

She fell back on dramatics.

"Tell me," she said, flinging out one arm. "Can a man really stand trial for murdering himself?"

The prosecutor was out of his seat and hopping up and down before my counsel had drawn breath to begin her next sentence. He needn't have bothered. The judge announced that yes, a man could.

Mr Dalkin sat down.

My counsel looked around her, noticed the number of cameras and the size of the crowd and decided she had to do more than just stand there opening and shutting her mouth. "This man," she said, pointing at me. "Used to be a gang boss. Until he was sued by his own clone. For reckless endangerment. Sued successfully."

I was sure the jury got that bit.

Because I was the man standing in the dock wearing a tatty jacket and being defended by her. And they'd buried the other me in a new silk suit and smothered his grave in enough orchids to fill a rainforest.

She made half a dozen mistakes in my life story but no one bothered to correct her, including me. The basics were there. Gang boss discovers he's due to be hit and grows clone to take the bullet instead. Clone stops off on his way to the hit, calls the police, the media and a lawyer he gets from a small ad in the back of that day's paper. The police and the lawyer could have been handled. The police, the lawyer *and* the media was one problem too many. Particularly as it was the out-of-state media my clone called.

The assassin was arrested.

I was sued by my clone. As my defence counsel said, successfully.

He took everything. The house, control of the gang, my bank accounts, my contacts book and a web of connections I'd spent most of my life building up. A dozen gangs had rolled over in the time I was boss; moving me up the ranks towards being boss of bosses. All the gangs got their autonomy back. Mostly it was the previous boss who simply stepped back into his old shoes. Sometimes his son, where an old boss had died in mysterious circumstances. Once it was the grandson; but that was the Lucianos and they were notoriously unlucky.

The map of the city went back to where it was before I came in. Jack Cogan kept me alive. That is, he let it be known he'd not been bought off or intimidated if anything happened to me and the best way to make sure nothing bad happened was keep me alive. I don't doubt I owe him. Equally, I don't doubt that at some point, he'd intended to collect.

Sighing deeply, my counsel retook her seat.

Whatever she'd been saying, it didn't look like the jury were convinced. A couple were even shaking their heads, as if they didn't know why she'd wasted her time trying to defend me in the first place. Only Jack Cogan was looking at me.

He nodded at the screen.

Then he glanced at his watch. When I shrugged, he did it again.

Maybe he had an appointment? A whore and a bottle of whisky waiting for him in some police apartment somewhere? I hoped so, one of us deserved to enjoy his afternoon and it didn't look like it was going to be me. Although there was probably someone out there sick enough to look forward to a couple of dozen machine-gun slugs to the chest. There are some sick people in this city.

And then, and this was weird, Jack Cogan stood up from his table and limped towards the restroom. Now Jack doesn't have a limp. I do, courtesy of whatever happened in those lost three days.

His leg was fine when he walked back to his seat.

It was my turn to speak. At least I assumed it was, from the way everyone was staring at me when I looked up from the dock.

"Well," said the judge. "Do you have anything to say before I pass sentence?"

By this point Jack Cogan was almost purple with ... It was hard to tell with what. I've only ever seen Jack with three expressions; angry, more angry, and angrier still, and all of these involved scowling. Now he looked almost anxious.

"Well?" the judge demanded.

"Yes," I said. "Can I see that tape again?"

You could tell from the judge's expression that he just thought I was digging myself into a deeper hole. The sneer on his face said he had no problems with me doing just that. As for Mr Dalkin, he was nodding like a toy dog before the judge even turned to him.

"No objections," he said.

As for Jack Cogan, he was looking relieved. Which told me what I needed to know. At least, it told me I was meant to know something, and that something was on this tape. So I watched the killer walk to the gate, slap his hand on the palm reader and listen to the gate click open.

"Sir," I said. "Can I see that again...?"

The judge sighed, but he let the clerk of the court rerun the sequence. As the killer tapped his hand to the plate, I tapped mine to the bulletproof glass in front of me, trying to mimic his movements.

He limped across the gravel, and he'd almost reached the front door before I realized the obvious. A glance round the court told me no one else had noticed it. So I kept silent as the front door opened itself and the killer made his way upstairs and along the corridor. I watched him drop his clip from the gun, check his watch, and decide against using a silencer.

We heard the shot and watched the man make his way back to the front door, shut it behind him and let himself through the gates, vanishing into the darkness beyond.

"And the tape stops after that?"

The prosecution lawyer looked up sharply, and the judge looked at the chief of police, who nodded reluctantly. My defence looked blank. No one had bothered to tell her. Why would they? And for the amount she was being paid, she hadn't bothered to ask.

"How long for?"

"Mr O'Brian?" The judge was staring at the police chief.

"An hour, your honour."

"And when the tape comes back on?"

Judges are not meant to ask questions like that. They're meant to leave it to the lawyers. But this was Judge Mallory's court and he'd obviously decided he was going to do what he wanted.

"Nothing, sir. It's all silent."

"How did you know?" Judge Mallory demanded. He was talking to me this time. "And what relevance does it have?"

"That's not me on film," I told him. "That's the clone."

Uproar filled the court. It was a big room and its ceiling was high and its walls were panelled in oak that muffled speech so effectively the main players were mic'd for sound. All the same, the noise of the crowd echoed off those oak walls and I watched at least a dozen sound men wince before turning down their dials.

"He's wearing his watch on the wrong wrist."

"You could have done that," shouted the prosecution lawyer. "You did do it. A cheap attempt to establish an alibi."

"And his hair's parted on the wrong side."

"Once again ..."

The judge waved the prosecution into silence. "Anything else?" he demanded, smiling sourly.

"He's limping on the wrong side."

"Run the bloody tape again," the judge told his clerk.

So the clerk did, and then the judge made me limp across the courtroom while everyone watched. He checked that my hair did indeed part on the other side, that I habitually wore my watch on a different wrist. He asked who could confirm this and Jack Cogan put up his hand.

"And the limp?"

"Recent," said the captain. "We had it examined. A cracked kneecap. It looks like a fall downstairs."

"In your opinion," the judge said. "How do you read what we've got here?"

Jack glanced towards the chief of police.

"I'm over here," the judge told Jack.

"Sorry, sir."

The judge grunted. "So," he said. "Talk me through what you think we've got. That is if your chief has no objections."

Chief O'Brian scowled.

"The clone used a photograph of the defendant to perfect his disguise. Only he dressed himself in the mirror and forgot to allow for things like the watch being on the opposite side. So when he came to faking the limp ..."

"He dragged the wrong foot."

Jack Cogan nodded. "Yes, sir. That's my reading."

"But he got through the gate and the front door and none of the weapons targeted him. That means ..."

"He shared DNA with the man in the dock."

"I know what it means," the judge said sharply. "You need to find out if there's a second clone."

There wasn't, and no one could come up with a reason why the first clone should want to commit suicide or decide to take me with him when he did. The next time I saw Jack Cogan he had gold braid on his uniform and arrived at the restaurant in a bulletproof sedan with *police* stencilled discreetly on the side. A driver so young he was barely out of diapers rushed to open the door.

"Chief," I said.

"Mr Capone ..."

We shook hands while his driver took up position beside the restaurant's front door and my bodyguards went round to protect the back. I owned the place and had chosen its staff myself. That was a while ago. All of them had since assured me, hand on heart, that they were delighted to see me back.

"The usual?" I asked Chief Cogan.

He nodded, unfolding his napkin and tucking one corner into his collar. In the three weeks since the court case his chest had lost its epic battle with his girth and resigned itself to losing. We ate squid, the little ones dropped into batter and dusted with paprika. Then we ate linguine and clams and washed it down with a bottle from my own vineyard in California. And then we ate whatever those little cakes are that are doused in rum and rolled in sugar.

"You had me scared," he said, when coffee finally arrived.

I waited for him to explain.

"Al ..." he said. "You had me scared. I thought you'd forgotten the plan and the man was about to send you down." He sat back and huffed like a horse. "Guess that's why I'm me and you're you. I don't have that kind of nerves."

He ate the sweet biscuit I passed him and reached into his pocket for a folded piece of paper. I let him reach. The chief had been searched long before he came into my presence.

"Thought you'd like to see this," he said.

It was a note from the city coroner. Three mob bosses had died by falling to their deaths from three different windows. The two goons who beat me up on arrest had saved everyone the trouble and shot themselves the afternoon the trial ended. The old chief of police was still alive, but he'd decided to leave town.

"You know where he's gone?" I asked.

Chief Cogan nodded.

"Good, then let it be known it wouldn't be good for his health to come back. Anything else?"

"Usual stuff," he said. "Clubs wanting licences, drive-bys in the ghetto and an unlicensed pimp trying to take over three blocks in the east city." He dumped his notes in front of me and listened intently as I told him what I wanted done in each case.

"You clear on that?"

"Sure thing," he said. "Completely clear."

So I glanced at my famous watch to show it was okay if he wanted to take his stomach somewhere else now. In fact, it would be good, because I had stuff to oversee. And Jack Cogan took the hint and pushed back his chair, dipping forward at the last minute to grab a chunk of bread that had been hiding in a basket under a napkin.

After stopping to butter it, he nodded apologetically and headed for the exit.

At the door, he turned back. "Can I ask you something?"

"Sure," I said. "Who knows? I might even answer."

"That night you came by my house and told me to smash your right knee. I thought you'd lost it." Chief Cogan shook his head at the memory. "But you had it planned, didn't you? Right from the start. All that getting drunk and being thrown out of bars. All those memory wipes. You were setting it up, so no one could say you'd had your memory wiped only the one time it mattered. After ... after ..."

"The other Mr Capone shot himself?"

"Yeah," said the Chief, wiping sweat from his forehead. "After that."

"Maybe," I said.

Jack Cogan grinned. He knew that was all he was going to get. The Chief let himself out and left me wondering. Maybe I had set it all up that carefully. Left myself little notes on the earlier occasions. Worked it all out down to the last memory wipe, wrong parting, misworn watch and shuffle of the wrong foot.

And maybe I hadn't. I couldn't remember.

THE HOUSE THAT GOT SHOT

Barbara Nadel

I NSPECTOR ÇETIN İKMEN cast his gaze slowly around the bloodied, shredded room before him and then, turning to his equally shocked female sergeant said, "What a mess."

"The whole house is the same, sir," Sergeant Ayşe Farsakoğlu replied. "Bullet holes everywhere."

"Do we know who she was?" İkmen said as he tipped his head in the direction of a blood-soaked body lying face downwards in front of him, its arms outstretched to each side clutching what looked like small lengths of rope.

"Not yet," Ayşe said. "Apart from this house the rest of the street has been empty for some months. This part of Haskoy is in the process of being redeveloped."

İkmen, looked down at the young woman with a cynical eye. As well as working as a police officer in Istanbul for over thirty years, he had lived in the city all his life. He'd seen a lot of metropolitan districts "redevelop" – not always for the better. Haskoy, a somewhat distant and rickety suburb on the northern shore of the Golden Horn was just the latest in a long line of "newly discovered" districts. Once home to a sizeable Jewish as well as a gypsy population, the little wooden houses of Haskoy had a certain shabby romance to them. Just not this particular one – not anymore.

"Well, whoever the victim was, she was only part of the assailants' target," İkmen said as he put his hand in his pocket and drew out a packet of cigarettes.

"What do you mean by that, sir?" Ayşe replied with a frown.

"Well, it's obvious," İkmen said. "Whoever did this was shooting the house as much as the occupant." Then after lighting up a cigarette he moved past the officer on guard at the front door of the property and went outside.

Over the course of the next few hours, many Istanbul police officials came and went from the house on the corner of Harab Cesme Sokak. Photographers, forensics and ballistics experts, ordinary officers and of course the police pathologist Dr Arto Sarkissian. The latter, who was a contemporary and old friend of Çetin İkmen, didn't take long to pronounce life extinct.

"What a thing to do to an old woman, eh?" he said when he came out to join İkmen in the street. "I've counted twelve bullet wounds so far and I'm sure I'll find more when I get her over to the lab. Insanity!"

"The whole house is shot to pieces," İkmen said as he looked across at the great wall that surrounded the once busy old synagogue opposite. "She's old, our victim. I wonder if she used to be a congregant over there."

"At the synagogue? Maybe," Arto shrugged. "The few Jews that remain around here do tend to be old. But whatever she may have been, one thing is for sure, this murder will not do the redevelopment around here much good. Especially if you add in our victim's slithery comrades and the possibility that they in turn may have more family somewhere nearby."

İkmen turned his dry thin face towards the rather more robust visage of his plump Armenian friend and said, "Slithery comrades?"

"The old woman was not the only living creature to die in that orgy of bullets." Arto paused to swallow rather nervously before he said, "She kept, indeed it would appear she was on friendly terms with, snakes."

"Snakes!"

"Two – so far," the doctor replied. "One in each hand. From the way that she fell it would seem that she was holding them up and out to both sides of her body when she was shot. I know that you hate them, but ..."

"Snakes! What kind of snakes?" İkmen asked as sweat began to visibly appear on his face.

"I don't know. I'm not a zoologist," the doctor replied. "Small, indeterminate serpents, now deceased."

"Happily."

"Depends upon your point of view," Arto continued. "Our victim, it would seem, was quite at ease handling them."

"That or she was preparing to throw them at her assailant," İkmen said.

"Either way she had the snakes for some reason and had to be comfortable with that," Arto replied. "I've told all of our people to be careful in case other slithery friends make unexpected appearances."

İkmen looked down instinctively at his own feet and then, anxiously, scanned the street to his left and right. Harab Cesme Sokak was a steep road that, as well as incorporating an elderly synagogue, also boasted a long row of wooden Ottoman houses amongst its treasures. What had been the last inhabited example of this type of property was İkmen's murder scene. It was also, he now knew, a possible source of snakes. Just the thought of snakes made him shudder. It was a phobia he had developed a long time ago. It was not one he had any interest in addressing now. He and snakes just did not meet – ever.

"Sir!"

A young man in a well-ironed blue uniform snapped to attention in front of İkmen.

"Constable Yıldız?"

"Sir, I've just been talking to the owner of the grocer's shop at the top of the hill."

Just as probably buying sweets as cigarettes, İkmen thought. Although not in reality *that* young, Hikmet Yıldız, with his baby face and his perfect shirts so obviously ironed by his sweet little headscarfed mother, was one of those boys who was taking a very long time to grow up.

"Yes? And?"

"Kemal Bey, the grocer, he says that all of this block of houses here has been bought by a foreigner," the young man said.

"Does he."

"Yes. Apparently, sir, all the occupants except the dead lady moved out when this new owner took possession about six months ago. I told him nothing, but of course like the whole district he has been watching us come and go here for hours. Kemal Bey of his own volition told me the dead lady's name. It was Ofis Hanım. Unusual name, isn't it?" he said as he looked at the Armenian for some possible explanation.

But Arto Sarkissian just shrugged. "It means nothing to me, constable," he said. "Did Kemal Bey tell you anything else about the lady?"

"Only that she almost never went out. Kemal Bey's son was in the habit of delivering groceries to Ofis Hanım's home once a week. But they never conversed. All Kemal Bey said was that a third party, another woman of the district, told him that Ofis Hanım did not, unlike her neighbours, have any intention of moving."

"I don't suppose that Kemal Bey said anything about snakes, did he?" İkmen asked.

The young officer frowned. "Snakes? No. Why?"

İkmen looked across first at Arto Sarkissian before he said, "Because constable, it would seem that Ofis Hanım had a particular liking for snakes. I do hope that your boots are securely laced."

Constable Yıldız, wide-eyed with horror looked down at his mercifully snake-free feet and said, "Allah!"

The following day brought further information about Ofis Hanım, although not as yet any actual suspect for her murder. In view of the fact that so many bullets had been found both in the old woman and in the fabric of the house, İkmen was surprised to learn that the weapon involved had been nothing more lethal or sophisticated than an ordinary shotgun.

"I would have thought that if whoever did this did so with the intention of wrecking the place, he would have saved himself a lot of effort and used a sub-machine gun," İkmen said to Ayşe Farsakoğlu as he looked down at the ballistics report on his desk.

"Depends what he was firing at, sir," the young woman replied.

"In spite of the fact that most of the residents of Haskoy are now obsessed by visions of murderous serpents, we have still only recovered the bodies of two snakes — neither of which was in the least bit dangerous."

"Non-venomous Whip Snakes," Ayşe said.

"Our assailant killed them and Ofis Hanım. Shot up the house maybe imagining more snakes ..."

"It's possible. I mean we, or rather I, had never heard of non-venomous Cypriot Whip Snakes until Forensics got back to us. Perhaps the killer thought that they were poisonous."

"Mmm." İkmen offered Ayşe a cigarette before lighting up himself and then said, "But to go to that house armed with a shotgun ... Ofis Hanım was a small, frail old lady. If somebody wanted to kill her all he needed to do was push her over."

"Assuming our assailant was a man," Ayşe said as she puffed delicately on the rough Maltepe cigarette her superior had just given her.

"Indeed."

"Yes."

"But male or female, the fact remains that someone killed Ofis Hanım and her snakes and wrecked her house," İkmen said. "Why?"

"Maybe Mr Lukash, the owner of that side of Harab Cesme Sokak will be able to tell us," Ayşe replied. "He and his wife are coming in at three."

"Maybe he will," İkmen replied. "And in the absence of any other motive, Mr Lukash's property empire or rather Ofis Hanım's effect upon it does put our Ukrainian friend in the frame. All of the other old residents moved away very quickly when he came into possession of that street."

"Redevelopment," Ayşe said sadly, "is not without its casualties."

"No." İkmen sighed. "And some of it is very good, but ... If only gangsters were not involved ..."

"We don't know that Mr Lukash is a gangster, sir. I know a lot of people here equate people like him from the former Soviet Union with gang activity, but the two don't always go together. Besides his wife is Turkish, from here in the city."

"Mmm," İkmen looked down at his desk gloomily. "I expect she's covered with gold chains and plastic surgery scars. They like their women like that."

"Who do?"

He looked up into a face that was taut with anger.

"Who likes their women 'like that'?" Ayşe reiterated. "Gangsters? Eastern Europeans? Or are gangsters always Eastern Europeans or ..."

"Ayşe, don't be angry ..."

"What, at you behaving just like the lowest, most prejudiced moron in the coffee house? Sir, you are better than that!' she said passionately. "You, of all people, know that you cannot judge anyone just on face value! You taught me that! You drummed that into my head from my very first day!"

İkmen rubbed a tired hand over his thin, middle-aged features. Ayşe was right of course. He was fifty-seven years old, he'd been in the police force for over thirty of those and he was both a father nine times over and a grandfather too. He'd seen a lot – enough to know that there was no "type" more able to commit murder than any other. Just because a man wore big chunky rings and a leather coat didn't make him a villain. Not necessarily.

"I apologise," he said, shaking his head miserably as he did so. "It's just that I've seen so much 'redevelopment' in my lifetime – so much of it to the detriment of this city and its people – in my opinion. You know what I mean, Ayşe. Great roads pushed relentlessly into once comfortable and tight-knit old communities, great big apartment buildings constructed on the foundations of once elegant Ottoman houses ..."

"Not all of those developments have been done by Eastern Europeans," Ayşe said. "In fact I think that very few properties have actually passed into foreign hands. And besides, sir, not everything that has been redeveloped has been bad. I mean some of the neighbourhoods that have undergone extensive redevelopment are actually better now than they were before. People who live there have a far superior quality of life."

"I know," İkmen nodded. "But the fact that everyone except Ofis Hanım moved out as soon as Mr Lukash bought those houses doesn't sit well with me. That area was poor. Where did all those poor people go?"

"We can find out," Ayşe said.

"Then that is what we must do," İkmen replied. "Find them. Talk to them."

"Yes, sir."

He looked up and smiled. "You know one place that has improved a lot in recent years?" he said. "Gulhane Park."

Ayşe knew the green and very pleasant park to the western side of the Topkapı Palace well. It was a nice relaxed place where she and her friends would sometimes go to walk about and eat ice-cream on sunny weekend afternoons.

"When I was young it was called Lunar Park," İkmen continued. "There was a sort of a fair there with cheap attractions; freak shows, grisly things. It was all swept away a long time ago."

"For the better by the sound of it," Ayşe said.

"Certainly for the better," İkmen replied firmly. "Most certainly."

Mrs Lukash had, it turned out, not disappointed. Or rather her appearance had not. She had been just as İkmen imagined she would – all bleached blonde hair and false breasts. Her almost totally silent Ukrainian husband had however been quite another matter. Old and world weary-looking, the most significant thing he'd said in his very halting Turkish was that he did not and had never owned Ofis Hanım's house. Unlike the other houses that Lukash had bought from the previous owner, a local man called Ali Koray, Ofis Hanım had owned her house and had not wanted to sell. İkmen took good note of this fact and, once the Lukashs had gone, instructed Ayşe to look into the Ukrainian's affairs. Ofis Hanım's house, he felt, had to have been a considerable thorn in the side of a man who was in the process, he said, of developing an elegant and valuable row of refitted houses.

Now, however, he was in the cramped and messy Haskoy office of Mr Ali Koray. On the basis that the landlord might have known Ofis Hanım and wishing to find out rather more about his dealings with Mr Lukash, İkmen now sat before a very battered desk behind which sat a short, thin man of about fifty.

"So you don't know where your old tenants went to after Mr Lukash bought your property?" İkmen asked as he lit up a cigarette.

"No, not really." Mr Koray shrugged in what appeared to be a very offhand manner. "I've seen one or two about. In local shops and … But no. I sold to Lukash, I will be honest with you, because I was sick of the whole landlord business. All the tenants ever did was complain! It was like living in a headache!"

"Mr Lukash gave you a good price?"

"Yes. He's redeveloping the houses. They look nice. I could never have afforded to do such a thing."

"Did the tenants know that their houses were going to be redeveloped for sale?" İkmen said.

Mr Koray shrugged again. It seemed to be some sort of habit. "I told them, yes. But I don't know whether they left or Lukash made them leave or what. Some were upset. But I needed the money and they, the tenants, they knew they'd have to go sometime."

"Yes," İkmen attempted a smile but then gave up. He'd met uncaring landlords before. It didn't get any easier. "I imagine Mr Lukash can't have been happy that he couldn't buy all the houses in the row."

"I don't know ..."

"Ofis Hanım ..."

"Oh, that shooting? Terrible business! Just awful!" Mr Koray shook his head violently at the thought of it.

"Did you know her?" İkmen asked.

Once again, Koray gave a shrug. "Not really."

"Strange that you owned all of the houses in the row except that belonging to Ofis Hanım. Mr Lukash's wife told us that her understanding was that you had inherited the row from your father. You have to know the area and its people well."

There was a pause, then Ali Koray smiled. "Ah," he said. "Mmm." He looked up at İkmen with his great wrinkle-wreathed eyes and said, "Look, inspector, the old woman, Ofis, she was, well, she was my father's mistress. A long time ago. He gave her that house and ..."

"I see."

"But since he died, back in 1988, my family and I, well we have left Ofis Hanım alone. My mother still lives. It is, was embarrassing."

"You or your family didn't try to buy the property back from Ofis Hanım."

"No." He shrugged. "What would have been the point?"

"To make more money from Mr Lukash."

He smiled. "I made plenty of money from Mr Lukash." He then looked, with what İkmen felt could not possibly be genuine pride, around his very small and shabby office. "I am content."

That evening, instead of going straight home to the İkmen family apartment in Sultanahmet, the inspector went to a bar in the nearby district of Cankurtaran. In the lee of one of the walls of the great Topkapı Palace the little bar where he met up with his friend Dr Arto Sarkissian was very basic, very local and almost empty. Just the way both İkmen and the doctor liked it.

Sitting at a rough table outside the bar, İkmen drank his beer with pleasure as he watched the sun begin to set behind a group of young children playing in the street. If he ignored the endless stream of traffic passing along Ishakpasa Caddesi, cutting through to the main coastal road, Kennedy Caddesi, he could almost imagine that he was back in the 1970s. The little unnamed bar they were sitting in front of certainly looked as if it came from that era, as did the innocent game of chase that the children were playing. Not a games console or item of designer clothing to be seen. Not that going back to the 1970s, even were that possible, was without its drawbacks.

"I'd far rather go back to the 1950s myself," Arto said as he drank his cola straight from the bottle. "There was so much political unrest in the 1970s. The 1950s were a lot, I suppose, simpler."

"Yes." İkmen who could also all too vividly recall the battles that had raged between the various left- and right-wing political factions in the 1970s, hadn't forgotten that either. He'd had to try to control some of it when he was a young constable. "But the trouble with the 1950s Arto, is that they were so primitive."

"Primitive?"

"Yes!" İkmen lit a cigarette. "Some parts of the city were so poor it was almost as if they were monochrome. Everyone wore the same dull clothes, in winter you choked on the fog from everyone's fires. In the summer the sewers stank."

"Oh, yes well ..."

"And on top of that we had to endure abominations just up the road here!"

Arto Sarkissian frowned.

"Lunar Park," İkmen said. "I was telling my sergeant about it earlier today. I said that since it became Gulhane Park it has improved enormously. One piece of good redevelopment if you ask me."

The doctor sat back in his chair and smiled. "Oh, I liked Lunar Park," he said. "It was quirky."

İkmen scowled. "Oh, yes," he said, "full of deformed dwarves, women with beards, cheap boring little side-shows ..."

"And of course snakes," his friend said as he watched İkmen's reaction to this out of the corner of his eye.

The policeman reddened. "Well ..."

"Even now, even when I told you about the dead snakes we found in the hands of the old woman in Haskoy, it got to you didn't it?"

İkmen let his head drop a little. "Yes."

"Çetin, the Lunar Park snake pit was just a hole filled with non-poisonous snakes. It was a silly attraction long since ..."

"It was a horrible, writhing mass of ghastly serpents with a girl in the middle of it!"

"Who you tried to 'rescue', yes," Arto said.

"I thought they were going to kill her. I put my hand down to her and they all slithered up my arm!" İkmen shuddered.

"While everyone else laughed because the girl was meant to be there. The Slave of the Snakes was part of the attraction."

"I was eleven, my mother had been dead for just six months and I couldn't look at death any more. I just couldn't!"

Arto Sarkissian, noting the tears that had welled up in his friend's eyes reached across the table and took one of his hands. "I know. I'm sorry."

He hadn't been in Lunar Park with Çetin when the Snake Pit incident occurred. Çetin's brother Halil had told him about it and, at the time, they had both had a good laugh at the strange antics of the younger boy. Until the early 1960s there had indeed been what amounted to a freak show in the shadow of the Topkapı Palace. One of the "attractions" had been a pit, lined with red silk, wherein lay a rather voluptuous woman who allowed herself to be writhed over by many non-venomous snakes. In the habit sometimes of writhing in time to the movements of her snakes, the so-called Slave of the Snakes looked to the eleven-year-old Çetin İkmen as if she was being attacked. By reaching down to her he had only been

trying to save her. But the effect that it had was to make the woman
and the man who owned the pit angry, cause the mainly gruff male
spectators to laugh and give the snakes someone new and exciting
to slither on to. It had also left Çetin with an almost hysterical fear
of snakes.

Çetin looked up at Arto and smiled. "I'm sorry," he said. "I over-
react where 'they', our legless, eyelid-less friends are concerned.
And this Haskoy investigation ..."

"What have you discovered so far?"

İkmen told him about Mr and Mrs Lukash as well as Mr Koray
and his admission with regard to Ofis Hanım and his father.

"She was Mr Koray senior's mistress according to the son," he
said.

"And he gave her that house?"

"Yes."

Arto Sarkissian shook his head slowly. "That must have been a
blow to Ali and his mother."

"Yes, although they had the other eight houses in that row, which
he sold to Mr Lukash. He said he got a good price and seemed
content."

"Yes, but the fact that your father set up his mistress in your own
district has to hurt. Many years have passed but I don't think that
one could easily accept such a scenario. Do you?"

But before İkmen could reply, his mobile phone began to ring. It
was Constable Yıldız from the crime scene at Haskoy. He had, he
said, found someone trying to break into Ofis Hanım's house.

In common with most people, he imagined, Çetin İkmen looked
down on the thief when Constable Yıldız presented her to him.

"She won't tell me her name," Yıldız said as he tipped his head
towards the tiny, ancient woman at his side.

İkmen looked steadily down into a pair of very dark, but very
clear, eyes. "Where did you find her constable?"

"In the bedroom," Yıldız replied. "Going through drawers."

"Were you?" İkmen asked the woman.

She turned her head defiantly to one side.

Suddenly angered by her stubbornness, Yıldız said to the old
woman, "Do you know who is talking to you? This is Inspector

Çetin İkmen Bey. He is the most famous police officer in this city. He can solve any crime. Any! You should not attempt to conceal anything from him, he ..."

"Yes, thank you constable," İkmen interrupted with a smile. "Your words are appreciated but ..." His voice fizzled out as his attention was caught by something that glittered at the old woman's neck. Yes, he was famous, if not rich to go with it, but he didn't always have exactly the right qualifications for every aspect of his job.

Briefly he looked at Arto Sarkissian and smiled. Then turning back to the old woman he said, "Madam I can see from the cross around your neck that you are a Christian lady. My friend here, Dr Sarkissian, is a Christian too. If you would like to speak to him ..."

"An Armenian?" the old woman growled, swatting the notion away with one hand as she did so. "Why would I want to speak to an Armenian?"

"Well ..."

She moved towards İkmen, withered hands on her thin, black-clad hips. "I am Greek," she said. "I lived here for all of my life until that bastard Koray sold us to the Russian Mafia!"

"Mr Lukash is Ukrainian ..."

"Russian, Ukrainian – what is the difference?" she said. "Koray sold us to him, he threw us out. Now I live in one stinking room in Balat. It's so damp it's like living in a hammam!"

"So why didn't you report Mr Lukash to the police?" İkmen asked, knowing full well what the answer would be.

"And have his men come and beat me to death?" the old woman said. "Famous you may be, Çetin Bey, but realistic you are obviously not!"

İkmen suppressed a smile. "Ah, but madam we are going off the point are we not?" he said. "You are, according to my constable here, a thief."

"Yes," the old woman said simply, "I am."

"What were you ..."

"Arrest me and I'll tell you everything," she said. She then held her arms out in front of her as if offering them for handcuffing. "Go on then, take me away!"

* * *

Her name, İkmen discovered was Irini Angelos. She was eighty
years old and came from one of the Istanbul Greek families, the
majority of whom had moved to Greece many years before. Irini
had stayed, she said, because, having seen pictures of Athens, she
found that it was not to her taste. "Too provincial," she declared in
that haughty Istanbul Greek way of hers. It made İkmen smile. The
old city Greeks had always been like that.

Irini Angelos was, of course, entitled to a lawyer, but she declined
the offer on the basis that what she had to say would, in time, prove
that she was only a minor villain in the story of Ofis Hanım and her
little house in Haskoy. However, she did finally agree that perhaps
if the "fat Armenian", as she dubbed Arto Sarkissian, would like to
sit in on her interview that might be for the best. Another witness to
her story, she said, would be quite a good idea. Even now late in the
evening, police headquarters beyond the door of the interview room
was still heaving with officers and those petitioning their ears and
services. In spite of this, İkmen, Yıldız and Arto Sarkissian listened
to the old woman's story with wrapt attention.

"When I heard that an elderly woman had been murdered in
Haskoy I feared that it was Ofis," she said. "But at first I didn't go
to Haskoy because for a little while I didn't really want to know the
truth. It is not always good to be right."

"You had reason to believe that Ofis Hanım was in danger?"
İkmen asked.

"As soon as Murad Koray died she was in danger. She had been
his mistress, he gave her that house."

"But Mr Koray died a long time ago, didn't he? That's what his
son told me."

"Yes. But while I still lived in Haskoy to keep my eyes on things,
that evil witch Emine, that is Murad Koray's wife, and her son
wouldn't make a move. I knew that once Ali Koray sold our houses
to that gangster, there was going to be trouble. I left, I had no
choice!"

"But then," İkmen said, "if, as I imagine you are saying Irini
Angelos, that Ofis Hanım was your friend, why didn't you go and
live with her when Mr Lukash evicted you?"

The old woman sighed impatiently. "Because that would have
exposed her secret!" she said. "And then we would both have died."

İkmen lit a cigarette and then said, "What secret?"

"About the house of serpents," Irini replied simply.

"The house of serpents?" İkmen looked across at Arto Sarkissian who just shrugged his shoulders.

"Oh, God, I suppose I'm going to have to go right back to the beginning aren't I?" Irini said, amid even more apparent irritation.

"Yes, I think so," İkmen replied. "In fact, Irini Angelos, I think that going back to the beginning of whatever tale you are telling is essential."

She asked for and was given a cigarette and a drink of water before she began.

"When I was thirty years old my husband died leaving me alone with three small children," she began. "It was the mid-1950s and most of my family, my brothers and sisters, had gone to live in Greece. So I was on my own, without money and no experience of life. I went to see my landlord, Murad Koray, who was not sympathetic in any way. I told him I would somehow get a job, but he told me that if my rent money wasn't on time as usual my children and I would have to go. I began to cry. I was not as tough then as I am now. But luckily for me my tears were not in vain. Overhearing our conversation from another room was Murad's mistress, a woman called Pembe. Murad loved her with all of his soul but once I had gone she upbraided him about his treatment of me and she suggested how I might be helped."

"How was that?" İkmen asked.

The old woman smiled. "Back in the 1950s, as well as having his houses in Haskoy, Murad Koray had an attraction in Lunar Park. Remember that? It is said that Murad's mother was a gypsy which was why he was involved with the fair. Anyway Murad owned something you may or may not remember, the Snake Pit."

Every bone, sinew and gram of flesh on İkmen's body shuddered. "Oh, yes I ..."

"You've gone a little pale," the old woman said as she squinted to look into İkmen's face. "You don't like snakes?"

İkmen first looked at Arto Sarkissian, who put a hand on his shoulder and then said, "You could say that, yes."

Irini stubbed out her cigarette before she continued. "I too was never that keen. But Pembe, now she was a different matter. She liked snakes, she lay in that pit in Lunar Park with the snakes quite happily. The only problem that she had was that sometimes she needed a break. She would, she said, feel uncomfortable and stiff from time to time down there in the pit. But Murad was a devil for money and wouldn't let her go while there were people to come and see the attraction, which was most of the time back in those days before television." She leaned forward smiling. "Pembe suggested I pay my rent by taking over from her for a couple of hours every day."

His eyes wide now, İkmen said, "And did you consent to this, this ..."

"What choice did I have?" Irini said. "I had children, I needed a roof over my head. And when poor old besotted Murad acceded to Pembe's suggestion I took my chance. Of course I was thin then as I am now and so I didn't look anywhere near as good amongst the snakes as Pembe did. The Slave of the Snakes they called her."

"Yes, I remember," İkmen said gloomily, or so the old woman felt. "But both of you at your different times were the Slave of the Snakes, surely?"

"Yes, except that I was only a poor imitation," the old woman said. "Pembe was the *real* slave of the snakes, she was their true love."

"Allah, but what a terrible way to have to make a living!"

Irini Angelos laughed. "Oh, you get used to it. You can get used to anything if you really want to – or have to. And besides, it did have its good side that awful job of mine. Pembe and I became great friends. She was so kind and beautiful and fun."

Even though he didn't often revisit that awful scarring encounter with snakes in Lunar Park, İkmen did know that the woman he had tried to rescue from the pit had been of a luscious and full-bodied type. It must have been Pembe. The real Slave of the Snakes.

"I called her Ofis, which means snake in Greek," Irini said.

Arto Sarkissian said, "Oh, but we all said what an unusual name that was! She wasn't Greek ..."

"No, she was a Turk," Irini said. "She was my very best friend. She never had children of her own but she treated my three as perfect pets. Nothing was too good for my children when Ofis was around. And she had money! Murad was besotted with her and gave her everything her heart desired."

"Including a house," İkmen said.

"Absolutely." She held one finger aloft. "But there were conditions on that that I will come to later. So Ofis and I worked at the park until eventually, as I am sure you know, it closed. Neither one of us was very young by then, but ... I did other things; cleaning people's houses, some work in shops. Murad continued to support Ofis, wouldn't let her work without him. And in spite of opposition from his wife and his son he wanted to set her up in a house near to his own. But there were problems."

"Like what?"

"Like the neighbours who knew her and what she was and who dubbed her a whore. Like the wife and son who did not want Murad to give what they felt was their property to Ofis."

"But he gave it to her anyway," İkmen said.

"Only on condition that it revert back to his family on Ofis' death," Irini said. "Ofis, bless her eyes, wanted to leave that house to my children. But she acceded to Murad's request. Not that the trouble stopped there."

İkmen frowned.

"Murad's wife as well as many of our neighbours resolved to persecute Ofis once she arrived in our street. I am not a fool and I have always and will always hear everything. If they could not prevent Ofis from living amongst them, they would frighten and cajole her so much that eventually she would have to leave or go insane. People, often those you live most closely to, can be vile," she said with what İkmen felt was a lifetime of experience just like this behind her voice.

"So," she continued, "it was then that I came up with the idea of the House of Snakes. The show at Lunar Park was over and I knew that Murad was going to have to find somewhere for the snakes. Ofis wanted to keep them which horrified Murad. But I told him to let her do it. I also told him to tell the world that she, Ofis Hanım the lover of snakes, had a whole houseful of the things, both venomous and non-venomous." She smiled.

"To keep people away," İkmen said.

"A place where snakes are loose on every surface is a place most people do not want to be," Irini said. "Even a sultan may be dissuaded in this way."

"The Mansion of Snakes!' Arto Sarkissian cried. "Of course!"

"You know," the old woman said, and then nodding her head towards İkmen she continued, "Tell him."

The doctor looked at İkmen and said, "In Bebek there is a mansion called the Mansion of the Snakes. It was built in the eighteenth century and belonged to one Mustafa Efendi. But the sultan of the day, Mahmud II was so taken with it that he told a friend of Mustafa Efendi, Said Efendi that he just had to have it. Knowing how much Mustafa Efendi loved his home and yet at the same time realizing that he could hardly deny anything to his sultan, Said Efendi made up a story to save his friend's home. He told the sultan that Mustafa Efendi was a great lover of snakes and that his wonderful home was full of them. The sultan changed his mind about the mansion immediately."

İkmen smiling said, "Allah! That's clever. I like that. So Irini Angelos you took this story and you used it to protect your friend."

"Ofis moved in and nobody came near," Irini said. "Murad would visit but people would assume that the snakes were put away when he was in residence. No other person would go inside. Not Murad's wife, his son or even me. I kept the pretence alive in order to protect her."

"So the house wasn't full of snakes?" İkmen said.

"Only the non-venomous ones from the pit and then later some small Cypriot snakes. The world apart from Murad, Ofis and myself thought differently however. Ofis, the snake woman, was left alone, which was just how she liked it. But then Murad died and Ali inherited everything. I knew he hated Ofis, she was like a needle in his pride, an insult to his mother. But he was still afraid to go anywhere near her and she was too poor and old by that time to move. I feared for her."

"Why didn't she move in with you?" İkmen asked. "If you felt that she was vulnerable?"

"Why should she?" Irini said. "The house was hers for the duration of her life and besides she liked living with her serpents. Unlike me she was truly a snake woman in every sense. And although her life was not exactly what it had been when Murad was still alive, it wasn't that bad until Ali Koray's debts began to overwhelm him. He gambles you see. Badly. He sold my house and the others with it to the foreigner just to pay off his debts."

İkmen, who had instructed Ayşe Farsakoğlu to look into Ali Koray's affairs said, "Go on."

"I moved. We all moved, we had to. But Ofis stayed and I became worried for her. Not because of the foreigner you understand. I mean he had been rough with us, the rest of the tenants, but then we knew that he would. He is a gangster. No, I worried about Ofis because of Ali Koray."

"Why was that?"

"Ali Koray, it was said, got into debt again very quickly after he sold his property. He is a lazy man who does nothing except sit in his father's office, drink tea and play cards," she said. "He doesn't work and so with no work and no property left to sell, what can he do? I'll tell you what I think," she said, "I think that he remembered Ofis' house and that it reverted back to him on her death. I'd lay money myself that he didn't mention that to you when you spoke to him."

"You think that Ali Koray killed Ofis Hanım?"

"Yes," she replied simply, "I do. I know the foreigner wanted to buy it originally but Ofis wouldn't sell. Ali Koray, however, needed to sell or do something."

"Can you prove it?" İkmen asked.

The old woman flung her withered hands to either side of her body. "Listen to what I say and see what you think," she said. "Whoever killed Ofis shot her house to pieces as you know. Whoever killed Ofis was making sure he killed all of her snakes along with her. He shot the house just to make sure that nothing was left alive in that place. There were no more than her two little snakes she'd had for years, but he wouldn't have known that. Now to my knowledge the foreigner didn't know anything about the snakes. But Ali Koray did and he was very afraid of them. Now Ofis' house is his and I think that if you ask the foreigner whether Ali Koray has approached him about it, you will find that he has indeed done so."

İkmen sat back in his chair and considered what had just been said to him. To say that Irini Angelos' story was strange was an understatement. But then Lunar Park and its inhabitants had been nothing if not strange as he well knew. There was a lot that puzzled about her story – like why Ofis Hanım preferred, actually preferred to live with snakes. There was also the problem of what Irini had been doing at Ofis' house when Constable Yıldız apprehended her.

"Irini Angelos," he said as he lit another Maltepe cigarette, "we still haven't established exactly why you were at Ofis Hanım's house this evening, have we?"

"No."

"So, you told me that you are a thief ..."

"Yes," she said, "in part that is true." Then she reached into the pocket of her long black coat and took out a brightly coloured piece of paper. "I stole this," she said as she laid it on the table in front of İkmen.

He leaned forward in order to look at what turned out to be a small poster. It showed a painting of a very voluptuous woman covered in thin, writhing snakes. Above the image was written "The Slave of the Snakes – the wonder and glory of Lunar Park". Pointing down to what to him was indeed a familiar image of a woman he said, "This is Ofis?"

"Yes," the old woman replied. "Lovely wasn't she? You know that years ago Ofis asked me if there was anything I would like from her should she die before me. I said I would like one of these old posters. A young boy who came to the park week in and week out, a poor thing with a hare lip, painted it and Murad had it copied. He made a very good likeness of Ofis."

"So if that is the case you're not stealing anything at all," İkmen said.

"I have no proof Ofis said that I could have anything," Irini replied. "And so ..."

"And so that wasn't the whole reason why you went to that house this evening was it, Irini Angelos?"

For a moment she looked as if she might be about to dissemble but then she shrugged again and said, "No, it wasn't. I wanted to tell you about Ali Koray too."

"So why didn't you just come down to the station and ask to see the inspector like everyone else?" Arto Sarkissian asked.

The answer when it came made both the Armenian and the policeman smile.

"Because I don't like the wait," Irini said with a considerable amount of tetchiness in her voice. "People wait for hours to see people like Çetin Bey. I'm far too old and tired to do that. Getting arrested really does cut out a lot of needless time-wasting."

The following day saw Ayşe Farsakoğlu confirm that Ali Koray did
indeed have gambling debts. He had also, according to Mrs Lukash,
approached her husband the previous evening about a possible sale
of Ofis Hanım's house. And although Ali Koray denied ever having
so much as set foot in Ofis Hanım's house, his shoes told another far
more sinister story.

"Condemned by snake as opposed to human blood," İkmen said
when he went to see Irini Angelos at her small room in Balat a few
days later. "It was all over his shoes."

"Ah well, you see the snakes always looked after Ofis," Irini said
as she placed a small glass of tea in front of her guest. "She was their
goddess."

İkmen smiled. "You know," he said, "that when we found Ofis
Hanım she had one snake in each hand."

The old woman nodded her head. "Like the snake goddess of
Knossos in Crete," she said. "It is a statue showing a voluptuous
bare breasted woman holding a writhing snake in each hand."

"Oh, yes," İkmen said, "I think I may have seen a picture of that
somewhere."

"It is a great treasure," Irini said. "And yet I imagine you probably
don't like it very much do you, Inspector?"

"You mean because of the snakes?" İkmen said. "You know,
Irini Angelos, there is a reason for my phobia about snakes."

"There is always a reason for everything," the old woman
replied.

He then told her about his childhood encounter with snakes –
and with their goddess Ofis Hanım. When he had finished his story
Irini said, laughing, "Oh dear, you poor little boy! You know that
people were always putting their hands into the pit, but not to save
the Slave as you did! They generally had a far more sexual motive.
Oh, you poor dear child!"

She put her thin arms around his neck and for just a few moments
she held him as he imagined she would have done her own children
many years before. In fact, he felt very sad that poor Irini had now
seemingly been deserted by her children. For her to end her days in
a damp little room in a rough part of Balat seemed both very harsh

and very sad. She was so vulnerable. He openly expressed his fears to her. Again she laughed.

"Oh, you don't want to worry about me, Inspector," she said. "I have accepted my fate. But I also have a little help now too."

Seeing the twinkle in her dark old eyes, İkmen said, "What's that Irini Angelos?"

"I've just simply followed Ofis' example," she said. "If you look behind you on top of the bookcase you will see."

İkmen was suddenly gripped by a terrible cold feeling. This was coupled with a genuine belief that turning around to see what might be on top of the bookcase was going to be a very bad idea. But he was a man and a police officer and so he couldn't just not do something so simple and seemingly safe as turn his head around. And so he did it quickly, sweating as he moved.

"Oh. Ah."

There were two little snakes on top of the bookcase. They had shiny skins and bright, inquisitive eyes. They were also loose.

"Non-venomous Cypriot Whip snakes, just the same as Ofis had," Irini said with a smile. "Everybody in the neighbourhood knows I have them and no one ever comes near or by. They are my new children. One is called Ofis and one Çetin, in honour of you and what you did for my old friend, Inspector."

"Oh, er, well," İkmen swallowed hard and then wet his bone-dry lips with his tongue. "It is I suppose quite an honour to be er, named alongside one who is a Snake Goddess ..."

"Ofis" and "Çetin" looked at him with a lot of sinuous approval.

"They like you," Irini said still smiling at the odd sight of her little pets and a man they were unconsciously tormenting. "You should make your peace with snakes you know Inspector. You, I feel, have a natural affinity with them."

"Yes, well, affinity, er ... I suppose that even snakes have their likes and dislikes, don't they?" he said.

"Absolutely," the old woman replied. "Would you like another glass of tea, Inspector?"

"Not just at the moment," İkmen said, as he tried without success to wrest his gaze from the strange eyeless stare of the serpent named especially for and after him. "I'm fine now. Absolutely ... fine."

THE OCTOPUS NEST

Sophie Hannah

IT WAS THE sight I had hoped never to see: the front door wide open, Becky, our babysitter, leaning out into the darkness as if straining to break free of the doorway's bright rectangle, her eyes wide with urgency. When she saw our car, she ran out into the drive, then stopped suddenly, arms at her sides, looking at the pavement. Wondering what she would say to us, how she would say it.

I assured myself that it couldn't be a real emergency; she'd have rung me on my mobile phone if it were. Then I realized I'd forgotten to switch it on as we left the cinema. Timothy and I had been too busy having a silly argument about the movie. He had claimed that the FBI must have known about the people in the woods, that it must have been a government relocation programme for victims of crime. I'd said there was nothing in the film to suggest that, that he'd plucked the hypothesis out of nowhere. He insisted he was right. Sometimes Timothy latches on to an idea and won't let go.

"Oh, no," he said now. I tasted a dry sourness in my mouth. Becky shivered beside the garage, her arms folded, her face so twisted with concern that I couldn't look at her. Instead, as we slowed to a halt, I focused on the huddle of bins on the corner of the pavement. They looked like a gang of squat conspirators.

Before Timothy had pulled up the handbrake, I was out of the car. "What is it?" I demanded. "Is it Alex?'

"No, he's asleep. He's absolutely fine." Becky put her hands on my arms, steadying me.

I slumped. "Thank God. Then ... has something else happened?"

"I don't know. I think so. There's something you need to have a look at." I was thinking, as Timothy and I followed her into the house, that nothing else mattered if Alex was safe. I wanted to run upstairs and kiss his sleeping face, watch the rhythmic rise and fall of his Thomas the Tank Engine duvet, but I sensed that whatever Becky wanted us to see couldn't wait. She had not said, "Don't worry, it's nothing serious." She did not think it was nothing.

All our photograph albums were on the floor in the lounge, some open, most closed. I frowned, puzzled. Becky was tidier than we were. In all the years she had babysat for us, we had not once returned to find anything out of place. Tonight, we had left one photo album, the current one, on the coffee table so that she could look at our holiday pictures. Why had she thrown it and all the others on the carpet?

She sank to the floor, crossing her legs. "Look at this." Timothy and I crouched down beside her. She pointed to a picture of Alex and me, having breakfast on our hotel terrace in Cyprus. Crumbs from our bread rolls speckled the blue tablecloth. We were both smiling, on the verge of laughing, as Timothy took the photograph.

"What about it?" I said.

"Look at the table behind you. Where the blonde woman's sitting."

I looked. She was in profile, her hair up in a pony-tail. She wore a sea-green shirt with the collar turned up. Her forehead was pink, as if she'd caught the sun the day before. Her hand, holding a small, white cup, was raised, halfway between the table and her mouth. "Do you know her?" asked Becky, looking at Timothy, then at me.

"No."

"No."

She turned a page in the album and pointed to another photograph, of Timothy reading *Ulysses* on a sun-lounger beside the pool. "Can't you read John Grisham like everybody else?" I'd said to him. "We're supposed to be on holiday." In the pool, the same blonde woman from the previous photograph stood in the shallow end, her hands behind her head. I guessed that she was adjusting her pony-tail before beginning her swim. She wore a one-piece swimsuit the colour of cantaloupe melon.

"There she is again," said Becky. "You didn't talk to her at all, in the hotel?"

"No."

"Didn't even notice her," said Timothy. "What's this about, Becky? She's just another guest. What's the big deal?"

Becky sighed heavily, as if, by answering as we had, we'd confirmed her worst fears. I began to feel frightened, as if something unimaginably dreadful was on its way. "She doesn't look familiar?"

"No," said Timothy impatiently. "Should she?"

Becky closed the album, reached for another one. This was one of our earliest, from before Alex was born. She flipped a few pages. Cambridge. Me, Timothy and my brother Richard outside King's College, sitting on a wall. I was eating an ice-cream. The day had been oven-hot. "Sitting next to you, Claire," said Becky. "It's the same person."

I looked at the blonde head. This woman – I was sure Becky was wrong, she couldn't be the same one – was turned away from the camera towards her bespectacled friend, whose face was animated. They looked as if they were having a lively conversation, utterly unaware of our presence. "You don't know that," I said. "All you can see is her hair."

"Look at the freckles on her shoulder and arm. And her earring. She's wearing the same ones in Cyprus – gold rings that are sort of square. Not very common."

I was beginning to feel a creeping unease, otherwise I might have pointed out that rings could not be square. "It's a coincidence," I said. "There must be more than one blonde woman with freckly arms who has earrings like that."

"Or it's the same woman, and she happened to be in Cambridge and then Cyprus at the same time as us," said Timothy. "Though I'm inclined to agree with Claire. It must be a different woman."

Becky was shaking her head as he spoke. "It isn't," she said. "When I looked at the Cyprus photos I noticed her. I thought I'd seen her somewhere before, but I couldn't place her. I puzzled over it for ages. Then later, when I was standing by the shelves choosing a DVD, I noticed the picture in the frame."

All our eyes slid towards it. It had been taken by a stranger so that all three of us could be in it: Timothy, Alex and me. We were in the grounds of a country house hotel just outside Edinburgh. It was the week of the book festival. Many of our trips, over the years, had revolved around Timothy buying books. Behind us were two large sash windows that belonged to the hotel's dining room. Clearly visible at one of them was the blonde woman from the Cyprus photographs. She was wearing a blue shirt this time, again with the collar turned up. Her face was small, but it was unmistakeably her. And the earrings were the same, the square hoops. I felt dizzy. This had to mean something. My brain wouldn't work quickly enough.

"That's why she looked familiar," said Becky. "I've seen that photo millions of times. I see it every time I come here. Alex is just a baby in it and … I thought it was an amazing coincidence, that the same woman was wherever you were in this picture four years ago and also in Cyprus this summer. It seemed too strange. So I got the other albums out and had a look. I couldn't believe it. In each one, she's in at least nine or ten of the photos. See for yourselves."

"Jesus." Timothy rubbed the sides of his face. When he removed his hands there were white spots on his skin. I began to turn the pages of another album. I saw the woman, once, twice. In Siena, at a taverna. Walking behind me in a street market in Morocco. Three times. She stood beside Timothy outside the Tate Modern, again with her short-sighted, frizzy-haired friend.

"But … this *can't* be a coincidence!" I said, expecting to have to convince Becky, or Timothy. Nobody disagreed with me. I felt sharp, piercing fear.

"What does it mean?" Timothy asked Becky. He rarely asked anybody for advice or an opinion, let alone a nineteen-year-old babysitter. His lips were thin and pale. "She must be following us. She's some sort of stalker. But … for nearly ten years! I don't like this at all. I'm ringing the police."

"They'll think you're crazy," I said, desperate to behave as if there was no need to take the matter seriously. "She's never done us any harm, never even drawn herself to our attention. She's not looking at us in any of the photos. She doesn't seem aware of our presence at all."

"Of course not!' Timothy snorted dismissively. "She'd try to look as innocent as possible as soon as she saw a camera coming out, wouldn't she? That's why we've not spotted her until now."

I turned to Becky. "Is every album the same?" I didn't have the courage to look.

She nodded. "Some, she's on nearly every page."

"Oh, God! What should we do? Why would someone we don't know want to follow us?'

"Timothy's right, you've got to tell the police," said Becky. "If something happens …"

"Christ!' Timothy marched up and down the lounge, shaking his head. "I don't need this," he said. "I really don't."

"Tim, are you *sure* you don't know her?" An affair, I was thinking. A jealous ex-girlfriend. I would almost have preferred that; at least there would have been a rational explanation, a clarifying link.

"Of course I'm sure!"

"Do you want me to stay?" asked Becky. What she meant was that she was keen to leave.

"She's not some woman I've slept with and discarded, if that's what you're thinking," Timothy snapped.

"You have to tell me if she is," I said. Neither of us cared that Becky was listening.

"Have I ever done anything like that?"

"Not that I know of."

"Claire, I swear on Alex's life: not only have I never slept with this woman, I've never even *spoken* to her." I believed him. Alex was sacred.

"I should go," said Becky. Our eyes begged her not to. She was a symbol of safety, the only one of the three of us who was not dogged by a stalker. We needed her normality to sustain us. I had never been so frightened in my life.

"I'll drive you," said Timothy.

"No!" I didn't want to be left alone with the photo albums. "Would you mind if we phoned you a cab?'

"Of course not."

"I said I'll drive her!"

"But I don't want you to go out!"

"Well, I want to get out. I need some air."

"What about me?"

"I'll be back in half an hour, Claire. Why don't you ring the police while I'm gone? Then we can talk to them when I get back."

"I can't." I began to cry. "You'll have to do it. I'm in no fit state."

He frowned. "All right. Look, don't worry. I won't be long."

Once he and Becky had left, I went upstairs and looked in on Alex. He was sleeping soundly, his hair covering his face. Despite my pleas, I found that I felt less afraid once Timothy had gone. I thought of one of our honeymoon photographs, one that could not possibly contain the blonde woman: Timothy in our en-suite bathroom at the Grand Hotel Tremezzo. He insisted on lavish holidays. Perhaps that was why we were always short of money. That and his book-collecting. In the picture, there is a mirror in front of him and one behind, reflecting an endless row of Timothies, each smaller than the last, each holding the camera to his eye, pressing the button. They dotted an invisible line that led from the foreground to the background. I knew why the picture had sprung to mind. It was the principle of magnification: seeing my own panic reflected in Timothy's eyes had added to my paranoia.

I went downstairs and began to look through all our photographs. This time I was methodical, unsuperstitious. I found the blonde woman with the upturned collars and the square hoop earrings again and again: on a boat, in a park, walking along a canal tow-path. Sometimes she was right behind us, sometimes nearby. Who was she? Why was she following us? I had no way of knowing. Neither would the police, not with only our photo albums to work from. Of course, they could track her down if they wanted to – they could appeal on television and somebody who knew her would be bound to come forward – but the idea of them doing such a thing was laughable. She had committed no crime. Stalking was against the law, I was fairly certain of that, but the direct accosting of one's prey was surely a pre-requisite. What, I wondered, would the police have to say about a stalker so unobtrusive that, were it not for Becky's meticulous eye, we might never have become aware of her? Her presence in our lives, unnoticed for all these years, felt more ghostly than criminal. I was suddenly very aware of myself, my thoughts and my actions, and looked around the room, up at the ceiling, half-expecting to find someone watching me.

I concentrated on the woman's face, trying to see a character or a motive behind it. She was either beautiful in a classical, well-proportioned way, or very bland-looking; I couldn't decide. I found it unsettling that, however hard I stared, I couldn't commit her face to memory; it was almost impossible to take in as a coherent whole. I looked at her features one by one and judged each of them regular, flawless, but together they made no lasting impression. I'd had this feeling before, usually about famous people: Sharon Stone, the late Jill Dando. They too had faces one could study in detail and still not know what they looked like.

In one photograph our blonde ghost was touching me. Her shoulder was pressed against mine in a crowded wine bar. Hay-on-Wye? No, Cheltenham. Another of Timothy's literary holidays. I was holding a tall cocktail, dark red and fizzy, like carbonated blood. I pointed to it, an apprehensive expression on my face. Timothy had labelled the photo "Am I really expected to drink this?" He assigned titles to all our pictures; his parents did it too. It was a Treharne family tradition.

The blonde woman had a book in her hand. It was on the edge of the picture, some of it missing. I screwed up my eyes to read the title. "The Octopus" – that was all that was visible. My heart jolted. "The Octopus Nest," I whispered. It was a novel I hadn't thought about for years. Timothy used to own it, probably still did. He'd tried to persuade me to read it, but I gave up. Sometimes it is apparent from the first page of a book that nothing is going to happen. A Timothy book.

I slammed the photo album shut and rang his mobile phone. It was switched off. I paced up and down the lounge, desperate to talk to somebody. I nearly rang Becky's mobile, but I didn't want her to make excuses when I asked her to babysit in the future. If I started to talk to her about obscure novels with strange titles, she'd think I was insane. Timothy had said he'd be back within half an hour. This could wait half an hour.

I forced myself to calm down, sit down, and think about how I was feeling. Was this surge of adrenaline justified? Seven years ago, the blonde woman had been in a wine bar, holding a novel that Timothy once raved about. It was a link, but then, I reminded myself, I did not need to look for a link. A woman we didn't know was in the backgrounds of dozens of our photographs; wasn't that connection enough?

Still, I was too agitated to do nothing. I searched all the book-shelves in our house. There was no copy of "The Octopus Nest". I tried Timothy's phone again, swearing under my breath, furious with impatience. How could he not have remembered to switch it on? He knew what a state I was in. Irrationally, I took my not being able to speak to him while he was out as an omen that it would take him much longer to return, that he might never come back. I needed to occupy myself, to drive away these groundless fears. That was when I thought of the internet.

I rushed to Timothy's study and switched on the computer, certain that Amazon, the online bookshop, would have "The Octopus Nest" listed. I wanted to know who it was by, what it was about. It might lead nowhere, but it was the only thing I had to go on. In none of the other photographs did our ghost have any identifiable accessories.

"The Octopus Nest" was available from Amazon, but not easily. Delivery might take up to six weeks, I read. This didn't matter to me. I didn't necessarily want a copy of the book. I just wanted to know more about it. The author was a K.V. Hammond. I clicked on the small picture of the novel's cover, a white background with one black tentacle running diagonally across it.

The book was number 756,234 in the Amazon chart. If Timothy and the blonde woman hadn't bought it all those years ago it would probably have been number 987,659, I thought, half-smiling. I was surprised I was able to joke, even inside my head. Somehow our ghost didn't seem quite so threatening, now that I had seen her holding a book that Timothy had once thought highly of, though I didn't understand why this should be the case. The optimist in me reasoned that she hadn't done us any harm in nearly a decade. Maybe she never would.

No description of the novel was offered. I had bought books from Amazon before, and there was usually a short synopsis. I clicked on the "Google" button and typed "K.V. Hammond" into the search box. The first result was the author's own website. Perhaps here I would discover more about "The Octopus Nest". I drummed my fingers on the desk, impatient for the home page to load.

A photograph began to appear on the screen, from the top down. A blue sky, a tree, a straw hat. Blonde hair. Gold, square hoop earrings. I gasped, pushing my chair away from the computer. It was her. A letter welcomed me to her site, was signed "Kathryn". Only minutes ago it had seemed out of the question that we would ever know her identity. Now I knew it beyond the slightest doubt.

I tried Timothy's mobile again, with no luck. "Please, please," I muttered, even though no one could hear me, even though a mechanical voice was already telling me to try again later. I felt as if Timothy had let me down badly, deserted me, though I knew he was probably too preoccupied to think about a detail such as whether his phone was on or off. He would be back soon, in any case.

Fear and excitement rioted in my mind, my whole body. I had to do something. Now that I was in possession of certain knowledge, calling the police did not seem such an absurd proposition. I didn't want to go into the whole story on the phone, so I said only that I wanted to report a stalker, that I knew who it was, that I had evidence. The woman I spoke to said she would send an officer to interview me as soon as possible.

Willing the computer to work faster, I moved from one section of Kathryn Hammond's website to another. She had published no books since "The Octopus Nest", but her newsletter said she was working on her next novel, the story of fifty years in the life of a ventriloquist's dummy, passed from one owner to another. Another Timothy book, I thought. The newsletter also informed fans (it seemed to take for granted that everyone who visited the site would be a fan) that Kathryn and her sister – the frizzy-haired woman, I assumed – were going on holiday to Sicily early next year.

For a second, I felt as if my blood had stopped moving around my body. We were going to Sicily too. In February. Kathryn Hammond and her sister were staying at the Hotel Bernabei. I had a horrible suspicion we were too. My terror returned, twice as strong as before. This was as real, as inexplicable as ever.

I rummaged through the drawers of the desk, thinking I might find a letter from Timothy's travel agent or a booking confirmation. There was nothing. I flew round the house like a trapped fly, opening drawers and pulling books off shelves. I couldn't understand it; there had to be some paperwork somewhere relating to our holiday.

I was crying, about to give up, when it occurred to me that Timothy kept a filing cabinet in the garage. "Why not?" he'd said.

"The thing's hideous and the house is too cluttered." I rarely went into the garage. It was dusty and messy, and smelled of damp, turpentine and cigarettes; since Alex was born, Timothy hadn't smoked in the house.

I had no choice but to go in there now. If the police arrived before Timothy got back, I wanted to be able to show them our holiday details and Kathryn Hammond's website. What more proof could they ask for? Even as I thought this, I was aware that it was not illegal for a novelist to go on holiday to Sicily. Terror gripped me as it occurred to me for the first time that perhaps we would never be able to stop her following us, never force her to admit to her behaviour or explain it. I didn't think I'd be able to stand that.

The cabinet wasn't locked. I pulled open the first drawer. A strangled moan escaped from my mouth as I stared, stunned, at what was inside. Books. Dozens of them. I saw the title "The Octopus Nest". Then, underneath it, "Le Nid du Poulpe". The same title, but in French. Numb with dread, I pulled the books out one by one, dropping them on the floor. I saw Hebrew letters, Japanese characters, a picture of a purple octopus, a green one, a raised black one that looked as if it might spin off the cover and hit me in the chest.

Kathryn Hammond's novel had been translated into many languages. I pulled open the next drawer down. More copies of "The Octopus Nest" – hardbacks, paperbacks, hardback-sized paperbacks, book club editions.

"Fifty-two in total."

I screamed, nearly lost my balance. Timothy stood in the doorway of the garage. "Timothy, what ...?"

He stared blankly at me for several seconds, saying nothing. I backed away from him until I was against the wall. I felt its rough texture through my blouse, scratching my skin.

"I was telling the truth," he said. "I've never spoken to her. I don't know her at all. She doesn't even know I exist."

The doorbell rang. The police. I'd said only that I wanted to report a stalker, that I knew who it was, that I had evidence.

WALKING THE DOG

Peter Robinson

THE DOG-DAYS CAME to the Beaches in August and the boardwalk was crowded. Even the dog-owners began to complain about the heat. Laura Francis felt as if she had been locked in the bathroom after a hot shower as she walked Big Ears down to the fenced-off compound on Kew Beach, where he could run free. She said hello to the few people she had seen there before while Big Ears sniffed the shrubbery and moved on to play with a Labrador retriever.

"They seem to like each other," said a voice beside her.

Laura turned and saw a man she thought she recognized, but not from the Beaches. She couldn't say where. He was handsome in a chiselled, matinee-idol sort of way, and the tight jeans and white T-shirt did justice to his well-toned muscles and tapered waist. Where did she know him from?

"You must excuse Big Ears," she said. "He's such a womanizer."

"It's nothing Rain can't handle."

"Rain? That's an unusual name for a dog."

He shrugged. "Is it? It was raining the day I picked her up from the humane society. Raining cats and dogs. Anyway, you're one to talk, naming dogs after English children's book characters."

Laura felt herself flush. "My mother used to read them to me when I was little. I grew up in England."

"I can tell by the accent. I'm Ray, by the way. Ray Lanagan."

"Laura Francis. Pleased to meet you."

"Laura? After the movie?"

"After my grandmother."

"Pity. You do look a bit like Gene Tierney, you know."

Laura tried to remember whether Gene Tierney was the one with overbite or the large breasts. As she had both, herself, she supposed it didn't really matter. She blushed again. "Thank you."

They stood in an awkward, edgy silence while the dogs played on around them. Then, all of a sudden, Laura remembered where she had seen Ray before. Jesus, of course, it was *him*, the guy from the TV commercial, the one for some sort of male aftershave or deodorant where he was stripped to the waist, wearing tight jeans like today. She'd seen it on a photo in a magazine, too. She had even fantasized about him, imagined it was him there in bed with her instead of Lloyd grunting away on top as if he were running a marathon.

"What is it?" Ray asked.

She brushed a strand of hair from her hot cheek. "Nothing. I just remembered where I've seen you before. You're an actor, aren't you?"

"For my sins."

"Are you here to make a movie?" It wasn't as stupid a question as it might have sounded. The studios were just down the road, and Toronto had almost as big a reputation for being Hollywood North as Vancouver. Laura ought to know; Lloyd ran a post-production company, and he was always telling her so.

"No," Ray said. "I'm resting, as we say in the business."

"Oh."

"I've got a couple of things lined up," he went on. "Commercials, a small part in a new CBC legal drama. That sort of thing. And whatever comes my way by chance."

"It sounds exciting."

"Not really. It's a living. To be honest, it's mostly a matter of hanging around while the techies get the sound and light right. But what about you? What do you do?"

"Me?" she pointed her thumb at her chest. "Nothing. I mean, I'm just a housewife." It was true, she supposed: "housewife" was about the only way she could describe herself. But she wasn't even that. Phaedra did all of the housework and Paula handled the garden. Laura had even hired a company to come in and clear the snow from the steps and the driveway in winter. So what did she do with her time, apart from shop and walk Big Ears? Sometimes she made dinner, but more often than not she made reservations. There were so many good restaurants on her stretch of Queen Street East – anything you wanted, Japanese, Greek, Indian, Chinese, Italian – that it seemed a shame to waste them.

The hazy bright sun beat down mercilessly and the water looked like a ruffled blue bedsheet beyond the wire fence. Laura was feeling embarrassed now that she had openly declared her uselessness.

"Would you like to go for a drink?" Ray asked. "I'm not coming on to you or anything, but it *is* a real scorcher."

Laura felt her heart give a little flutter and, if she were honest with herself, a pleasurable warmth spread through her lower belly.

"OK. Yes, I mean, sure," she said. "Look, it's a bit of a hassle going to a café or a pub with the dogs, right? Why don't you come up to the house? It's not far. Silver Birch. There's cold beer in the fridge and I left the air conditioning on."

Ray looked at her. He certainly had beautiful eyes, she thought, and they seemed especially steely blue in this kind of light. Blue eyes and black hair, a devastating combination. "Sure," he said. "If it's OK. Lead on."

They put Big Ears and Rain on leashes and walked up to Queen Street, which was crowded with tourists and locals pulling kids in bright-coloured carts, all OshKosh by Gosh and Birkenstocks. People browsed in shop windows, sat outdoors at Starbucks in shorts drinking their frappucinos and reading the *Globe and Mail*, and there was a queue outside the ice-cream shop. The traffic was moving at a crawl, but you could smell the coconut sunblock over the gas fumes.

Laura's large detached house stood at the top of a long flight of steps sheltered by overhanging shrubbery, and once they were off the street, nobody could see them. Not that it mattered, Laura told herself. It was all innocent enough.

It was a relief to get inside, and even the dogs seemed to collapse in a panting heap and enjoy the cool air.

"Nice place," said Ray, looking around the modern kitchen, with its central island and pots and pans hanging from hooks overhead.

Laura opened the fridge. "Beer? Coke? Juice?"

"I'll have a beer, if that's OK," said Ray.

"Beck's all right?"

"Perfect."

She opened Ray a Beck's and poured herself a glass of orange juice, the kind with the extra pulp. Her heart was beating fast. Perhaps it was the heat, the walk home? She watched Ray drink his beer from the bottle, his Adam's apple bobbing. When she took a sip of juice, a little dribbled out of her mouth and down her chin. Before she could make a move to get a napkin and wipe it off Ray had moved forward just as far as it took, bent forward, put his tongue on the curve under her lower lip and licked it off.

She felt his heat and shivered. "Ray, I'm not sure ... I mean, I don't think we should ... I ..."

The first kiss nearly drew blood. The second one did. Laura fell back against the fridge and felt the Mickey Mouse fridge-magnet that held the weekly to-do list digging into her shoulder. She experienced a moment of panic as Ray ripped open her Holt Renfrew blouse. What did she think she was doing, inviting a strange man into her home like this? He could be a serial killer or something. But fear quickly turned to pleasure when his mouth found her nipple. She moaned and pulled him against her and spread her legs apart. His hand moved up under her long, loose skirt, caressing the bare flesh of her thighs and rubbing between her legs.

Laura had never been so wet in her life, had never wanted it so much, and she didn't want to wait. Somehow, she manoeuvred them towards the dining-room table and tugged at his belt and zip as they stumbled backwards. She felt the edge of the table bump against the backs of her thighs and eased herself up on it, sweeping a couple of Waterford crystal glasses to the floor as she did so. The dogs barked. Ray was good and hard and he pulled her panties aside as she guided him smoothly inside her.

"Fuck me, Ray," she breathed. "Fuck me."

And he fucked her. He fucked her until she hammered with her fists on the table and a Royal Doulton cup and saucer joined the broken crystal on the floor. The dogs howled. Laura howled. When she sensed that Ray was about to come she pulled him closer and said, "Bite me."

And he bit her.

"I really think we should have that dog put down," said Lloyd after dinner that evening. "For God's sake, biting you like that. It could have given you rabies or something."

"Don't be silly. Big Ears isn't in the least bit rabid. It was an accident, that's all. I was just a bit too rough with him."

"It's the thin end of the wedge. Next time it'll be the postman, or some kid in the street. Think what'll happen then."

"We are not having Big Ears put down, and that's final. I'll be more careful in future."

"You just make sure you are." Lloyd paused, then asked, "Have you thought any more about that other matter I mentioned?"

Oh God, Laura thought, not again. Lloyd hated their house, hated the Beaches, hated Toronto. He wanted to sell up and move to Vancouver, live in Kitsilano or out on Point Grey. No matter that it rained there 364 days out of every year and all you could get to eat was sushi and alfalfa sprouts. Laura didn't want to live in Lotus Land. She was happy where she was. Even happier since that afternoon.

As Lloyd droned on and on, she drifted into pleasant reminis-cences of Ray's body on hers, the hard, sharp edges of his white teeth as they closed on the soft part of her neck. They had done it again, up in the bed this time, her and Lloyd's bed. It was slower, less urgent, more gentle, but if anything, it was even better. He was a good kisser, and the tip of his tongue found a sensitive spot at the front between her upper lip and gum that connected directly with her loins. She could still remember the warm ripples and floods of pleasure, like breaking waves running up through her loins and her belly, and she could feel a pleasant soreness between her legs even now, as she sat listening to Lloyd outline the advantages of moving the post-production company to Vancouver. Plenty of work there, he said. Hollywood connections. But if they moved, she would never see Ray again. It seemed more imperative than ever now to put a stop to it. She had to do *something*.

"I really don't want to talk about it right now, darling," she said.

"You never do."

"You know what I think of Vancouver."

"It doesn't rain that much."

"It's not just that. It's … Oh, can't we just leave it be?"

Lloyd put his hand up. "All right," he said. "All right. Subject closed for tonight." He got up and walked over to the drinks cabinet. "I feel like a cognac," he said.

Laura had that sinking feeling. She knew what was coming.

"Where is it?" Lloyd asked.

"Where is what, darling?"

"My snifter, my favourite brandy snifter. The one my father bought me."

"Oh, that," said Laura, remembering the shattered glass she had swept up from the hardwood floor. "I meant to tell you. I'm sorry, but there was an accident. The dishwasher."

Lloyd turned to look at her in disbelief. "You put my favourite crystal snifter in the *dishwasher*?"

"I know. I'm sorry. I was in a hurry."

Lloyd frowned. "A hurry? You? What do you ever have to be in a hurry about? Walking the bloody dog?"

Laura tried to laugh it off. "If only you knew half the things I had to do around the place, darling."

Lloyd continued to look at her. His eyes narrowed. "Had quite a day, haven't you?" he said.

Laura sighed. "I suppose so. It's just been one of those days."

"This'll have to do then," he said, pouring a generous helping of Rémy into a different crystal snifter.

It was just as good as the one she had broken, Laura thought. In fact, it was probably more expensive. But it wasn't *his*. It wasn't the one his bloody miserable old bastard of a father, God rot his soul, had bought him.

Lloyd sat down and sipped his cognac thoughtfully. The next time he spoke, Laura could see the way he was looking at her over the top of his glass. *That* look. "How about an early night?" he said.

Laura's stomach lurched. She put her hand to her forehead. "Oh, not tonight, darling," she said. "I'm sorry, but I have a terrible headache."

She didn't see Ray for nearly a week and she was going crazy with fear that he'd left town, maybe gone to Hollywood to be a star, that he'd just used her and discarded her the way men did. After all, they had only been together the once, and he hadn't told her he loved her or anything. All they had done was fuck. They didn't really *know* one another at all. They hadn't even exchanged phone numbers. She just had this absurd feeling that they were meant for each other, that it was *destiny*. A foolish fantasy, no doubt, but one that hurt like a knife jabbing into her heart every day she didn't see him.

Then one day, there he was at the beach again, as if he'd never been away. The dogs greeted each other like long lost friends while Laura tried to play it cool as lust burned through her like a forest fire.

"Hello, stranger," she said.

"I'm sorry," Ray said. "A job came up. Shampoo commercial. On the spot decision. Yes or no. I had to work on location in Niagara Falls. You're not mad at me, are you? It's not as if I could phone you and let you know or anything."

"Niagara Falls? How romantic."

"The bride's second great disappointment."

"What?"

"Oscar Wilde. What he said."

Laura giggled and put her hand to her mouth. "Oh, I see."

"I'd love to have taken you with me. I know it wouldn't have been a disappointment for us. I missed you."

Laura blushed. "I missed you, too. Want a cold beer?"

"Look," said Ray, "why don't we go to my place. It's only a top floor flat, but it's air-conditioned, and ..."

"And what?"

"Well, you know, the neighbours ..."

Laura couldn't tell him this, but she had got such an incredible rush out of doing it with Ray in *her own bed* that she couldn't stand the thought of going to his flat, no matter how nice and cool it was. Though she had changed and washed the sheets, she had fancied she could still smell him when she lay her head down for the night, and now she wanted her bed to absorb even more of him.

"Don't worry about the neighbours," she said. "They're all out during the day, anyway, and the nannies have to know how to be discreet if they want to stay in this country."

"Are you sure?"

"Perfectly."

And so it went on. Once, twice, sometimes three times a week, they went back to Laura's big house on Silver Birch. Sometimes they couldn't wait to get upstairs, so they did it on the dining-room table like the first time, but mostly they did it in the king-size bed, becoming more and more adventurous and experimental as they got to know one another's bodies and pleasure zones. Laura found a little pain quite stimulating sometimes, and Ray didn't mind obliging. They sampled all the positions and all the orifices, and when they had exhausted them, they started all over again. They talked, too, a lot, between bouts. Laura told Ray how unhappy she was with her marriage, and Ray told her how his ex-wife had ditched him for his accountant because his career wasn't exactly going in the same direction as Russell Crowe's, as his bank account made abundantly clear.

Then, one day when they had caught their breath after a particularly challenging position that wasn't even in the *Kama Sutra*, Laura said, "Lloyd wants to sell up and move to Vancouver. He won't stop going on about it. And he never gives up until he gets his way."

Ray turned over and leaned on his elbow. "You can't leave," he said.

It was as simple as that. *You can't leave.* She looked at him and beamed. "I know," she said. "You're right. I can't."

"Divorce him. Live with me. I want us to have a normal life, go places together like everyone else, go out for dinner, go to the movies, take vacations to Florida every winter."

It was everything she wanted, too. "Do you mean it, Ray?"

"Of course I mean it." He paused. "I love you, Laura."

Tears came to her eyes. "Oh my God." She kissed him and told him she loved him, too, and a few minutes later they resumed the conversation. "I can't divorce him," Laura said.

"Why on earth not?"

"For one thing, he's a Catholic. He's not practicing or anything, but he doesn't believe in divorce." Or more importantly, Laura thought, his poor dead father, who *was* devout in a bugger-the-choirboys sort of way, didn't believe in it.

"And ...?"

"Well, there's the money."

"What money?"

"It's mine. I mean, I inherited it from my father. He was an inventor and he came up with one of those simple little additives that keep things fresh for years. Anyway, he made a lot of money, and I was his only child, so I got it all. I've been financing Lloyd's post-production career from the beginning, before it started doing as well as it is now. If we divorced, with these no fault laws we've got today, he'd get half of everything. That's not fair. It should be all mine by rights."

"I don't care about the money. It's you I want."

She touched his cheek. "That's sweet, Ray, and I wouldn't care if we didn't have two cents between us as long as we were together, honest I wouldn't. But it doesn't have to be that way. The money's there. And everything I have is yours."

"So what's the alternative?"

She put her hand on his chest and ran it over the soft hair down to his flat stomach and beyond, kissed the eagle tattoo on his arm. She remembered it from the TV commercial and the magazine, had thought it was sexy even then. The dogs stirred for a moment at the side of the bed, then went back to sleep. They'd had a lot of exercise that morning. "There's the house, too," Laura went on, "and Lloyd's life insurance. Double indemnity, or something like that. I don't really understand these things, but it's really quite a lot of money. Enough to live on for a long time, maybe somewhere in the Caribbean? Or Europe. I've always wanted to live in Paris."

"What are you saying?"

Laura paused. "What if Lloyd had an accident? No, hear me out. Just suppose he had an accident. We'd have everything then. The house, the insurance, the business, my inheritance. It would all be ours. And we could be together for always."

"An accident? You're talking about—"

She put her finger to his lips. "No, darling, don't say it. Don't say the word?"

But whether he said it or not, she knew, as she knew he did, what the word was, and it sent a delightful shiver up her spine. The word was *murder*. *Murder* was what they were talking about. After a while, Ray said, "I might know someone. I did an unusual job once, impersonated a police officer in Montreal, a favour for someone who knew someone whose son was in trouble. You don't need to know who he is, but he's connected. He was very pleased with the way things worked out and he said if ever I needed anything ..."

"Well, there you are, then," said Laura, sitting up. "Do you know how to find this man? Do you think he could arrange something?"

Ray took her left nipple between his thumb and forefinger and squeezed. "I think so," he said. "But it won't be easy. I'd have to go to Montreal. Make contact. Right at the moment, though, something a bit more urgent has come up."

Laura saw what he meant. She slid down and took him in her mouth.

Time moved on, as it does. The days cooled, but Ray and Laura's passion didn't. Just after Thanksgiving, the weather forecasters predicted a big drop in temperature and encouraged Torontonians to wrap up warm.

Laura and Ray didn't need any warm wrapping. The rose-patterned duvet lay on the floor at the bottom of the bed, and they were bathed in sweat, panting, as Laura straddled Ray and worked them both to a shuddering climax. Instead of rolling off him when they had finished, this time Laura stayed on top and leaned forward, her hard nipples brushing his chest. They hadn't seen each other for a week because Ray had finally met his contact in Montreal.

"Did you talk to that man you know?" she asked after she had caught her breath.

Ray linked his hands behind his head. "Yes," he said.

"Does he know what ... I mean, what we want him to do?"

"He knows."

"To take his time and wait for absolutely the right opportunity?"

"He won't do it himself. The man he'll put on it is a professional, honey. He knows."

"And will he do it when the right time comes? It *must* seem like an accident."

"He'll do it. Don't worry."

"You know," Laura said, "you can stay all night if you want. Lloyd's away in Vancouver. Probably looking for property."

"Are you sure?"

"He won't be back till Thursday. We could just stay in bed the whole week." Laura shivered.

"Cold, honey?"

"A little. Winter's coming. Can't you feel it?"

Ray smiled. "I can definitely feel something," he said.

Laura gave him a playful tap on the chest then gasped as he thrust himself inside her again. So much energy. This time he didn't let her stay in control, he grabbed her shoulders and pushed her over on her back, in the good old missionary position, and pounded away so hard Laura thought the bed was going to break. This time, as Laura reached the edges of her orgasm, she thought that if she died at this moment, in this state of bliss, she would be happy forever. Then the furnace came on, the house exploded, and Laura got her wish.

"TWO DOGS PERISH IN BEACHES GAS EXPLOSION," Lloyd Francis read in the *Toronto Star* the following morning. "HOUSE-OWNERS ALSO DIE IN TRAGIC ACCIDENT." Well, they got that wrong on two counts, thought Lloyd. He was sitting over a cappuccino in his shirt-sleeves at an outdoor café on Robson Street, in Vancouver. While the cold snap had descended on the east with a vengeance, the west coast was enjoying record temperatures for the time of year. And no rain.

Lloyd happened to know that only one of the house's owners had died in the explosion, and that it hadn't been an accident. Far from it. Lloyd had planned the whole thing very carefully from the moment he had found out that his wife was enjoying a *grande passion* with an out-of-work actor. That hadn't been difficult. For a start, she had begun washing the bedsheets and pillow cases almost every day, though she usually left the laundry to Phaedra. Despite her caution, he had once seen blood on one of the sheets. Laura had also been unusually reluctant to have sex with him, and on the few occasions he had persuaded her to comply, it had been obvious to him that her thoughts were elsewhere and that, in the crude vernacular, he had been getting sloppy seconds.

Not that Laura hadn't been careful and cleaned herself up well. Lord only knew, she had probably stood under the shower for hours. But he could still tell. There was another man's smell about her. And then, of course, he had simply lain in wait one day when she thought he was at the studio and seen them returning together from the beach. After that, it hadn't been hard to find out where the man, Ray Lanagan, lived, and what he did, or didn't do. Lloyd was quite pleased with his detective abilities. Maybe he was in the wrong profession. He had shown himself to be pretty good at murder, too, and he was certain that no one would be able to prove that the explosion in which his wife and her lover had died had been anything but a tragic accident. Things like that happened every year in Toronto when the heat came on. A slow leak, building over time, a furnace not serviced for years, a stray spark or a naked flame, and BANG!

Lloyd sipped his cappuccino and took a bite of his croissant.

"You seem preoccupied, darling," said Anne-Marie, looking lovely in a low cut white top and a short denim skirt opposite him, her dark hair framing the delicate oval face, those tantalizing ruby lips. "What is it?"

"Nothing," said Lloyd. "Nothing at all. But I think I might have to fly back to Toronto today. Just for a short while."

Anne-Marie's face dropped. She was so expressive, showing joy or disappointment, pleasure or pain, without guile. This time it was clearly disappointment. "Oh, must you?"

"I'm afraid I must," he said, taking her hand and caressing it. "I have some important business to take care of. But I promise you I'll be back as soon as I can."

"And we'll live in that house we saw near Spanish Beach?"

"I'll put in an offer before I leave," Lloyd said. "It'll have to be in your name, though."

She wrinkled her nose. "I know. Tax reasons."

"Exactly. Good girl." It was only a little white lie, Lloyd told himself. But it wouldn't look good if he bought a new house in a far away city the day after his wife died in a tragic explosion. This called for careful planning and pacing. Anne-Marie would understand. Marital separations were complicated and difficult, as complex as the tax laws, and all that really mattered was that she knew he loved her. After the funeral, of course, he might feel the need to "get away for a while", and then perhaps Toronto would remind him too much of Laura, so it would be understandable if he moved the business somewhere else, say Vancouver. After a decent period of mourning, it would also be quite acceptable to "meet someone", Anne-Marie for example, and start anew, which was exactly what Lloyd Francis had in mind.

* * *

Detective Bobby Aiken didn't like the look of the report that had landed on his desk, didn't like the look of it at all. He worked out of police headquarters at 40 College Street, downtown, and under normal circumstances, he would never have heard of Laura Francis and Ray Lanagan. The Beaches was 55 Division's territory. But these weren't normal circumstances, and one of Aiken's jobs was to have a close look at borderline cases, where everything *looked* kosher but someone thought it wasn't. This time it was a young, ambitious beat cop who desperately wanted to work Homicide. There was just something about it, he'd said, something that didn't ring true, and the more Bobby Aiken looked at the files, the more he knew what the kid was talking about.

The forensics were clean, of course. The fire department and the Centre for Forensic Sciences had done sterling work there, as usual. These gas explosions were unfortunately commonplace in some of the older houses, where the owners might not have had their furnaces serviced or replaced for a long time, as had happened at the house on Silver Birch. An accident waiting to happen.

But police work, thank God, wasn't only a matter of forensics. There were other considerations here. Three of them.

Again, Aiken went through the files and jotted down his thoughts. Outside on College Street it was raining, and if he looked out of his window all he could see were the tops of umbrellas. A streetcar rumbled by, sparks flashing from the overhead wire. Cars splashed up water from the gutters.

First of all, Aiken noted, the victims hadn't been husband and wife, as the investigators and media had first thought. The husband, Lloyd Francis, had flown back from a business trip to Vancouver – giving himself a nice alibi, by the way – as soon as he had heard the news the following day, and he was doubly distraught to find out that not only was his wife dead, but that she had died in bed with another man.

No, Lloyd had said, he had no idea who the man was, but it hadn't taken a Sherlock Holmes to discover that his name was Ray Lanagan, and that he was a sometime actor and sometime petty crook, with a record of minor fraud and con jobs. Lanagan had been clean for the past three years, relying mostly on TV commercials and bit parts in series like *Da Vinci's Inquest*, before CBC canned it, and *The Murdoch Mysteries*. But Aiken knew that didn't necessarily mean he hadn't been up to something. He just hadn't got caught. Well, he had definitely been up to one thing – screwing Lloyd Francis's wife – and the penalty for that had been far more severe than for any other offence he had ever committed. He might have been after the broad's money, too, Aiken speculated, but he sure as hell wasn't going to get that now.

The second thing that bothered Aiken was the insurance and the money angle in general. Not only were the house and Laura Francis's life insured for hefty sums, but there was the post-production company, which was just starting to turn a good profit, and Laura's inheritance, which was still a considerable sum, tied up in stocks and bonds and other investments. Whoever got his hands on all of that would be very rich indeed.

And then there was Lloyd Francis himself. The young beat cop who rang the alarm bell had thought there was something odd about him when he had accompanied Lloyd to the ruins of the house. Nothing obvious, nothing he could put his finger on, of course, but just that indefinable policeman's itch, the feeling you get when it doesn't all add up, like when the soundtrack doesn't synchronize with the picture in a movie. Aiken hadn't talked to Lloyd Francis yet, but he was beginning to think it was about time.

Because finally there was the one clear and indisputable fact that linked everything else, like the magnet that makes a pattern out of iron filings: Lloyd Francis had spent five years working as a heating and air-conditioning serviceman from just after he left school until his early twenties. And if you knew that much about gas furnaces, Aiken surmised, then you didn't have to bloody well be there when one blew up. You could be in Vancouver, for example.

Lloyd felt a little shaken after the policeman's visit, but he still believed he'd held his own. One thing was clear, and that was that they had done a lot of checking, not only into his background, but also into the dead man's, Ray Lanagan. What on earth had Laura seen in such a loser? The man had petty criminal stamped all over him.

But what had worried Lloyd most of all was the knowledge that the man, Aiken, seemed to have about his own past, especially his heating and air-conditioning work. Not only did the police know he had done that for five years, but they seemed to know every job he had been on, every problem he had solved, the brand name of every furnace he had ever serviced. It was all rather overwhelming. Lloyd hadn't lied about it, hadn't tried to deny any of it – that would have been a sure way of sharpening their suspicions even more – but the truth painted the picture of a man easily capable of rigging the type of furnace in the Silver Birch house until it blew up on the first cold snap of the year.

Luckily, Lloyd knew they had absolutely no forensic evidence. If there had been any, which he doubted, it would have been obliterated by the fire. All he had to do was stick to his story, and they would never be able to prove a thing. Suspicion was all very well, but it wasn't sufficient grounds for a murder charge.

After the funeral, he had lain low in a sublet condominium at Victoria Park and Danforth, opposite Shopper's World. At night the streets were noisy and a little edgy, Lloyd felt, the kind of area where you might easily get mugged if you weren't careful. More than once he had had the disconcerting feeling that he was being followed, but he told himself not to be paranoid. He wouldn't be here for long. After a suitable period of mourning he would go to Vancouver and decide he couldn't face returning to the city where his poor wife met such a terrible death. He still had a few colleagues who would regret his decision to leave, perhaps, but there wasn't really anybody left in Toronto to care that much about Lloyd Francis and what happened to him. At the moment, they all thought he was a bit depressed, "getting over his loss". Soon he would be free to "meet" Anne-Marie and start a new life. The money should be all his by then, too, once the lawyers and accountants had finished with it. Never again would he have to listen to his wife reminding where his wealth and success came from.

The Silver Birch explosion had not only destroyed Lloyd's house and wife, it had also destroyed his car, a silver Toyota SUV, and he wasn't going to bother replacing it until he moved to Vancouver, where he'd probably buy a nice little red sports car. He still popped into the studios occasionally, mostly to see how things were going, and luckily his temporary accommodation was close to the Victoria Park subway. He soon found he didn't mind taking the TTC to work and back. In fact, he rather enjoyed it. They played classical music at the station to keep away the hooligans. If he got a seat on the train, he would read a book, and if he didn't, he would drift off into thoughts of his sweet Anne-Marie.

And so life went on, waiting, waiting for the time when he could decently and without arousing suspicion, make his move. The policeman didn't return, obviously realizing that he had absolutely no chance of making a case against Lloyd without a confession, which he knew he wouldn't get. It was late November now, arguably one of the grimmest months in Toronto, but at least the snow hadn't come yet, just one dreary cold grey day after another.

One such day Lloyd stood on the crowded eastbound platform at the St George subway station wondering if he dare make his move as early as next week. At least, he thought, he could "go away for a while", maybe even until after Christmas. Surely that would be acceptable by now? People would understand that he couldn't bear to spend his first Christmas without Laura in Toronto.

He had just decided that he would do it when he saw the train come tearing into the station. In his excitement at the thought of seeing Anne-Marie again so soon, a sort of unconscious sense of urgency had carried him a little closer to the edge of the platform than he should have been, and the crowds jostled behind him. He felt something hard jab into the small of his back, and the next thing he knew, his legs buckled and he pitched forward. He couldn't stop himself. He toppled in front of the oncoming train before the driver could do a thing. His last thought was of Anne-Marie waving goodbye to him at Vancouver International Airport, then the subway train smashed into him and its wheels shredded him to pieces.

Someone in the crowd screamed and people started running back towards the exits. The frail-looking old man with the walking-stick who had been standing directly behind Lloyd turned to walk away calmly through the chaos, but before he could get very far, two scruffy-looking young men emerged from the throng and one took him by each arm. "No you don't," one of them said. "This way." And they led him up to the street.

Detective Bobby Aiken played with the worry beads one of his colleagues had brought him back from a trip to Istanbul. Not that he was worried about anything. It was just a habit, and he found it very calming. It had, in fact, been a very good day.

Not because of Lloyd Francis. Aiken didn't really care one way or another about Francis' death. In his eyes, Francis had been a cold-blooded murderer and he had got no less than he deserved. No, the thing that pleased Aiken was that the undercover detectives he had detailed to keep an eye on Francis had picked up Mickey the Croaker disguised as an old man at the St George subway station, having seen him push Francis with the sharp end of his walking-stick.

Organized Crime had been after Mickey for many years now but had never managed to get anything on him. They knew that he usually worked for one of the big crime families in Montreal, and the way things were looking, he was just about ready to cut a deal: amnesty and the witness relocation plan for everything he knew about the Montreal operation, from the hits he had made to where the bodies were buried. Organized Crime were creaming their jeans over their good luck. It would mean a promotion for Bobby Aiken.

The only thing that puzzled Aiken was why? What had Lloyd Francis done to upset the Mob? There was something missing, and it irked him that he might never uncover it now the main players were dead. Mickey the Croaker knew nothing, of course. He had simply been obeying orders, and killing Lloyd Francis meant nothing more to him than swatting a fly. Francis's murder was more than likely connected with the post-production company, Aiken decided. It was well-known that the Mob had its fingers in the movie business, often for the purpose of money-laundering. A bit of digging around might uncover something more specific, but Aiken didn't have the time. Besides, what did it matter now? Even if he didn't understand how all the pieces fit together, things had worked out the right way. Lanagan and Francis were dead and Mickey the Croaker was about to sing. It was a shame about the wife, Laura. She had been a good-looking woman, from what Aiken had been able to tell from the family photographs, and it was a pity she had died so young. But those were the breaks. If she hadn't being playing the beast with two backs with Lanagan in her own bed, for Christ's sake, then she might still be alive today.

It was definitely a good day, Aiken decided, pushing the papers aside. Even the weather had improved. He looked out of the window. Indian Summer had come to Toronto in November. The sun glinted on the apartment windows at College and Yonge and the office workers were out on the streets, men without jackets and women in sleeveless summer dresses. A streetcar rumbled by, heading for Main station. Main. Out near the Beaches. The boardwalk and the Queen Street cafés would be crowded and the dog-walkers would be out in force. Aiken thought maybe he'd take Jasper out there for a run later. You never knew who you might meet when you were walking your dog on the beach.

THE VELOCITY OF BLAME

Christopher Fowler

"THE BEST WAY to get rid of a really big Cambodian cockroach is to wrap it in tissue paper, drop it in the toilet and pour Coco de Mer Body Butter over it so it can't climb the walls of the bowl, because the buggers have clawed feet and can really shift. Even then, they sometimes manage to shuck off the paper and use it to climb back up out of the toilet into your bathroom." That's what Dorothy's guidebook said. She was always reading me passages from the damned thing. It had a bunch of tips for dealing with the kind of problems you encounter over there. When they didn't work, she added her own twists. It was one of those guidebooks obsessed with hygiene and the strength of the dollar, and so paranoid about being ripped off that you lost faith in human nature the longer you kept reading it. I made her throw it away when we decided to stay on.

I'll admit, it took us a while to get used to the bugs in South East Asia, but I thought they'd turn out to be the least of our problems. There would be other issues to deal with. The food, the people, the heat, the past, the politics. I should have added another problem to that list; lack of communication.

We came to Siem Reap to do the tourist thing, hire bikes and see the temples of Angor Wat at sunset, climbing over the temples of Ta Keo and Ta Prohm, where great tree roots entwine the carvings until it's impossible to tell what is hand-carved and what is natural. We wanted to ride elephants, hang out in bars where you could still smoke beneath slow-turning fans, drive along the endless arrow-straight roads to the floodplains of the Tonle Sap Lake, eat fat shrimps in villages that had survived through the horrors of the

Khmer Rouge, but no one had told us about the people, how kind, placid and forgiving they were. No other country in the world could have survived so many horrors and still have found such power to forgive. It didn't make sense to me, but then I come from a land that specializes in Christian vengeance.

It was our first visit to South East Asia, and we immediately fell in love with the place.

Siem Reap was little more than a dusty crossroads crowded with ringing bicycles, lined with cafés and little places where you could get a foot and shoulder massage. There were covered markets at each end of the town selling intricate wooden carvings, pirated books and gaudy silks, and barns where farmers sat on the floor noisily trading their produce, with their kids running everywhere, laughing and fooling around, the closest definition I'd ever seen of real community. That's a word we're fond of using at home, but there it means something entirely less friendly.

After watching Chinese dealers testing precious stones that had been dug out of the mountains, running little blowtorches over gems to prove their integrity, I bought Dorothy a ruby for thirty dollars.

"I'm not going to have this made into anything," she said happily, "I just want to keep it somewhere in a box so I can look at it and remember.'

Instead of frying ourselves by the hotel pool we wandered around the streets, where every merchant was calling out, trying to lure us into their store with special offers. Not so pushy that they were annoying, just doing business and quickly leaving us alone as soon as they realized we didn't want to buy. Now that Cambodia was finally stable, the Russians and the French were competing to build along the town's main road, and ugly concrete blocks were going up behind the 1930s colonnades. No plumbing, no drainage but plenty of internet access; welcome to the new frontier, where you could use an ATM machine but still had to step over duelling scorpions to do so. A national museum had opened, absurdly high-tech, half the interactive exhibits not functioning, as though some rich outsider had insisted that this was what the town needed to draw tourists. Less than a decade of peace and the nation was embracing its future with a kind of friendly ferocity, but you feared for the transition process, knowing that everything could still be lost overnight.

And I was finally vacationing with my wife. Gail and Redmond had married and left home and were now living in Oakley, Virginia, which left me and Dorothy rattling around the house in Washington with too many bedrooms and memories. I'd been promising Dorothy that we'd eventually travel, but it proved harder to get away from work than I'd expected. After thirty-seven years of marriage, during which time we'd hardly ever left the country, I decided enough was enough and applied for two months' leave, although I eventually had to take it unpaid. Of course, whatever time you pick to go away is never the right time, and this proved to be the case; there was an election pending and everyone was expected to help, but Dorothy put her foot down and told me she'd go by herself if I didn't step away this time and make good on my promise to her. She said: "Politicians are like policemen, the work never stops and they never make much of a difference, so take a vacation."

So I booked the tickets and off we went.

When I first saw the officials at Siem Reap airport emptying their collected visa-cash into leather suitcases right in front of the tourists who paid them, I'll admit I thought the worst, that the corrupting influence of past dictators lived on – and maybe it does in other ways – but after that day I saw nothing else like it and we had a wonderful time.

On one of our last trips out beyond the river we found ourselves in a town almost completely surrounded by dense jungle. The Tonle Sap lake is tidal. For most of the year it's barely three feet deep, but during the monsoon season it connects with the Mekon River and reverses its flow, flooding the surrounding plains and forests, filling a vast area with breeding fish. The Vietnamese families living in the floating villages at the lake's edge aren't much liked by the Cambodians, but on the whole everyone rubs along. The effluvial soil is rich and the landscape is lush with vegetation. On that day we stopped in a village so small that no one living in it could decide what it was called, and that was when we saw the house.

It was just a white brick box in a small square of cleared grass, but the surrounding forest canopy glowed emerald even at noon, and it looked like the happiest place on earth. What's more, the little house was available to rent. I mentioned it to Dorothy, who dismissed the idea at once, but I could see she was excited. A light had come into her eyes that I had not seen in years. Dorothy never went out without makeup and jewellery. She cared about appearances, and what people thought of her. She was concerned about making a good impression. It's a Washington habit. But I could tell she relished the thought of not having to bother, even if it was just for a month.

"Well, I guess it wouldn't hurt to take a look," she said finally, so we visited the owner, a tiny little old lady called Madame Nghor, and she showed us around. It was just about as basic as you can get. There was really just one room with a single small window, because the kitchen and toilet were kind of outside. They stood on a half-covered deck with a wood rail that overlooked the fields and the forest. There was also a plank terrace at the front facing the road. Life was lived mainly out of doors.

The monsoon had recently ended, leaving the jungle green but foetid. On its far side, palms had been cleared to build a factory, but the breeze-block building had never been finished. The village was so perfect that it could even keep progress at bay. Madame Nghor agreed to rent us the property for one month. The price seemed absurdly low, but maybe it was extortionate to her. We didn't really care.

We checked out of the Borei Angkor, the fancy hotel where we had only met other Americans, and moved right in to the tiny house. When we got in the taxi to leave, the driver automatically assumed we were heading to the airport and very nearly dropped us there. He was real surprised when we redirected him into the countryside.

Our tickets home were open so there was nothing else to do but tell our family that we had decided to stay on awhile. Gail thought we were behaving kind of weirdly but Redmond congratulated us when we told him.

"I won't be making many more calls," I warned him. "The charger we brought with us doesn't work out here. But we have our health and our money, and the change is doing Dorothy a world of good."

"Just don't go native on us, Dad," Redmond laughed.

Obviously, staying in the house was very different to being in the hotel. There were no fresh towels or little gifts on the pillow, and there was no room service or air conditioning, but we loved it all the same. Madame Nghor offered to prepare food for us, and we took up her kind offer. On our second day, she called around with the other villagers to formally welcome us. The women peeped shyly around the door and wouldn't come in. The men sat in a circle outside and offered us a strong, sour yellow drink they'd made themselves. I didn't like it much but it wouldn't have been right to refuse it.

We were sad to see so many of their children missing an arm or a leg. They danced about dextrously with just a stick or two to lean on, and Dorothy and I felt compelled to give them a few coins even though we knew we shouldn't. There was this kid called Pran, a skinny little runt about seven years old, who had lost both his legs and one arm. There were still thousands of landmines buried in the countryside around the village, and we were warned about straying from the marked paths when cycling to the next village for provisions. The damage of war always outlives the fighting, sometimes in ways we can never imagine.

The younger villagers spoke some English, and all were anxious to ensure that we would have a happy stay. Madame Nghor was especially thoughtful, and would bring us small gifts – a mosquito coil, candles, a hand fan – anything she could think of that might make our stay more comfortable. Her husband had died in tragic circumstances – I heard from one of the villagers that he had been murdered by a Khmer resistance unit about fifteen years earlier – and pain was etched deeply in her face, but now her life was simple and safe and she made the best of it; her story, we felt, was to have a happy ending. She and the villagers lived by the principles enshrined by their religion, peace and acceptance and harmony, and we found it a humbling contrast to the way we lived at home. You try to do the right thing but life in the West is complicated and hypocritical.

There were times when we felt like disoriented Westerners, not understanding what we were seeing. On a trip into Siem Reap we saw a fight explode out of nowhere between two men who were whisked away so quickly by police that I feared for their survival in the cells. Then, an hour later, we saw them in a café together laughing and drinking. Some of the food gave us fiery stomach cramps – we weren't used to eating such quantities of spiced vegetables without any dairy products – and the insects particularly plagued Dorothy, who would find herself bitten even though she tightly wrapped herself at sunset from head to foot. One night as I watched this ritual of protection, I found myself fearing for her. She seemed so much more fragile here. Dorothy caught me looking, and told me not to fuss. She always had confidence in me.

The bugs were at their worst after a humid rainstorm broke across our new home one night. They flew into the shutters at such a lick I thought they might crack the wood. The next morning the warm, still pools under our decking were filled with giant centipedes and every type of crawling creature, some with pincers, some with horns and stingers, many as big as an adult fist. I shifted one multi-legged horror from the bedroom with a stick, and it caught me by surprise when its shiny black carapace split open and two vibrating iridescent green wings folded out. It lifted lazily into the air like a cargo plane, and I guided it toward an open window.

The following evening we opened a bottle of warm red wine and sat beside each other on the rickety wooden terrace, watching the sunset, Dorothy and I. Silence fell easily between us, but it was also a time for asking things we had avoided discussing all of our married life.

"Tell me," she said after a long pause for thought. "Do you ever regret working for the doctor?"

It was a question I had asked myself many times. "I was young," I replied. "I was ambitious. We were denied information. We didn't know many of the things we know now."

"But if you had known, would you still have worked for him?"

"Why do you need to know?"

"Because there were others who stood their ground." There was no reproach in her voice.

"They knew more than I ever did. He kept us in the dark."

"You knew about the carpet bombing. Everyone in Washington knew."

"We didn't know what it would lead to. How could we? But to answer your question – no, I wouldn't have worked for Kissinger."

As we were dressing, Madame Nghor brought us a ceramic pot and shyly set it on the low dining table. She looked uncomfortable about bringing it. "This for protection – for—" and here she rolled one forefinger over the other in an explanation I could not understand. I looked into the pot and found it contained an oily red butter that smelled like copper and petrol.

"How do I use this?" I asked.

"Not for you," she told me gently, "for your wife."

I figured that explained her awkwardness. For the last day or so Dorothy had been suffering from cramps. Madame Nghor held her hand out over the edge of the floor and made a soothing flat-palmed gesture.

"Put it on at night. You rub it like this to stop them from coming," and again she did the finger-rolling thing that I took to be an indication of cramps. "You have no trouble from them after, they stop and die. You must keep lid on pot tight. You want me to show?" I thought she looked mighty uncomfortable with what she regarded to be a personal subject, and by this time her embarrassment had spread to me, so I hastily thanked her and showed her out.

We were planning our first trip into the jungle, but Dorothy had not slept well, and was still in some pain. "We'll postpone it to another time," I told her. "Besides, it's been raining and now it's hot again, so God knows what kind of insects will be out and about."

"No, we'll go. I feel a lot better now, really. I'm not going to be a killjoy on this trip." I explained to her about rubbing on Madame Nghor's home-made potion but it seemed too oily and liable to stain, so she decided it would be better to use it when we got back. After tucking our shirts and socks tightly into our trousers and boots so that no insect could find a way in, we set off into the woodlands, clambering over great tree roots, stopping to listen to the calling of birds in the jungle canopy. The going was a lot tougher than we had expected, and after an hour we decided to turn back.

We had been hoping to stumble across one of the many overgrown temples that lay almost entirely buried by the returning jungle, and in one patch of cleared ground I rubbed away a layer of thick green moss to find the scarred stone face of an Apsara dancer staring up at me through the soft soil. With her raised eyes appearing above the leaves, it looked like she had been swimming through the grass and had just broken through the surface. As if she had been waiting for someone to come along and awaken her.

"You've let the sunlight fall on her face again," said Dorothy.

"We could uncover the rest of her," I suggested.

"You don't understand. The moss was protecting her from damage."

We walked on. Dorothy was particularly exhausted by the journey, so we stopped by a stream and listened to the sounds of the forest.

"We should have done this years ago," I said, taking her hand. Dorothy's hair had greyed a little and she had tied it back into a ponytail, but in the yellow light that fell through the branches she looked blonde again.

"The time was never right before, you know that," she replied. "At least we got to do it now."

She looked down at her boots, lost in thought. There was a leathery scuffle of wings, and a bird screamed high above us, then it was silent once more. The stream was so clear that you could count the pebbles on the bottom. Dorothy looked down at her white tube sock and began to rub it. "Damn."

"What's the matter?'

"Nothing, maybe a scratch." I looked and saw a small crimson stain the size of a penny. "I don't think anything could have got in, these socks are really thick. I'd have felt it."

"Better let me have a look." I rolled down her sock. It was full of blood. "I think you got a leech in there," I told her. "It won't hurt, but we'd better get you back." I knew that leeches produced an anaesthetic in their bite so they could continue to suck their host's blood without being felt. They also have an anticoagulant in their saliva, so they can carry on feeding until they're fully gorged. Then they drop from the body to seek water, through which they can travel to find a new host.

"It could have carried on and on without me knowing it was there," said Dorothy.

"No," I told her. "In the natural world parasites don't kill their hosts, because they'd ultimately kill themselves."

"You mean it's only humans who do that."

Soon the cover thinned out and the jungle opened on to a road that led back to the village. As soon as we reached the house we took off our socks and shoes. I found one leech attached to my ankle, and Dorothy had two. They were small and black, as soft as slugs but far more elastic and lively. They left splattery trails of blood as they twisted about on the bathroom floor. I stamped on their bloated bodies, sacs of blood that burst messily over the cracked white tiles. I had a sudden suspicion that there might be more of them on us.

"Turn around," I told Dorothy. "Take off your shirt." As she peeled off the wet cotton, I saw two more on her back, between her pale shoulder blades.

When she saw the thin streaks of unclotted blood in the mirror, Dorothy yelped. I picked off one of the creatures and examined it. As I did, it stretched and swung around, trying to bite me. I was surprised at the speed with which it moved. I could see two sets of tiny hooks like pinpoints, set on either end of its body. When I dropped it on to the sink it flipped over, end to end, like a slinky. It climbed the sheer sides of the bowl in seconds and disappeared into a wet corner.

"Let me light a cigarette," I told Dorothy, "I think you're supposed to burn them off.'

"No," she said, trying to sound unpanicked, "they bite deeper if you do that and tear the skin when you pull them. I think you're meant to flick them off with a fingernail." She had read about them in her travel guide, and was right. A nail under the leech's body was enough to make it come away. My back was clear – I think they found Dorothy's blood sweeter. The harder part was catching them once they fell. You expect anything that looks like a slug to move slowly. I placed my finger above one and watched as it stretched and waved about like an antenna, desperate to reach me. There was something grotesque about its obviousness, as if I was automatically expected to forgive its uncontrollable hunger.

The sun was setting and the sky had turned a spectacular shade of crimson. Out on the balcony, the warm moist air was thick with flying insects. I felt as if our environment had subtly turned against us, as if it was saying *We've nearly had enough of you tourists now, time to go home. You've pretended to be like us but you really don't belong here.*

Dorothy was tired and in unusually low spirits. She hardly ate anything from the tray of pork and noodles Madame Nghor had left for us. She was still suffering from muscle cramps, and opened the pot of oily rust-coloured ointment, patiently rubbing it into the tops of her legs and over her belly until the room stank.

My calves and thigh muscles were sore from the expedition. We were not so young now, I thought, and would have to make adjustments to the way we behaved. It had been foolish of us to just take off into the jungle like that without telling anyone where we were going – what if we had gotten lost, what would we have done? Just how quickly could things go wrong here?

I turned out the lights and we went to bed. The blackness was complete, but soon I saw lightning crackle above the treeline. It looked like an electric trolley was running through the forest. The temperature started to climb, and within minutes it was unbearable. Dorothy was twisting and turning in her narrow bed. I was sweating heavily, and could not get comfortable. I went for a smoke on the terrace and stood at the rail, listening to the noises of the night.

Dorothy's questions about my life had bothered me. There were no easy answers. Had Kissinger's illegal bombing of this astonishing country opened the way for everything that followed? We went into other countries and created a vacuum that had to be filled by something. Every day took us further away from being the innocents we had so long pretended to be.

I reached the end of the Marlboro packet. I left the terrace door wide to let some air in and came back inside. It seemed more stifling than ever. I lay down on top of the bed once more.

An hour later, rain broke and fell hard, pounding on the roof of the little house. The temperature began to fall. It rained and rained until the sky wore itself out. Calm returned, and I must have dozed.

Dorothy cried out suddenly, making me start. I tried to find a light, but it seemed the electricity was out, and the candles were somewhere in the other room. I knew at once that something was amiss.

Dorothy was struggling to sit up. She called for me and I grabbed at her wrist, only to find her skin slick with sweat. "What's the matter?" I kept asking. I probably frightened her with my shouting. I found my lighter, flicked it and tore back the thin sheet. Her nightdress was stained scarlet, and the material was shifting as if alive. I could smell something bad, like an infected open wound. She and I scrabbled to tear off the wet material.

As it ripped, I saw what was wrong; the area from her navel to the tops of her thighs was a black squirming mass of tiny bodies, slick and shiny with her blood. Leeches, it seemed that there were hundreds of them, sucking her life away from her.

I thrust my hand into them and instantly they began to flip on to my wrist and arm, attaching themselves, finding veins and biting hard. Dorothy screamed as I grabbed at them, trying to squeeze whole handfuls at a time, but they slipped through my blood-slick fingers. As fast as I flicked them away they came back, driven by their hunger for blood.

I needed something else. Finding the lighter, I struck it and thrust the flame into the wriggling slimy nest. Too late, I remembered that the ointment contained petrol. There was a soft pop of ignition and she was enveloped in thin blue flames. I grabbed my shirt and threw it over her stomach.

In the moment before the flickering flames were extinguished, I saw the horrific mess on her body, blood and burned leeches writhing everywhere, Dorothy shaking in pain and terror, and I ...

It shames me to think back to that moment. All I could think about when I saw her was the roaring anger of the blame, someone to blame. Madame Nghor had given us the oil, she had somehow discovered who I was, who I had worked for in Washington, and had made up this concoction to draw the leeches to us. She was taking revenge for the loss of her husband, for the destruction of her country, for me being an American. That was my first reaction, the seeking of blame.

The screams brought Madame Nghor – and half the village – to our door. She put on the light, and I realized that in my panic I had simply failed to find the switch. I thought she had come to gloat and take pleasure in this bizarre revenge, and I must have rushed at her. I remember grabbing her thin shoulders and shaking her very hard. Two men who turned out to be her sons ran forward and pulled me away from her.

"What did you do to my wife?" I yelled in her face, "What did you do?" I said some other things that it pains me now to remember. When she saw the pulsing mass of leeches that still quivered and crawled on Dorothy, Madame Nghor ran back down the steps and returned with something that looked like a can of lighter fluid, squeezing it wildly all around until every last one of the leeches had fallen away and shrivelled up.

Chaos. In the exposing glare of the overhead bulb, my wife lay sobbing, bloody and naked on the bed before the shocked villagers. I stayed frozen in one place until Madame Nghor had pulled a sheet over her.

"You stupid man," she scolded, wagging a cartoonish finger at me. "This all your fault, not mine! This! This!" She picked up the pot she had given us. "You put it on—" and when she made the smoothing gesture again I realized she meant I should put the oil on the floor, along the edges of the room, to keep the leeches out after the storm. It was not meant to be put on the skin. And the rolling fingers, she was simply showing us how the leeches moved and why it must be applied. I had misinterpreted so blindly, so badly. One of her sons dipped his finger in the mixture to show me. The thick red oil had cattle blood in it. The coppery smell attracted them, and they got stuck.

In shame and shock I started to laugh. I couldn't stop myself. Was this really how things went wrong in the world? Were mistakes always this fundamentally stupid? How could I have thought this tiny village woman might know I once worked for a political oppressor? It was absurd. Guilt, like some barely-visible fish resting in deep water, could surface without warning.

We took Dorothy to the hospital, but the burns themselves were superficial and there was no real damage from them. However, a ragged black patch of discoloured skin was left behind from the burned edges of the unhealed wounds, and her blood could not coagulate over the scratches my fingernails had left as I tried to dig the leeches from her. The doctor told her she would be left with scars.

Dorothy hardly spoke to me that day. We returned to Washington as soon as we could get a flight, slinking out of the village like criminals. The villagers watched us go in silence and embarrassment.

Seven months later my wife became ill and died. To this day I do not believe what the doctor said, and have convinced myself that her death was the result of some kind of blood poisoning, a delayed reaction to what happened that night.

Just before the year ended, I took early retirement. A new phalanx of eager young recruits was entering politics for the first time, and the thought just made me tired. I know at heart that I am a good man. I have made mistakes in my life, but the worst that night was the speed with which I sought to blame.

SOMEONE TAKE THESE DREAMS AWAY

Marc Werner

WHEN *CONTROL* OPENED at the Cornerhouse, the nights were getting longer. Most days, it was dark by half past four. Anton Corbijn's biopic of Ian Curtis was the film of the year; everybody went to see it (apart from me), even Nick. But while the rest of our colleagues from English and Film would have allowed themselves to become immersed in Corbijn's recreation of late 1970s Manchester, marvelling at Martin Ruhe's black and white cinematography, Nick would have been sitting there in the dark thinking of another British film with only a handful of scenes shot in black and white, the rest in colour.

Nick has a thing about black and white. He's fond of quoting Christopher Walken's line from Donald Cammell's *Wild Side*. "Life is black and white. Have you ever seen grey squares on a chessboard?"

I'm sitting in front of his computer in the office we've shared since I recommended him for a vacant lecturer's post, and I'm wondering where to look first. I don't even know how much stuff he keeps on his desktop machine. I hardly use mine at all, preferring my laptop. The office is tiny – the university has a problem with overcrowding – but it's surprising how sitting at Nick's desk gives me an entirely different perspective on it. The difference between it and the view from my desk is like the difference between the way *to* somewhere and the journey *back*. I spin slowly round to look at Nick's shelves. Two books by Roy Armes, *A Critical History of British Cinema* and

The Ambiguous Image. Roger Manvell's *New Cinema in Britain.*
Danny Peary's *Cult Movies.* (I have a copy of that somewhere, too.)
A few annual-sized hardbacks – *Thriller Movies, A Pictorial History
of Crime Films, Photoplay Film Yearbook 1976.* I was struck by
how many of these titles dated back to the 1970s. Among the newer
stuff: Chris Darke's *Light Readings,* Ali Catterall and Simon Wells'
book about British cult films *Your Face Here,* and a recent edition
of the *Time Out Film Guide.* An eclectic library.

It's very quiet in the office, which it rarely was when Nick was
around. He'd either be banging away at his keyboard ("Touch-
typing's for puffs. No offence!") or complaining loudly into his
phone about the standard of the technical equipment in the lecture
theatres. Or he'd have a student in for a tutorial. Three people in an
office designed for one. Admin, teaching, dealing with students –
that's only half of what we're supposed to be doing. The rest – our
so-called research – is what brings in the real money. But if we want
a quiet space in which to write, there's no point looking anywhere
near the university.

> *18.8.87 [morning]*
> *In a TV studio where I've been interviewed. The Queen
> turns up. Then we all go out to a tube station. The
> Queen looks nervous. On the train a man is smoking a
> cigarette and a cigar. His fat cigar looks like a knob with
> the foreskin pulled back. Arriving at Cambridge
> University (!?) I am shown with one other person (?) to
> my room, which is room B at school. I am given keys,
> though the door is of the saloon bar type.*

On the upper shelves behind Nick's desk, the beautifully tactile,
plastic-sheathed cases of DVDs. *Elephant, Old Boy, If....., Zéro de
Conduite.* Beautiful things, DVDs. Simple, full of promise. How
many have you bought and never watched? In case you ever needed
to see something again, to write about it, you told yourself, but
really it was just to possess them. Like a director hoarding prints
of his own films. A sense of ownership, a piece of marketing
genius. At least half the DVDs in anyone's collection have never
been watched.

I notice the line from *Wild Side* written on a yellow sticky note stuck to the side of Nick's inkjet printer. Also, on another note alongside: "When do we live? That's what I want to know." I knew the quote. It was a line spoken by Mick Travis, the Malcolm McDowell character in *If....*, near the beginning of the film. I might not have known it had it not been for Nick's interest in the film. His obsession with the film.

I've been covering for him for a week now. Delivering a lecture to undergraduates, running a workshop with his MA students. His absence has been noticed, but has not yet become a serious problem. It will, though. The conference he's organized – *Run in the Corridor: the Politics of School Shootings on Film*, which he's been working towards for several months – is only a week away.

A couple of times in the last few days I've been convinced things have switched around on his desk and have wondered if he's been in during the night. I know he has a good relationship with Byron, the dreadlocked security guard who wanders in from Moss Side towards the end of the afternoon. I've seen the two of them sharing a roll-up, huddled against the autumnal chill and standing a cautious distance from the main entrance to the building. One of them sources the gear and supplies the other. My guess is Byron is the supplier, if only because Nick, for all his strengths, is not very streetwise. But he can turn on the charm. One afternoon while he was waiting for a female student to turn up for a tutorial, he told me she was dyslexic. Listen to this, he said, reading from the student's Learning Support Document, "'Linzi has difficulty with planning work, prioritizing tasks and concentrating when there is background noise. She has poor short-term memory and may lose flow when interrupted.'" He looked up at me. "For fuck's sake," he said, "Do you think *I'm* dyslexic, then."

"Sounds like we all are," I said.

When Linzi came in and sat down across the desk from Nick, he held up a print-out and said to her, "This is your Learning Support Document." He immediately crumpled it into a ball and threw it at the bin. When she looked shocked, he said, "It's bollocks. I don't care how you spell encyclopaedia – consensus – liaison. Whatever. I'm interested in the *content* of what you write, not its *appearance*." She looked uncertain. "Don't worry," he said with a resigned smile. "I can always print off another copy."

In the quiet of the early afternoon, the phone rings on Nick's desk. I look at it, wondering whether to pick it up. I don't look at it for very long.

"Hello? Nick's phone," I say, strongly hoping the caller will not respond by saying, "Hello, Nick's phone."

"I'm looking for Nick," says a female voice.

You and me both.

"He's not at his desk at the moment, I'm afraid," I say. "Would you like to leave a message?"

"That's OK," she says, and before I know it she is gone.

I press 1471.

We are sorry. We do not have the caller's number.

I remember my own student days. One of my lecturers, Roger Huss – one of the few I really liked – had invited me to call him by his first name, and maybe I did a couple of times, but it never felt right somehow. *Excuse me, Roger. Thank you, Roger.* Now it's different. It's *Hey Nick* and *Laters dude.* Student reps sit on staff committees and complain bitterly if they think they're not getting their money's worth.

> *7.1.96*
> *At school, a gang of lads gathers round. I bristle but say nothing. Another lad comes in and tells us what we have to do – look back over all the films of the year and see which one God would have made differently(!).*

In my mind, as I hang up the phone, is a picture of Helena Swan, one of Nick's postgraduate students, a well-built and undeniably attractive woman in her early fifties. I've noticed her hanging around at the end of Nick's seminars, laughing at his jokes during a staff-students social event. I've had to start leaving the room when she comes for tutorials. It was her voice on the phone, I'm sure of it.

I switch his computer on. I know Nick's log-in because he dictated it to me over the phone one day when a system error was blocking mine and I couldn't use the photocopier. I enter it and the prompt asks for a password. I have a few weak guesses – anderson, mcdowell, oldboy, elephant (if.... doesn't have enough characters, even with the four-dot ellipsis) – but don't get lucky.

I stand up and go over to the window. Looking out at the wind-swept junction of side roads, I am reminded for some reason of another time I stood in exactly the same position and looked out to see Nick sauntering towards the building and talking on his mobile. He was smiling. I didn't often see him smile. As he approached the barrier, which was lowered to keep out unauthorized vehicles, he ended the call and dropped the phone into his jeans pocket. In front of him, the barrier suddenly rose as if, grandly, permitting him to enter. Nick looked up and gave a great guffawing laugh, which was even rarer than a smile and made him look a lot younger than his forty-five years. I could hear it, two floors up and through double-glazing. I laughed as well and felt momentarily light-headed as well as light-hearted. It felt like the first time we'd really connected in years, perhaps since school, though of course he hadn't seen me watching, and by the time he'd reached our office, his face had settled into its semi-permanent grimace of disapproval.

I go to the department admin office on the third floor. On the left as you go in is a series of filing cabinets. I open the one labelled S–Z and flick through until I find what I want. I leaf through a file, make some notes, and leave.

I stop by our office to pick up my bag and am about to leave when I have a thought. I walk over to Nick's shelves and take down the DVD of *If….* and a couple of books and slip them into my bag.

> 22.1.96 [morning]
> *Attending hospital. Very soon it's become our old school*
> *– it's assembly time. We're all in uniform. There's a boy*
> *in a wheelchair near me. He's got a glass of Coca-Cola*
> *with ice. Another boy comes along and sits in another*
> *wheelchair, sliding a big brown suitcase underneath the*
> *chair. I know the suitcase contains weapons.*

The bus is full of students. I stare out of the window and find myself thinking about Iain Constable's recent lecture on research methods. He was coming across as rather pedantic with his insistence on correct presentation. Footnotes, quotations, bibliographies. Every-thing had to be just so, or the student would lose marks. "Right down to the number of dots in an ellipsis," he said, and Nick spoke up, saying, "What about *If....*? What if you need to mention the title of Lindsay Anderson's 1968 film *If....*, which famously has four dots in its ellipsis? What then?" Iain laughed and Nick said he wasn't joking, it was a serious point. Taking Nick's interruption as a challenge, Iain entrenched and said an ellipsis with four dots was a mistake and would be marked as such in any work he came across. "Good job I'm not your student, then," Nick said, as he got up and walked out of the lecture theatre.

I found him later in our office, in tears.

"What is it?" I asked, shocked.

"Nothing. Leave me alone," he snapped, then softened slightly. "Just give us a minute, Mike."

I went to see the head of department about a timetabling issue. When I came back, Nick had dried his eyes, but his face was red as it jutted towards his computer screen.

"Are you going to tell me what's wrong or shall I mind my own business?" I asked.

"Something I read in here," Nick said, picking up Ali Catterall and Simon Wells' *Your Face Here*, which I knew had a chapter on *If....* He opened the book and flicked through the pages. "Page sixty-four," he said and chucked the book across the office.

I caught it and turned to the right page.

"Last para," Nick said. "'There were plans for a school reunion'."

Writing about Anderson's idea for a proper sequel to *If....* (as distinct from the fluff that was *O Lucky Man!*), the authors caught the reader up on what had happened to key cast members. Christine Noonan (the Girl) had left the profession and gone into teaching, David Wood had become a children's writer and McDowell, of course, had moved to Hollywood. Two, however, were dead. Richard Warwick (Wallace) had died from an AIDS-related condition in 1997, and Rupert Webster (Bobby Phillips) had been knifed to death on the New York subway in the 1980s.

I felt a lump in my throat as I instantly recalled one of their scenes from the film, shot in black and white, in which they slept side by side in Wallace's bed. Although Malcolm McDowell's scene with the Girl at the Packhorse Cafe, in which they had ended up play-fighting naked on the floor, again in black and white, had been remarkably effective in its insistence that fantasy was very much a part of the film's reality, it was clear where the director believed the emotional heart of the film was to be found. The camera's slow glide across the dorm, showing first Bobby Phillips and then revealing Wallace lying next to him, had made that very clear. Earlier, Phillips had watched admiringly as Wallace, after flashing a smile at the younger boy, performed slow-motion acrobatics on the high bar.

Although the scene in the Packhorse Cafe was sexually explicit, even allowing a glimpse of pubic hair, the film's erotic peak was to be found later, Nick had once patiently explained to me, in another black and white sequence. The one in which the blonde Mrs Kemp, housemaster Arthur Lowe's wife, played by Mary McLeod, walks naked down an empty corridor towards the camera, and then, away from the camera, through a boys' dormitory, trailing a hand along a line of washbasins and turning, finally, to look back over her shoulder at the viewer, her stance recalling that of the Girl in the café as she looked round from under a curtain of thick, dark hair while making coffee for Mick and Johnny. Mrs Kemp looked over her right shoulder, the Girl over her left. One of these shots looked as if it was meant to be erotic, but was merely a tease, a stock pose, a nod to the classic black-and-whites; the other, exploiting the full-figured vulnerability of the childless and lonely Mrs Kemp, actually was and powerfully so.

"If only Mary McLeod knew how many adolescent boys' wanks she was responsible for," Nick said.

This comment comes back to me as I get off the bus in West Didsbury. The anonymous Edwardian conversion across the road, once home to Factory Records, reveals no trace of its cultural significance. I cross Lapwing Lane and keep walking. The address I'm looking for is located within a grid of quiet residential streets to the west of Palatine Road. Helena Swan is not quite another generation, as Mrs Kemp had been to Mick, Johnny and the other boys ("Do you need this, Mrs Kemp," Mick had asked, in one of the refectory scenes, with a provocative thrust of the sauce bottle), but she is an apparently available woman some ten years older than Nick, of a similar build to Mary McLeod in 1968. She could easily be a stand-in, a body double.

Dusk is turning the lit front rooms of these imposing three-storey Victorian terraced houses into sound-stages, sets dressed and waiting for actors. A narrow footpath runs down the side of Helena Swan's property. Barely wide enough for two people to squeeze past each other, it offers a convenient spot from which to observe the back of the house. Some lights are burning; no noise can be heard. There must be a better way to go about what I'm trying to achieve. Do I really expect to see Nick suddenly appear silhouetted in a bedroom window? To knock on the front door and explain my quest would embroider unnecessary complications on to an already elaborate tapestry. I decide to wait for a while.

> *Wednesday, 15 January 1997*
> *At a swimming baths, there are three pools but they're short and narrow, barely bigger than normal bathroom baths. The one in the middle has two people in it: someone on the left who remains still, and a young black man who is swimming lengths. There would just be room for me to swim to his right. I'm perched on the rim about to dive in but I worry that my arms or legs might disturb other diners because now it's a restaurant as well. Also the black lad has just smiled at me and he's naked and I'm worried there isn't enough room.*

My thoughts turn to the DVD in my bag. Assuming a lack of success in my current endeavour, I will play the film when I get home. I've seen it a number of times and my familiarity with it has been enhanced by Nick's frequent allusions and references, but to watch it again under these particular conditions might just throw up an idea or two. I could never forget the grey echoing corridors down which Mick, Johnny and Wallace confidently stride, three abreast, to meet their punishment at the hands of the Whips. Vicious lashes of the cane in the school gymnasium, the wooden floor pounding with the lengthy run-up of the sadistic Rowntree. How similar that gym was to our own, in the grammar school. How different were the relationships of abuse, yet how familiar, really.

I take out my notebook, then my mobile, and key in a number. I hear a faint ringing, then another light comes on in the kitchen window and Helena Swan appears. She picks up the phone.

"Hello?" she says. "Hello?"

I hold my breath.

"Who is this?"

Still I say nothing.

Then, her voice shrinking to a whisper: "*Nick?*"

I thumb the red button to break the connection and breathe out and quickly breathe in again. I watch as Helena Swan turns away from the phone and stares into the air in front of her face, which looks as if it has just been slapped. I wish at that point I hadn't done what I have done, in spite of the information gained from it.

I asked Nick once if he was frustrated by the confusion surrounding the use of black and white sequences in *If....*, for the most part a colour film. Every commentator seems to have a different take and all claim to be reflecting the position of director Lindsay Anderson. Some say it was done to save money, others that a consistency of colour tone in the chapel, with its great stained-glass windows, could not be achieved. Still others argue that the choice was aesthetic, that it had to do with reminding the viewer of Anderson's links to Free Cinema, that it was part of a general push for Brechtian alien-ation, that it was intended to heighten the tension between fantasy and reality.

"It's all of those things and none of them," he'd said. "Art's impossible without ambiguity."

4 May 1997

Standing at a urinal in our school, but in Scotland. A man stood too close to me so I moved along and he muttered that the only person I'd have something to worry about in that department would be Ian somebody. I challenged him. He shook water at me, which I soon realized was his piss. I grabbed him and demanded to know his name and where he worked – Iain Grant, lab technician, he said. Somehow I knew they were two different Ians and that this one spelled his name the Scottish way.

When I get back home, I pour myself a large glass of wine and watch the film again. Every shot of the school reminds me of the one Nick and I both attended, he five years ahead of me. A couple of years ago there was a reunion. It was the last opportunity to visit the school, as the governors had finally admitted defeat in a long battle against time and announced that the school would move to new premises at the beginning of the next academic year. I asked Nick if he was going.

"Am I fuck."

I went; I was curious. You were supposed to get a boy to show you around, but I slipped up the back stairs and prowled the upper corridors on my own. I wasn't hugely keen to catch up with old faces and was attracted more by the fabric of the building itself. There were textures and shapes I had forgotten, but which came back to me with startling clarity once I saw them again after two decades. The painted notice boards pierced by thousands of pin holes. The grey plastic roller doors on boys' lockers outside classrooms.

The swimming pool was unrecognizable. Gone were the cold, green tiles, the constant drip of freezing water from the concertina glass ceiling. The pool had always been my most hated part of the school, even after optional wearing of trunks was introduced half-way through my time there. Until I was fourteen or fifteen all boys swam naked, and all boys found it humiliating and degrading. Mature adolescents, late developers – I was never sure which subset found it more embarrassing.

In the refectory I saw Corky – Mr McCorkindale, games master – and felt a sudden jolt of discomfort. I hovered on the edge of a group of old boys to overhear the conversation between them and Corky, who looked older (obviously), but also considerably smaller, than I remembered him. I already knew that he had left teaching, and I heard him say he had retrained as a psychotherapist. One of the old boys burst out laughing. Corky laughed, too, but then asked what was funny.

"Well, you created your own client base, didn't you?" said the former pupil. "With the school's policy on swimwear."

We could see the funny side now, but it had been nothing to laugh about at the time. Some had got over it, others were left with intimacy issues. I know one old boy turned Sunday league foot-baller who has never felt comfortable showering with his team-mates after a game. *I just can't get naked in front of other men*, he told me, paraphrasing Woody Allen. Not a problem I've ever had.

Nick never asked me about the reunion and I didn't volunteer anything. Part of me wanted to tell him that I had tried the door at the back of the school theatre, but that it had been locked.

Rewatching *If....* reminds me of the importance of Bobby Phillips. Not only do he and Wallace share a bed but the younger boy finds himself up on the roof with Mick, Johnny, Wallace and the Girl at the end of the film, bristling with guns and ammunition. A loaded gun won't set you free? Depends who you're pointing it at.

> *Sunday, 31 October 1999*
> *[Halloween.] I was back at school. The corridors and*
> *great hall were familiar, but everywhere there were*
> *orange plastic girders and supports appearing to hold up*
> *the ceilings. I knew these would be unsuitable to bear*
> *any loads, yet they could have no other use that I could*
> *fathom.*

The film has given me no clearer idea how to find Nick. From my bag I take out the books I borrowed from his shelves – a short BFI monograph on the film and his copy of *Your Face Here*, which falls open at page sixty-four and the paragraph about Rupert Webster and Richard Warwick. I have a look at the chapter on *If....* and then the BFI book, by Mark Sinker, which is intelligently written and packed with ideas and different approaches to interpretation. I notice that *Your Face Here* records the location of the motorcycle showroom, from which Mick and Johnny steal the motorbike they drive to the Packhorse Cafe, as being in South Wimbledon, whereas the BFI book and other sources, both print and internet, maintain it's in Shepherd's Bush. I look up *Your Face Here* on Amazon and am interested to see it has nine five-star reader reviews, all posted by "A Customer". None of them goes into much detail. On a hunch, I Google Richard Warwick: died at the age of fifty-two with a form of dementia brought on by AIDS. For Rupert Webster, however, I find a couple of sources claiming he's still alive. Either Anderson or McDowell spread a rumour that he'd been killed, they said. The internet is notoriously unreliable and it's only sentimentality that makes me place more trust in the printed page. I don't know what to believe, but I do hope that the boys who wrote *Your Face Here*, a

lively and enjoyable read, are wrong and that Rupert Webster, who
for a short time forty years ago was Bobby Phillips, is alive.

More to the point, I hope Nick is alive.

I'm narrowing down my options. I realize I have to do something
I should have done days ago.

I grab my stuff and leave the house.

The building containing Nick's flat is only a couple of streets away
from Helena Swan's house. I'm wondering if she knows this, as I tell
a resident on the top floor I'm delivering pizzas. The door clicks open
while he's still asking his girlfriend if they've ordered any.

> *Sunday, 27 November 2005*
> *Looking through old copies of the school newspaper, I*
> *see one with a picture of a girl on the front page. I*
> *recognize her, but the name given – something Schneidor*
> *– is not familiar. There are pictures of me, black and*
> *white, milking the applause from a huge crowd. There*
> *are other pictures of crowds on the fields at the front of*
> *the school, among them a young Mike, looking at me*
> *and waving. He moves as the picture comes to life.*

I've never been to Nick's place – he's never invited me – but I know
he lives on the first floor. There are two doors on the first landing.
The one on the right has pounding music coming from within, so I
knock once on the door on the left, wait a moment, then lean my
shoulder against it. I feel it give very slightly, so I treat it to a shove,
then another, and I'm inside. I push the door to behind me and lean
against it as I wait for my heartbeat to return to normal.

Straight ahead is a tiny bathroom, to the left of that an equally
small bedroom. Facing the bedroom is a combined kitchen and
living room. The size of the flat, a professional would be able to toss
it in two minutes and leave with either what they came for or the
knowledge that it wasn't there to be found. I'm not a professional,
but I do know Nick. I check out the bookshelves. More film books.
Novels about cinema: *Flicker*, *Throat Sprockets*, *The House of
Sleep*. A *Halliwell's Film Guide*. I take it down and look up *If....*,
which Halliwell appears to admire but still attacks for its "fash-
ionable emphasis on obscure narrative", concluding that "the film

as a whole makes no discernible point". Halliwell just couldn't help himself.

On the next shelf down are copies of Nick's books. His studies of Westerns and Eastern European SF and fantasy cinema for Wallflower Press and the experimental novel that was published in a limited edition by a local independent outfit. There are not many of us who have read it.

There's a decent-sized plasma-screen TV, but nothing leaps out at me from Nick's collection of DVDs and tapes, and there's no sign of a laptop (and no room for a desktop). The bedroom is dominated by an unmade double bed, on the far side of which a fat, well-thumbed notebook sits on a little set of drawers. It appears to be a dream diary. I flick through it and read random entries.

> *24 January 2006*
> *In school, towards the end of the day, I find myself near an empty staircase leading up, so I go up, thinking I'll just have a look around. I end up in a maths classroom full of small boys. The uniform is different and there are variations. I see one boy in a tight-fitting blazer and trousers that's very dark grey with silver symbols in a regular pattern all over it. The boys are getting up to go. I want to leave before them. I pass the teacher who has grey hair and who I think I recognize from my time at the school. He has his back to me. Then I'm looking for the door and I can't find it. Finally I do, but it's hidden and to get through it you have to push drapes aside and step over a threshold of broken bits of wood – it feels like a trap.*

They're not *all* about school, but enough of them are.

I put the notebook back down. On an impulse I open the top drawer and immediately wish I hadn't.

I was going to hail a cab, but when I get back to Palatine Road there's a bus coming, so I stick my hand out. I imagine everyone on the bus can see the way my jacket is weighed down on one side, but I doubt I'm the first person to catch the forty-three bus with a loaded gun in his pocket. I wonder how he got hold of it, though when I think about it, there must be a hundred ways to get tooled up in Manchester these days.

I get off a couple of stops early and walk. I haven't been back since the reunion. The fence by the old biology block never was much of a barrier. I approach the main buildings from the side – much less conspicuous than using the front entrance. I don't know what plans exist for the disused school. Demolition and a highly lucrative land sale, I presume. For now it stands empty. I enter via the ramp down to the basement on the west side. One of the double doors at the bottom opens at my touch. If the signs posted by a security company are anything other than an empty threat, I'd be surprised. I pick my way past a line of toilets, not a single door remaining, broken glass on the concrete floor flashing in the weak light of my mobile phone. I climb the stairs to the corner of the maths and geography corridors, where I stop and listen. All I can hear is the thumping of my heart and a steady drip-drip-drip somewhere behind me.

I creep past the Great Hall and main stairs. The shadows are grainy, alive with glittering motes. I hesitate outside the Masters' Common Room, the smooth stones of the corridor floor carpeted with white dust and flakes of paint. In the theatre, the individual wooden blocks that make up the parquet floor are all loose. The door at the back is no longer locked, but Nick is not inside. I enter a room I have not been inside for almost thirty years, at least not outside my dreams. Night after night, sometimes, for several days at a time, I have found myself back here. Twice, at the most, we were here together, but in my mind the narratives of those two occasions have become intertwined with the many, many times I have dreamed myself back. If the closest I can get to Nick in reality is sharing duties and an office, in my fantasy life we have remained locked into an infinite variety of positions on two turquoise vinyl-covered chairs pushed together as a makeshift couch in this tiny room – props cupboard? Wardrobe department? – at the back of the theatre. The first time, early May 1980, he had a little Philips cassette player and a badly recorded tape of bass-heavy music, dark and threatening, but utterly compelling. I asked him what it was and he smiled as he said it was called *Unknown Pleasures*. Even with the unsophisticated musical tastes of a twelve-year-old, I could tell it was special.

The way the drummer played just off the beat, the fact that the bass player carried the melody more often than not. Nick described the singer to me, told me he suffered epileptic fits, sometimes during performances.

When he touched me, it felt both wrong and right at the same time, but he was tender and patient. I liked his smile and the smell of his neck. When he held my face with his hands and kissed me, I imagined the east and west wings of the main school building somehow wrapping themselves around this tiny room at the back of the theatre and keeping us safe.

The second time, just before the Whit week holiday, Nick told me that the singer from the band had killed himself. He played the album again and we sat in the dark listening to it, the lyrics scattered with clues that should have foretold the singer's suicide. Nick also told me about a film he had seen on television just over a year ago in which four schoolboys and a girl staged a bloody revolution at their boarding school, shooting the headmaster and killing dozens of pupils and teachers. *We're in that film*, he told me. *You and me. One day you'll see it and you'll see what I mean.*

As I reach out an arm to steady myself against the wall, I feel the weight of the gun in my pocket.

I re-enter the auditorium and head for the swing doors that lead back to the main corridor. The eroded hollows in the steps cushion my footfalls as I climb the main stairs. The upper corridors are lit by moonlight. I stop and look out across the quad towards the windows of the adjacent corridor where a moving figure catches my eye. The pale, wide-hipped body, silvery white hair. Black holes for eyes. I don't need to be any closer to know that Helena Swan is playing Mrs Kemp, which would place Nick most likely at the end of her corridor at the junction with mine. I keep walking, the weight of the gun tugging at my right shoulder.

When I reach the junction of the two corridors, Nick is not there. I figure he'll be halfway up the next one, so that in a moment he can have Helena Swan walk away from him and look back, just as Mrs Kemp does. I doubt he's gone to the trouble of bringing a camera, but am aware that if I approach now I will ruin his shot. So be it.

He steps out from behind a bank of lockers twenty yards away.

"I wondered when you'd come," he says.

Helena Swan falters and stands still, uncertain how to react.

"You shouldn't be walking around with that in your pocket," Nick says calmly. "Give it to me."

I take the gun out of my pocket. Helena Swan, on seeing the dark shape in my hand, turns and runs towards the far end of the corridor.

"Who is it for?" I ask.

Nick smiles. "You brought it," he points out.

"I couldn't leave it in your flat with the door off its hinges," I say. "But if I give it to you, I'm worried you just might use it. Whether here and now or next week at your conference, in a dramatic re-enactment of a certain film."

"'One man can change the world with a bullet in the right place'," he says, quoting Mick Travis. "I'm not sure I can face that conference. All those academics."

I remain silent, thinking. He has a secret he can't live with. I am it.

"So," he says. "Stalemate."

Slowly, I bend at the knee and place the gun carefully on the floor. I straighten up and place the toe of my shoe against the mouth of the barrel and give the gun a gentle kick so that it slides several yards along the corridor to a position roughly halfway between us.

"Indeed," I say.

ANIMAL INTELLIGENCE

Alexander McCall Smith

1

MICHAEL MOVED EMPTY-HANDED into the house in Belfast. Most people have at least the contents of a small van to move in; he had nothing, just a suitcase, and not a large one at that.

It was not that he was poor. His bank account, although not over-full, was solvent, and he had a reasonable amount stashed away. The lack of possessions was a temporary state – brought about by an entirely amiable divorce.

"You can have the lot," he said to his wife. "I really don't need to take anything."

She had tried to persuade him otherwise. "But you can't give me *everything*," she said. "You need to take something. What about some pictures?"

But he had grown tired of the pictures, and if he removed them, he pointed out, there would be squares of discolouration on the walls and she would need to call in the decorators.

Such generosity, she said, was typical of him. "You're such a kind man," she said. "It breaks my heart to see you go. It really does."

And he replied. "It breaks mine too. But there we are. We're different, aren't we? And I want you to be happy." To which she replied that she wanted him to be happy too.

She took his hand in hers. She should not have fallen in love with that other man, but she had, and she realized that she loved him more than she loved Michael. And he was unhappy in London; he would do far better to return to Belfast.

"You never really liked London, " she said. "You never settled, did you?"

He shook his head. "It's nothing to do with Londoners." (She was one.) "It's just so large and the ... and the very air is sixth-hand. Or that's what it feels like."

She had sniffed, without really thinking; air was air. "The smell of home," she said to him.

"I want to go back to Belfast," he said. "I miss it. Everything about it, I miss. Black Mountain. The lough. The red brick. The pubs. Everything."

2

By good fortune, and co-incidence – which sometimes come together neatly – an aunt had died and left him the house off the Malone Road, a well-heeled part of the Northern Irish city. She was an archetypical Malone Road aunt – slightly disapproving and of firm convictions – but he had been fond of her and she of him. There were other nephews and nieces who might have benefited from a share in the house, but she favoured him. "I'm leaving this place to you," she said. "I see no point in leaving it to the whole lot of you. One room each. Absurd."

That conversation took place a couple of years before she died. He returned to look over the place and to make arrangements for it to be looked after by a postgraduate student from the university down the road, who made desultory efforts at keeping the garden in order, but who at least was assiduous in maintaining the interior. Michael preferred a short-term arrangement of this nature, as he already sensed that he and his wife were drifting apart and that he would leave London. Now he had a place to come back to.

3

He thought that he might remarry – he was forty-five and there was still plenty of time, even to start a family, if he was lucky. But he did not want to hurry things. He found it easy to adjust to being on his own, but it did occur to him that he might get a cat. A dog would tie him down too much; a cat could be left to fend for itself for the occasional weekend. A cat gave a house a more lived-in feel. A cat would become a familiar spirit, like a benign ghost.

"Try and get hold of an intelligent cat," advised a friend. "Burmese, preferably. They're very intelligent."

He agreed that this was a good idea; one would not want to live with a cat that found life too much of a challenge. A breeder was located in Fermanagh and Michael made the trip out to collect his allocated kitten.

"These are very clever creatures," said the breeder. "You won't be able to teach this wee fellow any tricks. He'll know them all already."

Michael looked at the diminutive cat, at its green eyes, which were already fixed on him. There was certainly a marked intelligence there; he was being assessed, he felt; weighed up in some obscure feline calculation. He felt slightly uneasy.

4

Michael worked from home, preparing complicated tax returns for clients whose faces he never saw. He did this from a study where he had a view of the stretch of garden that lay behind the house. The cat loved this miniature jungle, and spent hours stalking creatures real and imaginary amongst the shrubs. Michael went out from time to time and watched the cat in its hunting, but this would usually stop the cat from doing what it was doing. It would sit down, and direct its disconcerting gaze in his direction. Only when he had gone back in would the game resume.

Burmese cats, he had been told, were affectionate, but this one was not. It appeared for meals, glaring at him if its food was late or if it in some way failed to meet its expectations. Then it would saunter off. If he tried to pick it up and stroke it, it would freeze and look at him with undisguised hostility.

"The cat doesn't like me," he remarked to the friend who had recommended the breed.

"Give it time," said the friend.

"I have, and it makes no difference. He seems to be getting increasingly hostile. It's almost as if he resents the fact that I live in the house with him."

The friend laughed. "He wants you out?"

"Don't joke about it," said Michael.

5

Some months after the cat's arrival, when it was almost fully-grown, it made its first attempt to trip Michael up. He saved himself from falling, but only just.

"You stupid creature," he muttered.

The cat looked up at him, with all the coldness of a psychopath, and then sauntered off. A dog, Michael reflected, always looks apologetic if it gets in its owners way; not so cats. Or not so *this* cat.

There were several more incidents of this nature, and each time it occurred Michael became more irritated. It seemed to him that the cat's behaviour was intentional, that it wanted him to fall and injure himself. In self-defence he tried to stand on its tail when it got between his feet – that, he thought, would teach it a lesson. But the cat spun round and dug its claws into his trouser leg, scratching him slightly. Then it looked at him with a murderous look in its eye, held his gaze for a few moments, and wandered away.

6

Michael spent long hours on the telephone to his ex-wife in London.

"I'm missing you terribly," she said. "Do you think we've done the right thing?"

"Ask your boyfriend," he said, and then changed the subject to the cat. "That cat."

"It looks so sweet," she said. "That photograph you sent me. Really sweet."

"Appearances can be deceptive," he retorted. "It is definitely not a sweet cat. Not at all."

"Are you being kind enough to it? You have to win their affection you know."

He explained about the tripping up. "Do you think it possible that a cat might decide to ... to harm its owner?"

There was silence at the other end of the line. "Are you all right, Michael?"

He sighed. "I know it sounds absurd, but I have the distinct impression that this cat is trying to ... Well, I don't know. Trying to get me, I suppose."

She laughed. "Impossible. Cats don't do that. No matter how intelligent. Cats know which side their bread's buttered on."

He agreed that this was generally the case, but then he posed the question: what if an intelligent cat, a really intelligent one, thought that it might inherit a house, once the human owners were disposed of?

7

Some days after this conversation, Michael returned to the house one night after being at a dinner party out of town. It had been a good evening and his hosts, although tactful about it, had clearly attempted a bit of match-making. He found that he liked the woman invited to sit beside him. She was also divorced and had a seven-year-old son. The father was in Dubai, working for an engineering firm. She and Michael got on well and telephone numbers were exchanged. He saw the hostess watching this with approval; why, he wondered, do people get pleasure in bringing others together? Was it because we feared loneliness, not only for ourselves, but for others?

He came back to the house in a state of elation. He was on top of his work; he was not short of money; he had the prospect of a date with that nice woman. But then there was the cat.

He retired to bed and turned off his light. He dozed off quickly, but was suddenly awakened by a noise downstairs, a yowling sound. He got up, rubbing the sleep from his eyes. It would be hungry, he supposed. That was the way it yowled when it wanted him to feed it.

It was a stair-rod that tripped him up. It was near the top of the stairs, and it had come out at such an angle that anybody would be bound to fall over it in the dark. He shouted out as he fell and reached out wildly for something to clutch. His hand found no purchase on the wall, but brushed against the light switch and inadvertently turned it on. As he fell, he saw the cat at the bottom of the stairs, looking up at him with its intense green eyes.

He was not injured; bruised, perhaps, but nothing more than that. The cat, after surveying the scene, walked calmly away, and out of its cat door. He sat there for several minutes, rubbing his left knee and thinking. He was positive that the stair-rod had not been out of place when he had gone up to bed; he would have noticed it if it had. He was sure. He was quite convinced.

There was only one explanation: the cat had moved the stair-rod deliberately.

8

He had nobody to speak to. If he tried to tell any of his friends about what had happened they would have concluded that he had lost his reason. Cats did not try to murder their owners, even if they had a motive. The idea was absurd. Cats had few intentions in this life; and as for motives, the very concept was inappropriate and misleading when applied to the animal world.

But Michael was sure, and the next morning he rehearsed his alternatives. He could give the cat away – there would be plenty of people who would willingly provide a home to such an elegant, exotic creature. Yet if he did that, he would be passing on to somebody a creature who might do to a new owner exactly what it had tried to do to him. So he could not do that.

He could take it to the vet, he supposed, and ask for it to be put down – that would be self-defence surely. But no vet would put down a perfectly healthy young animal just because the owner had taken a dislike to it. And that is what the vet would conclude; he would think that it was a matter of personal dislike.

He decided that he would have to do something to bring the cat under control. Even if he could not reform it, he could let it know that he was aware of what it was up to. And that is the line of reasoning which produced his brilliant idea.

He looked out of his window. The cat was in the garden, sitting on a patch of grass, looking back at him in its superior manner. He pointed a finger at the animal and mouthed the words: "I'm on to you, kitty!"

9

He timed his arrival back at the house very carefully. He wanted the cat to be in when he returned, so that he could witness the impact of his plan. So he made sure that he came back at a point in the day when he knew that the cat would be hungry and would be waiting indignantly to be fed.

And his new dog was chosen carefully too. He was a recently-retired police dog, still in good shape, who had been living with his former handler in Dunmurry. The handler and his wife were moving into a flat and wanted somewhere more suitable for the dog.

"He's a great chap," said the handler. "When I was in the force he solved a lot of crimes, so he did."

"Just what I'm looking for," said Michael.

He led the dog into its new home. When it saw them come in, the cat arched its back and retreated on tip-toes to the back of the room. Every hair on its body was electrified, standing straight in terror and outrage.

"I think we understand one another very well now," said Michael.

The cat said nothing.

12 BOLINBROKE AVENUE

Peter James

IT WAS A pleasant-looking mock Tudor semi, with a cherry tree in the front garden and a wooden birdbath. There was nothing immediately evident about the property to suggest a reason for the terror Susan Miller felt each time she saw it.

Number twelve. White letters on the oak door. A brass knocker. And in the distance, the faint sound of the sea. She began to walk up the path, her speed increasing as she came closer, as if drawn by an invisible magnet. Her terror deepening, she reached forward and rang the bell.

"Susan! Susan, darling! It's OK. It's OK!"

The dull rasp faded in her ears; her eyes sprang open; she gulped down air, staring out into the darkness of the bedroom. "I'm sorry," she whispered, hoarsely. "The dream. I had the dream."

Tom settled back down with a grunt of disapproval and was asleep again in moments. Susan lay awake, listening to the steady, endless roar of the traffic on the M6 pouring past Birmingham, fear roaring like an icy flood-stream through her.

She got out of bed and walked over to the window, afraid to go back to sleep. Easing back the edge of a curtain, she stared out into the night; the large illuminated letters advertising IKEA dominated the horizon.

The dream was getting more frequent. The first time had been on Christmas Eve some ten years back, and for a long while it had recurred only very occasionally. Now it was happening every few weeks.

After a short while, exhaustion and the cold of the late October air lured her back into bed. She snuggled up against Tom's unyielding body and closed her eyes, knowing the second nightmare which always followed was yet to come, and that she was powerless to resist it.

Christmas Eve. Susan arrived home laden with last-minute shopping, including a few silly gifts for Tom to try to make him smile; he rarely smiled these days. His car was in the drive, but when she called out he did not respond. Puzzled, she went upstairs, calling his name again. Then she opened the bedroom door.

As she did so, she heard the creak of springs and the rustle of sheets. Two naked figures writhing on the bed swirled in unison towards her. Their shocked faces stared at her as if she was an intruder, had no right to be there. Strangers. A woman with long red hair and a grey-haired man. Both of them total strangers making love in her bed, in her bedroom. *In her house.*

But instead of confronting them, she backed away, rapidly, confused, feeling as if it was herself who was the intruder. "I'm sorry," she said. "I'm so sorry. I'm—"

Then she woke up.

Tom stirred, grunted, then slept on.

Susan lay still. God it was so vivid this time, it seemed to be getting more and more vivid just recently. She had read an article in a magazine recently about interpreting dreams, and she tried to think what this one might be telling her.

Confusion was the theme. She was getting confused easily these days, particularly over time. Often she'd be on the verge of starting some job around the house, then remember that she had already done it; or rushing out to the shops to buy something she had already just bought. Stress. She had read about the effects of stress, in another magazine – she got most of her knowledge from magazines – and that it could cause all kinds of confusion and tricks of the mind.

And she knew the source of the stress, also.

Mandy. The new secretary at the Walsall branch of the Allied Chester and North East Building society, where Tom was deputy manager. Tom had told her about Mandy's arrival a year ago, and had then never mentioned her since. But she had watched them talking at the annual Christmas party last year, to which spouses and partners were invited. They had talked a damned sight too much for Susan's liking. And they e-mailed each other a damned sight too much.

She had not been sure what to do. At thirty-two she had kept her figure through careful eating and regular aerobics, and still looked good. She took care over her short brown hair, over her makeup and her clothes. There wasn't much else she *could* do, and confronting Tom without any evidence would have made her look foolish. Besides, she was under doctor's orders to stay calm. She had given up work in order to relax and improve her chances of conceiving the child they had been trying for these past five years. She *had* to stay calm.

Unexpectedly, the solution presented itself when Tom arrived home that evening.

"Promotion?' she said, her eyes alight with excitement.

"Yup! You are now looking at the second youngest ever Branch Manager for the Allied Chester and North East Building society! But," he added hesitantly, "it's going to mean moving."

"Moving? I don't mind at all, darling!" *Anywhere*, she thought. *The further the better. Get him away from that bloody Mandy!* "Where to?"

"Brighton."

She could scarcely believe her luck. In their teens, Tom had taken her for a weekend to Brighton; it was the first time they had been away together; the bed in the little hotel had creaked like mad, and someone in the room below had hollered at them and they'd had to stuff sheets into their mouths to silence their laugher. "We're going to live in Brighton?"

"That's right!"

She flung her arms around him. "When? How soon?"

"They want me to take over the branch at the start of the New Year. So we have to find a house pretty smartly."

Susan did a quick calculation. It was now mid November. "We'll never find somewhere and get moved in within a month. We've got to sell this place, we've got to—"

"The Society will help. They're relocating us, all expenses paid, and we get a lump sum allowance for more expensive housing in the south. They're giving me the week off next week so we can go there and look around. I've told the relocations officer our budget and she's contacting some local estate agents for us."

The first particulars arrived two days later in a thick envelope. Susan opened it in the kitchen and pulled out the contents, whilst Tom was gulping down his breakfast. There were about fifteen houses, mostly too expensive. She discarded several, then read the details of one that was well within their range, a very ugly box of a house with a *small but charming* garden, close to the sea. She liked the idea of living close to the sea, but not the house. Still, she thought. You spend most of your time indoors, not looking at the exterior, so she put it aside as a possible and turned to the next.

As she saw the picture, she froze. *Couldn't be*, she thought, bringing it closer to her eyes. *Could not possibly be.* She stared hard, struggling to control her shaking hands, at a mock Tudor semi identical to the one she always saw in her dream. Coincidence, she thought, feeling a tightening knot in her throat. *Coincidence*. Has to be. There are thousands of houses that look like this.

Twelve Bolinbroke Avenue.

Number *twelve*, she knew, was the number on the door in her dream.

The distant roar of the sea she always heard in that dream.

Maybe she had seen the house when they had been to Brighton previously. How long ago was that? Fourteen years? But even if she had seen it before, why should it have stuck in her mind?

"Anything of interest?" Tom said, reaching out and turning the particulars of the ugly box round to read them. Then he pulled the details of the semi out of her hands, rather roughly. "This looks nice," he said. "In our bracket. *In need of some modernization*. That's estate agent-speak for a near wreck. Means if we do it up it could be worth a lot more."

Susan agreed that they should see the house. She had to see it to satisfy herself that it was not the one in the dream; but she did not tell Tom that; he had little sympathy for her dreams.

The estate agent drove them himself. He wore a sharp suit, white socks and smelled of hair gel. "Great position," he said. "One of the most sought-after residential areas of Hove. Five minutes walk to the beach. Hove Lagoon close by, great for kids. And it's a bargain for this area. A bit of work and you could increase the value a lot." He turned into Bolinbroke Avenue, and pointed with his finger. "There we are."

Susan bit her lip as they pulled up outside number twelve. Her mouth was dry and she was shaking badly. Terror was gripping her; the same terror she previously experienced only in her dreams, gripped her like a claw.

The only thing that was different was the For Sale board outside. She could see the cherry tree; the wooden bird bath. She could hear the sea. There was no doubt in her mind; absolutely no doubt at all.

She climbed out of the car as if she were back in her dream, and led the way up the path. Exactly as she always did in her dream, she reached out her hand and rang the bell.

After a few moments the door was opened by a woman in her forties, with long red hair. She had a pleasant, open-natured smile at first, but when she saw Susan, all the colour drained from her face. She looked as if she had been struck with a sledgehammer.

Susan was staring back at her in amazement. There was no mistaking, absolutely no mistaking at all. "Oh my God," she said, the words blurting out. "You're the woman I keep seeing in my dream."

"And you," she replied, barely able to get the words out, "Y– you – you are the ghost that's been haunting our bedroom for the past ten years."

Susan stood, helpless, waves of fear rippling her skin. "Ghost?" she said finally.

"You look like our ghost; you just look so incredibly like her." She hesitated. "Who are you? How can I help you?"

"We've come to see around the house."

"See around the house?" she sounded astonished.

"The estate agent – made an appointment." Susan turned to look at him for confirmation, but could not see him or Tom – or the car.

"There must be a mistake," the woman said. "This house is not on the market."

Susan looked round again, disoriented. Where were they? Where the hell had they gone? "Please," she said. "This ghost I resemble – who – who is – was – she?"

"I don't know; neither of us do. But about ten years ago some building society manager bought this house when it was a wreck, murdered his wife on Christmas eve and moved his mistress in. He renovated the house, and cemented his wife into the basement. The mistress finally cracked after a couple of years and went to the police. That's all I know."

"What – what happened to them?"

The woman was staring oddly at her, as if she was trying to see her but no longer could. Susan felt swirling cold air engulfing her. She turned, bewildered. Where the hell was Tom? The estate agent? Then she saw that the For Sale board had gone from the garden.

She was alone, on the step, facing the closed front door.

Number twelve. She stared at the white plastic letters; the brass knocker. Then, as if drawn by that same damned magnet, she felt herself being pulled forward, felt herself gliding in through the solid oak of the door.

I'll wake up in a moment, she thought. *I'll wake up. I always do.* Except she knew, this time, something had changed.

APPETITE FOR MURDER

Simon R. Green

I NEVER WANTED to be a detective. But the call went out, and no one else stood up, so I sold my soul to the company store, for a badge and a gun and a shift that never ends.

The Nightside is London's very own dirty little secret; a hidden realm of gods and monsters, magic and murder, and more sin and temptation than you can shake a wallet at. People come to the Nightside from all over the world, to indulge the pleasures and appetites that might not have a name, but certainly have a price. It's always night in the Nightside, always three o'clock in the morning, the hour that tries men's souls and finds them wanting. The sun has never shone here, probably because it knows it isn't welcome. This is a place to do things that can only be done in the shadows, in the dark.

I'm Sam Warren. I was the first, and for a long time the only, detective in the Nightside. I worked for the authorities, those grey and faceless figures who run the Nightside, in as much as anyone does, or can. Even in a place where there is no crime, because everything is permitted, where sin and suffering, death and damnation are just business as usual … there are still those who go too far, and have to be taken down hard. And for that, you need a detective.

We don't get many serial killers in the Nightside. Mostly because amateurs don't tend to last long among so much professional competition. But I was made detective, more years ago than I care to remember, to hunt down the very first of these human monsters. His name was Shock Headed Peter. He killed 347 men, women and children, before I caught him. Though that's just an official estimate; we never found any of his victims' bodies. Just their clothes.

Wouldn't surprise me if the real total was closer to a thousand. I caught him and put him away; but the things I saw, and the things I had to do, changed me forever.

Made me the Nightside's detective, for all my sins, mea culpa.

I'd just finished eating when the call came in. From the *H.P. Lovecraft Memorial Library*, home to more forbidden tomes under one roof than anywhere else. Browse at your own risk. It appeared the Nightside's latest serial killer had struck again. Only this time he'd been interrupted, and the body was still warm, the blood still wet.

I strode through the library accompanied by a Mister Pettigrew, a tall stork-like personage with wild eyes and a shock of white hair. He gabbled continuously as we made our way through the tall stacks, wringing his bony hands against his sunken chest. Mister Pettigrew was Chief Librarian, and almost overcome with shame that such a vulgar thing should have happened in his library.

"It's all such a mess!" he wailed. "And right in the middle of the Anthropology Section. We've only just finished refurbishing!"

"What can you tell me about the victim?" I said patiently.

"Oh, he's dead. Yes. Very dead, in fact. Horribly mutilated, Detective! I don't know how we're going to get the blood out of the carpets."

"Did you happen to notice if there were any … pieces missing, from the body?"

"Pieces? Oh dear," said Mister Pettigrew. "I can feel one of my heads coming on. I think I'm going to have to go and have a little lie down."

He took me as far as the Anthropology Section, and then disappeared at speed. It hadn't been twenty minutes since I got the call, but still someone had beaten me to the body. Crouching beside the bloody mess on the floor was the Nightside's very own superheroine, Ms Fate. She wore a highly polished black leather outfit, complete with full face mask and cape; but somehow on her it never looked like a costume or some fetish thing. It looked like a uniform. Like work clothes. She even had a utility belt around her narrow waist, all golden clasp and bulging little pouches. I thought the high heels on the boots were a bit much, though. I came up on her from behind, making no noise at all, but she still knew I was there.

"Hello, Detective Warren," she said, in her low smoky voice, not even glancing round. "You got here fast."

"Happened to be in the neighbourhood," I said. "What have you found?"

"All kinds of interesting things. Come and have a look."

Anyone else I would have sent packing, but not her. We'd worked a bunch of cases together, and she knew her stuff. We don't get too many super-heroes or vigilantes in the Nightside, mostly because they get killed off so damn quickly. Ms Fate, that dark avenger of the night, was different. Very focused, very skilled, very professional. Would have made a good detective. She made room for me to crouch down beside her. My knees made loud cracking noises in the library hush.

"You're looking good, detective," Ms Fate said easily. "Have you started dying your hair?"

"Far too much grey," I said. "I was starting to look my age, and I couldn't have that."

"I've questioned the staff," said Ms Fate. "Knew you wouldn't mind. No one saw anything, but then no one ever does, in the Nightside. Only one way in to this Section, and only one way out, and he would have had blood all over him, but ..."

"Any camera surveillance?"

"The kind of people who come here, to read the kind of books they keep here, really don't want to be identified. So, no surveillance of any kind, scientific or mystical. There's major security in place to keep any of the books from going walkabout, but that's it."

"If our killer was interrupted, he may have left some clues behind," I said. "This is his sixth victim. Maybe he got sloppy."

Ms Fate nodded slowly, her expression unreadable behind her dark mask. Her eyes were very blue, very bright. "This has got to stop, detective. Five previous victims, all horribly mutilated, all with missing organs. Different organs each time. Interestingly enough, the first victim was killed with a blade, but all the others were torn apart, through brute strength. Why change his MO after the first killing? Most serial killers cling to a pattern, a ritual, that means something significant to them."

"Maybe he decided a blade wasn't personal enough," I said. "Maybe he felt the need to get his hands dirty."

We both looked at the body in silence for a while. This one was different. The victim had been a werewolf, and had been caught in mid-change as he died. His face had elongated into a muzzle, his hands had claws, and patches of silver-grey fur showed clearly on his exposed skin. His clothes were ripped and torn and soaked with blood. He'd been gutted, torn raggedly open from chin to crotch, leaving a great crimson wound. There was blood all around him, and more spattered across the spines of books on the shelves.

"It's never easy to kill a werewolf," Ms Fate said finally. "But given the state of the wound's edges, he wasn't cut open. That rules out a silver dagger."

"No sign of a silver bullet either," I said.

"Then we can probably rule out the Lone Ranger." She rubbed her bare chin thoughtfully. "You know; the extent of these injuries reminds me a lot of cattle mutilations."

I looked at her. "Are we talking little grey aliens?"

She smiled briefly, her scarlet lips standing out against the pale skin under the black mask. "Maybe I should check to see if he's been probed?"

"I think that was the least of his worries," I said. "This must have been a really bad way to die. Our victim had his organs ripped out while he was still alive."

Ms Fate busied herself taking samples from the body and the crime scene, dropping them into sealable plastic bags, and tucking them away in her belt pouches.

"Don't smile," she said, not looking round. "Forensic science catches more killers than deductive thought."

"I never said a word," I said innocently.

"You didn't have to. You only have to look at my utility belt and your mouth starts twitching. I'll have you know the things I store in my belt have saved my life on more than one occasion. Shuriken, smoke bombs, nausea gas capsules, stun grenades ... A girl has to be prepared for everything." She stood up and looked down at the body. "It's such a mess I can't even tell which organs were taken; can you?"

"The heart, certainly," I said, standing up. "Anything else, we'll have to wait for the autopsy."

"I've already been through the clothing," said Ms Fate. "If there was any ID, the killer took it with him. But I did find a Press Pass, tucked away in his shoe. Said he worked for the *Night Times*. But no name on the pass, which is odd. Could be an investigative reporter, I suppose, working undercover."

"I'll check with the editor," I said.

"But what was he doing here? Research?"

We both looked around, and Ms Fate was the first to find a book lying on the floor, just outside the blood pool. She opened the book, and flicked quickly through it.

"Anything interesting?" I said.

"Hard to tell. Some doctoral dissertation on the cannibal practices of certain South American tribes."

I gestured for the book, and she handed it over. I skimmed quickly through the opening chapter. "Seems to be about the old cannibal myth that you are what you eat. You know; eat a brave man's heart to become brave, a runner's leg muscles to become fast ..."

We both looked at the torn-open body on the floor, with its missing organs.

"Could that be our murderer's motivation?" said Ms Fate. "He's taking the organs so he can eat them later, and maybe ... what? Gain new abilities? Run me through the details of the five previous victims, Detective."

"First was a minor Greek godling," I said. "Supposedly descended from Hercules, at many removes. Very strong. Died of a single knife wound to the heart. Chest and arm muscles were taken."

"Just the one blow to the heart," said Ms Fate. "You'd have to get in close for that. Which suggests the victim either knew his killer, or had reason to trust him."

"If the killer has acquired a godling's strength, he wouldn't need a knife any more," I said.

"There's more to it than that." She looked like she might be frowning, behind her mask. "This whole hands-on thing shouts ... passion. That the killer enjoyed it, or took some satisfaction from it."

"Second victim was a farseer," I said. "What they call a remote viewer these days. Her head was smashed in, and her eyes taken. After that; an immortal who lost his testicles, a teleporter for a messenger service who had his brain ripped right out of his skull, and finally a minor radio chat show host, who lost his tongue and vocal chords."

"Why that last one?" said Ms Fate. "What did the killer hope to gain? The gift of the gab?"

"You'll have to ask him," I said. "Presumably the killer believed that eating the werewolf's missing organs would give him shape-changing abilities, or at least regeneration."

"He's trying to eat himself into a more powerful person ... Hell, just the godling's strength and the werewolf's abilities will make him really hard to take down. Have you come up with any leads yet, from the previous victims?"

"No," I said. "Nothing."

"Then I suppose we'd better run through the usual suspects, if only to cross them off. How about Mr Stab, the legendary uncaught immortal serial killer of Old London Town?"

"No," I said. "He always uses a knife, or a scalpel. Always has, ever since 1888."

"All right; how about Arnold Drood, the Bloody Man?"

"His own family tracked him down and killed him just last year."

"Good. Shock Headed Peter?"

"Still in prison, where I put him," I said. "And there he'll stay, till the day he dies."

Ms Fate sniffed. "Don't know why they didn't just execute him."

"Oh, they tried," I said. "Several times, in fact. But it didn't take."

"Wait a minute," said Ms Fate. She knelt down again suddenly, and leant right over to study the dead man's elongated muzzle. "Take a look at this, Detective. The nose and mouth tissues are eaten away. Right back to the bone in places. I wonder ..." She produced a chemical kit from her belt, and ran some quick tests. "I thought so. Silver. Definite traces of silver dust, in the nose, mouth and throat. Now that was clever ... Throw a handful of silver dust into the were-wolf's face, he breathes it in, unsuspecting, and his tissues would immediately react to the silver. It had to have been horribly painful; certainly enough to distract the victim and interrupt his shape change ... while leaving him vulnerable to the killer's exceptional strength."

"Well spotted," I said. "I must be getting old. Was a time I wouldn't have missed something like that."

"You're not that old," Ms Fate said lightly.

"Old enough that they want to retire me," I said.

"You? You'll never retire! You live for this job."

"Yes," I said. "I've done it so long it's all I've got now. But I am getting old. Slow. Still better than any of these upstart latecomers, like John Taylor and Tommy Oblivion."

"You look fine to me," Ms Fate said firmly. "In pretty good shape too, for a man of your age. How do you manage it?"

I smiled. "We all have our secrets."

"Of course. This is the Nightside, after all."

"I could have worked out your secret identity," I said. "If I'd wanted to."

"Perhaps. Though it might have surprised you. Why didn't you?"

"I don't know. Professional courtesy? Or maybe I just liked the idea of knowing there was someone else around who wanted to catch murderers as much as I did."

"You can depend on me," said Ms Fate.

Our next port of call was the Nightside's one and only autopsy room. We do have a CSI, but it only has four people in it. And only one Coroner, Dr West. Short, stocky fellow with a smiling face and flat straw-yellow hair. I wouldn't leave him alone with the body of anyone I cared about, but he's good enough at his job.

By the time Ms Fate and I got there, Dr West already has the werewolf's body laid out in his slab. He was washing the naked body with great thoroughness and crooning a song to it as we entered. He looked round unhurriedly, and waggled the fingers of one podgy hand at us.

"Come in, come in! So nice to have visitors. So nice! Of course, I'm never alone down here, but I do miss good conversation. Take a look at this."

He put down his wet sponge, picked up a long surgical instrument, and started poking around inside the body's massive wound. Ms Fate and I moved closer, while still maintaining a respectful distance. Dr West tended to get over-excited with a scalpel in his hand, and we didn't want to get spattered.

Dr West thrust both his hands into the cavity and started rooting around with quite unnecessary enthusiasm. "The heart is missing," he said cheerfully. "Also, the liver. Yes. Yes ... Not cut out, torn out

... Made a real mess of this poor fellow's insides; hard to be sure of anything else ... Not sure what to put down as actual cause of death; blood loss, trauma, shock ... Heart attack? Yes. That covers it. So; another victim for our current serial killer. Number six ... how very industrious. Oh yes. Haven't even got a name for your chart, have we, boy? Just another John Doe ... But not to worry; I've got a nice little locker waiting for you, nice and cosy, next to your fellow victims."

"You have got to stop talking to the corpses like that," I said sternly. "One of these days someone will catch you at it."

Dr West stuck out his tongue at me. "Let them. See if I care. See if they can get anyone else to do this job."

"How long have you been Coroner, Dr West?" said Ms Fate, tactfully changing the subject.

"Oh, years and years, my dear. I was made Coroner the same year Samuel here was made detective. Oh yes, we go way back, Samuel and I. All because of that nasty Shock Headed Peter ... The Authorities decided that such a successful serial killer was bad for business, and therefore Something Must Be Done. It's all about popular perception, you see ... There are many things in the Nightside far more dangerous than any human killer could ever hope to be, but the Authorities, bless their grey little hearts, wanted visitors to feel safe, so ..."

He stopped and looked at me sourly. "You'd never believe he and I were the same age, would you? How do you do it, Samuel?"

"Healthy eating," I said. "And lots of vitamins."

"Why haven't you called in Walker?" Ms Fate said suddenly. "He speaks for the Authorities, with a voice everyone has to obey; and I've heard it said he once made a corpse sit up on a slab and answer his questions."

"Oh, he did, he did," said Dr West, pulling his hands out of the body with a nasty sucking sound. "I was there at the time, and very edifying it was too. But unfortunately, all six of our victims had their tongues torn out. After our killer had taken the bits and pieces he wanted. Which suggests our killer had reason to be afraid of Walker."

"Hell," I said. "Everyone's got good reason to be afraid of Walker."

Dr West shrugged, threw aside his scalpel and slipped off his latex gloves with a deliberate flourish, as though to make clear he'd done all that could reasonably be expected of him.

Ms Fate stared into the open wound again. "Our killer really does like his work, doesn't he?"

"He's got an appetite for it," I said solemnly.

"Oh, please," said Ms Fate.

I moved in beside her, staring down into the cavity. "Took the heart out first, then the liver. Our killer must believe they hold the secret of the werewolf's abilities. If he is a shape-changer now, he'd be that much harder to take down."

Ms Fate looked at me thoughtfully, and then turned to Dr West. "Do you still have all the victims' clothes and belongings?"

"Of course, my dear, of course! Individually bagged and tagged. Help yourself."

She opened every bag, and checked every piece of torn and blood-soaked clothing. It's always good to see a real professional at work. Eventually she ran out of things to check and test, and turned back to me.

"Six victims. Different ages, sexes, occupations. Nothing at all to connect them. Unless you know something, Detective."

"There's nothing in the files," I said.

"So how were the victims chosen? Why these six people?"

"Maybe the people don't matter," I said. "Just their abilities."

"Run me through them again," she said. "Names and abilities, in order, from the beginning."

"First victim was the godling Demetrius Heracles," I said patiently. "Then the farseer, Barbara Moore. The teleporter, Cainy du Brec. The immortal Count Magnus, though I doubt very much that was his real name. The chat show host, Adrian Woss, and finally the werewolf, Christopher Russell."

"This whole business reminds me unpleasantly of Shock Headed Peter," Ms Fate said slowly. "Not the MO, but the sheer ruthlessness of the murders. Are you sure he hasn't escaped?"

"Positive," I said. "No one escapes from Shadow Deep."

She shook her masked head, her heavy cloak rustling loudly. "I'd still feel happier if we checked. Can you get us in?"

"Of course," I said. "I'm the detective."

* * *

So we went down into Shadow Deep, all the way down to the darkest place in the Nightside, sunk far below in the cold bedrock. Constructed ... no one knows how long ago, to hold the most vicious, evil and dangerous criminals ever stupid enough to prey on the Nightside. The ones we can't, for one reason or another, just execute and be done with. The only way down is by the official transport circle, maintained and operated by three witches from a small room over a really rough bar called "The Jolly Cripple". If the people who drank in the bar knew what went on in the room above their heads ... they'd probably drink a hell of a lot more.

"Why here?" said Ms Fate, as we ascended the gloomy back stairs. "Secrecy?"

"Partly, I suppose," I said. "More likely because it's cheap."

The three witches were the traditional bent-over hags in tattered cloaks, all clawed hands and hooked noses. The great circle on the floor had been marked in chalk mixed with sulphur and semen. You don't want to know how I found out. Ms Fate glowered at the three witches.

"You can stop that cackling right now. You don't have to put on an act; we're not tourists."

"Well, pardon us for taking pride in our work," said one of the witches, straightening up immediately. "We are professionals, after all. And image is everything, these days. You don't think these warts just happened, do you?"

I gave her my best hard look, and she got the transport operation underway. The three witches did the business with a minimum of chanting and incense, and down Ms Fate and I went, down to Shadow Deep.

It was dark when we arrived, completely dark with not a ghost of a light anywhere. I only knew Ms Fate was there with me because I could hear her breathing at my side. Footsteps approached, slow and heavy, until finally a pair of night vision goggles were thrust into my hand. I nearly jumped out of my skin, and from the muffled squeak beside me, so did Ms Fate. I slipped the goggles on, and Shadow Deep appeared around me, all dull green images and fuzzy shadows.

It's always dark in Shadow Deep.

We were standing in an ancient circular stone chamber, with a low roof, curving walls and just the one exit, leading into a stone tunnel. Standing before us was one of the prison staff; a rough clay golem with simple pre-programmed routines. It had no eyes on its smooth face, because it didn't need to see. It turned abruptly and started off down the tunnel, and Ms Fate and I hurried after it. The tunnel branched almost immediately, and branched again, and as we moved from tunnel to identical tunnel, I soon lost all track of where I was.

We came at last to the governor's office, and the golem raised an oversized hand and knocked once on the door. A cheery voice called out for us to enter, and the door swung open before us. A blinding light spilled out, and Ms Fate and I clawed off our goggles as we stumbled into the office. The door shut itself behind us.

I looked around the governor's office with watering eyes. It wasn't particularly big, but it had all the comforts. The Governor came out from behind his desk to greet us, a big blocky man with a big friendly smile that didn't touch his eyes at all. He seemed happy to see us, but then, he was probably happy to see anyone. Shadow Deep doesn't get many visitors.

"Welcome, welcome!" he said, taking our goggles and shaking my hand and Ms Fate's with great gusto. "The great detective and the famous vigilante; such an honour! Do sit down, make yourselves at home. That's right! Make yourselves comfortable! Can I offer you a drink, cigars?"

"No," I said.

"Ah, Detective," said the Governor, sitting down again behind his desk. "It's always business with you, isn't it?"

"Ms Fate is concerned that one of your inmates might have escaped," I said.

"What? Oh no; no, quite impossible!" The Governor turned his full attention and what he likes to think of as his charming smile on Ms Fate. "No one ever escapes from here. Never, never. It's always dark in Shadow Deep, you see. Light doesn't work here, outside my office. Not any kind of light, scientific or magical. Not even a match … Even if a prisoner could get out of his cell, which he can't, there's no way he could find his way through the maze of tunnels to the transfer site. Even a teleporter can't get out of here, because there's no way of knowing how far down we are!"

"Tell her how it works," I said. "Tell her what happens to the scum I bring here."

The Governor blinked rapidly, and tried another ingratiating smile. "Yes, well, the prisoner is put into his cell by one of the golems, and the door is then nailed shut. And sealed forever with pre-prepared, very powerful magics. Once in, a prisoner never leaves his cell. The golems pass food and water through a slot in the door. And that's it."

"What about—?" said Ms Fate.

"There's a grille in the floor."

"Oh, ick."

"Quite," said the Governor. "You must understand, our prisoners are not here to reform, or repent. Only the very worst individuals ever end up here, and they stay here till they die. However long that takes. No reprieves, and no time off for good behaviour."

"How did you get this job?" said Ms Fate.

"I think I must have done something really bad in a previous existence," the Governor said grandly. "Cosmic payback can be such a bitch."

"You got this job because you got caught," I said.

The Governor scowled. "Yes, well ... It's not that I did anything really bad ..."

"Ms Fate," I said, "Allow me to introduce to you Charles Peace, villain from a long line of villains. Burglar, thief, and snapper up of anything valuable not actually nailed down. Safes opened while you wait."

"That was my downfall," the Governor admitted. "I opened Walker's safe, you see; just for the challenge of it. And I saw something I really shouldn't have seen. Something no one was ever supposed to see. I ran, of course, but the Detective tracked me down and brought me back, and Walker gave me a choice. On the spot execution, or serve here as governor until what I know becomes obsolete, and doesn't matter any more. That was seventeen years ago, and there isn't a day goes by where I don't wonder whether I made the right decision."

"Seventeen years?" said Ms Fate. She always did have a soft spot for a hard luck story.

"Seventeen years, four months and three days," said the Governor.

"Not that I obsess about it, you understand."

"Is Shock Headed Peter still here?" I said bluntly. "There's no chance he could have got out?"

"Of course not! I did the rounds only an hour ago, and his cell is still sealed. Come on, Detective; if Shock Headed Peter was on the loose in the Nightside again, we'd all know about it."

"Who else have you got down here?" said Ms Fate. "Anyone ... famous?"

"Oh, quite a few; certainly some names you'd recognize. Let's see; we have the Murder Masques, Sweet Annie Abattoir, Max Maxwell the Voodoo Apostate, Maggie Malign ... But they're all quite secure, too, I can assure you."

"I just needed to be sure this place is as secure as it's supposed to be," said Ms Fate. "You'd better prepare a new cell, governor, because I've brought you a new prisoner."

And she looked at me.

I rose to my feet, and so did she. We stood looking at each other for a long moment.

"I'm sorry, Sam," she said. "But it's you. You're the murderer."

"Have you gone mad?" I said.

"You gave yourself away, Sam," she said, meeting my gaze squarely with her own. "That's why I had you bring me here to Shadow Deep, where you belong. Where even you can't get away."

"What makes you think it was me?" I said.

"You knew things you shouldn't have known. Things only the killer could have known. First, at the library. That anthropology text was a dry, stuffy and very academic text. Very difficult for a layman to read and understand. But you just skimmed through it and then neatly summed up the whole concept. The only way you could have done that, was if you'd known it in advance. That raised my suspicions, but I didn't say anything. I wanted to be wrong about you.

"But you did it again, at the autopsy. First, you knew that the heart had been removed *before* the liver. Dr West hadn't worked that out yet, because the body's insides were such a mess. Second, when I asked you to name the victims in order, you named them all, including the werewolf. Who hasn't been identified yet. Dr West still had him down as a John Doe.

"So, it had to be you. Why, Sam? Why?"

"Because they were going to make me retire," I said. It was actually a relief, to be able to tell it to someone. "Take away my job, my reason for living, just because I'm not as young as I used to be. All my experience, all my years of service, all the things I've done for them, and the authorities were going to give me a gold watch and throw me on the scrap heap. Now, when things are worse than they've ever been. When I'm needed more than ever. It wasn't fair. It wasn't right.

"So I decided I would just take what I needed, to make myself the greatest detective that ever was. With my new abilities, I would be unstoppable. I would go private, like John Taylor and Larry Oblivion and show those wet-behind-the-ears newcomers how it's done ... I would become rich and famous, and if I looked a little younger, well... this is the Nightside, after all.

"Shed no tears for my victims. They were all criminals, though I could never prove it. That's why there was no paperwork on them. But I knew. Trust me; they all deserved to die. They were all scum.

"I'd actually finished, you know. The werewolf would have been my last victim. I had all I needed. I teleported in and out of the library, which is why no one saw me come and go. But then ... you had to turn up, the second-best detective in the Nightside, and spoil everything. I never should have agreed to train you ... but I saw in you a passion for justice that matched my own. You could have been my partner, my successor. The things we could have done ... But now I'm going to have to kill you, and the governor. I can't let you tell. Can't let you stop me, not after everything I've done. The Nightside needs me.

"You'll just be two more victims of the unknown serial killer."

I surged forward with a werewolf's supernatural speed, and grabbed the front of Ms Fate's black leather costume with a godling's strength. I closed my hand on her chest and ripped her left breast away. And then I stopped, dumbstruck. The breast was in my hand, but under the torn open leather there was no wound, no spouting blood. Only a very flat, very masculine chest. Ms Fate smiled coldly.

"And that's why you'd never have guessed my secret identity, Sam. Who would ever have suspected that a man would dress up as a super-heroine, to fight crime? But then, this is the Nightside, and like you said; we all have our secrets."

And while I stood there, listening with an open mouth, she palmed a nausea gas capsule from her belt and threw it in my face. I hit the stone floor on my hands and knees, vomiting so hard I couldn't concentrate enough to use any of my abilities. The governor called for two of his golems, and they came and dragged me away. They threw me into a cell, and then nailed the door shut, and sealed it forever.

No need for a trial. Ms Fate would have a word with Walker, and that would be that. That's how I always did it.

So here I am, in Shadow Deep, in the dark that never ends. Guess whose cell they put me next to. Just guess.

One of these days they'll open this cell, and find nothing here but my clothes.

THE OTHER HALF

Mick Herron

WHEN SHE'D FINISHED with the computer she returned to the bathroom, set the boiler's timer to constant, and collected the shirt: a black silk collarless affair evidently saved for special occasions. She carried this downstairs, turning the thermostat up as high as it would go as she passed, then hung it on the kitchen door while she sorted out her remaining tasks. The clock on the wall read Nearly Time To Go, but she didn't need telling; her body already sending out signals – pinpricks at the back of the neck, a fizziness in the blood; the on-the-edge messages the primal self transmits at useful moments. She'd promised herself ten minutes, max, and they were almost up. Kitchen jobs done, she retrieved the shirt and let herself out the back door, locking it behind her with the key from the hook next to the cooker. For a moment she stood fixed to the spot, gauging the quality of the neighbourhood noise. Nothing seemed out of the ordinary. She released the breath she'd been holding, then placed the key on the windowledge, before looking down at the shirt in her hand. "Now, what are we going to do with you?" she asked; though if the truth were told, she already knew.

"Reformatted," Joe repeated.

"The hard drive, yes."

"Which is bad," he ventured.

"You don't get computers, do you, Joe?"

Joe Silvermann shook his head regretfully. While he didn't mind that he didn't get computers, he hated disappointing people.

Tom Parker said, "Basically, Tessa wiped it. Erased all the work stored in the machine plus all the software loaded on it, which, trust me, comes to an expensive piece of damage on its own. Even without her other party pieces."

"Such as the heating."

"I was only away two days. Imagine if I'd been gone all week? Or a fortnight?"

"Or a long cruise," Joe suggested. "Four weeks, sometimes six. Two months, even. I've seen adverts."

"It doesn't bear thinking about," Tom said. "House was like a heatwave as it was. The bill'll be ruinous. Then there were the kitchen japes. Fridge and freezer doors swinging open, oven on full blast. And the phone, she'd left the phone off the hook. After dialling one of those premium rate chatlines. Jesus!"

"It's not good," Joe agreed, shaking his head. "Not good at all."

"And what she did with my shirt ... "

He'd been steadily growing redder through this recital, and Joe was worried Tom Parker might accidentally have a seizure or something; perhaps a mild apoplectic episode requiring medical intervention. He was a youngish man, so this wasn't desperately likely, but as Joe's first-aid expertise stopped at dialling 999, he thought it best to steer conversation away from the shirt. "You'll forgive my saying so, I know," he said. "Not only because we are friends, but because you're a fair man. But you keep saying Tessa did this. Did she perhaps leave a note? Or some other declaration of some description?"

"Of course she didn't, Joe. We're talking criminal damage here."

"She seemed a nice young woman," he mourned.

"Well," Tom Parker said, "don't they all? To start with."

He'd first met Tom Parker three months previously, at a French market in Gloucester Green, where they'd fallen into conversation over the relative merits of the olives on offer. Tom had been with Tessa – Tessa Greenlaw – and Joe, in the way of such meetings, had assumed them an established couple. He himself had been with Zoë at the time, and for all he knew, Tom and Tessa made the same assumption about them. Not that Zoë had been on the spot when the conversation started, of course – she had a way of bringing such encounters to an early close – but by the time she returned from a nearby wine stall, Joe was already ushering his new friends in the direction of a coffee bar.

"You'll never stop collecting strays, will you?" she'd said later.

"Hardly strays. He runs a language school? She is an NHS, what are they calling them now? Managers? Hardly strays, Zoë."

"It's the kind of thing old people do."

Joe would never get to be old, but neither of them knew that yet. Besides, as he said, the pair weren't strays: Tom Parker was mid-thirties, with a relaxed, confident way which expressed itself in his clothing, his smile, and the direct expression he wore when he shook Joe's hand. "Joe," he'd said. "Good to meet you. This is Tessa." Tessa was a few years younger: a sweet-faced blonde woman whose small, squarish, black-framed spectacles gave the impression that she was trying to look less attractive than she was, though to Joe's mind they made her look rather sexy. While waiting for coffee, the group swapped life details.

"I've never met a private detective," Tom had said.

Joe shrugged modestly.

"Well, now you've met two," Zoë told him.

"Do you solve many crimes?"

"That depends on what you mean by 'solve'," Joe said carefully. "And also 'crimes'."

"It sounds fascinating," Tessa said. She had a rather breathy voice, to Joe's ear.

"It sounds fascinating," Zoë echoed sarcastically as they made their way home later.

"She was trying to show an interest, that's all. I thought they were a nice couple."

Though as it turned out, they were no longer a couple by the time Joe next encountered Tom.

This had been in a bar in the city centre, where Joe had been watering a police contact of his, one Bob Poland, who had no useful information on a young runaway case Joe was working on, but managed to drag it out to five large scotches anyway. Joe himself had been nursing a beer, because there was no point getting competitive with a thirsty cop. He was only halfway through it when Bob had to leave – his shift was up – so was unfolding his newspaper when Tom Parker walked through the door. His language school, Joe remembered as he raised a hand in greeting, was just round the corner.

"You remember me?"

"Of course – Joe, isn't it?"

"Silvermann."

"From the olive stall."

"Well—"

"The private eye – don't worry, I remember."

He often dropped in here for a drink once the working day was done, he told Joe. The pair settled at a table by the window.

"And Tessa, how is she?"

"Oh, I'm not seeing her any more."

"Tom! No! What happened?"

"Well, nothing. Christ, Joe, it's not the death of romance or anything. We dated for a while and now we're not. Simple as that." Something in his expression, though, suggested it wasn't that simple.

"But ..."

"But what?"

But nothing, Joe had to admit. Nothing he wanted to say out loud. That they had seemed a nice couple, and that nice couples ought to stick together, if only to set an example to everyone else. "Should I – would you like another drink?" When all else failed, offer hospitality. "Should I go to the bar?"

"Joe, they have table service." Tom raised a hand for the waitress. "Why do it yourself when you can pay someone else to do it? How about you, you want the other half?"

"Perhaps I will."

Tom ordered their drinks, then went on, "Besides, she's unstable. Was right from the start."

"Unstable?"

"I used to get phonecalls from her in the middle of the night. Checking up. That I was alone, and where I ought to be."

Joe clucked his tongue, shook his head. "Late night phonecalls. Zoë and I, we had a spate a while back. They get tired, they give up. You're sure this was Tessa?"

"Sometimes she'd arrive on my doorstep unexpectedly, or be waiting when I left work. You ever been stalked, Joe?"

"Is it stalking, this? Not just ..."

"Just what?"

Joe shrugged. "Perhaps she just wants to be with you."

"Feels like stalking to me, mate." He shook his head. "It's a hell of a world, Joe, I'm telling you. And most of its problems caused by women."

Well, maybe half, Joe conceded. If you ignored war and famine and stuff.

They fell to talking about other things. The next Joe heard about Tessa, Tom was in his office, outlining the damage.

He had taken a cigarette from a pocket but didn't light it; just held it between finger and thumb as he spoke. "Those phone calls? They never stopped. Oh, she wouldn't speak, but it was her. Middle of the night, and I'm getting woken up to be given the silent treatment. Or not woken up, if you know what I mean."

"Sometimes you're already awake," Joe guessed.

"Not alone, either. You can imagine the damper that puts on proceedings."

"She sounds unhappy."

"And I care? She's fucking nuts, Joe. And driving me crazy while she's at it."

"Have you been to the police?"

"What good would that do? Look. I know it was Tessa, you know it was Tessa. Bloody Tessa knows it was Tessa. But knowing isn't proving. We get into an I said-she said situation, the best that'll happen's she'll get told to watch her step by the boys in blue. Meanwhile, I'm still paying the bills on her domestic terrorism, thanks a bunch."

"How did she get in?"

"In?"

"To your house," Joe explained. "She didn't look, pardon my saying, like a housebreaker."

"Oh, right. No, she didn't need to be. We'd swapped keys, but she never gave it back. Claimed she did, but she didn't."

"And your locks? Have you changed your locks?"

"Well I have now, Joe. But that's a little late to help."

Joe nodded, as a change from shaking his head. There'd been a crime, and Tom seemed certain he'd identified the culprit. But it wasn't clear what Joe was expected to do about it.

Tom said, "That was my favourite shirt, too. Bought it in Italy. It's not like I can just pop out and buy another."

"It's not … salvageable? No, sorry, forget I spoke. Of course it's not."

Tom leaned forward. His unlit cigarette jammed meaning into every syllable. "She blocked the sewer pipe with it, Joe. First I knew about it, the toilet's backing up. Course it's not bloody salvageable."

"Would you like coffee? Tea?"

"Neither. Not right now."

"You're upset, yes. Your shirt and all the rest, plus the sense of being invaded. I can see you'd want to talk to somebody about it."

"But why you."

"That's what I was wondering, Tom, yes. Why me?"

So Tom told him.

A homeless man had made his pitch by an entrance to the covered market: teatowel in front of him for contributions to his wellbeing, he sat crosslegged, back to the wall, face obscured by a hood. A young Alsatian lay next to him, its head on his knee. Lots of homeless people – and there were lots; they seemed to multiply faster than any housing shortage could account for – lots of them had dogs, Joe had noticed, which was a detail which, if not a silver lining, at least provided a little insulation, he liked to think. There was comfort in knowing that no matter how hard you'd fallen, love was still available. He'd said as much to Zoë once, and she'd looked at him as if he were mad, which wasn't an unusual expression for Zoë.

"They don't keep dogs for something to love, Joe. They keep dogs so they've something to shout at. Something they can get angry with, which just has to sit and take it."

Which might or might not have been true, but one thing was certain: having heard it said, Joe would never look at a homeless man and his dog in quite the same way again.

"The glass is always half-empty, isn't it, Zoë?" he'd said sadly.

"No, the glass is cracked," she'd told him. "And there's no way I'm drinking from a cracked glass."

Anyway, the dog he was looking at was the same one he'd seen yesterday, because this was the homeless guy's regular hangout, and this particular entrance to Oxford's covered market was right by the doorway to Tessa Greenlaw's gym. Or the gym Tessa Greenlaw was a member of. Joe had spent long enough watching it to make such pointless clarifications to himself, as if somewhere inside his own head was a not entirely bright third party, in constant need of updating. Tessa Greenlaw came here once her workday was done, or had done so both days Joe had been following her. *Surveilling*, he amended. "Following" had a stalkerish air. And yesterday, after leaving, she'd done nothing more complicated than head straight home, giving Joe a tricky moment when he'd found himself boarding the same bus – but it had been crowded, and he'd sat where she couldn't see his face, and besides, they'd only encountered each other once, months ago. Chances were, all she'd have would be one of those vague city moments at the sight of a face from a forgotten context. And if that happened, she hadn't let on.

Tonight, though, there was no rush for the bus. Instead, on leaving the gym Tessa Greenlaw headed south, down St Aldate's. Giving her a moment to get ahead, Joe peeled himself from his hiding place, thought for a moment about popping over the road to slip a quid to the boy with the dog, decided he didn't have time, and set off in Tessa's wake.

It was hardly a surprise. How many places could she have been headed? Well, okay, she could have been going anywhere – but a short distance down St Aldate's, then a left turn off the main road, and what you reached was the building that housed Tom Parker's language school.

This wasn't a busy thoroughfare. Joe couldn't have followed Tessa along it without being spotted. But opposite the lane's entrance, on St Aldate's itself, was a bench for the weary, from which Joe had a clear view of Tessa Greenlaw coming to a halt by the language school; of Tessa checking her watch, then leaning against the wall of the building opposite, looking up at the second-floor window where Tom had his office.

Joe spread his newspaper over his knees, in case Tessa noticed him.

He timed it at eleven minutes. Eleven minutes before Tom Parker came out. During this time, Tessa grew restless; checked her watch a number of times; fiddled through her bag for something she didn't find. She was wearing the same glasses Joe had admired the first time he'd met her – only time, he amended; you couldn't call this "meeting" – and her hair was shorter, but what he mostly noticed was that she seemed, what might the word be – frazzled? Yes: she seemed frazzled. As if things were not going her way lately, and the directions they had chosen instead were stretching her thin ... Zoë would probably point out that Tessa had just been to the gym, which might account for it. But still: she looked frazzled.

Joe was staring straight at her when she looked his way. He dropped his eyes to the newspaper; made a bit of a thing about turning a page. When he risked another glance, Tom was in the lane too.

"You saw?"

"I saw, yes."

"That's the fourth time. No, *fifth*. She's mad, Joe. Complete mentalist."

"Mentalist." Joe wasn't sure he'd encountered the term. "Certainly, she does not give the impression of being, ah, stable."

He hadn't been able to hear everything, but that she'd been shouting was clear enough. *Bastard* had floated Joe's way. And all the while Tom had been making soothing gestures in the air; smiling softly but never quite touching her, as if Tessa were a cornered animal in spitting mood, unclear of its own best choices. When he'd reached at last for her sleeve she'd pulled her arm away angrily and stormed down the lane, away from Joe. Slowly, he'd folded his newspaper and stood. When Tom reached him, he led the way to the bar without a word.

Now he said, "And has there been any *pattern*, any particular sequence to the way in which she comes and, ah, lurks outside your workplace?"

"I'm not sure. Would it make a difference?"

"Probably not," Joe admitted.

"You're thinking some kind of PMT thing?"

Uncomfortable with this direction, Joe shook his head. "Not really." Truth was, he had no idea what questions to ask, or what answers would help. Insights into the female psyche weren't his specialty. And if he'd ever claimed them to be, it wasn't like the notion would withstand five minutes of Zoë's scrutiny. "Did you confront her about her invasion of your property?"

"Did she give the impression of being up for a discussion?"

"I couldn't hear," Joe explained. "Traffic. Distance. Plus, she was shouting and you were speaking softly. Neither was an ideal volume."

"Well trust me, she was in no mood for answering questions. More than likely, she'd find a way of blaming it on me, anyway. You had much to do with mad women, Joe?"

Loyally, Joe denied it.

"Lucky you."

She'd looked frazzled, he remembered. It wasn't such a stretch to colour her mad. "What was she saying?"

Tom Palmer ran a hand through his hair: a boyish gesture, not without charm. "That we belong together. That I was just being stupid, and should come to my senses. That *I* should come to *my* senses." He shook his head in wonderment. "A bloody baby. We're not even in a relationship, for god's sake."

"Does she have parents? Someone who could perhaps talk to her—"

"Well I don't know, do I? We weren't playing happy families, Joe. We were only together for a couple of weeks."

"An official complaint, perhaps? Now that I've been a witness to this stalking, this harassment, perhaps you want me to … accompany you to the police station?"

Tom barked a sudden laugh. "You've never actually been a copper, have you, Joe?"

"Never. Not ever."

"But you talk the talk. No, I don't want you to accompany me to the station, thanks anyway. I want something more direct than that. I want you to put a stop to it. To all her crap."

Joe had been afraid that's where this was leading. "You think she'll listen to me?" He was older than Tessa, true – could easily be her father – and perhaps a little elder wisdom was what she needed: but still, he was afraid. Not of confronting a madwoman; more of being mortally embarrassed. "There is a law," he suggested. "The Protection from Harassment Act?"

"I know," Tom said. "You think that's going to carry weight? Quote section thirteen, paragraph six at her, and watch enlightenment dawn?" He leaned forward. "She's barking, Joe. You've seen what she's like, waiting round my office to harangue me when I leave. Not to mention she seriously messed me about, wiped my computer. I like things ordered, Joe. This was out of order. So. Are you going to help or not? I mean, that's what you do, right? You're a private eye. You take on clients."

"Yes," Joe sighed. "It's what I do. I take on clients."

"Good." Tom passed a key across the table. "I want you to mess her place up, Joe. Same way she messed mine. Fair's fair, right?"

"I suppose it is," Joe agreed. "Fair's fair. Yes."

Tessa left home for work at 9.15. It was all right for some, Joe noted, a judgment tempered by the knowledge that if he himself didn't reach the office before eleven, it wasn't like anyone would notice. As it was, this morning he'd been up at seven; by half-past, had been slumped twenty yards down the road from Tessa's front door, his trusty newspaper on the car seat next to him, in case a disguise was called for. Was it really necessary for him to observe, first-hand, Tessa's departure? Yes, it was. If he was going to let himself into her place with the key Tom had given him, he wanted proof positive she was off the premises. He figured that was the way Philip Marlowe would have played it, "What would Marlowe do?" being Joe's regular mantra. Marlowe wouldn't take unnecessary risks. Well, that wasn't true. But it was the answer Joe wanted, which was substantially more important.

"You still have this?" he had asked Tom on being given Tessa's doorkey. "Won't she have changed the lock?"

"Trust me, that'll get you through the door."

"But—"

"Trust me."

So Joe's hand had clamped round the key as if his fist were taking an impression.

Now he straightened in the driving seat as Tessa reached the corner, crossed the road, and headed for her bus stop.

Give her another ten minutes, he thought. It was likely she'd be waiting at least that long; time enough to remember she'd left her purse behind, or her paperback, or any one of a hundred items she never left home without. But his body was in unwilled motion, eager to get this part finished whatever excuses his mind could conjure; his body was excavating itself from its car, brushing the creases from its coat; was pulling its collar up in a completely unsuspicious attempt to obscure its face for the benefit of anyone curtain-twitching, wondering what the guy in the car was up to. Housebreaking in broad daylight was not a game for the nervous. So if he was engaged in it, he couldn't be nervous: QED. Unnervously, then, Joe made his way to Tessa's house; unnervously fished her key from his pocket as he did so; unnervously dropped it as he tripped on the kerb, then had to frantically scrabble before it disappeared down a drain.

Now *that*, Joseph – he chided himself – could so easily have ended in farce.

He looked around. Weirdly, there was nobody in sight; or maybe it was normal – what did Joe know about this particular street at this particular time of the morning? Key safely in his fist, he released a breath just as a bus passed the end of the road, on its way to collect Tessa Greenlaw and transport her out of the area. There was no more room for hesitation. He had the key in hand, the door in his sights. What he was about to do was illegal, but would only look unusual if he farted about while doing it. Farting about was not something Marlowe would do. Again, QED.

Nobody shouted as he walked directly to Tessa's door; no sirens blared as he slid the key into its lock. It turned. The door opened.

He was in.

This was only the second time he'd let himself into another person's house without their knowledge – not without help, either time. But this was different. He was here to do damage: well-deserved damage, he reminded himself, as his conscience threatened to kick in – this wasn't random vandalism; it was a message. That's what it was. A message.

Nothing immediately suggested itself as Joe scouted round the ground floor, but once he'd climbed the stairs and discovered what was evidently an office, his next move became clear.

He set to with a will.

"So why did you break into Tessa's place?"

"I wanted to see if the key worked," Joe explained. He took it from his pocket: a recent copy, shiny and unscratched. "They exchanged keys. He told me that. But when they broke up, he made an extra copy of hers before giving it back. That's why he was so sure she wouldn't have changed the locks. She didn't know he had it."

"It was Tom stalking Tessa, wasn't it?" Zoë said flatly. "Not the other way round."

"It's a creepy thing to do, isn't it? Keep a copy of your ex-girlfriend's key. Except he had me doing the actual stalking," Joe said. "There's the crux, you might call it. The nub." He recalled his self-clarification, following Tessa: that this wasn't *stalking* but *surveillance*. "Prior to persuading me to – I think the word would be – *trash* her place. Yes, trash." He recalled for her Tom's words in the bar: "Why do things yourself when you can pay someone else to do them? He was talking about fetching drinks. But ... "

"You discerned a principle," said Zoë.

"You don't seem surprised."

"I didn't much like him."

"Yes, but ..."

"But what?"

"You don't much like anyone, Zoë," Joe explained. "It's not like you were making an exception."

They were in the office, which was the most neutral ground of their marriage.

"Point," Zoë said. "But I thought you were his friend."

"I was, but was he mine? What sort of friend sends you off on a job like that?"

"The kind who's taking revenge."

"On poor Tessa, yes. She dumped him, I'm assuming."

"Guess so," Zoë said. "And he called her, didn't he? Asked her to meet him after work, once he'd arranged for you to be following her. Then blew her off when he eventually came out. So what you saw was her quite reasonably losing her rag, and you never did hear what he was saying."

"I think so, yes. There are ways someone clever could find out, probably, with phone records and technological trickery, but for myself, yes, I'm sure he faked it."

"Can't think why she went."

"Sometimes women are gentle like that," Joe suggested. "She

would have been feeling guilty, perhaps, about dumping him. He maybe made an overture of friendship, or offered to apologise for something."

"And you're not worried she trashed his place first?"

Joe smiled kindly. "Don't you get it? He made that up so I'd be on his side. It didn't happen, Zoë. Not before today. And even if she had – well. I don't like stalkers."

"Me neither," Zoë said. And meant it. Tom had made a pass at her shortly after that meeting in the market, and evidently didn't take rejection well, hence the spate of late night calls she and Joe had suffered a while back. But Joe had been right about one thing; there were ways, with technological trickery, that someone clever could find out who'd been making phonecalls, no matter that they thought they'd shielded their number. Trashing Tom Parker's place had been her reasonable response. It hadn't occurred to her he'd think Tessa had done it, but the more she listened to Joe, the more she was sure he'd thought no such thing. He'd known it was Zoë. Using Joe – steering him to where he'd do to Tessa what Zoë had done to Tom – was the typical stalker's revenge: manipulative, distant, pleased with itself. His hard luck Joe had seen through him. Not that she was about to share any of this. "How'd you get into his place anyway?"

His second break-in. Harder when you don't have a key.

"Bob Poland helped," he said. For a fee. "Policemen know the strangest things. Like getting through locks."

Zoë nodded. Getting through locks was a skill she'd been tutored in by a local tearaway. "And what did you do?" she asked, curious. "Once you were in?"

There'd been a moment when he'd almost turned and left, overcome by the enormity of it: of breaking in, of wreaking havoc. But then he'd seen Tom's office. *I like things ordered, Joe*, he'd said. And there, to prove it, stood his filing cabinets, with its reams of carefully alphabetized records that Joe had carefully, randomly, reordered. Tom would be hours straightening that lot out. Hours. Maybe days.

"It's better you don't know," he told her.

He was sure that's what Marlowe would have said.

SWORD LILIES

Sally Spedding

SINCE CHRISTMAS, THE Rue des Platanes in Villerchamp has become known as the Rue des Morts.

Old Monsieur Renaud in number ten succumbed to liver failure on Millennium Eve, while further up, next to the public telephone, Madame Pla had fallen senseless from her bed. On February 14, young Thierry Santos had mounted his moped only to be struck by a VW camper van belonging to a German couple from Kohl. They'd been too hysterical to park it safely afterwards, so the street was blocked off for at least half an hour.

Now, as always, Madame Laval was busy by her front window, wiping over the inner shutters with a new chamois leather, and rearranging the plastic gladioli in their faux Sèvres vase. It was already mid-April, and soon more tourists from the north would be passing through the village to the famous gorge and its chapel cut deep into the rock. No, she'd never written in its Book of Supplication to the Blessed Virgin, preferring to keep her wishes private. Besides, one way and another, most of them had been granted without Divine intervention.

It was more important that this retired school teacher kept a continual and visible presence in the street, something for which the Dreille family opposite were always grateful, seeing as their absences were growing more frequent. They had a sole remaining relative in Brittany, and were no doubt hoping their solicitous attentions would soon be paying off.

She'd be the first to know of any decease by the inevitable brand new car parked outside, complete with tinted glass and fancy wheels. Even an *A Vendre* sign, she guessed, presaging a move to the better side of the town. That's when her smile would become a little less warm, her gift of *confiture aux framboises* proffered in a smaller pot than usual ...

She looked out again, the morning sun glancing in on her grey head. The church bells clanged eleven and here on the dot was old Monsieur José from number four with his terrier. Why in God's name did a man in such poor health keep such a handful as that? She asked herself as the dog roamed from left to right, oblivious to its owner's feeble whistling. Then horror of horrors, it squatted outside her door. She watched as a brown coil extruded from under its tail, sending up a fuzz of steam.

Dilemma. Monsieur José's son Yves was the electrician. She needed him to upgrade the wiring in her house and put in an extra point for her special new equipment arriving next week. She sighed. All she could do was stare at the aberration and remove it as soon as Monsieur José had struggled by.

She put on her coat, for although the sun was warm in a clear sky, a northerly breeze still persisted. Two pieces of kitchen roll and a plastic bag lay ready in her basket, and mercifully, the turd proved a clean lift. Then, with the bundle still exuding its own rich smell, she set off up the street and rounded the bend by the *poubelles*.

To the right lay steps up to another row of houses which could only be reached by foot. A mere three were occupied, the rest had been for sale for months, their handwritten notices bleached by the sun. An unpruned rose together with an array of terracotta pots stood outside number four. She squeezed the smelly package to fit the letterbox and pushed it in, then with the agility of someone ten years younger descended the steps and walked home as if nothing was amiss. She made herself a *tisane* of honey and elderberry, before sitting down once more by the window with the accoutrements of her trade.

She had a fine-nibbed pen, royal blue ink and an empty mustard pot for water, in which rested a pastry brush. However, her paper was the common variety found in any *tabac* or kiosk, each page a pattern of fine turquoise squares.

"For the peasants," she told herself, but anything more personal or special was out of the question.

As always, before the first word, she drained the surplus ink into a piece of white blotting paper and watched as its stain spread and darkened.

* * *

In the *boulangerie* next morning, she learned that the elderly and fragile Mademoiselle Bertrand in number fifty-two had died after lunch the day before. A fact she later recorded on her *Fleurs de Campagne* calendar, and not without a quiet satisfaction. For Renée Bertrand was, like many in that rundown part of the town, ready enough to take her charity, whether it was a clutch of violets or a carton of ready-mashed potato, but unwilling to give anything in return. And since her son's win on the Lotto – whereby 50,000 francs had trickled her way – she'd withdrawn even more behind her fly-speckled curtains.

Madame Laval never had need of a thesaurus or dictionary, for her words flowed like the irrigating water in the local *jardins*. She knew exactly how to infer, emphasize or simply leave to the imagination whenever that was more effective. It was her craft, after all, just like tapestry work or crochet, perfected over the years ...

Her pen paused between sentences as she watched Simone Dunoine wrestle with her three children on the way home to dinner from the nursery school. Probably nothing worth eating on their table, she mused, but what else could you expect from an unmarried mother who worked part-time at the Esso pumps? They'd be better off coming to *her* for tuition, except she couldn't abide anyone bringing in the street on their shoes, or the clamour of youthful ignorance.

Sweat built up under her latex gloves as she folded the paper in two, eased it into the envelope and brushed water under the flap.

"*Voilà*." The same with the stamp. The pile of letters was growing. It was all very satisfying, and never failed to give her an appetite. One o'clock.

The street was quiet. Everyone's tucking in, she smiled to herself, and as it's Thursday it'll be ham and leeks with fruit tart to follow. She could smell the pig meat wafting from nearby chimneys as she went to buy her croissant. How these people could afford a joint of meat and a *pâtisserie* day in day out, was nobody's business. Even those on Social Security.

She opened her larder door on a crust of cheese and two pickled dills in a cloudy liquid at the bottom of the jar. There was a knob of baguette and a scraping of margarine from the economy-sized tub.

Small wonder Renée Bertrand hadn't lasted. She reminded herself to write in the Book of Condolence which the woman's son had left outside their front door. Of course, her sympathies would be in an entirely different hand with a different pen.

After lunch, she washed up, leaving the solitary plate to dry in the rack, then, with her mail in her handbag went down the tiled steps to the garage. Most people in the street had converted what had once been stabling into utility rooms with boilers, freezers and unwanted gifts, keeping their cars outside but to her this space was a necessary cool and sombre womb for her most inventive notions.

Her white Renault Clio was a common enough car and it was the reason she'd bought it. In fact, she'd once sat by the window all day checking the tally of all the various makes, and this far outstripped the rest. Thus would she merge more anonymously with the region's traffic as she travelled from letterbox to letterbox.

Today it was the Ariège. A department dotted with sizeable towns sufficiently far away, yet plausible, for most of Villerchamp's residents had relatives within 200 kilometres. The bird must stay close to the worm, she told herself, unlocking the car door. And what worms they were ...

She could hear next door's telephone as she checked her black leather gloves were handy. More news, no doubt, for Monsieur and Madame Vouziez, who spent their days in their garden at the top of the street. It was probably their former lodger, a student at Montpellier university, who phoned once a week on Thursdays.

Her car nudged its way into the daylight and she left the engine running while she closed the garage door. There was no one around, just the buzz of afternoon television through the shutters. Everyone was digesting the news and weather. She was soon out of Villerchamp and picking up speed between the pruned plane trees that lined the route. She tuned in to France Musique and a heated debate on Berlioz, then hummed along to excerpts of *"L'Enfance du Christ"* as the road climbed up away from Quillan and into the high pastures.

The bells were chiming five o'clock as she returned to the Rue des Morts, and immediately she recognized Madame Vouziez with her wheelbarrow, and her other next door neighbour, Madame Baro standing by the new phone booth shaking their heads.

They beckoned her to join them and dispensed the news that old Monsieur José had been rushed to hospital with a defibrillator attached to his heart.

"*Mon Dieu*. It never ends." Sybille Vouziez sighed. "Soon there'll be none of us left."

"But he's had a bad heart for years." Madame Laval feigned concern, yet her eyes were unchanged. "His sister told me he had a funny turn last *Toussaint*. I could hardly believe he'd once played rugby for Béziers. It's a good job we don't know what's round the corner, that's for sure ..."

The other two nodded, staring in at passing cars. "I expect Yves has already had a valuation on it," she added, looking up the street.

"But his Papa's not dead yet." Madame Baro gave her a sharp look. "He may come back fit as a flea."

"Well let's hope so, but I say it's too much for someone like him having a house here, a *Maison Bourgeoise* in Perpignan, *and* a farm near Toulouse, as well as that dog ..."

"Maybe that's what's kept him going. But I've never understood why he chose to stay in this old street," Madame Vouziez removed her hat and shook it. "Unless it's to be near his son, and of course he's always got us, his friends ..."

"Exactly. We've never let him down, have we?"

"No. That's why I've already offered to look after little 'Chipie' for him while he's away."

Madame Vouziez forgot to return her hat to her head as an all-too-familiar figure had emerged from number twenty-three. The now childless widow Pauline Santos.

It was impossible for Madame Laval to make her excuses and leave. That would have been too obvious. Instead, she fixed her mouth in a rictus of pity while holding out both hands.

"Paulette, *chérie*, how are you?" she said. "We've all been so worried. We've not seen anything of you for weeks."

The woman looked ill, her skin as grey as the tombs in the cemetery, and she kept her eyes downcast, refusing Madame Laval's kindly gesture. The former schoolteacher noticed a *télécarte* in her hand for as well she knew, the Santos had never had their own phone.

"Not good. It gets worse," sighed the widow. "Each day I think, dear Thierry wouldn't want to see me like this, that his Mama should be strong, but no. I must be a terrible disappointment to him and it cannot be otherwise ..."

Madame Vouviez reached into her wheelbarrow and pulled out a big celeriac with leaves still bearing a few beige slugs.

"Have this, Paulette. Better than pills any day."

However the woman barely noticed. Her tired eyes began to water.

"I'm just on my way to telephone the police." That last word made Madame Laval flinch. "I've been meaning to since it happened, you know," she gulped. "The accident ..."

"Police?" Madame Baro looked shocked. "Why?"

"I'll show you." Pauline Santos dug in her pocket and pulled out a long white envelope which had obviously been studied many times. She then extracted the note and held her breath.

"Go on. What is it?" Madame Laval tried to get a closer look. Tried to keep her voice steady.

"It arrived the day he ..." the younger woman broke off, unable to continue.

"We're your friends," encouraged Madame Laval in her carefully rehearsed caring tone. "You can trust us."

"Well, after reading it, he went round like a mad thing, yelling, slamming doors, not like him at all." She sniffed. "He should never have taken his moped out in that state, but there it is. He did."

A silence fell over the small group, broken only by sparrows in a nearby plane tree.

"Please, let's see it." Madame Vouziez reached for the sheet of expensive paper, but Pauline Santos held it fast.

"Fingerprints. I've got to be careful. They'll want to examine it, and so far, there's only mine and ..." She began to sob and Madame Laval put a hand on her arm.

"You read it then. We're your friends. We want to help ..."

And in that sunlit street with the birdsong overhead, the women listened as a pure and terrible wickedness passed from the page to taint the late afternoon.

"It's impossible anyone could be so wicked." Madame Laval's eyes threatened to pop from her face.

"Fancy telling the poor boy he'd failed his army tests. Who would do such a thing?"

"The worst is, if he'd checked properly, he'd have realized the letter wasn't on army headed paper, and the postmark was Céret. It's just that he wanted army life so much ..." Madame Santos buried the letter back in her pocket and excused herself.

The women watched as she headed for the telephone, her shadow still touching them, and while the other residents finished their discussion, Madame Laval noted her eight minutes, twenty-two seconds in the phone booth, and when she got home, contacted the florists to send her a spray of gladioli. It was the most her pension would allow.

Twenty-four hours to go before the computer keyboard would become mightier than the pen. Madame Laval was in the public *lavabo*, rubbing at her washing with extra vigour. The imminence of an e-mail address using Madame Baro's name, reaching a wider readership, turned her fingers red and her towels cleaner than ever before, so that the two Leboeuf sisters walking past like elderly crabs seemed amused.

"*Bonjour*." They chorused. "Someone's energetic today."

"Ah *oui*. I'm tired of looking at dingy laundry. And it's such a fine morning to make a difference."

They nodded their old heads in unison, but then, instead of continuing their trek home as she'd have preferred, they stopped to peer down at their reflections in the dark water.

"Is anything wrong?" Madame Laval looked up. Since Pauline Santos had made that call, she was a little, but not overly, on edge.

"Well, we don't know if it's true or not, but ..." Cecile Leboeuf began, just as Madame Laval's soap slid from under her palm and plopped into the current.

"What is?" She fished for it, to no avail. "Damnation!"

Both spinsters stepped back in astonishment at hearing this respectable retired schoolteacher swear so vehemently.

"I'm sorry," she didn't look up. "It's my only bar ..."

But the wind had gone from their sails and they turned away, whispering. She steadied herself, aware that something had changed. They would gossip as sure as night follows day. It would get round the town that she wasn't the woman they all thought. But worse, in her correspondence, that particular swear word was her most favoured, even some might say, her hallmark. She watched her soap glide away out of reach, wrung out her towels and returned to the house, anger quickening her steps.

Her wrist was still damp but no matter, and the brief letter took half the normal time. It was as if her special Muse had landed on her shoulder. The sentiments to the Leboeufs were perfect, the promise her best yet. She would make one more trip, this time to Chalabre in the morning, and then be ready for her new era …

She glanced up to see a gendarmerie car passing then slowing to a crawl along the gravelled edge. It stopped at number twenty-three, whereupon two officers got out and rang Madame Santos' bell, all the while looking up and down the Rue des Platanes.

She froze. Could they see her through the floral net? Did they suspect anything? She looked round at her equipment, the envelope ready to be sent. She'd only need a minute to burn it all and set some books on the table instead. Her little stove was nearly out, however, she tore up the exercise book and together with the pen and blotting paper, crammed it into the fire.

Strange coloured flames leapt into life followed by short bursts of the pen exploding. But then, quite unexpectedly, as if this intrusion had been too sudden, the fire died, leaving her crucial evidence unburnt. She panicked. Should she go and get new wood or stay on guard? She decided to stay, for after all, should the gendarmes knock on her door, she could always pretend to be out.

She turned off the kitchen light and went upstairs to view the scene from above. Clutching her throat, she hardly dared breathe until as anticipated, the gendarmes reappeared, one carrying a large manila envelope. Her heart felt like a stone in her chest. It had never been particularly strong since a childhood pneumonia, and teaching at secondary schools had further strained it.

"*Merde!*"

They were focused on her house. Staring, in fact. And now, without bothering to turn their car round, were coming her way. She gripped the bed end. The wood felt cold. Its familiar rustic carving of corn sheaves hard and unforgiving. Suddenly the pain whipped round her chest like cask bands, then down her arm, her side, until her whole body buckled in a final deathly spasm.

"Madame Laval?" One of the officers called through the letterbox. "We'd like a word. Won't keep you a moment ... It's just that as we were around in the street, Madame Santos asked us to thank you for her flowers ..."

LOVE HURTS

Bill Kirton

H ELEN DIPS THE spoon into the jar, twists it to collect the honey and lets a long, golden teardrop fall on to the bread. She slides the knife across the glistening surface. The small Sabatier has a wide blade, perfect for the fat smooth flow of the spread. Honey was one of the first things she'd tried Ben on when she began to wean him off the breast. Eighteen and a bit years ago.

She smiles as her eyes lift to look through into the dining room with its big bay window. Outside, the sky hangs between pale blue and the peach wash of the sunset's beginning. Ben is in his usual place on the window seat. Six feet two of him, folded into a corner of the sky. She marvels yet again that she has carried that tall, handsome man inside her.

After it happened, she was interviewed by a man and two women.

"It was so sweet when I started feeling him moving and prodding inside. He was so gentle. Never hurt me."

She laughed, reached across and tapped Fraser on the arm.

"You know, I'm sorry for you," she said.

"Really?"

"Yes. You'll never have a baby inside you."

"No fear of that," said Fraser.

He smiled, but Helen didn't notice. She was lost in thoughts of how, in the darkness inside her, she'd made the bones and tissues of a man. Fraser studied her, saw an image of his mother or one of his aunts, only more refined. They didn't have her quiet careful tones, each word sculpted by her mouth, correct.

Helen was proud of her taste, proud of the room to which she'd invited them, with its elegant prints and Monart glass. She'd settled

Fraser in a velvet-covered armchair and gestured for the two women to sit on the chaise longue as she took the window seat.

"He was only four when Iain left us, you know. Four," she repeated, as if to herself. "I was sitting here reading him a story."

She looked down at the tasselled cushion on the box seat and began to stroke it.

"He loved it here; it was our favourite place."

"Tell us about Iain," said Fraser.

The name brought a quick, sudden frown and a shake of the head.

"He just came in and said that he was going. That was it. It was no surprise. Made no difference to me. But for poor little Ben ... What a cruel thing to do: take away a wee boy's father to spend more time with a receptionist."

There was a curl in her lip as she spoke the word. She leaned forward again, wanting them to understand.

"I was so angry. He just held Ben out in front of him and said, 'This is what it's all about. This.' Fancy that. Calling his own son 'This'."

She gave a little shake of her head and made some punching gestures against the cushion. They were sharp, hard. She became calm again but Fraser noticed that her fingers started picking at the hem of her jumper as she spoke. Fast, angry movements. She took a tissue from the small box beside her and dabbed at her eyes.

"Can we talk about Ben?" he asked, very gently.

She puts the slice of bread on the plate and reaches for another. Again the spoon dips, the golden blob falls. Beyond Ben's dark shape, outside the window, the peach wash has thickened to a buttermilk gold.

She feels the joy of her overwhelming love for Ben. Remembers teaching him to read, soothing him through aches, pains and illnesses, leaving him at the school gate that first, agonizing day, watching him throw himself into tackles on the football field. She aches with the pride of seeing her son grow from funny, stumbling toddler to archetypal schoolboy with eyes full of mischief, and then on into his beautiful, graceful youth.

* * *

"About Ben," Fraser insisted, the gentleness still in his voice.

"I never deceived myself," she said, with a shake of the head. "I knew I'd have to share him. He's such a handsome boy. I knew they'd start chasing him and coveting him and wooing him."

She made "coveting" and "wooing" sound pornographic.

"I knew there'd be girlfriends. But, you know, he told me all about them. We'd sit in the window here and he'd talk about kissing them and ask all sorts of questions. I was his friend as well as his mother, you see." She gave a little giggle. "Like the first time he touched a girl's breast. It was an accident. He stretched across to take a book from the desk beside here and she moved and he suddenly felt … 'this lump' he called it."

Fraser smiled his understanding although he found it all rather genteel. His own first contact with a breast had been very deliberate and given both himself and Lorna, whose breast it was, the biggest thrill of their twelve-year-old lives.

"He used to tell me the sort of things girls said and did," Helen went on. "And I'd explain to him what they really meant. All the little secrets that women have. Even when we're very young."

She sought the agreement of the two women. They contented themselves with sympathetic little smiles. The older of the two, Anne Baxter, was about the same age as Helen. The younger, Gillian McKay, had only just turned thirty.

"Tricky business, sex education," said Fraser, dragging himself back from memories of Lorna on the grass in Hazlehead Park.

"Oh, he'd never make love to any of them," said Helen. "That was out of the question. I mean, the time I'm talking about, he was only fifteen or sixteen. He knew it could ruin his life. But then, this year … April, it was … Well, he started to change. It was Alice. He met her at a party. Told me about her and we made silly jokes about Wonderland. But by the end of May … Oh, I don't know. He was different."

She tapped the surface on which she sat.

"I used to see him here, on the window seat, day after day. All hunched up. And so quiet."

Her eyes lifted to Ben and the sky beyond him, where the gold is being burnished to the darker, copper tones of early evening.

"It was wonderful this summer," she said. "He'd been grumpy, hardly speaking to me. Then, suddenly, one night, he came home and gave me a huge kiss. Put his arms round me and said, 'Sorry, Mum. I've been a pain, haven't I?' It made me so happy. After that, it was just like old times. Sitting in the window together, chatting, laughing."

She paused. Her voice dropped.

"Then he brought her home."

She was almost whispering, feeling again the twisting inside her at Alice's loveliness. Wide hazel eyes and a smile that promised secret things. She'd been sweet but Helen had heard her laughter when she was out of the room and felt that there was a sort of triumph in it.

"It was frightening how quickly he fell in love," she said. "He burned with it, right from the start. Poor Ben. She wasn't worth it."

Her fingers were now stroking the material of her jumper with little caresses.

"It changed him so much. He ... wasn't my Ben any more. Out of reach. And the tantrums ... I'd say just the slightest thing and he'd jump up and shout and fling himself about."

The caresses became little tappings.

"You love your children so much, don't you?" she said. "You can't help it."

She stopped tapping her fingers and seemed to settle into a complete stillness.

"That's why I asked her to come and see me. Alice, I mean. September, it was. We sat in the window here. Ben was away. We had a long talk."

She stopped. They waited and Fraser was eventually forced to ask, "What about?" She looked at him, the smile long gone, her eyes narrower.

"Ben," she replied. "I told her she was hurting him, making him suffer. I asked her if she loved him. She just shrugged."

"So what did you do?"

Helen gave a deep, angry sigh.

"Oh, there were all sorts of things I wanted to do. If she couldn't love my Ben the way he deserved, well ..."

Fraser saw a tear in her left eye. It didn't form fully enough to brim over on to her cheek but stayed there, shining.

"I told her lies," she said.

"Lies?"

She gave a little nod.

"About Ben."

"What sort of lies?" asked Fraser, his voice almost a whisper.

"Epileptic," she said.

Fraser looked at his two colleagues. Both shrugged.

"Epileptic?" he repeated.

"Yes. I told her that's what Ben was."

"But he wasn't, was he?"

"No. He's perfect."

The image of her beautiful Ben brought a little smile to her mouth. The tear still trembled.

"I just wanted to frighten her off. I told her that he shouldn't get excited."

Fraser heard the catch in her throat. McKay reached across, took a tissue from the box and handed it to her. She pushed the tissue hard against each eye in turn, then shuddered.

"And she believed me, the stupid girl. How could she? How could she believe such nonsense?"

She dabbed fiercely at her nose, controlling the little sobs that had come into her voice.

"I made her promise not to tell him I'd said anything," she said at last. "But she must have said something."

She waved her hand; a feeble, lost little gesture.

"Ben started crying. I could hear him. Almost every night, sobbing away in his room."

She shook herself, trying to shrug off the echoes of his tears.

"There was no need to ask him. I knew."

Suddenly, the tears came back. She spoke through them, her words pulled apart by sobs.

"One night, I was driving home. And there he was. My poor Ben. Just ... just standing under the trees. Opposite her house. All alone."

The memory was too much. McKay got up, sat beside her and put her arm around her shoulders. Helen accepted the comfort but then shifted slightly, re-establishing a space between them before she started speaking again.

"It was Hallowe'en. I phoned her. She said ... she said she was sorry. Said she'd tried to make a clean break but that Ben became greedy, possessive. Silly, selfish girl."

A heaviness settled in Fraser as he listened. He just had to wait as she worked through it all. There was nothing he could say. He'd seen the photographs: the blood, the young body spread-eagled, the cuts and slashes in the chest and shoulders, the deep wounds in hands and arms that had been raised to stop the assault.

"Ben said some very ... unkind things," Helen was saying. "I knew he'd be sorry when he thought about them."

Her hands were moving back and forth over her skirt. Fraser couldn't guess at the sights she saw as she looked down at them.

"It was just nonsense," she said. "Wanting to leave home, things like that."

Her face was turned away from all of them. A stillness came over her and, when she looked at them again, it was obvious that she'd changed. Her eyes had died. The Helen they'd been talking to so far was Ben's mother; the caring, loving soul of the years they'd had together. But this woman was the Helen that had taken over that evening in early November.

That was when Ben said he hated her, that she'd ruined his life. He was out of his mind with grief, shouting and swearing. It was too much for Helen. She left the room and stood sobbing in the kitchen as he continued to scream at her. He followed her through, called her names that sliced into her, saying that he was leaving and that he'd be glad when he never had to see her again. He even grabbed her arms and spun her round to face him.

"You're evil. A selfish, evil bitch."

He pushed her back against the cabinets.

"You think you did it from love. You're wrong. Love doesn't do that. Dad was right."

He turned and stamped out. Her head was spinning with the words of this rude, angry monster that had taken Ben's place. She picked up the Sabatier knife, ran through and started hitting Ben again and again.

When the police reponded to her call, they found her calm once more. Ben's body lay along the window seat, his face turned towards the garden, his blood pooling deeply in a dark, sticky layer around him.

Helen has stopped spreading the honey. She picks up the plate of bread, carries it through to the dining room and puts it on the window seat. The sky oozes with the crimson of the disappearing sun. The plate is piled high with bread off which the honey flows, its amber darkening as it seeps over the edge on to the walnut surround ...

Fraser didn't think she was a danger to anyone. She could easily be in one of the bigger wards. But her quiet, determined actions might eventually unsettle the others and, for the moment, he wasn't prepared to take the chance. When he, Dr Baxter and Nurse McKay had left her room and locked the door, he'd stopped to watch her through the small observation panel. The walls of the room were a dull cream, unrelieved by any colours. Helen looked round at them, smiled, then started the routine which he'd seen her follow over and over again. Her hand reached forward and began to make motions as if she were spreading butter. When she'd finished, she walked to a corner of the room, the same one every time, and stood looking at the wall. She stayed there for several minutes, then returned to her bed and started all over again. These were the actions that filled all her days.

FUNERAL WEATHER

Kate Ellis

D EATH CAME SILENTLY to Flora Politson on Friday the thirteenth of April.

At sixty-one years of age, Flora – the plump widow of a wealthy Liverpool merchant and mistress of a grand stucco villa in Fulwood Park, some three miles from the smells of the city and the bustle of the docks – had appeared to be in the best of health. But Dr Willis knew that good health is often no defence against a visit from the Grim Reaper.

Willis, with his great mutton chop whiskers and his battered leather bag, was more adept at charming wealthy ladies than he was at diagnosis, but he gave his verdict with the certainty of holy writ. Flora Politson had died of heart failure. A sudden and merciful end.

The small, pale young man with sandy hair who accompanied the doctor looked no older than the butcher's boy who came whistling up the drive of Mortaber Villa each day on his bicycle. However, from his manner of dress and the leather doctor's bag he clutched in his right hand, Biddy – the late Mrs Politson's maid – guessed that he was assisting Dr Willis in some way. But it wasn't her place to ask questions.

Biddy stood near the bedroom, smoothing her crisp, white apron with restless fingers as the doctor and his companion bent over Mrs Politson who lay, as though asleep, on the bed. Biddy thought her mistress looked so peaceful lying there, her arms crossed neatly on her chest. The snowy lace counterpane was pulled up to her scrawny neck and her hair, spread out on the pillow, was iron grey and fluffy like the rain clouds that hung over the River Mersey that morning.

Biddy gazed out of the sash window at the gardens below with their bushy laurels lining the sweeping drive. It had begun to rain, a thin, miserable drizzle. Funeral weather, her mother used to say. Weather for death.

Dr Willis interrupted Biddy's thoughts by touching her arm and she flinched. He'd touched her before, his large, clammy hand patting her small rough one. Lingering too long. The younger man was still standing by the bed, silent and thoughtful, studying Flora's dead face and Biddy doubted he'd have noticed Dr Willis's over-familiar gesture. And even if he had seen, he would no doubt have kept his opinions to himself – as underlings and servants must.

Biddy cleared her throat. "Begging your pardon, sir," she said, lowering her eyes. "But how did the mistress die? She wasn't ill or nothing."

The doctor gave Biddy a small, patronizing smile. "Your mistress has suffered with a weak heart for many years." He didn't bother elaborating further. Why should he, for a maidservant with a round, pudding face and lank, mousy hair tucked up under her cap.

"The undertakers will be here presently," the doctor said. A speck of saliva escaped his lips and Biddy looked away. Something about him reminded her of George, the footman at the house on Catherine Street where she'd once worked. She had been fourteen then and she'd had no experience of men ... until she caught George's lecherous bloodshot eye. She imagined she could smell him now, the scent of his sweat as he had held her close to him – when he did what he liked to do when the cook's back was turned and the staff were all busy with their chores. Biddy felt her body trembling at the very thought of George's touch ... of his clammy hand thrusting up her skirts, touching and kneading the places her mother had told her nobody but her husband should be privy to. She glanced at the dead woman on the bed, trying to banish the memories of her humiliation.

Dr Willis gave her a businesslike smile. "I shall sign the death certificate and leave it here. Mr Politson will be here shortly. I have sent word that his mother has passed away."

"Mr Politson called this morning, sir," Biddy said, almost in a whisper.

The doctor looked at her, frowning. "I didn't know."

"He stayed about half an hour, sir. Him and the mistress ..." She stopped herself. It wasn't her place to gossip about her betters and she was aware that she'd said enough already.

Dr Willis shuffled his feet. "I don't think that's any concern of ours, Biddy." He turned and addressed the young man. "Dr Carson, there's nothing more we can do here."

The young man made no move to leave but looked straight at Biddy with an intensity that made her uncomfortable. "Please go on, Biddy. What were you saying about Mr Politson and your mistress?" He glanced at the corpse on the bed as though he expected it to rise at any moment and join in the conversation.

"If you please, sir, they ... they had words, sir. That's all." Biddy sounded wary.

"What kind of words?"

"Harsh ones, sir. We could hear them in the servants' hall. But it's not my place to say any more."

"Indeed," Willis interrupted, impatient.

"I don't suppose you caught the, er ... sense of these harsh words, did you?"

"Not the sense, sir. I just heard raised voices. As though they were quarrelling, sir."

"Doctor Carson, it is time we were going," Willis said firmly. "This unfortunate girl can hardly be expected to pass judgment on the affairs of her employers. The death was natural and that is an end to the matter."

Dr Willis looked at the corpse again, a little uneasy. Flora Politson had quarrelled with her son – and a few hours later, Flora Politson had been found dead by her maid. But Willis had known the family for years and, as far as he was concerned, people of the Politsons' standing in the community were above suspicion. It was high time young Dr Carson, his assistant of three months, learned this before he committed the grave sin of insulting his betters. "Dr Carson, come. We have patients to see."

But Carson ignored the order. He walked back to the bed and bent over the dead woman, sniffing the air around her. Alongside an empty bottle marked laudanum on the bedside table, stood a half-drunk cup of tea, the milk formed into dead swirls on the surface. He sniffed at it before placing his hand beneath the dead woman's head and lifting it gently. For a few moments he studied the pillow closely, then he lowered the head again.

"Is anything the matter, sir?" Biddy asked, craning her neck to see what was going on.

Before Carson could answer, Willis spoke again, impatient. "Come, Carson, we have calls to make. Biddy, tell Waggs that the undertaker is expected."

Biddy scurried from the room and made for the servant's hall where she knew the butler, Mr Waggs, was polishing the silver. As she reached the foot of the stairs she heard Dr Carson's voice. "I'm not satisfied, doctor," he was saying. "I wish to make a more thorough examination."

"Nonsense," Willis barked as he swept down the staircase, almost colliding with Biddy who had stood aside with her head bowed, ready to see the medical men off the premises.

Biddy watched the younger doctor hesitate at the front door. Then he turned to address her. "Biddy, just one thing, if you please. Had your mistress pricked herself at all ... a finger perhaps ... or some part of her face or ...?"

Biddy frowned in an effort to remember. Then she nodded. "She pricked her finger yesterday, sir, when she was sewing. Drove a needle in almost to the bone, sir."

"Indeed."

"Oh yes, sir. It bled something awful."

Carson nodded. "Come, Biddy. Show me if you will."

Biddy hesitated for a few moments before returning upstairs to Flora's bedside. She watched while the doctor uncovered the dead woman's hands. Sure enough, on her left forefinger was a pinprick wound, half-healed now but still visible. Unexpectedly, Carson picked up the cup containing the dregs of tea and poured a little of the liquid into a small glass vial which he popped into his waistcoat pocket before thanking Biddy again and hurrying out to join his colleague downstairs in the hallway. Biddy saw Dr Willis shoot the young man a hostile glance. His professional opinion had been questioned. Or his incompetence had been discovered.

Biddy bobbed a curtsy as the two doctors left then she hurried across the hall and pushed open the green baize door that led to the servants' quarters.

Death had visited the house. And death meant more work. Until the arrival of the police brought everything to a sudden halt.

* * *

Reginald Politson was the only son and heir of Flora Politson and the late Septimus Politson Esquire. Septimus himself had been a man of ambition and by the time of his death seven years ago, he had made a fortune supplying the voracious needs of the Liverpool shipping industry. Reginald had been a disappointment to him – all the servants knew that – and after her husband's death, Flora had kept her dainty hands on the company's tiller. But now she was dead, Reginald would have free rein to run the business as he thought fit. And there were many, servants' hall gossip had it, who thought that he would run it into the ground.

Reginald was a swarthy man in his mid-thirties. And he was unmarried which some in the servants' hall took as a sign of dissipation. A respectable young man in Reginald's position should take a wife and those that didn't were definitely suspect. Biddy had overheard one of the footmen telling Daisy the parlour maid that Mr Politson preferred the company of men but Biddy was uncertain what he had meant by that. At least he didn't pester the female servants like some. At least she didn't have to go about the house in fear that he might creep up on her, pull her into a room and use her to satisfy his desires, panting like an animal above her, hurting her like her old master at the house in Canning Place had done.

Biddy served tea to Mr Politson and the family solicitor, Mr Jaques, in the drawing room. The house was now in deep mourning – black crêpe everywhere and a large black bow tied to the front door. The undertakers, with their long, serious faces and discreet footsteps, had called and Mrs Politson had been laid out properly in her bed, receiving visitors in death as she had done in life.

Flora Politson's only son and her solicitor wore suitably solemn expressions as they discussed whatever they were discussing. As Biddy set down the tray, Mr Politson looked restless and uncomfortable and perhaps, she thought, also a little guilty. But she told herself that the man had just lost his mother suddenly and he was probably in shock.

The policemen arrived at six o'clock. Mr Waggs admitted the inspector and the plump uniformed constable through the front door with plain disapproval. As far as Mr Waggs was concerned, policemen should use the tradesmen's entrance. Mr Waggs had once worked for a titled gentleman and was a stickler for the proprieties.

The inspector, a large man with a bald head and ruddy cheeks, was closeted with Mr Politson and his solicitor for a full half hour before Biddy was summoned from the servants' hall to the dining room. Inspector Always wished to speak with her.

Biddy hadn't had dealings with the police before but her brothers said that they were best avoided. Police meant trouble and her brothers were usually right about that sort of thing. They'd had to be. Their parents had travelled to Liverpool from County Mayo on a crowded boat to be packed into a cellar in one of the mean, filthy courts that lay between St James Street and the docks with their children and the rats. Four of their children had died. But Biddy and her two brothers had survived.

She entered the dining room and saw the constable sitting awkwardly in the corner of the room, his notebook at the ready, while the inspector sat in one of the dining chairs at the huge polished table. The inspector smiled as he invited her to sit. He had a kind face. But she'd known men with kind faces before – and they sometimes weren't what they seemed.

"Now, Biddy, you must tell the truth, do you understand?"

Biddy nodded.

"There was a small bottle by your mistress's bed. Do you know what it contained?"

"Her laudanum, sir. Took it every night without fail, she did … to sleep."

"Dr Carson suspects there was some in her tea. He's saying the dose might have killed her."

Biddy's hand went to her mouth in horror. "She never took it in tea, sir. She took it in water last thing at night."

"Would you say anything had upset your mistress recently, Biddy? Think carefully."

Biddy frowned. "She had words with Mr Politson … her son. They were arguing like …" She stopped herself. She mustn't say too much.

"You didn't overhear what they were saying by any chance?" The inspector gave her a knowing wink. Servants listened at keyholes. Servants knew things.

Biddy blushed. "I heard the words … immoral … and unnatural. And the mistress asked him why he didn't get himself a wife. I couldn't make out everything Mr Politson said in reply, sir. But he sounded angry. He said she'd be sorry."

"Were those his exact words?"

Biddy considered the question for a few moments. "Those or something very like them, sir."

The inspector smiled again. He reminded her of the priest at the church near where she used to live – he had always made her feel guilty too. She swallowed hard. "Will that be all, sir?"

The inspector nodded. "For the moment," he said.

Biddy made straight for the servants' hall. And by the end of the day word had spread that the police thought Flora Politson had been poisoned.

And when Biddy piped up that she was sure she'd taken an overdose by accident, nobody believed her.

On her afternoon off Biddy was grateful to escape from the heavy blanket of mourning that had enveloped the house from scullery to attic. The mistress' death was the only topic of conversation in the servants' hall and, as nothing more had been seen of the police for several days, everyone assumed that the initial suspicion about the cause of Flora's death had been dispelled, to the disappointment of some. There had already been an inquest and the coroner had given his verdict. Accidental death. Mrs Flora Politson had taken her usual laudanum then she had taken a further dose, no doubt distracted by her quarrel with Reginald, her only son.

The funeral arrangements, a little delayed by the inquest, were now in progress and Reginald Politson was playing the grieving son to perfection, receiving the condolences of Liverpool society who paid their dutiful calls with solemn faces and tearful eyes.

It was to be a grand funeral, as befitted a woman of Flora's standing, held in a few days' time at St Anne's church. Cook was working herself up into a state of near hysteria about the catering arrangements. But Cook worked herself up about most things.

At one o'clock that afternoon, Biddy left the bustling house by the servants' entrance, securing her new hat firmly with a hat pin. The wind was blowing in strongly from the River Mersey and you couldn't be too careful as far as new hats were concerned. She made for Sefton Park, walking purposefully towards the new bandstand.

She was meeting Michael there and she didn't want to be late. Michael was her favourite brother, always smiling, always ready with a quip. She didn't care that he'd been in trouble with the police, or that he earned what money he had playing cards with strangers in pubs. He was her Michael. Her darling big brother.

She hurried onwards past the park lake. It looked like paradise with all those trees and the water glistening in the weak sunlight and she was unaware of being followed, of the footsteps behind her echoing her own on the new stone path. So when she heard someone calling her name softly, she swung round, bringing her hand to her breast as if to still her pounding heart.

Reginald Politson stood there, shifting from foot to foot. His dress was immaculate as usual but he looked pale and there were dark rings beneath his eyes as though he hadn't slept. And he looked frightened. "Biddy." He spoke with his habitual smooth charm but Biddy sensed his anxiety. "I'm glad I caught up with you. I need to speak to you."

Biddy said nothing. She stared at his shoes. They were shiny. You could almost see the reflection of the grey clouds overhead in them. He offered his arm and she hesitated before taking it. Gentlemen were dangerous. She'd thought Mr Politson was different somehow – but now she wasn't so sure. She slipped her arm through his stiffly.

"It's a delicate matter," he began as they walked. "The police wish to see me again. Look, Biddy, they might want to talk to the servants too. And if they do, I need you to tell them I never entered her bedroom that day." He stopped suddenly and looked at her with wide, pleading eyes. Like a child … or a dog.

Biddy straightened her back. For the first time in her life she had power. And she wasn't sure how to use it.

But after a few moments she shook her head. "I've got to tell the truth, sir. I don't want to go to hell, do I?"

She spotted Michael, sheltering in the trees, waiting, watching impatiently. "I'm sorry, sir," she said, pulling her arm away. "I'm meeting someone. I've got to go now."

As she hurried off towards the trees, it began to rain.

* * *

Henry Carson MD had calls to make. Not that anybody was ill, but there were things he had to check. He had looked through all the notes Dr Willis had made during his years working as a physician in the town of Liverpool. Willis, he knew, worked chiefly amongst the wealthy that dwelled in considerable comfort in the fine Georgian houses around Rodney Street and Catherine Street. Carson himself, after a few weeks of assisting Willis in his work, had taken to salving his sensitive conscience by helping at a clinic for the poor of the squalid courts – so close to the mansions of the rich but in a different and lower world.

But today it was the rich who concerned him. Three of Dr Willis' wealthy patients to be precise. He spread the records of their deaths before him on his desk and moved the oil lamp a little closer. The similarities were unmistakable. But he had no evidence. Only vague suspicions.

He turned down the lamp and left the room. It would be better by far if Dr Willis knew nothing about what he was preparing to do. Henry Carson crept down the staircase of Willis' house in Rodney Street and let himself out, careful not to disturb the household.

He had questions to ask. And it was usually servants who knew the answers.

Biddy hurried back to Fulwood park. Talking to Michael, walking with him arm in arm, listening to the news of the family – how dad was still drinking, how mam was growing thinner by the day and how Patrick's cough was no better – had made her lose all track of time.

She began to run but when she reached the park lake she spotted Reginald Politson walking, deep in conversation, with a flamboyantly dressed young man. She slipped behind the trunk of the nearest tree and once Politson and his companion were out of sight she hurried back, her heart thumping, and hurtled down the steps leading down to the servants' quarters, mouthing a silent prayer that Mr Waggs wouldn't see her and scold her for her lateness.

When she saw there was nobody about, she paused in the lobby to catch her breath, took off her coat and hat and walked casually through the kitchen where Cook was too preoccupied to notice her. Then she hurried up the back stairs and shot into the sparsely furnished bedroom she shared with Sally the parlour maid, shutting the door softly behind her.

And as she drew the cheap cardboard suitcase from beneath her iron bed, she felt her body was trembling. She knew she was in danger and she was afraid.

"I have just paid another visit to Mrs Politson's house in Fulwood Park."

Dr Willis looked up at his assistant who stood on the other side of the huge oak desk like a schoolboy summoned to his headmaster and felt a wave of irritation. "I see," he said, trying to stay calm. "I should have accompanied you, Dr Carson. It is not your place to ..."

"I think Flora Politson was murdered."

Willis stood up, knocking a stack of papers to the floor. "This is outrageous. How dare you intrude on the grief of a family of the Politsons' standing with unfounded accusations. If you wish to keep your reputation in this town ..."

"If this matter is not dealt with promptly, doctor, your own reputation might suffer. If it emerged that a crime was ignored ..."

Willis stroked his mutton chop whiskers, considering the implications. "You have evidence?"

"I have discovered three similar cases."

Willis raised his eyebrows.

"I have visited all the houses concerned and interviewed the servants. The victims were all wealthy widows and the deaths were identical. The laudanum by the bed tends to deflect suspicion. The blood on the pillow, easily explained away ..."

He had Willis's complete attention now. "You have re-examined Mrs Politson's body?"

Carson nodded. "And my examination confirmed my theory."

"But the motive? What can your killer gain from these deaths?"

Carson explained patiently and Willis' eyes widened. "You can prove nothing."

"I have already sent the maid to fetch Inspector Always."

Willis swallowed hard, looking like a man who was about to face the gallows. "I fear, doctor, that you are about to make a fool of yourself," he said weakly.

When Henry Carson arrived at Mortaber Villa in Dr Willis' brougham, seated opposite Inspector Always, he felt a little apprehensive. But he had considered the facts carefully and he knew that the murderer was clever and had been responsible for the deaths of at least four women. Maybe more.

Carson alighted first and marched straight to the front door. A black crêpe mourning bow was fixed to the brass knocker and the doctor's pounding on the door was enough to wake the dead. The door was opened by a butler with hostile, suspicious eyes who announced in chilly tones that Mr Politson would be with them presently.

"It's not Mr Politson we want to see this time," said Inspector Always. "It's you, Mr Waggs. We'd like to ask you some questions." Always had acquired the skill over the years of making even the most innocent statement sound menacing to instil fear into the hearts of Liverpool's criminal fraternity.

Carson saw panic in the butler's eyes. The haughty looks had disappeared only to be replaced by fear.

Waggs led them to the butler's pantry where they spoke in hushed whispers. When the three men emerged, Waggs led Always upstairs and Carson followed, wanting to be in at the end.

But when they reached the room it was empty. Their bird had flown out into the rainy night.

Two years later.

It was a grey, rainy day in New York and Mrs Van Dutton was snoring slightly in her drugged sleep, unaware that her maid, Rosa, was standing by the bed watching her.

As Rosa stared at the unconscious woman, her mind began to wander. She heard again the clank of the anchor being raised, felt the thrill of standing on the deck with her brother watching Liverpool fading into the distance, bound for a new world full of new opportunities. America.

She had used the name Biddy then, of course. But she was accustomed to changing her name. At Mrs Ventnor's house in Canning Place she had been Sarah, at Mrs Hobson's establishment in Catherine Street she had been Daisy and at Mrs Tregellis' she had been Mary. Forging references was a simple matter – Michael had a deft touch with words

– and money made lonely old women gullible so it had been easy to steal the wealthy widows' jewels, little by little. A ring here, a brooch there. Until discovery was imminent and action had to be taken.

She and Michael had thought America would be different – their Promised Land where they could make their fortune. But when the money had started to dwindle, she'd been obliged to fall back on her tried and trusted way of raising the necessary funds.

She took the hat pin from the pocket of her skirts and felt the point with her finger. The pin was an old friend. What policeman would consider that the pin securing her hat could possibly be a murder weapon. Every woman possessed one. But not many considered its murderous possibilities.

She turned the drugged woman over gently and lifted the hair until the nape of the scrawny neck was exposed. That young doctor in Liverpool – Carson his name was – had noticed a spot of blood on the pillow so now she was careful to place a handkerchief beneath the head to prevent any telltale mark being left. Then she arranged the scene carefully. The half-empty bottle of laudanum by the bed and the remains of a night-time drink which also contained the drug – Mrs Van Dutton had taken it to help her sleep and taken a double dose accidentally. Her maid, of course, would confirm that she was in the habit of using it to prevent disturbed nights. No questions must be asked. And no doctor would dream of examining the area beneath the hairline at the back of the dead woman's neck.

The maid gritted her teeth and thrust the hat pin upwards into the unconscious woman's brain. So neat. Now the charade would begin. She would discover that the old lady had died in her sleep and call the doctor after helping herself to any jewels and cash that might not be missed by the victims' neglectful relatives.

It was a full hour before the doctor came that day – plenty of time to arrange things. It had all gone smoothly. Mrs Van Dutton's usual physician was otherwise engaged but a new doctor was coming in his place so that was better still. She felt rather pleased with herself and, as she waited for the doctor to arrive, she gazed out of the window, avoiding the sight of the wizened corpse on the bed. It was raining again. Funeral weather.

* * *

The doctor arranged his features into a solemn expression as Mrs Van Dutton's footman answered the door.

"I was expecting Dr Brown," the servant said as he led the way upstairs.

"He's been unavoidably detained."

The footman turned. "You sound English, sir."

"I am. I only arrived in New York three weeks ago. Carson's the name. Dr Henry Carson."

A YEAR TO REMEMBER

Robert Barnard

"MY, *HOW TIME flies!*" wrote Annette Bigsby, as she sat down on December 13 to compose the round-robin that, immaculately word-processed, would accompany her Christmas cards to friends and relations all around the world.

"This last year has been one of all sorts. Some of the usual, which my correspondents will recognize: holidays in Majorca and Las Vegas, visits to Brighton, London and Morocco, and then some of the unusual to balance them.

One high spot of the unusual occurred in May. What could be nicer and more heartwarming than opening the door to a relative unseen for more than fifteen years? And how lovely that we could immediately strike up a rapport! That's what happened with my second cousin Malcolm Watts – only a teenager, but wise and generous beyond his years."

Annette put down her pen. She would have to say more of Malcolm, but she wanted to strike the right note from the beginning. On reading it through she thought she already had struck a nice balance (as she would have put it) between the true and the misleading.

When she opened the front door on that memorable day in May 2007 her main emotion was not the surprise which her letter, quite cleverly, led her readers to assume she felt. She had already had contact with Malcolm through the Families United website. She had responded unwillingly to his appeal, and in fact had only done so because it had been made clear that if he did not get the facts of his birth from the website he would get them from his adoptive mother, who was obviously as weak and indiscreet as Annette had always feared.

"More than fifteen" was also true but misleading. It was over seventeen years since mother and baby had been allowed home from hospital, three days after Malcolm's birth. After overnighting at cousin Caroline's home she had kissed the boy goodbye (cousin Caroline seemed to insist on it) and gone back to her own home in Peterborough.

"Am I what you expected?" asked Malcolm in his eager-puppy way.

"I'm not sure ... I don't think I *expected* anything."

"I thought I might remind you of my father."

"Oh dear – that's so long ago. He was dead before you were born." And in truth Annette could hardly remember anything about him.

"Dead? He must have been very young. How did he die?"

"It was a car crash. Tragic. Absolutely tragic."

"But you've married since?"

"*Been* married. At the moment I'm in a relationship. We're planning to marry, but we've just not got around to it yet."

"And you'd rather he and I didn't meet."

Annette flounced a little.

"I don't know why you say that."

"Because you specified times when I could come so exactly. They were obviously when he was at work."

"Well ... well yes. I didn't think Grant was quite ready yet."

"Ready?"

"Ready to be told."

Annette licked the tip of her Uniball pen and continued writing.

"*Professionally – on the job front, I mean – everything has gone like a dream. I am now well entrenched as head buyer at the Peterborough M and S, and enjoying enormously the work and the challenge. So much has been done in the last year or two to improve and brighten the store's women's clothing, and I am happy and proud to have been part of this. Grant, in his challenging and demanding job in securities, goes from strength to strength, and both of us seem to be on a steep upward curve.*"

"Who was round here today?" Grant asked, when he got in in the early hours.

"Round here?"

"There were two cups and saucers on the draining board."

"Oh, that. That was Peggy Hartley from marketing. She's been on to me to see the house, because she'd love to move to this area."

"What's so fucking special about these houses?" Grant asked. He had never so much as nodded to any of the neighbours, or shown any consciousness that they lived in a desirable neighbourhood. "It's just a fucking house."

"Well, it's two or three steps up from anything Peggy Hartley can afford. We do very nicely, Grant."

Grant grunted, and got down to what he did very nicely.

Annette nearly swallowed her Uniball before she got down to the first crux in her account of 2007. This needed careful handling.

"So those are the main outlines of my year. One of the joys has been the way the two strands have meshed. No sooner did Malcolm and Grant meet than they seemed to form a partnership – both taking enormous pleasure in each other's company. Grant has no family to speak of, unlike most Londoners. He has lost them through emigration, death and spending long periods away." (She thought, then crossed out the last six words and inserted an "or" before *"death"*). *"So it was a particular joy to see how one of my few remaining relatives got on with the man who will be my husband. Goodness! We must make arrangements for the wedding soon!"*

When Annette got back from work at twenty past five one July evening, Grant and Malcolm were eyeing each other up like two dogs meeting each other for the first time in a park. This time what she noticed about Malcolm was not his puppyishness but his incipient manhood. The moment she came in Grant started getting together his gear for work: the tightly-buttoned suit jacket over the padded waistcoat and the swagger stick. There was no sign of any refreshment having been offered to Malcolm.

"You've got a visitor," said Grant, pausing bulkily by the door, an expression of disgust on his face. "I'll leave you to it."

"We can manage," said Malcolm.

"Yes, I'll give Malcolm a cup of coffee and then I have a lot of work on my plate for tomorrow. Be careful, darling."

"Oh, I'll be careful. Ain't I always? If I wasn't I'd be on Disability, and I wouldn't be able to keep you in the manner to which you are accustomed." He leered. "Have fun."

Annette busied herself in the kitchen to get her thoughts together, then brought coffee into the lounge.

"You arranged this, didn't you?" she said accusingly. "Coming here at a time when you knew I would be at work and Grant would be at home."

"How would I know that? You never told me he was a night worker." Seeing her thoughts Malcolm changed his tactics. "All right, all right. You told me when not to come. And I kept watch on the house."

"What did you do that for?"

"To be able to come and see Grant in his natural habitat."

"I would have asked you to meet him eventually."

"You'd have given him directions how to behave, covered over all his rough edges."

"Does Grant look like somebody I could tell how to behave?"

"He might have made an effort. I wanted to meet the real him."

"Well, now you have." She didn't ask what he thought of him, but he told her just the same.

"Mum—"

"Don't call me that."

"We're alone, Mum. And I didn't tell him. I'm your cousin Caroline's son as far as he's concerned. He's a violent man, Mum. There's aggression bubbling away under the surface the whole time. Does he hit you?"

"No, he doesn't! The idea!" lied Annette.

"Well, I wonder at you. You've got loads of class, and he's just a common nightclub bouncer."

"Casino. That's quite different. He's in charge of security at a very well thought of casino, part of a chain."

"Well, swipe me. Actually, Mum, I don't give a damn what he does for a living. What I care about is the atmosphere of violence he carries around with him. He's an eruption waiting to happen. And then he spouts a lot of nonsense about keeping you in the lap of luxury."

"He earns a very good wage. It's a dangerous job. And the house takes a lot of upkeep. It's the age when the plumbing and the electricity start going wrong, and the Council Tax is horrendous."

Light dawned.

"It's yours, isn't it, Mum? Your house."

"Yes. What of it? I got it with my divorce settlement – *with* a mortgage to match. If it hadn't been for Grant I'd have had to sell it."

"How did you meet him?"

"At the casino. It's a nice place to go. You don't have to be a big gambler. There's a really good restaurant, and it's the same to them if you bet high or if you're cautious, like me. I like it there."

Malcolm came over and took her in his arms.

"Mum, you were lonely, weren't you? After your divorce. You were just a well-off widow waiting for some lounge lizard to get his claws into you."

"Grant is not a lounge lizard," Annette said weakly.

"A lounge Rottweiler then." Malcolm pushed her away so that he could look into her eyes. "Mum, I worry about you. I don't care how violent he is towards the other punters—"

"Don't be silly. You're ignorant. How could he be violent towards the casino's best customers? He'd be out on his ear in no time."

"All I'm saying, Mum, is: you need someone to protect you. I'm glad I came along in time."

Annette smiled satirically.

"Malcolm dear, you're seventeen. I'm sure one day you'll be a very capable man, but at the moment you're not—"

"I'm not taking him on at all-in-wrestling, Mum. He's got all the muscle. What I've got is brain."

Annette said nothing. She really didn't know about his brain one way or the other. Malcolm drew her closer to him.

"Mum, you've got me to rely on."

"One sadness was Malcolm's inability to come on our holiday with us. He was just too busy looking for a job. I know he's going to find one where he will do well, and he's quite right to be choosy, because he's a very personable young man. We went back to Vegas – as I call it now – where we were so happy last year. It's not the gambling that attracts us: Grant gets enough of that in his job. It's the whole

atmosphere, the feeling of something exciting going on all the time. So we don't lose much money – in fact, Grant made a very nice 'killing' this year. But that's not something we'd rely on doing another year – we're not so daft."

"This is better than having your tame puppy along," said Grant as the plane neared the US coastline and he opened his third little bottle of whisky.

"He's a very nice puppy," said Annette, who was herself slightly squiffy from white wine.

"Tell me again what relation he is."

"He's my cousin Caroline's son."

"Legitimate is he? All fair and square? Not wrong side of the blanket, or adopted, or babynapped from some unsuspecting couple?"

"Of course he's legitimate. What kind of daft idea are you getting?"

"Only when you've mentioned your cousin Caroline earlier, you've never mentioned any husband."

"Can't we give Malcolm a rest? You've gone on about him quite enough in the last few weeks. We're off on holiday."

"Right. And it's going to be a cracker. I'm mainly going to watch. That's how you become a winner in casinos. You keep your eyes open. I've got all the background now, from A to Z – or zee as those Yanks say. Just watch me!"

Strangely enough, his exultation did not make Annette feel happy.

But in the next few days she did what he'd ordered: she watched him. They played the tables a little, made a few friends among the English contingent in the hotel, and Grant kept his eyes open. By the second day he was concentrating on one of the croupiers, occasionally playing at his wheel, more often watching from a distance. It was slow work. They only had ten days, but it was the seventh day before Grant said to Annette, whose uneasiness had been growing.

"That croupier is bent."

"Oh Grant! I'm sure he's not. It's the best-run casino in Vegas – everyone says so."

"Makes no difference. He's bent. And I know what he's been doing."

"But Grant – be careful! Please, please be careful. It could be dangerous. There could be large sums involved."

"You're mental, woman. Of course there are large sums involved. There better be. Why do you think I'm interested? Just do exactly – and I mean exactly – what I tell you. That, and nothing more."

The following evening, when Annette was dressing for dinner, Grant said:

"Don't bother to dress. You're staying in this room tonight. I need you to be here."

"But Grant, I—"

"Ring room service if you're hungry. And make sure everything is packed. Yours and mine. Everything."

"But Grant, it's only Tuesday. We don't go until—"

"DO WHAT I SAY! Can I be clearer than that? Do what I say and we're made."

And he left the room.

It was inevitable, only a matter of time, that she would follow him and find out what he was up to. If he had understood her better he would have known this, but he had known her mainly in bed, when he came home until she went to work, and on her occasional visits to the casino. She was already dressed, so she used half an hour to pack as he had ordered her to do, then thought it was safe to go out. She knew the table he would be watching, or playing at, and she stood in the shadow of a plastic marble pillar to watch. He was playing and he was losing. But he was not getting bad-tempered, aggressive, as he usually did. He was watching carefully, especially when the croupier's eyes were turned away from him. He exuded, to Annette's experienced eye, an air of enormous satisfaction.

The croupier changed at ten, and true to habit he went off to one of the many bars. Annette watched from a distance, and saw Grant nonchalantly follow him – casually, as if he could have chosen any other of the bars to go to. Annette went closer, and Grant, holding a glass of lager – he despised cocktails, and thought spirits dangerous when he was on a job – was apparently just having a breather between sessions. But in fact he was watching the croupier exchanging low words with a thickset man who seemed to talk with both his hands – an Italian, Annette felt sure. When he had said goodbye the croupier looked at his glass, seemed about to down it, but found a man by his left shoulder.

It was Grant. Annette, who had taken her eyes off him, was as surprised by his move as the croupier. Grant's mouth went towards the man's ear and he began talking. Annette saw the man swallow (his Adam's apple did a high-jump), then she saw fear in his eyes, saw him clutching a brief-case, protectively, clearly fighting back but on a losing wicket.

That was the danger signal. Ten minutes later she was back in the hotel room, languidly seeming to read a book. Then minutes after that Grant was back, clutching a briefcase very like the croupier's.

"OK. The hotel bill's been settled up. We're out of here. Taxi to the airport. Right?"

"Oh yes, Grant. But I don't see why—"

"You don't have to. No time for questions. We'll get any plane going to Britain. Or to Europe if we have to. Right. Away."

Two hours later they were on a KLM plane going to Amsterdam. Annette had not asked any more questions and Grant certainly had not explained unprompted. But once the plane took off he was in high good humour, drinking in moderation (a good sign) and chaffing the hostesses.

"We're made," he said, as once more they flew over the East Coast and out to the Atlantic. "Well, not made. But we will be. It worked!"

She still didn't ask any questions. She didn't need to.

"We were just settling down again, modestly enjoying our little windfall, and back at our dear old home – because we're both home-birds at heart, in spite of demanding jobs – when Grant was selected for the sort of job that you can't refuse, if you're ever going to get ahead in the organization you work for. It was opening a new branch in Peking, which has a new name I can't spell. We talked it over, back and forth, but in the end there was no choice: he had to go. It was upsetting, but I knew our love would survive a period of separation. I sobbed and I kissed him goodbye in a little patch of woodland off the A15, which meant a good deal to us. Malcolm drove me back home, sobbing my heart out."

"Malcolm, it's awful. I don't know what to do. He's so *changed*. It's all this money. I keep warning him. What if they don't accept what's happened? What if they send someone after him? A – what do you call it – a hit man? He just shrugs and says it wasn't that much money. But I've seen it in his briefcase. It's thousands and thousands. I'm so *afraid*."

"Would it be so dreadful if he did take off for a bit? Let things cool down?"

"Leaving me here if the hit man arrives. You hear of things happening – people being tied up and tortured for what they know."

"You could insist he takes you with him."

"Well ... no. No, I couldn't." Ringing in her ears was Grant's response to that suggestion: "Time I had a change. Swapped you for a newer model. Well past that time, if the truth were known."

"Right. So the scenario is: you're here terrified while he swans off to places unknown. He probably won't even tell you where he's gone. Safer .... I did warn you about him, Mum."

Annette's mouth had dropped.

"But that would be awful. If they were torturing me to find out where he'd gone, and I didn't even *know*," wailed Annette.

"Better for him, though. When's he thinking of going?"

"End of the week. He wants to stay in with the casino people. He says that they're the basis of his future prosperity."

"Just leave it to me, Mum. Leave it to me."

The next day Malcolm rang the front doorbell at two o'clock, just about the time, he knew, when Grant woke up to a new day.

"What do you want, squirt?" Grant asked, with elephantine jocularity.

"I've got a bit of a proposition for you," said Malcolm.

"Oh yes? What kind of proposition would interest me, coming from you? But I suppose you'd better come in." Once Malcolm was in the lounge Grant reluctantly asked: "Want a drink?"

"Coffee would be fine."

"Oh? Too early in the day for a Scotch?" But he went into the kitchen and gave Malcolm the time to do what he had to do with the half-empty bottle of whisky on the shiny new bar in the corner.

"It's instant. I can't do with fucking percolators," said Grant, coming back. "Now what's this proposition?"

"Look, I'm only in this for my mother. I want to spare her heartbreak."

Grant, pouring himself a Scotch, turned round with a sneer on his face.

"Heartbreak? Spare me the sobbing violins. I could ask you what dear cousin Caroline has to do with this, but I've always suspected. I'm not as dim as people think."

"I knew you would have guessed. You're very good at jumping to obvious conclusions I would think. Now, I imagine you're going to slink out of here on Thursday or Friday, while Mum is at work, and I guess you have plans to take anything in the house that will fetch a bit of money. It would be against your nature to leave anything of value behind."

Grant had downed his neat Scotch, and now poured himself another.

"Why would I bother? I've got the Vegas money."

"Very nice, I'm sure. But when did having money stop people like you from wanting a bit more, if it was easy pickings? .... Are you all right?"

Grant sat down heavily.

"I don't know ... I've never—"

"No, I don't suppose you have," said Malcolm. He sat still and waited. There were coughs, heaving stomach, dribbles from the mouth, and Grant never regained anything that could be called consciousness. When he was at last undeniably dead Malcolm began the difficult business of dragging the body through the house then through the connecting door that led to the garage – making his task blessedly easier – then stuffing Grant on the floor of the back seat of the car, Grant's own BMW. Everything was nice and tidy by the time Annette came home.

"Malcolm – what are you doing here?"

"Solving your problem." He smiled, with the satisfaction of a young achiever. "He was never any good for you, was he, Mum? You got involved, and then you found you were up to your ears, and with no means of escape."

"Well, I—"

"He used you and abused you. It's been a nightmare for you. It's over now, Mum. Now all we have to do is get rid of him."

Annette swallowed.

"You mean the body, don't you?"

"Of course I mean the body. It's not going to be easy, digging the grave. The ground's still hard. I shall need your help. Know any piece of land where we could be private?"

"There's a bit of woodland, just off the A15. It has ... associations. It was where—"

"Don't go into that, Mum. It'll be dark by half past five. We'd better leave it a bit later, though. It'll be a piece of cake, you'll see."

And it was. They put on old clothes (cast-offs from the separated husband for Malcolm) and brought spades from the garden shed. Annette knew the way to the little wood by heart, and they had the grave ready after an hour's digging. She kissed the lips of the corpse (an unnecessary touch, Malcolm thought), and they rolled him in and covered him over. Then Malcolm trailed brambles and ivy over the earth he had stamped flat, and they set off for home. Malcolm stayed the night, in one of the spare bedrooms.

"I thought I was going to be lonely, and of course I do miss Grant so very much, but, by coincidence, my nephew Malcolm has been doing work experience in Peterborough, in the dispensary of Boots the Chemist's, and he has moved in, at least until Christmas, when he will have to make a decision about his future. He's a lovely boy, and he's invaluable about the house. He keeps saying he's going to take care of me, and it's lovely that he wants to!

It only remains to wish you all—"

Annette, as she wrote the last words, was conscious of a presence behind her, and she looked round to see a smiling Malcolm. He had just come down from counting, for the umpteenth time, the dollar notes in the late Grant's briefcase. There were plenty of them, in fifties, but with the exchange rate having plummeted of late he wondered if there was enough to finance his plans, whether something else substantial, say property, might not be needed.

"That's lovely, Mum," he said when he had read through the letter. "We'd better cut out that bit about the A15, but you've got the tone just right. Everyone will be happy to receive that. And the last words are spot on. You've got me now, and I'm really going to take care of you."

She felt his young hand caressing her shoulders and arms, and felt wonderfully, deliciously, safe.

TIME OF THE GREEN

Ken Bruen

F<small>AKE CITY</small>
Yeah, trot 'em out
  A phony
  A con man
  Grifter
Flim-flam guy
I know 'em all
Been 'em all
To
Varying degrees of success
Currently, I'm washed up in the West Of Ireland
Time on my hands
But not on my wrist
That I'm gonna fix
Bring that sucker to the bank
Shooting craps
And
Dude, I can sure shoot the shit
You'll have noticed … my accent … see, I'm … talking real slow
so you can keep up
  Accents
More changes than a Brixton hooker on one of them wet
November evenings, I've been there, Brixton too.
I flit from accent like an alky on down gear
And you're thinking
"Why?"

'Cos I can.

Failed actor

Yeah, maybe that's it. Try it on for verification. I hadn't what it takes, for acting. That zombied sponge ability to soak it up

And odd to tell, I'm not real good at taking direction. But hang me out to dry, shoot me now, I fess up.

I wanted the kudos without the graft

Is that so wrong? Seems to me to be the spirit of the zeitgeist.

I left London in a hurry, hung some paper and it was coming back to bite me in the ass and hard.

Got me a cheapo flight outa there, in like, jig time. Just a carry on.

If I'd a little more of a window, I'd have gone to Prague, they like me there

But Galway was first up and like I said, speed was of the essence.

I'd never been to Ireland, swear to God.

My periods Stateside, I knew lotsa Micks.

Mad demented bastards

And like, I mean, do they ever – ever, shut the fuck up?

A woman asked me

"Don't you love their lyricism?"

She was kidding, right? Wasn't she?

The Harps, all the swearing

   Fook this, fook that

   By jaysus

   Yah bollix

What's with that?

You want a crash course in cussin', get you in the Mick mode, watch *Deadwood*. The effing and blinding, set you right up.

Our plane circled over Galway airport, no sign of us landing. A middle-aged woman at the window seat, smelling of Chanel and stale gin, said

"Seagulls on the runway."

I asked

"And that tells us what?"

She gave me a cursory glance, then

"We might be diverted to Knock, now that'd be a hoor."

As in whore?

Then she let out a breath, said

"Ah, there's Tommy, he's shooing them."
For a moment I thought he was shooting them. I asked
"And Tommy, that's his job?"
She clucked her tongue, said
"Don't be an eejit, he's the Air Traffic Controller."
Right
With a final look at me she said
"You must be English."
Welcome to Ireland.

I had two credit cards, good for tops, twenty days, then the flag
went up. With about a hundred in sterling.

Man, I love a challenge.

I was wearing my Armani suit, the real job. Not one of those
knock-off units. Most times, let the suit do the talking, gets you
halfway there. In the lounge, I changed my cash to euros and had to
check the time on the airport wall. My one aim, well, first one
anyway, was a Rolex Oyster, the whole nine.

My old man, the original loser, wore a Timex, plastic strap, to
accessorize his soul, once, between beatings, said to me

"A man's arrived when he wears The Oyster."

Stuck with me.

I'd never quite got it together to attain one. And hey, I didn't
want it to fulfil his dream

Fuck him

It was solely to roar

"This is for you Pops."

To stick it up his ass

We buried him two years ago, cheap box, cheap service. My
Mom, glass-eyed on valium, threw a dead rose into the hole, said

"He was a good man."

I looked right in her eyes, said

"You stupid cunt."

Liar too

Last I heard, she was down in Boca, working on her skin cancer.

Coming out of Arrivals, I hailed a cab, took a moment and decided
to go American. The flag still flew for the Micks. The Brits, now

they were always thin ice. The driver, his face a riot of broken veins, purple blotches, asked

"How's it going?"

I never quite worked out the 'it'. Was it life, the weather, work?

Most times in Ireland, it was the weather. I was sorely tempted to answer

"It's a hoor."

Went with

"Going good buddy, and you, how you doing?"

Lots of vim in there

Worked

He put the cab in gear, no automatic for this guy and he asked

"Yank, right?"

"Outa Boston."

Why not? The Kennedys owned it and they still had sainthood here. He asked

"Where to?"

"A good hotel, in the city centre?"

"Ah, you'll be wanting The Great Southern."

It would be neither southern nor great but it certainly had notions. The driver lit a cigarette. I asked

"Don't you guys, like, have a smoking ban?"

Blew a cloud of smoke at the Sacred Heart Medallion on the dash, said

"Ary, fuck that."

My kind of country

I used my American Express at the Hotel and it was hard to focus for a moment, my British birth always got me those moments, despite how I'd immersed myself in America, damn near raised there, the homeland still sang in me, if anything British can be said to sing. The receptionist provided me with a spacious room, overlooking Eyre Square, the heartbeat of the city. I booked for a week and they seemed delighted.

The porter who showed me to the room reminded me of the first man I ever killed, he didn't even look remotely like him but something in his gestures, I dunno. A Mexican, named José, he'd tried to stiff me on a deal and it was the first time I got to use a knife. I wasn't very adept then and it was messy, stuck him in the throat first and of course, geyser of blood, been a time since then but they say, you never forget your first. He sometimes came in my dreams, a gouging spilling hole in his brown neck. I'd kinda liked old José, made me laugh.

The porter was showing me the amenities and I slipped him ten euros, got rid of him.

I unpacked my hold-all, one white shirt, black Levis and my Converse. Picked up the phone, got room service, ordered a bottle of Jameson, club sandwich, ice and they said it would be along in jig time.

I was in the shower when it came and I shouted

"Kick ten bucks on for your tip."

Heard warm appreciation.

Clean, change of clothes and double Jameson over ice, I let my breath out, said

"Good to go."

Had me a warm-up jacket from the Yankees and slipped that on, checked my reflection in the full-length mirror

Tousled blond hair, even features, bordering on bland and tall-ish. My beer gut holding, barely. Crinkled my eyes, gave me that warm look, your regular affluent but not showy guy.

Next three days, I hit the shops, hit them hard. Galway's a walking town and suited me. Lots of quaint pubs, some cobbled streets and a definite carnival buzz. It was May, summer walking point.

Brown Thomas, a department store, with prices to rival Fifth Avenue, took care of my wardrobe. The American gig was gold, I'd go

"Charge?"

Flash the plastic and they even delivered the shit to my hotel. Got me all the G.Q. designer crap, and what the hell, a pair of Ray-Bans.

Through the shades, I stared at Hartmann's, an old-time family jewellers with a sign to light me up

"Exclusive Rolex Dealers."

I like a touch of tradition

The cops, called guards, were unarmed

I fucking loved Ireland

Third night, I was in the pub, one of the ones advertising the craic.

Not the dope, the Irish term for a good time, party on. I had a table by the wall, tipped the waitress and she protested, placing a pint of black and Jameson back before me

"You don't need to do that."

Dragging up that boyish smile, I said

"But I want to."

Bitch lapped it up

She wasn't bad looking, had that Irish colleen vibe going. Good legs, good breasts and nice pert arse ... shit ... ass ... gotta focus. Her age, late twenties I'd hazard.

She'd do

Her name was Aine, pronounced, you ready for this, Awn-neh ... Jesus, I thought maybe she was Hebrew. I've no beef with them, you understand. I asked her what it meant, like I gave a fuck, she said

"'Tis Irish for Ann."

Nearly fucked up by asking

"So I can call you Ann then?"

Got the look and

"Why on earth would you want to do that?"

Why indeed-y?

You throw the green around, let that *"gee shucks"* mojo out there and the predators gather, chum in the water. Near closing when a skel made his strike. Slipped into the chair beside me, like a quiet virus, said

"Welcome to Ireland."

Different country, same species, bottom feeder. He was late thirties and most of them bad, worse teeth and a worn combat jacket. His hair was in full recession, the eyes, cold and cash-registered

I put out my hand, said

"Thanks buddy, I'm Teddy."

Yeah

His handshake was the cold fish school. He said

"Ah, shure we still love Ted, with all his crosses."

I offered him a drink and he allowed he might try a small brandy, Martell if they had it. Aine brought it and I caught the rapid look between them, double act, just the way I liked it

Ever catch that Mamet movie ... *House of Games?*

Man, I studied it, the line ... *and two to take 'em,* carved on my heart.

I put a fifty on her tray, said

"One for you, hon."

She gave a radiant smile, not a bad-looking babe after all and gushed

"Aren't you the terrible man?"

She had no fucking idea.

That Kraut poet, Rilke, got himself a line, *Each angel is terrible* ... meant me.

The shark gave his name as Seamas. I didn't ask for translation, I knew that was Jim. He worked in communications and I wanted to go

"You're a natural."

Second brandy in, my shout of course, he made the pitch

"Well now Teddy, *cara*, they treating you all right over in that Great Southern Hotel?"

He leaned a little on the *Great*

Fun guy

I hadn't mentioned where I was staying

Game on.

A time, they had me in that secure facility, yeah, the madhouse, the home for the bewildered, and the shrink, he's giving me all these tests, leaned back, said

"You show latent sociopathetic tendencies."

The shite these guys talk

So I went with, asked

"Gimme fifty bucks."

"Excuse me?"

"Give me fifty bucks or I'll slice your jugular."

The alarm bell right there on his desk, his hand hovering and he asked

"Are you serious?"

I stared at his hand, said

"Depends on how latent those tendencies are."

Ah, for the good times

Seamas was waiting for my answer. I peered at his combat jacket,

First Airborne and Paratroopers insignia. I needled a tad, let his balance stay precarious, asked

"You were in the Service?"

Nailed the fuck but he rallied, said

"My, am ... own small tribute to the boys doing their bit."

The sarcasm leaking all over the words

Good, I like a player.

Was going to run with

"The grunts in Baghdad, the nineteen-year-olds from Idaho and Montana, I'm sure it helps, knowing you're sitting there, slurping cognac, talking garbage."

But I needed him

He was on the same hymn sheet, went for flattery, smiled, glanced at my feet, his teeth accessorizing his jacket, green in neon, said

"I like your trainers."

I'd briefly zoned

Happens

I go away sometimes, like a white blankness, a space apart, with some episode from the past narrating on the side.

A college broad I was fleecing, trust fund mama, met her on that spring break gig they do. I was in my professor year-out sabbatical, writing the novel schtick, right down to the leather patches on my corduroy jacket.

Easy role

Crib some Updike, Cheever, sprinkle with Blake, it's a lock

Blake I learned from Thomas Harris, *Red Dragon*

Go figure

Blake is a shoo in, they suck that right up

Took her nine large but it went south

Had to drown the bitch and in the shower, you think that's easy, damn soap makes everything slippy and you're a bit woozy after the sex. The upside, it's a clean kill.

My own reading stretched to Julia Philips, *You'll Never Eat Lunch In This Town Again*. She has a story in there, hanging with Coppola, him doing forty shots of espresso daily ... the fuck kind of jones is that?

I snapped back, levelled my eyes on Seamas, said

"Converse Originals, Chuck Taylor endorsed."

They were.

He went

"Who?"

"Never mind, my hotel is good, they're treating me real fine."

He finished the brandy, relaxed, said

"You need anything, anything at all, I'm yer man."

The hook

Before I could launch, he said

"In Ireland, we speak Irish English, like the Brit version but loaded, you with me?"

How complicated was it? I nodded and he continued

"For example, we say *They saw you coming*", means, you're ripe to be ripped off. Now I wouldn't want that to happen to a nice fellah like yer own self."

I said

"I'm here to spearhead a major distribution deal in ..."

I gave him the full look, ribbed my nose with my index finger

He nodded, he was a clued-in guy and I continued

"And ... we need some people we can rely on. We ask them to front a small amount of cash, say two large, and entrust them with a sizable package to see how they manage. The profits are enormous ..."

I rubbed my eyes, getting that sincerity in there, then

"The people I select need to prove their worth so we ask them to come up with the cash in 24 hours ... most don't, or can't and we know from the off, they're not the people we need."

I let him digest this. The guy hadn't seen two large in one place in his whole lousy life. He asked

"What's to stop you taking off with the cash, if I could produce the readies?"

I smiled

"See, you're the kind of guy I feel I'm seeking. You're thinking outside the box. As a sign of my good faith, I'll let you hold my passport and drivers licence. Where am I going to go without them?"

I ordered a last round of drinks, let him see a mess of credit cards, and thick wedge of notes. He gulped his drink then

"Twenty-four hours, Jesus, hard to come by two large in that time."

I raised my glass, said

"Well, we move on, you've had a nice evening, we say good luck and I move on."

His hand was up and he protested

"No, no, I'm in, I'll get it."

I indicated Aine and said

"If she can raise similar, you're in for twice the payoff."

Now he smiled, asked

"What makes you think I know her that well?"

"It's my speciality to know people."

He was impressed.

One, as they say ... *jarring note*. Apart from the zoning out that happens to me, I'm pretty much on top of my game, I've been doing this shit a long time and am, like, very good at it. As Seamas and I finished off our drinks, a guy who'd had one too many nearly smashed into our table. He had that highly concentrated drunk walk of watching every step and then it suddenly gets away from you and you're doing a reel and a hornpipe. He hit the table hard and as he was that rarity, a good-natured souse, he was all apologies and he'd buy us fresh drinks, the whole pathetic nine and, being caught unprepared, I said

"No sweat guv, don't worry about it mate."

In full glorious Brit/London voice

Fuck

What it sounded most like was natural, like my real tone

I laughed it off as I got an odd look from Seamas. I said

"I do a lousy Brit accent, you think buddy?"

A heartbeat then he said

"Don't we all."

It nagged at me but then I reasoned, Seamas was a dumb schmuck, why I picked him.

We agreed to meet the following evening. I'd bring the product and he and Aine, they'd bring whatever cash they raised.

He said he had a van and would pick me up on Shop Street around seven, we could do our business without prying eyes.

I clinked my glass against his, said

"Here's to the Galway connection."

And he said

"God bless the work."

My basic scam is hit a place, select some skels, lay a line of patter, offer a slice of the large pie, let 'em in for two, three Gs and five times out of ten, I hook. Mainly, I get about half what I asked and four towns later, I'm usually ten to the good.

The beauty is ... who they gonna call?

Sure it's fraught but I relish the edge, love the mind fuck.

Women are best, get a few of 'em, get a bitch-fest brewing.

Next day was R-day, Rolex time. My mouth was dry, I was hitting the precipice, going out on the wing, not entirely sure if the plastic would take the weight

But, it went like, dare I say ... *clockwork*

Walked outa the jewellers, the gold Rolex on my wrist and Mont Blanc in my jacket.

I'd pushed it, got cocky, adrenaline roaring in my ears, blinding me to the risk. And too, I was fucking dazzled by the watch. You'd shit a brick to hear the price. Lemme say, a town's worth of scam.

Sitting in a coffee shop after, wolfing a Danish, double espresso to chase, I eased a notch. I was going to have to split sooner than planned. The credit card would be flagged. I'd, maybe, forty-eight hours to the good

Maybe.

Dublin would be next, do some sightseeing, pluck some fresh meat.

For the rendezvous, I dressed to impress, my new leather Boss jacket, Tommy Hilfiger chinos and soft tan loafers, Italian of course.

That afternoon, I'd arranged some protection, level the playing field. I'm not too big on trust. There's a lot of shysters out there

Got me a knife.

I had a younger brother, Darren, snivelling little bastard, always in my face and worse, getting the shine from my folks. Back then, their attention seemed worthy of merit.

So, I drowned him

Doesn't take long, you do it right, even looks like you tried to save them, like you were trying to help.

Tragic accident

Golly gosh, gee whiz.

Backfired

After, the old man got sucked into the bottle and never came back.

His belt began to appear and my mom, she found mother's little helpers and that's all she wrote.

I think of cute Darren sometimes, the look in his eyes, those moments before the close. I learned then, a plea is a piece of shit.

Wished he could have seen the Rolex though.

Shop Street, the main pedestrian gig in Galway, they have a camping store. Got me a fine blade, hand-tooled and the guy asked

"You backpacking?"

I'm wearing a fucking Rolex, was he blind? I said

"Packing alright."

If Seamas had any other alternative, I'd gut him like a Galway salmon.

Learnt the finer points in Brixton, have a scar on my abdomen to prove it.

Hit real low, rip up, fast, steady and then buddy, pull way the fuck back. Those entrails are going to splash

And Aine, who knew?

This were a novel, the critics would say ... the female character is only a cipher ... are they kidding, aren't all women? What's to describe? They nag, end of story.

I could ball her, have me some Irish but it wasn't a priority. She got lippy, well, I'd use my hands, watch the Rolex catch the light as I squeezed.

As you can see, I was primed.

They picked me up off Shop Street, in a van that needed a major overhaul, not to mention a decent wash, fucking nowhere people.

Seamas, in the driver's seat, and I squeezed in beside Aine, got a little hip action grinding, she was hot

Aine said

"Looks like rain."

The Micks and the forecasts.

Seamas said

"We'll drive out a ways, no need for prying eyes."

We pulled up on the outskirts of the city, Galway Bay spread before us. Seamas produced a flask, said

"'Tis poteen, we call it *Uisce beatha*, Holy Water and it's a miraculous bevy all right."

He offered me the flask and seeing my hesitation, Aine whined

"You won't drink with us?"

What the hell, I grabbed it, took a healthy wallop and it kicked. I gasped, asked

"That's what, like Irish moonshine?"

Aine gave me a glorious smile, said

"More like goodnight."

Came to with my head on fire, throbbing like a bastard and then the cold, my whole body frozen.

My naked body

I sat up and pebbles were embedded in my ass. I was on a beach, not a shred of clothing and checked my wrist

No Rolex.

Dawn was breaking, the light creeping over the bay. I began to get slowly to my feet, dizziness and nausea hitting in waves, saw the note, wedged under a stone. I grabbed it, read

> Teddy, mate, guv
>> We saw you coming. We're Irish but

Not green ...

And that knife ...

Not nice

> We confiscated it, lest you hurt yerself. Now, that would be no way to treat a Brit, would it?

> You better get your arse in gear, rain is forecast.

I crumpled it and said aloud

"Always with the bloody weather talk."

VIVISECTION

Bernie Crosthwaite

THEY SHUFFLE INTO the room, half a dozen of them. They reek of cheap deodorant and alcohol ... and sex. White coats flap open to reveal their scruffy clothes. My gaze fixes on a boy with spiky blonde hair, laughing with a girl in a short skirt and flip-flops whose knees are already turning blue. Serves her right.

I'm just about to make a start when another one lurches in, chewing gum, talking on his mobile phone, and wearing – I can hardly believe my eyes – a *hat*.

The ripple of chatter swells into a wave. Such appalling manners.

"Pay attention. I'm about to begin."

A serious-looking young lady in glasses turns to me expectantly, but the rest take no notice whatsoever. A surge of bile rises in my throat. I pointedly walk to the door, left gaping open by the latecomer, and shut it firmly. My action serves two purposes: the temperature in the room drops once more, and there is silence. At last.

I return to my position behind the metal table. I know that deep down, despite the rudeness, they are in awe of my powers.

"I trust you have switched off your mobile phones?" I take care not to look directly at the gentleman with the knitted headgear. "Last time, someone forgot. The ring tone was so loud my knife slipped and ..." I hold up my bandaged finger so they can see the damage, then carefully pull on a pair of disposable gloves.

In fact, it didn't happen quite like that – I don't even remember how I got the cut, only that there was a lot of blood – but it gets their attention and I'm gratified to see them all check their phones, reluctantly cutting themselves off from their lifelines. Young people seem to think that their electronic devices are a kind of umbilical cord and that without them they will die.

When the flutter of activity has settled down I peer over my half-moon glasses, looking straight at the boy this time. "You – the one with the woolly hat – take it off."

"But it's cold in here," he whines.

"What do you expect? This is a mortuary, not an overheated seminar room. Can you imagine the smell if we had full central heating?"

"Whatever." He pulls the hat off with a flourish, revealing his premature baldness. "Happy now?"

I note the telltale nodules of fat around his eyes. High cholesterol. He'll be dead of a heart attack before he's fifty. "Ecstatic."

Titters of laughter flare up, die away. They won't be laughing soon.

The time has come.

"Like you, I have never seen this specimen before. Normally I read the notes first." I indicate a manila folder lying on the bench behind me. "But I'm under great pressure at the moment – so much to deal with." I grind my teeth, a habit I've got into lately. "So together, our job will be to find the cause of death."

There is complete hush as I peel back the sheet. The cadaver lies supine, quiet and obedient. That's something I admire about the dead, their beautiful quiescence. Most of the corpses I use for demonstrations, after several days in a chilled drawer, have a musty metallic smell, like thawing meat. But this one is fresh and has an odour of the sea – ozone and tissue salts in their last frantic throes of activity. Its recent demise suggests this might be an urgent police matter. Perhaps I should have read the notes after all ...

I detect movement to my left, something twitching or flickering just out of vision. I jerk my head round but there's nothing. It must be that damn tic in my left eyelid that has plagued me for a couple of weeks now. Tiredness, that's all it is. I haven't been sleeping well.

"Right. What do we have here?" I cast a professional glance over the specimen. "Female. Late thirties, I'd say. Any initial observations?"

No one answers. I'm an expert at silences. Some are thick with embarrassment from sheer lack of knowledge. Others are syrupy and lazy, the speciality of the *can't be bothered* merchants. This one twangs with hostility, a reaction no doubt to my firm handling of

Mr Woolly Hat. I suspect they have the answers, but they are going to make me extract them by force, like pulling teeth.

"Come on. Come on. That's the easiest question you'll get all afternoon. If you can't answer that, it's going to be a very long session indeed."

I can hear the drip from a tap, the distant buzz of a fly. I note that the bare feet of the girl in the mini skirt have turned a mottled mauve that perfectly matches the lividity of the skin six hours after death. She sees me staring, which must be what prompts her to speak up.

"She dyed her hair?"

I wait until the muffled laughter has run its course.

"*She dyed her hair ...*" I glance down. I really should have cleaned my spectacles – they are smeared with dust and fingerprints. Squinting, I see that the woman's hair, now dulled by death, had once been a theatrical shade of red. A long strand of it has caught across her neck like a wound. I look away. Julia was a redhead too. Did she dye her hair? That's a question I cannot answer. "This is the School of Forensic Medicine," I say sharply. "You'll find Beauty Therapy at the Further Education College down the road."

The corners of the girl's mouth turn down like those of a petulant five-year-old. She mutters something I don't catch. There are low mutters, shuffling of feet.

"Can we see any external signs of the cause of death? Is there evidence of disease? Any open wounds, operation scars, swellings, needle marks?"

They stare at me open-mouthed. I can see I'm rolling a ball uphill with this lot. Perhaps their silence is the ignorant kind after all. I've credited them with far too much intelligence. I won't make that mistake again.

"No external signs, then."

Woolly Hat raises his hand. "But what about the—?"

"Please don't interrupt." I'm beginning to find him as irritating as that fly buzzing somewhere in the room. "So how do we proceed?"

No response. *Quelle surprise.*

"I intend to start at the top." I move to the end of the table and stand behind the head.

My instruments are laid out neatly on a trolley beside me. With an electric shaver I remove a circular area of the woman's hair, like a monk's tonsure. "Now I'm going to use a saw in order to trepan the skull. Some pathologists use an electric one with oscillating safety blades, but I prefer the old-fashioned manual kind." I pick up the fine-toothed instrument and begin to score through the skull cap. Once I've cut all the way round, I use a cranium chisel to lift off the bowl-shaped section of bone.

"Now watch how I sever the nerves and the blood vessels so that I can remove the brain."

I enjoy the mesmerized looks on their faces as I lift the organ out. No shuffling of feet now, no laughter, barely any breathing.

"Look at it. Just a wrinkled pile of jelly. Yet hidden within is the most sophisticated circuitry in the universe." I strike a pose. I always relish this bit. *"Is this a dagger which I see before me, the handle towards my hand? Come let me clutch thee: I have thee not, and yet I see thee still ... Art thou a dagger of the mind, a false creation, proceeding from the heat-oppressed brain?"*

I have been known to get a round of applause at this point, but there is dead silence.

"No doubt you all recognize the quote?"

It seems not.

"It's from *Macbeth*. By William Shakespeare," I add drily.

"Personally I prefer *Rumble in the Bronx*," mumbles Woolly Hat.

"What's that? Speak up."

"You know, the Jackie Chan film?"

"Jackie Chan? I've never heard of her."

The boy with the blonde spikes covers his mouth. Is he going to be sick?

"You." I glower at him, holding out the brain. "Take it."

"What for?"

I nod towards the scales that hang above the dissecting table. "We weigh every organ and record the weight. Put some gloves on and get on with it."

Grimacing, he tips the mass of jelly into the steel pan while I address the other members of the group. "A woman's brain is slightly smaller than a man's. No less effective, of course. In fact, in many ways, more devious and cunning. Take Lady Macbeth."

I retrieve the brain from the cream-faced poltroon, and selecting a knife with a twelve-inch blade, dissect the organ in half.

"Any abnormalities?"

They stare dumbly.

"I'll tell you then. The answer is no."

Woolly Hat is craving attention again, his hand flapping like a flag in the wind. "But there are tiny—"

"Be quiet! I was rather hoping for a tumour, perhaps an astrocytoma grade four. A swift and silent killer that may have explained this specimen's untimely end. But no such luck. So what do we do next?"

A spotty youth raises a tentative hand. "Cut her open?"

"I assume you mean *make an incision*?"

The boy's skin flares up as if his whole face is covered with acne rosacea. "I suppose so."

"Splendid. But what kind of incision?"

He shrugs his puny shoulders. Bad diet. Too much refined carbohydrate. A candidate for diabetes if ever I saw one.

"We have three choices. We can use a T-shaped or a Y-shaped cut. These give easy access to the body cavity. But who wants to take the easy way? I favour the single straight cut, right down the middle. Like so ..."

The knife slices through the chilly flesh, which in a refrigerated specimen has the consistency of soft leather. But a fresh corpse retains its springy muscle tone, and because the bones are not yet dry and brittle, they can be surprisingly resistant.

"*Unseamed him from the nave to the chaps*. That's how Shakespeare describes Macbeth's favourite method of despatch. We go in the other direction, starting at the neck, taking a brief detour round the tough tissue of the navel and ending up at the pubis ... There we are. Done." I wave the knife two-handedly like a claymore. "*With his brandished steel that smoked with bloody execution*."

I contemplate them over my spectacles, but I have failed to make a dent in the lumpen demeanour of the group. Surely some of them must have studied the Scottish play at school? Or even – radical thought – seen it performed in the theatre?

Apparently not.

"Of course, Macbeth was a violent man, a killer. I'm a mere pathologist. Generally speaking, I only unseam those who are already dead."

Someone – I can't see who – mutters, "That's a matter of opinion."

I ignore the impertinence and plough on. "It's an interesting fact that the real Macbeth, a tenth-century Scottish king, was an exemplary ruler, not a tyrant at all." Despite the cold, my face feels clammy. "Another interesting fact: I met my wife at a performance of the Scottish play. We got talking during the interval. I was enthusiastic about the production. Julia wasn't so sure – too violent, she said. In the final scene she had to cover her eyes when they brandished Macbeth's severed head, dripping with blood. Excellent stuff." I wipe my sleeve across my damp brow. Maybe I've caught something, probably from one of the students. Walking germ carriers, most of them.

"Now where was I?" The body has been slit open to reveal the bright yellow subcutaneous fat, the salmon-coloured muscle. "Now I need my bone cutters ..." I turn to the trolley. My hand falls on an instrument. I pick it up. A pair of forceps. Damn.

"Some pathologists prefer scissors to cut the ribs," I tell them, to cover my undignified scramble amongst the steel blades. "But I favour a good pair of bone cutters." I hold them aloft in triumph.

There is a satisfying crack as the first rib snaps. Without glancing up from my work I say, "I've known students to faint at this point. I think it's the noise." I let a few heavy seconds pass. But there is no telltale thud as a body hits the floor. "Splendid," I say, though in truth, I'm rather disappointed.

"Now I can remove the chest plate and expose the internal organs ... And there they are. Packed in like a box of chocolates, the assorted kind, all shapes and sizes. The arrangement never fails to amaze me, such an excellent use of space." I wipe my forehead again. "Talking of chocolate, a word to the wise. I prefer dark chocolate. If funds allow, go for the best, with a minimum of seventy per cent cocoa butter. But no end of term presents of that hideous milky stuff, or, god help us, *white* chocolate."

I'm breathing faster than normal. It's surprisingly hard work, dealing with a dead body. "My wife was very fond of white chocolate." There's a buzzing in my brain as if that damned fly has got inside. I shake my head violently to dislodge the infernal noise. "So plain chocolate every time. Understood?"

Fortunately I've given up expecting a response.

"Let's get on. What am I holding now?"

"Lungs?" The serious-looking female, the one with the unflattering glasses.

"Good heavens, someone spoke. And a correct answer to boot. The lungs indeed. Think of them as a couple of flabby balloons inflated by the heart. Tireless workers, the lungs. The heart gets all the headlines, but where would it be without these backroom boys?"

Just as I'm chalking the weight of the lungs on the board I hear the thud I've been waiting for. Who is it? I turn round. The girl in the skimpy skirt? No. She's shivering with cold, but upright. Blondie? No, he's still standing too. The girl with the glasses? That attention-seeking baldie? No, both present and correct.

Ah, now I see. It's Spotty. His colleagues cluster round him, unbuttoning his shirt, placing a rolled-up white coat under his head.

"Leave him alone! Let him lie there until he wakes up. He won't come to any harm, not unless someone steps on him."

They stare at me with what seems like one unified malevolent eye.

Feeling almost jolly I continue the post-mortem. I even start to hum. I'm on a roll now.

"The lungs are a little distended, but there's no sign of disease. She obviously wasn't a smoker."

"And the pinhead haemorrhages?" Woolly Hat doesn't even bother to raise his hand this time.

"Did I ask for a comment? Moving on to the heart." Although I'm sweating profusely I begin to shiver with cold. My fingers feel stiff and clumsy as they wield the knife to slice through the connecting blood vessels. But finally I lift out the heart and hold it in the palm of one hand.

"Notice that the Valentine cards get it all wrong. It's basically nothing more than a bicycle pump. It's the colour of uncooked liver and shaped like a builder's backside. And as you can see, it's a heavy, floppy blood-congested lump of flesh that might well ache – angina is the usual culprit – but can never be described as *broken*."

Angina ... perhaps that's what's wrong with me. That heaviness in my chest like someone standing on it, the tiredness, the shortness of breath, the restless nights.

"Nothing sentimental about it. Can't bear sentimentality. My wife took me to the ballet on my birthday a fortnight ago. Never again. Sickly saccharine stuff. She gave me a rather splendid present though – a large bottle of what they used to call Kensington Gore, the artificial blood they use in the theatre, now known rather more prosaically as Pro Blood. A leaving present, she said. After all those years together ... *Out, out, brief candle ...*"

Someone coughs.

Where am I? Of course – the mortuary, the cadaver on the dissecting table, the woman with dyed red hair. Straight hair. Julia's had a natural and untameable kink, sprouting tendrils of copper wire when the light was behind her.

"Time's getting on. Who can tell me what this is? You – the boy with the blonde spikes."

"The oesophagus?" he asks sullenly.

I sigh deeply. "Where were you during basic anatomy? No doubt doing unspeakable things with your girlfriend in some grubby squat?"

He doesn't deny it.

"No, it is not the oesophagus. It is the trachea. This is the oesophagus. Now for the abdominal organs."

As each body part is removed I check it for disease, weigh it, record the weight. First the liver, then the stomach and the kidneys. And the pesky little thing known as the gall bladder, which can cause no end of trouble.

"Now we come to the uterus. The womb. From whence we all came. This remarkable organ resists putrefaction longer than any other. Women, it would appear, are more durable than men." I tip the surprisingly small pear-shaped organ into the bucket under the table with all the rest. I doubt this woman had any children. Nor did Julia. And now she never will.

My glasses are misty with sweat. "So, cause of death. I'm tending towards sudden unexplained heart failure. Any other theories?"

True to form, Woolly Hat's arm snakes up like a cobra rising from its basket.

"Could the ligature mark around her neck have anything to do with it?"

Ligature mark?

I squint at the corpse, barely able to see through the smeared lenses. Surely it's a strand of red hair? I touch it. A groove in the flesh. Damn him.

"I was wondering when someone would notice that. What does it suggest?"

"Death by hanging?" offers Miss Flip-Flop.

"Suicide," says the studious girl.

I nod approvingly. Suicide, of course. No signs of disease or trauma elsewhere. An excellent theory.

"Or murder made to look like suicide," says Woolly Hat.

I take up the challenge. "Let's examine the hyoid bone, shall we?" I point to a spot under the chin. "It's so fragile it breaks during strangulation, but not when the body has been hanged. Take a close look."

The bald one comes round to my side of the table. He leans over the corpse and prods the bone.

"Is it broken?"

"No," he admits. "But look at the ligature mark. No sign of inflammation."

"Therefore?"

"She was dead before the rope was put around her neck."

"Now you're being melodramatic."

"Why won't you admit what's staring you in the face?" he shouts.

"Staring …?" I glance down at the body but the eyes are closed, thank god.

"The woman's face is blue."

"It's cold in here," I insist.

"And there are tiny haemorrhages in her brain and her lungs."

"Exactly. Consistent with lack of oxygen, caused by self-inflicted hanging."

"So where's the inflammation round the neck?"

"We've been through this. The hyoid bone is unbroken. So it cannot be murder."

That shuts him up.

Suddenly his features change. It's like watching Toshiro Mifune in that particularly savage Japanese version of *Macbeth*. His face becomes taut, his eyes narrow to slits. He thrusts out his hands, one in front of the other, the sharp edges facing me like blades. He springs at me like someone demented. One hand stops dead at the side of my neck. If he'd gone just a millimetre further ...

"Pressure on the vagus nerve stops the heart," he says quietly. "Look in the police file. I bet her partner was ex-army, SAS probably, or some sort of survival freak." He reels his hands backwards. "Or a karate expert. Like Jackie Chan."

I remove my half-moon spectacles and place them in the top pocket of my coat. "You could have killed me. What's your name? Who's your personal tutor? I intend to report you!"

He just laughs. "You're the one who should be reported. Have you thought about early retirement?"

An almighty hubbub breaks out. Before I can quell the riot a deep groan emanates from the floor and does the job for me.

A couple of students haul Spotty to his feet. He's pale and groggy with dark smudges for eye sockets. Supported by his friends like a drunk, he glares at me.

I wag my finger at him. "Are you sure you're cut out for forensic medicine, young man? It takes a certain type of character, you know. The ability to detach is essential. You failed to detach."

"That's it, I've had enough," says Woolly Hat. "I'm off." He shoves his headgear back on and strides out, followed by his pathetic cohort.

For a few minutes I can hardly breathe. I feel as if I've been punched in the stomach. Then I rub my aching eyes, put my glasses back on.

The room looks like a butcher's shop. The cadaver is a hollow gourd, its innards scooped out and discarded. There are bloody organs spilling out of the bucket, the floor is slippery with body fluids. The stench of death is overwhelming. Vagal inhibition. I wish I'd thought of that. Far less messy. But that night, after the ballet, sheer force of professional habit made me reach for a knife ...

"*I have supped full with horrors,*" I murmur.

Taking a deep breath I peel off my scarlet-stained gloves and pick up the manila folder. *Threatened to leave abusive partner ... found hanging ... partner served in Gulf War ... extensive collection of martial arts films ... is death suspicious? Report needed asap.*

I fish my dictaphone from my pocket. I outline the findings of the post-mortem and state my interpretation of the evidence. "I conclude that lack of inflammation at site of rope marks indicates deliberate compression of neck leading to inhibition of the vagus nerve, stopping the heart and causing death within seconds."

It takes some time to tidy up and finish my paperwork. When everything is done I stroll out to the car park.

It's cold outside, colder than the mortuary, and already growing dark. A flock of rooks circle high over the grounds and land in perfect sequence on the branches of the tall tree they have made their home. Their cawing cries sound like the cackling of witches on a misty heath.

Or the scrape of knife on bone.

Shaking my head I muse on the events of the afternoon. Young people, these days. Quite frankly, I could cheerfully murder the lot of them.

STAR'S JAR

Kate Horsley

————————————————

Conrad Mulondo slouched into Kisendi one hot Wednesday when the red dust stuck to the sweat of knees and napes and the blue turaco called raucously from the thorn tree. His wife, Star, hadn't seen him in weeks. She blinked at the shine of his black shoes in the sunlight, the glare of his white dress shirt.

Conrad always wore nice clothes when he came back to her. They hugged and Star felt ashamed of her scruffy pink *gomesi* and cropped hair. Conrad let go of her and sat on the sofa, his hand smoothing the doilies Star's mother had given them for their *kwanjula*. He cast an eye over the cement walls he'd been promising to paint, the wheelbarrow full of baked-mud bricks.

"Been moving round trying to make a shilling so you can fix this place."

"*Kulikayo*, Conrad. Thought you were lost," said Star and walked to the cupboard of a kitchen.

She'd been calling Conrad all the names God didn't like her using, but as she emptied the sachet of powder into a jug, she hummed under her breath. There was a mirror sticker on the side of the clapped-out fridge. She peeked round and saw the blue-black sheen of her cheeks, her straight white teeth.

"Still pretty."

Over the scent of hot earth and burnt grass, Star could smell roasting maize. She kicked the back door open, waved to the bicycle vendor blaring speeded-up Uganda gospel down the potholed main road. Her boys kicked a saggy football across the scrub-grass yard and the baby wailed in a washtub.

"Joyce, rinse the soap from her eyes!" shouted Star to her eldest girl.

Star would take a jerry can bath then spend the afternoon making love to Conrad. That's what hot days were for. She stirred the orange soda with a spoon and pulled two Daffy Duck glasses from the washing tub. With a glass in each hand and her big toe curled round the edge of the living-room door, Star stopped like lizard caught in torchlight.

"I need to change for tonight," said a woman's voice.

"Well, keep your bum there and gossip with her while I get the money."

Star bit her lip and walked into the living room. Conrad started up when he saw her then sat back slightly away from the girl Star recognized as Mukasa Olive. She pushed one glass into Conrad's hand, pushed the other at Olive who looked down in disgust at a fly creeping round the rim.

"Hello, Mrs Mulondo," said Olive. Her smooth, brown face was framed with crisp curls of fake hair, silver-beaded at the scalp. Conrad saw Star looking Olive up and down and smirked.

"She's beautiful out of her school uniform," he said.

Star held her back very straight as if she might get taller by doing so. Conrad set his drink down on the table next to him.

"Can I wash my hands, Star?"

A baby cockroach slurped at the sweat balling off Conrad's glass.

"If you can find the tub."

Conrad usually fought with Star, but she'd seen him be polite to dupes. She wilted on to the edge of the armchair and Olive started in.

"We're taking that place across from you so Conrad can be near ..."

"I'd better find him some soap," snapped Star.

He wasn't in the bathroom, but belly down on the dirt floor of the messy bedroom. The lid of their money tin clunked and he wriggled from under the bed. Star sat down on the bed and began to cry.

"I can't even afford *matoke*, Conrad."

He sat next to her and hugged her awkwardly while she wiped at her eyes.

"Life's tough, Star. Robert hasn't paid me yet ..."

"You said there's cash in Kisendi for those in the know ..."

Conrad laughed. "That's true. Give me time." He kissed her on the nose.

Star took Conrad's face between her hands and kissed his mouth. She lay back on the pink, plush coverlet with Goofy stitched into it and pulled him on top of her. He kissed her, pushed his hand between her thighs. She tugged his shirt up and stroked his back.

"Conrad!" shouted Olive from the living room.

"I have to go," said Conrad. He tucked in his shirt. "*Welaba*, Star."

Star lay where she was, her skirt round her hips. The wind-up radio was gone. Olive's shrill giggle sounded through the window. Star reached under the bed for the tin. It was empty. Her family would go hungry tonight. Conrad had left her six times and given her a child on every return.

"This time he won't come back. And he won't pay me back either."

Star went to the kitchen and found a *Royco* jar with the label half washed off. She dumped the beef powder into a five-shilling bag and stuffed it in the rusted metal rack with her tubs of this and that spice.

"You'll be better off in here," she said.

In the living room, their faded wedding photo was the one ornament. There the happy couple stood: Star in her gold changing dress and Conrad in his blue suit that everybody said looked smart. Star laughed as she lifted the photograph down, felt happy yanking the picture from its frame and ripping it in two. She made small tears around Conrad's body until she had a jagged cut out of her husband. He fitted perfectly in the *Royco* jar.

With the old T-shirt of Conrad's she used as a dish rag, Star rubbed at the white bottom of the label till the jar came clean and she could see her husband's wedding day face.

For the other ingredients, Star had to wait until night when her children were jumbled together in bed. Odd sighs and belly rumbles told her that none of them were really asleep. They hadn't eaten more than *posho* for a week and the smell of Mama Esther frying chicken next door had them drooling on their bed sheet.

Star took a black plastic bag and crept into Esther's unkempt sorghum patch. She caught a grasshopper – more by luck than skill – and dropped it *cricicring* into the bag. Nearby, a white stone shone in the moonlight, so she picked that too, then a pinch of red clay, a chicken feather, a henna flower crushed between her fingers 'til it bled.

On the smoothed-mud doorstep she swept so carefully each morning, Star made her mother's recipe: the cricicring *nsenene* (like a tiny chicken when you roasted it), the *chicoco* feather smeared with orange henna, the white stone blooded with red earth.

The thorn tree in her yard had snared the moon.

"Don't feel stressed," Star told it, "you always slip out of that tree."

It was an old moon, half chewed down. Beneath it, Conrad once bit her ear and told her he loved her. Star took Conrad from his glass house and ran her thumb over his face. A sob shook her by the ribs and the last ingredient fell into the *Royco* jar, bitter and salt. She put him back and screwed the lid shut.

"What's Tata's picture doing in there?"

It was Joyce. She sat down next to Star and pulled her nightshirt over her knees. Star wiped her wet face on the sleeve of her T-shirt and thought. At thirteen, Joyce was in the church choir and loved Jesus like a brother, nothing like either of her parents.

"Tata left us again," said Star.

She pulled Joyce's beaded braid, but the stubborn girl moved her head away.

"Promise you're not going to hurt him, Mama?"

"Of course I won't hurt him, Joyce. I love him," she replied, aware that her mother had spoken those very same words the week Star's own Tata died.

Star waited until Joyce was back in bed. She didn't want to hurt anyone, but the rent was overdue and Conrad would be too busy with Olive to find food for them. He was always bragging that there was a pile of money to be found in Kisendi and rubbing the side of his nose to show he knew where. He just needed a push. She fished in her bra for her last 300 shilling and placed them on the lid of the *Royco* jar.

Clutching Conrad and the shillings to her breast, Star went round the back of her house where bitter tomatoes grew wild. She dug down to the roots and in a shallow grave, buried the money and the jar.

"Draw him to money," she told it.

The image she held in her head sent chills through her guts and made her heart pound.

Conrad and the boys were outside the one-room police station playing poker on a fold-out table. Clumps of black hair blew across from Sandra's Salon and gathered at the belly of a dog dying in the middle of the dirt path. The mutt's demise was the closest thing to action since the pool hall caught fire. Conrad had a book on how long the corpse would stay there.

There was no crime in Kisendi because two years back Paddy the thief stole Robert's TV and ended up gut-shot in the swamp. No one stole after that except for Robert. It was said he kept wads of bills down the toilet and hidden in his roof. He was Chief of Police, so he took what he liked from the villagers. Right now he was doing the bribe-rounds on the *Celtel* shacks that mildewed the main road.

Conrad thought about Paddy's body, the sour papyrus stench, how the bloated face gleamed when their torches flicked over it. Robert told them where to start looking and arrested no one for the crime.

"He wouldn't got burned anyhow if he'd stayed in Kisendi."

Conrad shuddered. The words *gut-shot* and *swamp* made him shit himself. Since that night Conrad and Jackson fenced the odd radio but mainly they just played cards. He stole a look at Jackson's hand – well, well, a pair of Queens! Jackson had been in the toilet for hours and he was holding up the game. But these days he was edgy, up to something for sure and not sharing it. Maybe he knew where Robert kept his stash. God knows, Conrad could use the money what with six kids and a new wife. Everybody seemed to get a piece except for him.

It would be funny to sneak up on Jackson, see what he was up to. Conrad didn't usually play jokes but today the urge was irresistible. He stuffed his cards in his pocket and went round the back. There was a row of cubicles with wooden doors and padlocks. The sow lived in one, her farrow making a motorcycle-engine noise every feeding time.

The toilet cubicle was next door to the pigpen and the door was ajar. Conrad drew out his revolver and used the muzzle to nose it open. A billow of flies hit him in the face but the cubicle was empty. Jackson must have taken a long call because it stank more than usual in there and he'd left the padlock on the ledge, the toilet roll unfurled and soaking piss from the floor. Robert would kill them if he found the place like this.

Conrad bent to pick the roll up and saw a flash of white down the squat hole. He set his gun on a plank and hunkered down to look closer. He could still hardly see it in the stinking dark, so he shut his mouth and pearl-diver-like ducked his head parallel with the hole. It was a Capital Shopper Market bag hanging from the back plank of the latrine.

There was his piece.

He reached in the hole and yanked the bag free. His foot slipped in a smear of shit and the gun flew in the hole with a splash. Conrad laughed at the sound. He felt drunk and later when he found himself up on the iron roof of Robert's barn, he giggled. This was a bold move and about time. He crawled over the corrugated metal slowly slowly, listened to it tick as the heat of day drained away. The banana leaves whispered to him and a gust of warm wind peppered his face with dust. There was another bag of money hidden in the storm drain. He peered at it, reached down.

Back at the house, Olive had her feet up in front of the TV. She was watching a Nigerian movie while the pink paint on her toenails dried.

"You're late," she said, "and you're filthy. Where've you been?"

"I dunno," said Conrad and began to cry like he sometimes did when he was badly hungover. He nuzzled the neck of her dress.

"Are you cheating on me?" Olive landed him one on the ear.

"Don't hit me. My head is paining!" he moaned.

Olive pushed him away with a cluck of disgust and switched off the TV.

What had kept him out 'til 10 o'clock? He struggled to sort his head out but couldn't make out more than an image here and there like strobes on dancing bodies in a karaoke club. He saw his fingers *brrr* a Nightjar's song through worn green bills. He teetered on a roof one minute and the next fell on his knees in the bush to dig.

Conrad looked at his dirty nails. Something else was horribly wrong. He groped his trouser waist.

Where in Jesus' name was his gun?

The next morning, Star woke with a nervous feeling. She didn't dress or even put on her flip-flops, just ran barefoot to the bitter tomato bush. With her hands, she dug around the roots. There, sure enough, was the black plastic bag full of money. She held it to her face. It was dirty, but she kissed it.

It rained for weeks after that. The wet charmed mosquitoes out of the papyrus swamp, drove the white ants from their hills and into the village. Men snatched ants from the air, pulled off the wings and ate the sweet flesh. Star's children caught them in cupped hands for her to fry.

Star pulled a yellow bag over her head to protect her new braids and went to the patch of dirt where green plantains and charcoal lay in sloppy piles. She bought coal and matches so she could light her burner without begging fire from Mama Esther. At the take-out shack, she got a bag of chicken and chapattis. When the power went out for load-shedding, they sat around the paraffin lamp and let it burn while they sucked the faintest flavours from thighbones.

Star wasn't in the habit of saving and most of the tomato-bush-money went into school fees. The first day her kids left for school, Star had time to make herself sweet porridge, feed the baby and scrub the step. She put on her new red dress with the patent leather pumps. Why not brag a little now that she could? She was tying the baby round her waist when a woman's voice shouted from the yard.

"Let me first come!" called Star.

"Eh, eh. I have all day," grumbled the voice.

Star finished the knot at her waist and went out. There in a blue plastic chair sat Olive. She was playing with a mobile phone Star recognized.

Olive looked over Star's red dress and shoes and clucked.

"I know he's paying you, Star. Your kids have new shoes while I can't get money for lard. You've fooled him and I'll find out how."

"What I have, I earned," Star retorted. She padlocked the door and went to the shops.

* * *

When Star returned a few hours later, Olive was in the blue chair drinking a can of soda. She'd placed the chair under the thorn tree to shade herself.

Star set her charcoal burner out and brought out the blue tub, a bag of potatoes and her knife. Olive watched Star peel with eyes half-closed and the neighbours peered around their net curtains. The baby crawled over to Olive and played with the strap of her sandal. Olive wasn't used to babies. As the moon rose, she stretched from the chair and stuffed the phone into her bra.

"You keep the ring, Star, I'll keep the man. I'll get that money back, too."

Olive kicked the soda can so hard it bounced off the step and hit the baby in the arm. Star cradled her and made soothing noises. She picked up the coke can and crushed it with her foot. In the bedroom, she laid the baby on the coverlet, then pulled out the jar and pressed her cheek against the cool lid.

"Your Olive is a bad woman, Conrad. She came to my house and hurt our baby."

The soda can had a coin-shaped flatness.

"Draw him from Olive," she told the jar and slipped the can underneath it.

She held a very pleasing image in her head.

When her children caught the *matatu* to school, Star went to the timber lean-to where Margret sold onions and green peppers. Later she would make a stew and cast into the pot the small bitter tomatoes that kept her pressure down.

Mama Esther was there before her, buying bread slices and gossiping with Margret.

"Did you hear? He found her with another man and beat her so bad she had to limp home to her parents' house in Luwero!"

"Are you sure?" asked Margret.

"Oh yes, Olive and Conrad are broken up. No doubt."

When they saw Star standing there, they turned to her and smiled. It was a bad look, as if Conrad would run straight back to her, as if she should be happy that another woman was hurt.

Star walked up to the soda kiosk. She'd just paid 300 shillings for powdered milk when Conrad appeared with a bag of empty coke bottles. His eyes were puffy and he had a cut on his cheek. He was wearing the ragged old jeans Star had washed so many times.

"How are you, Star?" he asked in a dull voice.

"I'm well," she smiled.

"You look pretty," said Conrad, eyeing her new red dress and shoes. "You must be eating."

As she walked away from him, Star smelled *waragi* on her husband's breath.

"If only he had a woman to take care of him ..." she whispered to the baby.

The truth was, Star missed the old dog and their nights together before the children were born. Now her house was almost empty. His too. She unlocked her back door and put the food away. The baby was fast asleep in her sling so Star laid her down on the mattress.

From the jar, the picture of Conrad seemed to wink at Star. She hiked her red dress up and pulled down her new polka-dot underwear. White stretch marks wriggled across the smooth black skin of her belly. She stroked them for a moment, then stepped out of her knickers and dropped them over the *Royco* jar. The leg-hole slid down the glass until the gusset framed Conrad's face.

"Draw him to me," said Star and held a familiar image in her head.

She walked through the bush until she came to the coffee plantation where Conrad's family was buried. Star liked graveyards and she'd hinted as much to Conrad, but the idea of making love a few feet above his ancestors' bones made him retch.

When Conrad emerged from the trees, a sprig of green beans in his hand, Star didn't waste time on sweet-talk. She pushed the dusty plastic flowers from his Grandma's headstone and stretched out to take him. His eyes were milky when he kissed her, like that half-wit with the cataracts who begged in the dust on Namirembe Road. He tugged her dress over her head and nuzzled her breasts, whispered Star in her ear as he bit her lobes. She'd been ready for him for weeks and when he entered her, she fastened on like a limpet.

Star walked to the yard where her kids were playing. Rose ran up and wrapped her arms round her mother's waist. Star ran a hand over her daughter's short hair and leaned to kiss her.

"You have a good Tata, don't you? He's even sent you to school. You think we'd be happy if he came back to live with us?"

"Yes!" said Rose, "Tata!" and ran back to her game.

Star went to the bed and reached for Conrad but the jar was gone. Her bedroom stank of body odour and toilet flies buzzed over the pillow. A hand closed round Star's throat and a cold circle pressed her temple.

"You're looking pretty pretty these days Star," growled a voice from behind her, "Looks like you're spending someone else's shillings. I heard your kids are even in school. I just went to find your idiot husband ... where's he gone?"

Conrad had gone for soda but somewhere along the way, the empties vanished. He found himself leaving the bush with his flies undone and scratch marks on his upper arm.

"I must've been in a fight," he thought, "and got knocked out, maybe. My head is paining."

He was avoiding the police station. Robert had been paranoid since his secret stash went missing. All the boys took a beating. Suspicion had first fallen on Jackson as the biggest liar and the most shifty person all round. Hadn't he been up to something secretive for weeks? Jackson's body turned up in the swamp near where they'd found Paddy's and deep down in Conrad a feeling of relief bubbled up with a *pop* like his friend's last breath.

The scratches on Conrad's arm were fresh. When he touched them he had such a strong image of Star in a hot red dress that he stopped in the road.

"I can even smell her," he muttered.

Star's scent reminded Conrad of the way it used to be on lazy Sundays when they should've been in church. He turned round and looked towards his old house. His kids were running about with some unreeled cassette tape tied on to a sheet of paper, pretending it was a parachute. The woman at the Dairy had said they were all in school now except for the baby, that God must have blessed his family with a windfall. He thought of his wife alone in her house in that red dress.

"Maybe I could visit her." He looked down at his ragged jeans. "I'll have to change first."

Conrad pushed open the back door of his house and walked into the kitchen. He hadn't tidied since Olive walked out and there were pans covered in flies and pools of milky scum by the freezer. A rotten stench, too, like old Nile Perch mingled with sweat, Robert's smell. Since Jackson's disappearance, the Chief was always slumped in front of Conrad's TV watching football. It would all change if he moved back in with Star. She liked to keep their lives in order. Conrad undid his belt, dropped his jeans and pulled his shirt over his head.

A cold circle jabbed Conrad's back.

"My latrine filled up, Conrad," said Robert. "You know how it gets when it rains and you have to call the shit-suckers in to drain it out?"

"Yeah," said Conrad, his shirt wrapped round his head. He stood there with his penis out, feeling a hazy terror. "So the latrine's back to normal now?"

"The latrine is. But some other shit I thought I sorted weeks ago is overflowing, 'cos you see some idiot dumped something so big it broke the drainage machine."

"What could do that?" asked Conrad and turned round to blink at Robert through the cotton of his shirt.

"Well maybe it's this thing in your back."

Star shook so badly she could barely think. She could still feel the imprint of Robert's hands on her neck. But worse, the jar was missing. Surely Robert wouldn't have taken it. Dumbly, she looked in the fridge. There was no *Royco*, just soda and onions.

"Have you seen a glass jar?" she asked Joyce.

Joyce paused, her hand an inch away from slapping Joseph's face.

"You mean the one with Tata's picture in it?"

"Yes!" said Star, trying to keep the panic from her voice.

Conrad kneed Robert in the balls. Robert doubled up and puked. He dropped Conrad's gun wrapped in a five-shilling bag, the only piece of evidence Robert had collected in his career. Conrad yanked his T-shirt over his head and went for the gun. He brought it down hard on the back of Robert's neck.

* * *

"Maama! Baby has the jar," called Rose and pointed to the culprit.

The baby sat with one buttock in a mud puddle, gurgling at the open *Royco* jar. Her fat little fist was around her father's paper head.

Conrad slid in the sick and across the floor. He landed under Robert. Robert punched him in the face.

"You idiot," he growled, "You're going to the swamp to join your friends, Paddy and Jackson …"

Conrad kicked Robert's gut and he fell to the floor on top of Conrad.

"Bad baby!" shouted Star.

The child wailed and reached for Star's dress, but for once, Star left her there. She picked up the jar and screwed back the lid, dusting the dirt from its grooves.

"Baby, I thought I'd lost you!" she said, cradling it.

Rose stood in the doorway and stared at her mother, her mouth slack. Star sat down in her plastic chair and placed Conrad on the dirt between her feet.

"Draw him home," she whispered.

Robert smashed Conrad's head against the floor. He pushed a thumb into Conrad's eye-socket. The gun was between them. Conrad's hand closed over the barrel just as Robert found the handle.

"Wrong end, my friend." growled Robert, "Your poor wife's going to miss you."

Star waited for the familiar image but none came. The kids kept their distance, playing quietly now with the baby. Star knew that behind her back they exchanged worried looks, wondering if Mama went mad when Tata left, whether she could manage. The sun set in a pink haze and kites circled overhead. She watched them then leaned down, her lips bent in a kiss. The *Royco* jar burst with a loud *pop* and the contents ran out in a blur of blue and brown. As the new moon rose over the thorn tree, all Star had left of Conrad were brightly coloured blotches that bubbled as the red earth swallowed them.

THERE'S NO SUCH THING AS A VICTIMLESS CRIME

Paul Johnston

THE BANKER'S HOUSE burned down the night after Beltane. It took only a few minutes for the fire chief to declare that it was a case of arson – there were three melted petrol cans at the front door and windows. Only one body was found, curled up foetus-like in a bedroom on the first floor. When the owner called the next day, hot under the collar, from the Caribbean, he said it was probably the Norwegian au pair. When he had taken his family away from Edinburgh, she had stayed to complete her advanced English course.

"So it's a murder case now," Detective Chief Superintendent Andrew Garvie said to his subordinate.

"Aye." Jimmy Bain was looking at the building like a fairytale castle next to Lothian and Borders Police headquarters. It contained one of Scotland's most exclusive private schools. "He went there, you know."

Garvie, thin and bespectacled, followed his gaze. "The banker? I'm aware of that." He turned to the other man, his expression hardening. "So did I, Detective Inspector."

Bain raised an eyebrow. "Is that right, sir? I didn't know."

Garvie would have bet his golf clubs that his least favourite but most effective investigator was perfectly aware of where he'd been educated, just as he knew that Bain had been at a bog-standard high school in Fife.

"Did you know him, then?" the inspector asked, running nicotine-stained fingers over his thin grey hair.

"I did not," Garvie replied coldly. "He was four years older and in a different house."

"I read in the paper that he was expelled for nicking a teacher's car." Bain's lips formed into a slack grin. "Started his thieving early then."

The superintendent frowned. "I don't know about that, but Sir Rory Ferguson doesn't have a criminal record." He wasn't going to tell the inspector that Rory was a member of his golf club, or that he had often sat late into the night drinking with the banker who had become globally notorious for the size of his earnings and pension.

"There was talk that he'd be stripped of his knighthood."

"I wouldn't listen to talk if I were you, Inspector." Garvie looked at the file on his desk. "Where do we stand with the investigation?"

Jimmy Bain shrugged. "The techies are still combing the ruins, but they're not too optimistic of finding anything that'll identify whoever started the blaze."

"Witnesses?"

"My people are still ringing doorbells. It was the middle of the night and that part of Morningside isn't exactly teeming with people."

The superintendent nodded. He'd been to the Ferguson house the previous Christmas. It was large, detached and separated from the neighbouring buildings by high walls.

"Campbell's looking at the internet. Customers whose investments were wiped out and workers who lost their jobs have set up websites. Some of them are quite threatening." Bain looked ostentatiously at his watch. "I'm meeting Sir Ronald's lawyer in half an hour, sir. He told me on the phone there had been abusive calls and letters."

Garvie stood up. "Right, on you go. And Inspector? Keep in touch this time. I don't want to find out about the case from the TV news."

Bain's lips twitched but didn't break into a smile. "What about the girl's father? He's flying in from Oslo at midday."

"I'm handling that," the superintendent said.

After the door had closed behind the inspector, Andrew Garvie took off his glasses and rubbed his eyes. The last thing he wanted was to meet the grieving parent, but the Chief Constable had told him to offer the Norwegian every courtesy. He was something high up in the oil business, and he was also bringing his daughter's dental records with him so that she could be identified.

The detective superintendent checked that his door was securely closed, then found the name Farrelly in his mobile phone memory and pressed connect.

Jimmy Bain finished looking through the file of letters and phone transcripts in the opulent New Town office.

"Mr Farrelly, do you take any of this seriously?" he asked, making his accent as heavy as he could.

"I do, and I sincerely hope you do too, Detective Inspector." The lawyer enunciated like an old-time BBC news-reader.

"It's just people letting off steam, isn't it? I mean, you cannae blame them for feeling aggrieved. They're out of pocket or on the dole, while your client's sailing his yacht in the sun."

Donald Farrelly W.S. rose from his chair and leaned towards the diminutive policeman. "It is my client who is the victim here, Inspector. He has lost his house and possessions—"

"Which, I'm sure, were well insured, unlike the au pair." Jimmy Bain got up. "All right, sir, I've got enough to work on. No doubt we'll be in touch."

"Make sure you are," the lawyer said. "I play golf with Superintendent Garvie."

"Is that right?" Bain said, on his way to the door. "Is he any good?"

Outside, in his car, he wondered if Farrelly had also been at school with his boss and Sir Rory.

Andrew Garvie stared at the letter that the Norwegian had handed him as soon as they got into the car at the airport. The police driver was taking them back into the city.

"Is this ... can we be sure this is genuine?"

The dead girl's father turned icy blue eyes on to him. "Certainly," he said. "Iris told her mother she was dating her employer."

The superintendent looked at the headquarters of the bank that had been one of Rory Ferguson's main competitors, before Rory's bank had crashed into bankruptcy. What on earth had his friend been doing? Servicing the hired help was one thing, but writing her a love letter was way beyond the pale.

"You realize what this means?" the Norwegian said. His cheeks and hands were weather-beaten, and he wasn't carrying a trace of fat. "This is a murder case."

"Quite so," Garvie said. "We're treating it as one."

"Really?" the oilman said. "So, are Sir Rory Ferguson and his wife on their way back for questioning?"

"I beg your pardon?" The superintendent's voice was faint.

"They are suspects, are they not?"

Andrew Garvie's eyes widened. "You mean ..."

"One of them arranged Iris's death, you can be sure of that." The Norwegian sat back in his seat, his fists tightly clenched.

Garvie considered placating the grieving father with platitudes, but decided that would be a waste of time. Then it struck him how much Jimmy Bain would enjoy this twist in the case.

The media had a field day when it was announced that the banker and his wife would be returning to Scotland. Donald Farrelly had refused to answer any questions after emphasizing how public-spirited his client was being.

"Public-spirited, my arse," Jimmy Bain said to his wife, as they watched the TV news. "The man was shagging the—"

"Language," Mavis Bain said. "This is not the police canteen."

The inspector raised his eyes to the ceiling. It certainly wasn't the canteen – the food there was better. "I'm going out," he said, heading for the door. "I might be late."

"That'll make a change," Mavis said sourly.

His mobile rang before he reached the pub at the end of the road.

"Detective Inspector Bain?" said a female voice.

"Aye. Who's this?"

"I'd ... I'd rather not say just now." The woman had the under-stated accent of the Scottish landed gentry. "Can we meet as soon as possible? It's to do with the fire at the Ferguson house."

Bain played ball with alacrity. An hour later, a tall, slim woman wearing a fedora pulled low and a black trouser suit walked into the bar in Newington. He nodded to her from the corner table. After he'd been to get a tonic water and ice for her and another pint of heavy for himself, he took in the tanned face.

"I know who you are," the inspector said. He'd seen plenty of photographs of Lady Angela Ferguson in the papers. She was involved with a charity that worked on famine relief in Africa.

"Don't bother saying my name," she said in a low voice.

Bain shrugged. "No problem. What can I do for you? I'd have thought you'd have seen enough police officers over the last few days." Garvie had kept him away from the interviews with the banker and his wife, but he assumed they'd been dragged over the coals. The Norwegian's evidence was hard to argue with. His daughter had been identified by her teeth, and he had signed an exclusive deal with one of the national dailies. But, as yet, no one had been charged.

Lady Angela took a dainty sip of her drink. "Who do you think set the fire, Inspector?"

Bain couldn't help his eyebrows heading ceiling-wards. "I can't discuss that with you," he said, taking refuge in his pint. The fact was, he and the team had checked all the individuals and groups who had abused and threatened the banker – none had been deemed serious and most of the people had alibis.

"You don't know, do you?" The woman held her eyes on him, finally shaking her head. "I don't know who actually did it, either." She paused. "But I know who was responsible."

"Really?" The inspector leaned closer. "And who's that?"

Lady Angela looked around and then met his eyes again. "Mrs Thatcher."

Bain let out a frustrated groan. "Oh, come on. I didn't have you down as a socialist."

"I'm not," the banker's wife said primly.

"You realize I could arrest you for wasting police time?" he said, his voice hard.

"Oh, I doubt you'll do that," she said, shaking her head. "You see, I'm not talking about the former prime minister."

Jimmy Bain felt the cold finger that always heralded a break-through slide up his spine. "You're not?" he said, his tone softening. "Who, then?"

"I think you know Donald Farrelly."

He nodded.

"If you check the partners in his firm, you'll see there is one named Mary Thatcher. She works with Donald on my husband's affairs." She gave a brittle laugh. "I mean, his legal affairs, though she's been sticking her snout into his private life, too. In fact, that's the point."

"It is?" The inspector was trying to keep his cool.

"You see, Mary Thatcher's had a thing about Rory for years. At first we laughed about it, but eventually we had to complain to Donald. Since then, she's been less apparent, but I still had my suspicions."

Jimmy Bain emptied his glass. "Are you saying this Mary Thatcher had something to do with the au pair's death?"

"Of course," the banker's wife said. "She said as much to Rory, but he's too much of a gentleman to betray her."

"What exactly did she say to your husband?"

Lady Angela looked around again. "That she'd arranged for the fire. She was quite unrepentant. As far as she was concerned, Rory had been seduced by the wretched girl and it was up to Mary to deal with her. I imagine lawyers know lots of unsavoury people to do jobs like that."

Various obscenities ran through the inspector's mind. Then he took out his phone and called Andrew Garvie.

Mary Thatcher denied everything. She was a lawyer, so she was good at denial. Sir Rory refused to corroborate Lady Angela's statement. In the lack of further evidence, no charges were brought. The media learned nothing about the development and interest in the case began to fade.

Jimmy Bain was summoned by his boss.

"I'm taking you off the case, Inspector," Garvie said. "It needs a fresh approach."

"It needs someone to question Mary Thatcher properly," Bain said, his cheeks aflame. "Why didn't you let me do it?"

The superintendent glanced at him. "Because the Chief assigned me."

The inspector had been doing some digging. "Does the Chief know that you play golf with Sir Rory Ferguson and Donald Farrelly?"

Garvie raised his shoulders. "Is that of significance?"

"Aye!' Jimmy Bain shouted. "It is of bloody significance! This is not a victimless crime. A girl was murdered!"

More words were exchanged before the inspector withdrew.

Three weeks later, Mary Thatcher, who had recently divorced, was bludgeoned to death in the garden of her weekend house in Berwickshire. Her four-year-old son was asleep upstairs. Suspicion immediately fell on the father of the dead au pair, but he had the perfect alibi – he had been shooting moose in the mountains east of Bergen with three friends. He never mentioned the anonymous e-mail he had received and immediately deleted, and he knew the former French Foreign Legion man he used for special operations would keep his well-paid mouth shut.

Jimmy Bain had also deleted the message after he sent it from a cyber-café in central Edinburgh. Next door was a branch of the bank Sir Rory Ferguson had run into the ground. It was being turned into an "Everything for a Pound" shop. The inspector didn't know that Mrs Thatcher was a mother.

AND HERE'S THE NEXT CLUE ...

Amy Myers

M R PERCY PIP had always yearned to be a crime writer. From his careful study of how to break into the market with an eye-catching potential bestseller, he realized that two obstacles lay in his path to stardom. The first was his name, which if displayed in large lettering across the dust-jacket would not instantly attract an enthusiastic readership. The second was somewhat more of a problem. He had learned that rule number one in achieving one's goal was to write about what you knew, but so far Percy had never committed a murder.

Percy Pip therefore took steps to remedy both of his shortcomings. First, he selected a nom de plume for his new occupation. This would be part-time of course, since rule number two for crime writing was not to give up the day job. When he became a household name, he might reconsider this decision but until then his employers could be reassured of his loyalty, especially as his job dovetailed nicely with his criminal purposes.

Secondly, he began to make meticulous preparations for his first murder. Unfortunately, this would have to be the first of several, since rule number three, so it appeared from his perusal of booksellers' crime sections, was that a serial killer was an essential feature. The golden days of the lone murder, or even of two (permitted in order to keep the investigation going for 256 pages), were long since over. No, three had to be the minimum, with the necessary clues, preferably gruesome, to indicate that a series was in progress.

"What do you mean, crime scene?"

Dr Jonathan Fuller, the director of Mystery Unravelled: Crime-writing Courses Ltd., looked aghast. He had put on several successful workshops all over the country without the intervention of a corpse, and the cause of his distress hovered between his own position and wondering who amongst his current group might be a real-life murderer. Janice Dove's dead body had just been removed from the hotel, having been found in her room by his assistant Mavis Sharp, after Janice had failed to appear for breakfast. Since then the workshop's peaceful discussion of the criminal viewpoint in fiction had given way to an all too real influx of police, doctors, and scientists clad in white scene suits.

"Just routine, sir," the investigating officer said reassuringly. "Suspicious death, you see."

"But surely it was a heart attack or perhaps food poisoning," Jonathan croaked. "The staff ... "

"Poisoning's possible," was the not so reassuring reply. "Was anyone else taken ill?"

"Not to my knowledge. After dinner at 7.30 some people prefer to go their own way or retire early," Jonathan explained, "but I heard nothing mentioned at breakfast about ill-effects."

Jonathan's weekend courses took place in hired conference facilities in a country house hotel in varied locations. In the current one, in Suffolk, the facilities had seemed the best yet, with his party of two dozen completely separated from the rest of the guests, although this, he realized, would focus the investigation on his own pupils. After all, Janice Dove was known from previous courses to several of the participants here. Many of them around him now were eager, no doubt, to pick up such gems of police procedure as they could. He found himself automatically answering the inspector's questions. No, this was not the first workshop that Miss Dove had attended. Yes, she was an aspiring writer.

"Such a gift," he added weakly. "She showed me her latest rejection slip, on which the agent had written *a personal encouraging comment.*"

The inspector was not interested in rejection slips. "We'll need all the information you have on Miss Dove. Do you know what she ate for dinner?"

Jonathan looked uncertain. "I expect it was the stew. It was a buffet. We were moving around – little tables, you know the sort of thing. Most people—"

"Fish," one of his group, Paul Merlin, interrupted firmly. "Janice chose the fish. It had *prawns* in it."

"She had stew," Mavis Sharp retorted equally firmly. "I saw this morning that Janice had been sick. It was *stew*, and plum crumble, I think."

"Sharp of eye as well as by name, eh?" the inspector said jovially. "You found the body, didn't you?"

"I did." Mavis looked modest. "Of course my profession helps." She was the author of six lurid whodunits, one of which had actually received a review in a newspaper.

"We make a strong team. Miss Sharp is cosy, whereas I am hard-boiled," Jonathan explained, receiving a strange look for his pains.

"The two types of crime novel," Mavis explained briskly. "The Agatha Christie school versus the tough brigade."

The inspector's brow cleared. "Rebus!"

As a hat had been thrown into the ring, Mavis felt the need to distance herself from the cosier cosies. "Of course, I am in the *modern* Agatha Christie school."

Another strange look, this time for Mavis. The inspector decided to move on. "And all of you were strangers to each other?" He cast a glance over the crowd before him.

"No." Jonathan steeled himself to speak for his little flock. "The venue and subject matter of these workshops change, but their value is so great that some of my students come to more than one. I believe there are about eight regulars here today."

To Jonathan's eye they all still looked unlikely candidates for the role of murderer, and none of them so far as he knew had had any close relationship with Janice Dove, who was in her fifties and hardly likely to catch the eye of an idealistic crime writer looking for a model moll.

Among the eight, three were prominent in terms of potential troublemakers, in Jonathan's opinion. One was David Patterson, an ex-policeman in his forties, who assumed his experience was an automatic gateway to publication. He wrote with enthusiasm, but the result, unfortunately, was not fiction. His stories were turgid dollops of "I proceeded north-west in an easterly direction".

Paul Merlin was in his early sixties at a guess, an accountant on the point of retiring, with an over-absorbing interest in what he called the psychological approach and Jonathan privately termed the sex-obsessed. He was the ferret breed of student, anxious to display his own superior knowledge while at the same time to winkle out every last drop of knowledge that might be lurking in the recesses of his instructor's mind.

Luke Hayward was twenty-nine, and a teacher with what seemed such a fanatical dislike of teaching that it was clear what drove him onwards towards the promised land of crime writing. A bad teacher, Jonathan decided, the sort who would demolish his pupils in order to rebuild them in his own image. Jonathan prided himself on his ability to pick out the achievers in his audience, a gift acquired from the auctions he conducted in his other occupation. Achievers were those whose willpower would drive them onwards, no matter what the opposition, and no matter whether they were Eton-schooled, state-schooled or unschooled. The chief achiever of the assembled company around him, including Mavis, would in his estimation be Paul Merlin, although he never underestimated the power of the non-achiever to throw a spanner in the works.

"I'm extremely sorry about Janice," Paul told him earnestly. "A terrible thing to die amongst strangers."

"We weren't strangers," Luke immediately objected. "We'd all met before."

"Yes, but we didn't know each other on a personal basis," Mavis quickly pointed out. Miss Marple always remained detached from her suspects.

"What did kill her?" Jonathan asked, after the inspector had vanished and they were being ushered back towards their own secluded workshop room for interrogation.

David almost visibly swelled with pride. "We won't know until the autopsy report."

"*We?*" Luke picked up sarcastically. "Didn't know you were with the Suffolk police."

David scowled. "Once a policeman, always a policeman."

"I dislike being treated as though we were all potential murderers," Paul muttered as a gimlet-eyed policewoman opened the door for them to enter. "How do they know she didn't take the stuff herself?"

"What stuff?" Luke pounced, as he would on an unfortunate sixth-former. "How do you know it was poison?"

"Even if it was," David said, "it could have been an accident."

Mavis drew herself up. "It could not."

"How—" David began.

"Because there was a distinctive supermarket plastic bag at her side full of some prickly fruit, a knife and spoon, a packet of disposable plastic gloves, and an open window and—"

"Still could have been an accident or suicide," David interrupted, annoyed at being outranked by a woman.

"And—" Jonathan prompted Mavis to continue.

"A peppermill taped to her chest."

There was a certain camaraderie about the Mystery Unravelled crime-writing course, held three months later and on this occasion in a Hampshire manor house. Those participants who had attended the previous course, five in all, enjoyed an enviable position so far as the somewhat nervous but excited newcomers were concerned, as they were able to speak with first-hand knowledge of a real-life crime scene.

David in particular came into his own, having come by privileged information gained by bribing former colleagues with beer, flattery and, regrettably, twenty-pound notes.

Even Mavis condescended to listen avidly, as they awaited lunch on the Saturday morning. "So what did poor Janice die of?" she asked.

"Hyoscyamine," David replied smugly. "Datura seeds grated in the peppermill over, probably, the stew. Clever, wasn't it? I understand there's no forensic evidence to indicate anyone else was involved."

"So it could have been suicide," Paul said triumphantly.

"Rather a let-down," Luke sneered, but was disregarded.

"Then why bother to tape the pepper mill on?" David grunted. "Daft. I'm just a straightforward cop. Something like that happens in old Agatha's stuff, not in real life."

Mavis took this personally. "Only in this case, it did," she snapped.

"Still suicide," Paul maintained, anxious to maintain his lead. "A killer couldn't guess exactly when she would die in order to creep in to attach the peppermill."

"The first person to find her could," Luke said meaningfully. Mavis had criticized the best short story he had ever written. And he knew why: she intended to steal his plot.

Mavis quelled him with a look. "I knew your thinking was wobbly, Luke, but *really*! Would I go along to Janice's room armed with a peppermill to check if my victim were dead and then stop to tape it on in order to draw attention to the fact that it was murder?"

Luke rallied. "Agatha might have done."

She capped him. "Agatha always had a rational explanation. I doubt if you do."

David entered the fray. "Of course, I'm just a plain cop, but in my experience, the first on the scene often *is* the killer."

Paul switched tack to leap on the passing bandwagon. "It's the psychology."

"Why," Mavis boomed savagely over him, "should *anyone* wish to tape a peppermill on to a victim?"

"It's easy," Paul persevered. "In the interests of her – or of course his – art." Two and two for a retiring accountant were permitted to make five.

"Eh?" David looked blank.

"To test us all," Paul explained. "If you understood the sexual perspective—"

"Balderdash," David interrupted. "It was a joke."

Mavis seized her chance. "As I explained in this morning's workshop, the death itself should *never* be a joke. A peppermill comes perilously close to it."

The workshop students took this to heart, and the peppermill at the buffet lunch remained untouched either by hand or in conversation. The wine bottles fared much better. They were all emptied and five more called for, and consequently when the students reassembled for the afternoon workshop, they were some way into discussion of the intricacies of the protagonist's responsibility towards readers before Charles Beeton, one of the five regulars, was missed.

"He'll be here somewhere," Jonathan said anxiously. "He's probably fallen asleep." Charles was a gentleman of mature years and girth, and after the lunch they had all enjoyed, this explanation seemed highly likely. "But I'll check his room to be on the safe side." When he arrived, however, he found it unlocked, but empty.

Mavis was not so lucky. En route to the ladies' room in the basement, she stumbled over Charles's dead body. Her scream could be heard by the group in the workshop, growing ever louder as she rushed back to summon help. "Attack," she gasped, as she reached the room, panting for breath. "He's dead. Chest."

"A heart attack?" Jonathan caught her words as he returned from his fruitless errand, and joined the rush downstairs, already reaching for his mobile phone.

"Attack on the heart certainly," Luke said soberly, as he reached the body and saw what awaited them. David immediately felt for a pulse, but without success. A knife was protruding from Charles's chest, and Jonathan could not avoid seeing something else too.

Not only was there a distinctive-looking plastic supermarket bag at Charles's side, but another knife, shiny and clean, was carefully taped to his sweater.

"Don't touch the bag," David ordered, as Luke peered curiously into it. "Evidence."

In his element, David took charge, seizing Jonathan's mobile to summon the police; he then deputed Mavis, Jonathan and himself to guard the body while the others should remain together in the workshop room. Any visits to the toilets would be accompanied, according to sex, by himself, Mavis or Jonathan.

The crime scene manager of the police team that speedily arrived fully agreed that the plastic bag was evidence. Inside was a pair of men's shoes, an old-fashioned plastic mac that appeared slightly stained with blood, and another packet of disposable gloves. The shiny knife too, he agreed, was evidence though its purpose naturally eluded him, as the knife that killed Charles was declaring its presence so obviously.

"What on earth was the second knife for?" Luke asked, a trifle shakily, after they had been dismissed from the crime scene and rejoined the other students round the table in the workshop room.

"The first one's easier to understand," David said ponderously. "Removing it would have covered the killer in blood."

"But the second?" Luke persisted.

"I think I can guess," Paul said, with what he hoped was quiet authority.

"Psychologically they carry a sexual implication?" enquired Luke innocently.

Paul stiffened. "It could be," he replied defensively. "However I am inclined to think these are deodands." He looked round at their blank faces, and added modestly, "As a solicitor, I have a knowledge of legal history."

"I thought everyone knew what they were," Luke immediately put in. "They're relicts of medieval law which held that the object was a guilty party in the crime and as such forfeit to the crown, sometimes being passed to the victim's family in compensation."

"Quite," Paul said patronizingly. "Not repealed until the middle of the nineteenth century, when a rail company objected to forfeiting one of their express trains. In the case of poor Janice and now Charles, the peppermill and the knife are to be held responsible for their deaths."

"Try telling that to the Old Bailey," David snorted. "No way. It's a copy-cat murder. You'll see."

They did. Or rather the Kent police did. This time, excluding Jonathan and Mavis, the number of regulars was down to three: David, who said he had a duty to be present because as an ex-policeman he could keep an eye on things; Paul, who was set on proving his deodand theory; and Luke who was set on disproving anything that anyone else suggested.

Jonathan had considered whether it would be wise to hold this course at all, but he had been heartened to find there was no such thing as bad publicity. So numerous were the applications from newcomers that he was forced to turn students away. Mavis Sharp had hesitated about instructing at another course, but on discovering that her young friend Beatrice Worthy wished to sign up she decided she would join her. Unfortunately on arrival at the Kentish hotel, she quickly discovered that Beatrice's motives for wishing to come were mixed. First, she wrung Mavis's mind dry of every detail about the murders at which she had been first on the scene. Thereafter, Beatrice devoted her attention to Luke, and from Mavis's glimpse of the canoodling at the rear of the room during the Saturday workshop, she had broadened her sphere of interest.

David, Paul and even Luke (when he could detach himself from Beatrice) were all eager to outdo each other in the "My theory about the murders" stakes, and the newcomers were equally eager to detect which of the regulars could have been the killer.

It made for an interesting forum and Mavis, having recovered from the shock of discovering two corpses earlier in the year, was in her element. Her nose twitched continuously with the sharpness the investigating officer had commented on over Janice's death.

Discussion continued almost until dinnertime on the Saturday, and then resumed over the meal. Jonathan had abandoned the buffet approach to dinner, to everybody's obvious relief, after much earlier debate about Janice's murder. With set places, he could more easily keep an eye on everyone's presence and prevent any lone excursions.

However, after dinner, he could exercise no such control. When Luke promulgated an evening walk, Beatrice eagerly accepted. Mavis gently insisted that she should accompany them, but when she returned after powdering her nose she was annoyed to find that they had left without her. A mistake she told herself firmly, and spent ten minutes chatting to Jonathan, Paul and David before they parted for their separate rooms.

David, through his special knowledge, had told them that the police were as baffled over Charles' murder as over Janice's, even though the Hampshire and Suffolk police forces had consulted their modus operandi files and were in constant contact with each other. Neither the knives nor the plastic mac nor the shoes had revealed any DNA or useful fibres, and thus there seemed to be little progress, though from time to time one or other of the witnesses was thoroughly grilled.

Jonathan himself had endured several such grillings, which was hardly surprising. After Charles's death, he had feared that the

Mystery Unravelled company would be ordered to suspend all further courses, but no such injunction was laid on him although his credit and company details had been checked. What he could not satisfy the police about, naturally enough, was whether any of the participants would have reason to murder any of the others. Was there jealousy over a publishing contract? These students were nowhere near that happy stage, he had explained. Were there any romantic affairs between them? If there were, he would hardly be privy to them, he had reasonably replied. Had he, with his expert knowledge, noticed anything untoward in any of his students' characters, especially the regular ones? Jonathan hesitated over this. Did Luke's edginess or Paul's sexual obsession count? Or David's need to be involved in police work again? He decided not, and did not mention them.

Breakfast on the Sunday morning was a quiet affair with people arriving in ones and twos between 7.30 and 8.30. Some chose to go for a run first "for inspiration", Luke had explained, since the workshop this morning would be a set exercise of a short criminal story of a thousand words. Others of the group ran nowhere, or in some cases attended early church services. They were fortunate, because it was Luke who therefore came across the dead body of Beatrice Worthy on the woodland path. His white-faced appearance back at the hotel as he blurted out the gruesome details put the latecomers entirely off their Full English breakfasts.

In the all but certain knowledge that this would surely spell the end for Mystery Unravelled courses, if only because no hotel would offer them any facilities in future, Jonathan alerted the police and the hotel manager, and bravely set off with Luke to guard the body. Mavis, rejoicing that it was not she who had found poor Beatrice, waited for the arrival of the police.

"Round the next bend," Luke instructed Jonathan, stopping abruptly on the path. At this stage Jonathan too decided to wait for the police, not sure he could face a corpse again. After their arrival, however, he and Luke followed them cautiously to the scene of the crime, watching from the sidelines as they proceeded with their grim task. Even from where they stood they could glimpse the tongue protruding through blue lips, and blood and froth on the face of what had once been an attractive girl. And even from here they could see the distinctive supermarket plastic bag. They could also see something far more horrible.

Taped to Beatrice's bosom were two severed human hands.

On this occasion by unspoken accord, the workshop was abandoned. No one had the stomach for the intricacies of the psychopathic mind (fictional version) when the factual version was all too prominent in everyone's thoughts. Nor was there much stomach for lunch either, particularly for those most concerned in the investigation: the regulars.

The Kent police were assiduously interviewing every member of the hotel staff, and everyone at the Mystery Unravelled course. In addition to Jonathan and Mavis, particular attention was paid to David, Luke and Paul as the three present at all the workshops where murders had occurred.

Again by unspoken accord, most of the group drifted back to the workshop after lunch, as if a black cloud separated it from the rest of humanity. As it was hard for the newcomers to voice any natural speculation as to the guilty party, there was silence reigning in the room when David returned from a trip to the crime scene. There he had successfully managed to infiltrate the crime scene and circulate for ten whole minutes until ejected by the crime scene manager.

"He left his socks in the bag this time," David told them. "And the shoes looked much larger than last time. There was a pair of leather gloves, but no disposable ones."

"So he went barefoot this time?" Luke asked.

"Or had spare socks with him."

"What else?" Mavis asked, having had the scene fully described to her by Luke. "An axe?"

Not having been first on the scene, she felt more objective about this murder, even though it was poor Beatrice. She had her suspicions about this case. Miss Marple always did, and even though Luke was the front runner, David and Paul were still *in the frame*. That phrase pleased her as it showed that she was keeping Agatha's tradition up to date.

"Yes." David glanced at Mavis' large capable hands. "But she was strangled manually."

"So it couldn't have been a woman," Luke sounded disappointed.

"It could. Sex," Paul announced darkly.

"Charles wasn't a sex object," David said scornfully.

"There's sexual jealousy of the young. *And* the change of life," Paul diagnosed.

Mavis bristled with fury. "As I explained, Paul, in yesterday's workshop, modern medicine and technology have rendered many crime clichés unusable. Real life has moved on. HRT disposes of such problems far more efficiently than carrying out axe murders."

"She wasn't murdered by an axe," Jonathan pointed out in the interests of accuracy. "The hands were taped on, not the axe."

Paul nodded solemnly. "I'm glad you're a convert to my deodand theory, Jonathan."

Mavis frowned. "You said the deodand was the object that committed the crime. But the hands were Beatrice's own. They'd been chopped off. Are you saying she strangled herself?" The awfulness of it caught up with her, and she began to weep.

Paul was not to be daunted by tears. "No, but it's part of the psychology of the killer. We all appear quite normal to each other, but so would the psychopath who committed these murders. Two different faces, one for us, and another one for himself."

His listeners stirred uneasily, avoiding looking at each other.

Pleased that he had made his point, Paul continued: "After all, look at Agatha Christie and her famous disappearance. She took time off to pretend she was someone else."

"But not a psychopath," Mavis said sharply. "Poor woman, she was simply—"

"Why?" David cut across the conflict. "Why the hands at all? It's plain evil."

"That's just what Miss Marple would have said," Mavis said, looking at him very carefully.

It was Mavis who by chance did prove to be an achiever after all. Sharp by name and sharp by nature, as the police had said. When she called in at her local police station over a very trifling point of false claims, it was her sheer perseverance and downright bullying that drove them to look into the matter. By subsequent patient tracking of phone records they reached their quarry and then through sheer chance they discovered the murderer of Janice, Charles and Beatrice.

Mr Percy Pip was rudely awakened from a peaceful doze in which he was being presented with the Crime Writers' Diamond Dagger award, and was shattered to find upon his doorstep a CID officer plus a uniformed police constable, holding up ID cards.

"Mr Percy Pip?" And when he nodded, he heard those familiar words: "We have a warrant here for your arrest …"

Percy's face was ashen. He had been given to understand that all policemen were either Plods and thus easily outfoxed, or drunk and disorderly with severe psychological problems. The three investigating officers he had so far met had given no indications to the contrary. What therefore had gone wrong?

"But there was no forensic evidence," Percy babbled. "No DNA. I was most careful. They were, I assure you, the perfect murders. All of them—"

He stopped, aware that they were looking at him in a strange way. "We'll look into that, sir, now you've mentioned it. Meanwhile, we're here to arrest you on a fraud charge, identity theft."

Percy Pip couldn't believe it. Caught through the mere matter of providing utility bills, driving licence, etc. to establish bank accounts, signatures, accommodation address and rented office and living space, mostly achieved through one simple house clearance. And, he remembered, a false doctorate.

"The identity theft of the late Mr Jonathan Fuller. I have to warn you …"

FRECKLES

Allan Guthrie

"I LOVE YOU," Freddy said. "Can I have a kiss?"

"Away and shite, Freckles," Karen said, the sole of one foot planted against the wall she was leaning against as she stared at the other kids in the playground.

Freddy bowed his head. "Why not?" he said, into his chest.

"You what?"

He looked up, whispered, "Why not?"

She breathed hard. "Cause you're an ugly fucker."

Freddy held back his tears. "I'm not," he said. "Mum says—"

"Aye, you are," Karen told him, turning her head to face him. "Those freckles. Dead fuckin' ugly, man."

He wanted to ask her why it didn't bother her that she didn't have any friends. But she'd turned away again and was looking straight ahead.

When he got home, he told his mum. Didn't use the words Karen had used, though. He'd have got smacked.

His mum laughed.

He went to his room and punched the stuffing out of Clown. When he was hot and sweaty he shoved the stuffing back in Clown and threw him out of sight under the bed where he couldn't see the bastard's smile. Freddy walked in front of his mirror, stood there and looked at his reflection.

He counted his freckles. Last time he checked, there were four hundred and thirty-seven. He didn't know many other kids his age who'd ever counted that high. Most of them didn't need to.

The knock at the door made him jump.

His mum walked in. "What's the matter?"

He shook his head.

"Freddy? Are you counting again?"

He looked at his feet.

"Don't listen to Karen," she said. "She's nothing but trouble, that one."

He didn't look up.

"You'll grow out of the freckles," his mum said. "When you get older, they'll disappear."

He looked at her. "Promise?"

She nodded.

Liar.

Ten years later, hundreds of the fucking things still dotted his face. They were worse in the summer, but they were pretty bad all year round.

Last summer, he'd taken to wearing make-up. You could tell he was wearing make-up but you couldn't tell he had freckles. At least, that's what he hoped. He was all set to pay Karen a visit with his new face, but his confidence had left him as he got off the bus. He was sure she'd be able to see through the make-up.

This summer, he'd felt braver. Or so he thought. But the summer passed, and he'd stayed at home. By autumn, though, he felt ready. No doubt about it. His freckles weren't so bad, and with the make-up, well, Karen would see an improvement. And that had to be good.

He knew where she lived. She'd moved into a flat with her big sister, Edie.

Twice he went to see her, but both times he turned back before he got there. His stomach played up when he was nervous.

Third time, he made it up the garden path. He stared at the door, practising what he was going to say. He fought back a rush of nausea, knocked, but she didn't answer.

No one home.

He ran back down the path and threw up by the side of the road.

Fourth time, he got lucky.

The door opened and he stared at her, blood rushing to his head, his ears ringing.

Part of him had hoped her sister would answer and he could just make his apologies and leave.

"Yeah?" she said.

He opened his mouth.

"What?"

He licked his lips. They were so dry they hurt his tongue. "It's me," he said.

"Yeah," she said. "Fuckin' Freckles. I can see that. Well?"

"I don't have freckles," he said.

"Aye, you fuckin' do," she said. "Under all that foundation, you fuckin' poof."

He shook his head slowly. He turned.

"The fuck did you want anyway?" she shouted after him.

He carried on walking till it started to rain. It was dark by then and he had no idea where he was.

Time passed. He heard she got pregnant. Then he heard she was getting married.

He celebrated by trying to kill himself with sleeping pills and whisky. Woke up to the stench of vomit and shit, and felt more revolting than ever.

Six months in a psychiatric hospital helped, though.

When he got out, first thing he did was to try various bleaching creams. He spent a fortune, and the cream did help lighten the freckles. Or so he thought until he bumped into her one night in a pub. An accident.

"Hey," she said. "How's it going?"

For a moment, he allowed himself to get excited. She remembered him. She was interested in him. She wanted to have a conversation. She hadn't called him Freckles.

But she turned to the guy sitting next to her, a man hardly five foot tall with large ears and a scarred bald head. "Ain't that the freckliest fuckin' face you've ever seen, Babe?"

She got pregnant again. Then she got divorced from the dwarf.

Freddy tried to persuade his doctor to prescribe tretinoin, even though he knew by now that freckles couldn't be treated on the NHS. He claimed it would help with his depression. No joy. So he got hold of some himself. It certainly helped lighten his freckles, but at a cost. His skin turned red, itched, flaked and became painful to the touch.

Substituting one blemish for another, that's all he was doing. Made him feel even uglier. He looked around for another option. Chemical peel. Cryosurgery. Laser treatment.

The chemical peel was likely to cause scarring, so that was easily dismissed.

It seemed that cryosurgery was considered inferior to laser treatment, so that was the way to go.

He paid for two treatments, eight weeks apart.

When he went back to see her again a year later, a guy he'd never seen before answered the door.

"Is Karen in?" Freddy asked.

"Fuck's it to you?" he said.

"I'm an old friend."

The guy nodded. "She's gone," he said after bit. "Fucked off with her brats."

"Do you know where?"

"Didn't ask."

Freddy shuffled his feet. "You think you might see her again?"

"Doubt it."

"If you do, could you tell her Freddy called by?"

"Freddy?" the guy said, and peered at Freddy. "Freckles? Fuck, aye," he said. "Heard about you. That's a fuckin' faceful of freckles, right enough."

Next time he saw her was almost two years later. She was walking down the street with her kids; one, a boy, running ahead, throwing punches at an invisible victim, the other in a pram. Karen didn't notice Freddy.

He followed her for the length of the street, sorely tempted to follow her further. But he stopped himself. He knew how it would look. Especially with tears running down his face.

Anyway, he had to get back to work. He was saving up for a new laser treatment, one that was guaranteed to remove all but the most stubborn of his blemishes.

And that's what it did. The new treatment resulted in minimal scarring, massive freckle reduction, and the few little bastards that remained were so light in colour that his mum said they really weren't noticeable. He was desperate to track Karen down and show her.

Took him five months. She'd moved, but that wasn't the reason. Just took him that long to get himself together.

Her ex-husband, the dwarf, opened the door. "Fuck's sake," he said. "Fuck you doing here, Freckles?"

Freddy hadn't known the dwarf was back on the scene. Freddy should have left, but he couldn't help himself. He said, "Is Karen in?"

"Fuckin' aye, she is," the dwarf said. "What's it to you?"

"I want to see her."

"Fuck for?"

"Because," Freddy said. He indicated his face. "Cause of my freckles."

The dwarf looked at him, shook his scarred head. He turned, shouted into the house, "Karen. That Freckles dickhead for you."

She came to the door, barefoot, dress hanging off her rail-thin torso. Her arms looked snappable. Her glazed-over eyes bulged in her shrunken face. "Eh?" she said.

Freddy wasn't surprised. "It's me," he said. "Freddy."

"And?" she said.

He forced a grin. "What do you think?"

"Eh?" she said.

He indicated his face. "The freckles," he said. "All gone."

"Oh," she said. "Aye."

The three of them stood in the doorway glancing at each other until the dwarf said, "That it?"

Freddy shrugged.

"You came here to show her your freckles?"

"I don't have any. Well, hardly any."

"And that's it?"

Freddy looked at his feet. "Well, no."

"What, then?"

About time he went for it. He had to. He might never get another chance. And he was bubbling with confidence. He could feel it pressing behind his eyes. "Do you love her?" he asked the dwarf.

The dwarf looked up at her, then looked up at Freddy. "Mind your own fuckin' business," he said.

"Well I do," Freddy said. "I love her with all my heart and soul."
He turned to Karen. "I love you," he said.

The dwarf leapt at him and smacked him on the mouth. Freddy
fell to the ground. His face felt wet and, curiously, it burned. The
dwarf jumped on top of him, swinging at him.

Another blow struck Freddy on the cheek.

And another.

He tasted blood. Warm, salty, thick.

Then he saw the blade glistening in the dwarf's hand, and his
tongue caught the loose flap of skin and the air in his mouth felt
cool where it slipped through the ripped skin of his cheek.

He caught Karen's gaze. She hadn't moved. She was staring at
him from the doorway.

He swallowed blood, choked, spat.

The dwarf was on him again, thrusting at his face with the blade.

Ten years passed before Freddy saw Karen again.

He'd left the city, but the memory of her never faded. He knew
he'd have to come back eventually.

And here he was. Ten years older. Ten years more afraid.

He adjusted his cap, shielded his face like he always did, even
though it was night-time. There were streetlights, though. He'd
have preferred total darkness for this.

Maybe then, though, she'd have recognized his voice. She might
do that anyway. Maybe she'd run away. His heart speeded up as he
got closer.

She noticed his approach, clipped towards him on her heels.

"You looking for some fun, big boy?" she asked him.

"That … yes."

She grabbed his arm, linked hers in his.

No sign of recognition. The contact made him want to cry.

"You got a car?" she asked.

"I'd like to kiss you."

She stopped. "I don't do kissing."

"Never mind," he said.

"What do you mean?"

"Forget it."

"I don't kiss."

"Okay."

"Anything else, though. Within reason."

"What's within reason?"

"Hand-job, blow-job, full sex – straight, full service. Greek, maybe, if you're not too big. Golden shower, if you like, but not reverse. No hardsports. And absolutely nothing without."

"Without what?"

"You done this before?"

"No kissing?"

"No chance."

"I love you," he said. "I've always loved you."

She tugged her arm away. "Who the fuck are you?"

"Freddy," he said.

She peered at him. "Freckles?"

"Yeah." He reached up, grabbed the peak of his cap. "But I got rid of my freckles. You know that." He took off the cap.

"Oh, Jesus," she said, putting her hand to her mouth but keeping her eyes fixed on him. "That's fuckin' hideous."

"Thanks," he said.

"I didn't mean …"

"I was sorry to hear about your husband."

"You were?"

He nodded.

"He was my ex."

"But you'd got back together."

"Yeah, but we'd split up again by then," she said.

"After what he did to you … It was hard to keep things going when he was inside."

"Must have hurt, though."

"They said it was instant. The car hit him—"

"I meant, must have hurt you. The loss of a loved one."

She turned her head away. "I didn't love him."

"But you once did."

"No," she said. "Never."

He paused. "Did they ever catch the driver?" He waited long enough for her to answer. She didn't, her eyes remaining fixed on the mess he called his face. "Did they?"

He knew the answer, of course.

Even in the dim light he could see her eyes sparkle.

He'd have liked to thank her for doing that for him.

"Oh my fuck," she said. "It never occurred to me."

He put on a puzzled expression, hoped she could see past the scarring enough to make it out.

"You did it, you fucker."

"No," he said. "God, no, I wouldn't—"

"I'm not blaming you," she said.

"Well," he said, and waited.

"He asked for it."

"Well," he said.

"I wish I'd had the balls to do it myself."

Freddy put his cap back on, angled it so that it hid the bad side of his face. "Can I buy you a drink? Somewhere quiet. Somewhere dark?"

Freddy married Karen two years later. Six weeks after their marriage he discovered a freckle on her shoulder one night when they were sharing a bath. The freckle grew rapidly over the next couple of days. By the time she went to see her doctor, it was dark and hard and the size of her thumbnail.

She lasted just under a month.

Neither of her children made it to the funeral. Her sister, Edie, turned up late, drunk. That was the only way she could be in the same room as Freddy without freaking out at the sight of him. So she told him.

Freddy spent that summer sunbathing, something he'd never done before. He went to the south of France, lay around on the beaches soaking up the sun, not giving a fuck how many kids he scared. His freckles returned, though, and with them, his depression.

He went back home, stared at the walls for a week and a bit. One night he went out, bought a bottle of whisky and some paracetamol, and booked himself into a top-floor room in a high-rise hotel.

Couple of hours later, full of drink and pills, he walked out on to the balcony.

One hundred and fifty-five. One hundred and fifty-six ...

Freddy sits in his wheelchair and stares at his reflection in the mirror. He gets angry if the nurses try to move him. He can't help it. Not even his mother can interrupt him while he's counting his freckles.

One hundred and fifty seven.

When he's done, he'll start over again. Got to keep checking, Karen says.

Not that he's got anything else to do. Everything below his neck is dead. But that doesn't matter.

Sometimes he feels Karen touch his cheek, her fingertips outlining his old wounds. When he closes his eyes he feels her lips on his brow. Sometimes she whispers to him. "Keep counting," she says. "I think they're fading, Freddy."

HAPPY HOLIDAYS

Val McDermid

I

A CHRYSANTHEMUM BURST of colour flooded the sky. "Oooh," said the man, his blue eyes sparking with reflected light.

"Aaah," said the woman, managing to invest the single syllable with irony and good humour. Her shaggy blonde hair picked up colour from the fireworks, giving her a fibre-optic punk look at odds with the conservative cut of her coat and trousers.

"I've always loved fireworks."

"Must be the repressed arsonist in you."

Dr Tony Hill, clinical psychologist and criminal profiler, pulled a rueful face. "You've got me bang to rights, guv." He checked out the smile on her face. "Admit it, though. You love Bonfire Night too." A scatter of green and red tracer raced across the sky, burning after-images inside his eyelids.

DCI Carol Jordan snorted. "Nothing like it. Kids shoving bangers through people's letter-boxes, drunks sticking lit fireworks up their backsides, nutters throwing bricks when the fire engines turn up to deal with bonfires that've gone out of control? Best night of the year for us."

Tony shook his head, refusing to give in to her sarcasm. "It's been a long time since you had to deal with rubbish like that. It's only the quality villains you have to bother with these days."

As if summoned by his words, Carol's phone burst into life. "Terrific," she groaned, turning away and jamming a finger into her free ear. "Sergeant Devine. What have you got?"

Tony tuned out the phone call, giving the fireworks his full attention. Moments later, he felt her touch on his arm. "I have to go."

"You need me?"

"I'm not sure. It wouldn't hurt."

If it didn't hurt, it would be the first time. Tony followed Carol back to her car, the sky hissing and fizzing behind him.

The smell of cooked human flesh was unforgettable and unambiguous. Sweet and cloying, it always seemed to coat the inside of Carol's nostrils for days, apparently lingering long after it should have been nothing more than a memory. She wrinkled her nose in disgust and surveyed the grisly scene.

It wasn't a big bonfire, but it had gone up like a torch. Whoever had built it had set it in the corner of a fallow field, close to a gate but out of sight of the road. The evening's light breeze had been enough to send a drift of sparks into the hedgerow and the resulting blaze had brought a fire crew to the scene. Job done, they'd checked the wet smoking heap of debris and discovered the source of the smell overwhelming even the fuel that had been used as an accelerant.

As Tony prowled round the fringes of what was clearly the scene of a worse crime than arson, Carol consulted the lead fire officer. "It wouldn't have taken long to get hold," he said. "From the smell, I think he used a mixture of accelerants – petrol, acetone, whatever. The sort of stuff you'd have lying around your garage."

Tony stared at the remains, frowning. He turned and called to the fire officer. "The body – did it start off in the middle like that?"

"You mean, was the bonfire built round it?"

Tony nodded. "Exactly."

"No. You can see from the way the wood's collapsed around it. It started off on top of the fire."

"Like a Guy." It wasn't a question; the fireman's answer had clearly confirmed what Tony already thought. He looked at Carol. "You do need me."

Tony smashed the ball back over the net, narrowly missing the return when his doorbell rang. He tossed the Wii control on to the sofa and went to the door. "We've got the post mortem and some preliminary forensics," Carol walked in, not waiting for an invitation. "I thought you'd want to take a look." She passed him a file.

"There's an open bottle of wine in the fridge," Tony said, already scanning the papers and feeling his way into an armchair. As he read, Carol disappeared into the kitchen, returning with two glasses. She placed one on the table by Tony's chair and settled opposite him on the sofa, watching the muscles in his face tighten as he read.

It didn't make for comfortable reading. A male between twenty-five and forty, the victim had been alive when he'd been put on the bonfire. Smoke inhalation had killed him, but he'd have suffered tremendous pain before the release of death. He'd been bound hand and foot with wire and his mouth had been sealed by some sort of adhesive tape. For a moment, Tony allowed himself to imagine how terrifying an ordeal it must have been and how much pleasure it had given the killer. But only for a moment. "No ID?" he said.

"We think he's Jonathan Meadows. His girlfriend reported him missing the morning after. We're waiting for confirmation from dental records."

"And what do we know about Jonathan Meadows?"

"He's twenty-six, he's a garage mechanic. He lives with his girl-friend in a flat in Moorside—"

"Moorside? That's a long way from where he died."

Carol nodded. "Right across town. He left work at the usual time. He told his girlfriend and his mates at work that he was going to the gym. He usually went three or four times a week, but he never showed up that night."

"So somewhere between – what, six and eight o'clock? – he met someone who overpowered him, bound and gagged him, stuck him on top of a bonfire and set fire to him?"

"That's about the size of it. Anything strike you?"

"That's not easy, carrying out something like that." Tony flicked through the few sheets of paper again. His mind raced through the possibilities, exploring the message of the crime, trying to make a narrative from the bare bones in front of him. "He's a very low-risk victim," he said. "When young men like him die violently, it's not usually like this. A pub brawl, a fight over a woman, a turf war over drugs or prostitution, yes. But not this kind of premeditated thing. If he was just a random victim, if anyone would do, it's more likely to be a homeless person, a drunk staggering home last thing, someone vulnerable. Not someone with a job, a partner, a life."

"You think it's personal?"

"Hard to say until we know a lot more about Jonathan Meadows." He tapped the scene-of-crime report. "There doesn't seem to be much in the way of forensics at the scene."

"There's a pull-in by the gate to the field. It's tarmacked, so no convenient tyre tracks. There's a few footprints, but they're pretty indistinct. The SOCOs think he was wearing some sort of covering over his shoes. Just like the ones we use to preserve the crime scene." Carol pulled a face to emphasize the irony. "No convenient cigarette ends, Coke cans or used condoms."

Tony put down the file and drank some wine. "I don't think he's a beginner. It's too well executed. I think he's done this before. At least once."

Carol shook her head. "I checked the database. Nothing like this anywhere in the UK in the last five years."

That, he thought, was why she needed him. She thought in straight lines, which was a useful attribute in a cop, since, however much they might like to believe otherwise, that was how most criminals thought. But years of training and experience had honed his own corkscrew mind till he could see nothing but hidden agendas stretching backwards like the images in an infinity mirror. "That's because you were looking for a burning," he said.

Carol looked at him as if he'd lost it. "Well, duh," she said. "That's because the victim was burned."

He jumped to his feet and began pacing. "Forget the fire. That's irrelevant. Look for low-risk victims who were restrained with wire and gagged with adhesive tape. The fire is not what this is about. That's just window dressing, Carol."

Carol tapped the pile of paper on her desk with the end of her pen. Sometimes it was hard not to credit Tony with psychic powers. He'd said there would be at least one other victim, and it looked as if he'd been right. Trawling the databases with a different set of parameters had taken Carol's IT specialist a few days. But she'd finally come up with a second case that fitted the bill.

The body of Tina Chapman, a thirty-seven-year-old teacher from Leeds, had been found in the Leeds–Liverpool canal a few days before Jonathan Meadows' murder. A routine dredging had snagged something unexpected and further examination had produced a grisly finding. She'd been gagged with duct tape, bound hand and foot with wire, tethered to a wooden chair weighted with a cement block and thrown in. She'd been alive when she went into the water. Cause of death: drowning.

A single parent, she'd been reported missing by her thirteen-year-old son. She'd left work at the usual time, according to colleagues. Her son thought she'd said she was going to the supermarket on her way home, but neither her credit card nor her store loyalty card had been used.

Carol had spoken to the senior investigating officer in charge of the case. He'd admitted they were struggling. "We only found her car a couple of days ago in the car park of a hotel about half a mile from the supermarket her son said she used. It was parked down the end, in a dark corner out of range of their CCTV cameras. No bloody idea what she was doing down there. And no joy from forensics so far."

"Anybody in the frame?"

His weary sigh reminded her of cases she'd struggled with over the years. "It's not looking good, to be honest. There was a boyfriend, but they split up about six months ago. Nobody else involved, it just ran out of road. Quite amicable, apparently. The boyfriend still takes the lad to the rugby. Not a scrap of motive."

"And that's it?" Carol was beginning to share his frustration. "What about the boy's real father?"

"Well, he wasn't what you'd call any kind of father. He walked out on them when the lad was a matter of months old."

Carol wasn't quite ready to let go of the straw she'd grasped. "He might have come round to the idea of having some contact with the boy."

"I doubt it. He died in the Boxing Day tsunami back in '04. So we're back to square one and not a bloody thing to go at."

Carol still couldn't accept she'd reached the end of the road. "What about her colleagues? Any problems there?"

She could practically hear the shrug. "Not that they're letting on about. Nobody's got a bad word to say about Tina, and I don't think they're just speaking well of the dead. She's been working there for four years and doesn't seem to have caused a ripple with other staff or parents. I can't say I share your notion that this has got anything to do with your body, but I tell you, if you come up with anything that makes sense of this, I'll buy you a very large drink."

Making sense of things was what Bradfield Police paid Tony for. But sometimes it was easier than others. This was not one of those occasions. Carol had dropped off the case files on Jonathan Meadows and Tina Chapman at Bradfield Moor, the secure hospital where he spent his days among the criminally insane, a clientele whose personal idiosyncrasies he did not always find easy to distinguish from the population at large.

Two victims, linked by their unlikelihood. There was no evidence that their paths had ever crossed. They lived thirty miles apart. Carol's team had already established that Tina Chapman did not have her car serviced at the garage where Jonathan Meadows worked. He'd never attended a school where she'd taught. They had no apparent common interests. Anyone other than Tony might have been reluctant to forge any link between the two cases. Carol had pointed that out earlier, acknowledging that her counterpart in Leeds was far from convinced there was a connection. Tony's instincts said otherwise.

As he read, he made notes. *Water. Fire. Four elements?* It was a possibility, but admitting it took him no further forward. If the killer was opting for murder methods that mirrored fire, water, earth and air, what did it mean? And why did it apply to those particular victims? Tina Chapman was a French teacher. What had that to do with water? And how was a garage mechanic connected to fire? No, unless he could find more convincing connective tissue, the four elements idea wasn't going anywhere.

He studied the file again, spreading the papers across the living room floor so he could see all the information simultaneously. And this time, something much more interesting caught his attention.

Carol stared at the two pieces of paper, wondering what she was supposed to see. "What am I looking for?" she said.

"The dates," Tony said. "October 31. November 5."

Light dawned. "Hallowe'en. Bonfire Night."

"Exactly." As he always did when he was in the grip of an idea, he paced, pausing by the dining table to scribble down the odd note. "What's special about them, Carol?"

"Well, people celebrate them. They do particular things. They're traditional."

Tony grinned, his hands waving in the air as he spoke. "Traditional. Exactly. That's it. You've hit the nail on the head. They're great British traditions."

"Hallowe'en's American," Carol objected. "Trick or treat. That's not British."

"It is originally. It came from the Celtic Samhain festival. Trick or treat is a variation of the Scottish guising tradition. Trust me, Carol, it only got to be American when the Irish took it over there. We started it."

Carol groaned. "Sometimes I feel the internet is a terrible curse."

"Not to those of us with enquiring minds. So, we've got two very British festivals. I can't help wondering if that's the root of what's going on here. Tina died like a witch on the ducking stool. Jonathan burned like a bonfire Guy. The murder methods fit the dates." He spun on his heel and headed back towards Carol.

"So I'm asking myself, is our killer somebody who's raging against Britain and our traditions? Someone who feels slighted by this country? Someone who feels racially oppressed maybe? Because the victims are white, Carol. And the killer's paid no attention to Diwali. OK, we've not had Eid yet, but I'm betting he won't take a victim then. I'm telling you, Carol, I think I'm on to something here."

Carol frowned. "Even if you're right – and frankly, it sounds even more crazy than most of your theories – why these two? Why pick on them."

Tony trailed to a halt and stared down at what he'd written. "I don't know yet." He turned to meet her eyes. "But there is one thing I'm pretty sure about."

He could see the dread in her eyes. "What's that?"

"If we don't find the killer, the next victim's going to be a dead Santa. Stuffed in a chimney would be my best guess."

Later, Tony's words would echo in Carol's head. When she least expected it, they reverberated inside her. As she sat in the canteen, half her attention on her lasagne and half on the screen of the TV, she was jolted by a newsflash that chilled her more than the November snow: SANTA SNATCHED OFF STREET.

II

It had been a long time since Tony had been a student but he'd never lost his taste for research. What made his investigations different from those of Carol and her team was his conviction that the truth lay in the tangents. An exhaustive police investigation would turn up all sorts of unexpectedness, but there would always be stuff that slipped between the cracks. People were superstitious about telling secrets. Even when they gave up information, they held something back. Partly because they could and partly because they liked the illusion of power it dealt them. Tony, a man whose gift for empathy was his finest tool and his greatest weakness, had a remarkable talent for convincing people that their hearts would never be at peace till they had shared every last morsel of information.

And so he devoted his attentions to identifying the unswept corners of the lives of Tina Chapman and Jonathan Meadows.

The first thing that attracted his attention about Tina Chapman was that she had only been in her current job for four years. In his world, history cast a long shadow, with present crimes often having their roots deep in the past. He wondered where Tina Chapman had been before she came to teach French in Leeds.

He knew he could probably short-circuit his curiosity with a call to Carol, but her gibe about the internet was still fresh in his mind so he decided to see what he could uncover without her help.

Googling Tina Chapman brought nothing relevant except for a Facebook entry describing her as "everybody's favourite language teacher", an online review of the sixth-form performance of "Le Malade Imaginaire" that she'd directed and a slew of news stories about the murder. None of the articles mentioned where she'd taught previously. But there was an interesting clue in one of them. Tina's son wasn't called Ben Chapman but Ben Wallace. "Lovely," Tony said aloud. If Wallace had been Ben's father's name, there was at least a fighting chance that his mother had used it at some point.

He tried "Tina Wallace" in the search engine, which threw out a couple of academics and a real estate agent in Wyoming. Then he tried "Martina Chapman", "Christina Chapman", "Martina Wallace" and finally, "Christina Wallace". He stared at the screen, hardly able to credit what he saw there.

There was no doubt about it. If ever there was a motive for murder, this was it.

Detective Inspector Mike Cassidy knew Carol Jordan only by reputation. Her major case squad was despised and desired in pretty much equal measure by Bradfield's detectives, depending on whether they knew they would never be good enough or they aspired to join. Cassidy avoided either camp; at forty-two, he knew he was too old to find a niche working alongside the Chief Constable's blue-eyed girl. But he didn't resent her success as so many others did. That didn't stop him showing his surprise when she walked into his incident room with an air of confident ownership.

He stood up and rounded his desk, determined not to be put at a disadvantage. "DCI Jordan," he said with a formal little nod. He waited; let her come to him.

Carol returned the nod. "DI Cassidy. I hear you're dealing with the abduction in Market Street?"

Cassidy's lips twisted in an awkward cross between a smile and a sneer. "The case of the stolen Santa? Isn't that what they're calling it in the canteen?"

"I don't care what they're calling it in the canteen. As far as I'm concerned, there's nothing funny about a man being kidnapped in broad daylight on a Bradfield street."

Cassidy took the rebuke on the chin. "As it happens, I'm with you on that one, ma'am. It's no joke for Tommy Garrity or his family. And apart from anything else, it makes us look like monkeys."

"So where are you up to?"

"Tommy Garrity was dressed in a Santa suit, collecting money for Christmas For Children when two men in balaclavas and blue overalls drove up the pedestrian precinct in a white Transit. They stopped in front of Tommy, bundled him into the Transit and took off. We got the van on CCTV, turns out it was stolen off a building site this morning." Cassidy turned to his desk and excavated a map from the stack of paper by the keyboard. He handed it to Carol.

"The red line's the route they took out of the city centre. We lost them round the back of Temple Fields. Once you come off Campion Way, the coverage is patchy."

Carol sighed. "Typical. What about the number plate recognition cameras?"

"Nothing. At least we know they've not left the city on any of the main drags."

"So, Tommy Garrity. Is he known?"

Cassidy shook his head. "Nothing on file. He works behind the bar at the Irish Club in Harriestown, does a lot of charity work in his spare time. He's fifty-five, three kids, two grandkids. Wife's a school dinner lady. I've got a team out on the knocker but so far Garrity's white as the driven."

Carol traced the line on the map. "That's what worries me."

Cassidy couldn't keep his curiosity at bay any longer. "If you don't mind me asking, ma'am, what's your interest? I mean, not to play down the importance of daylight abduction, but it's not major in the sense of being up your street."

Carol dropped the map on Cassidy's desk. "Just something somebody said to me a couple of weeks ago. Can you keep me posted, please?"

Cassidy watched her walk out. She was more than easy on the eye, and normally that would have been all that registered with him. But Carol Jordan's interest had left him perturbed and anxious. What the hell was he missing here?

News generally passed Tony by. He had enough variety in his life to occupy his interest without having to seek out further examples of human shortcomings. But because he'd floated the suggestion of Santa as potential victim, he was more susceptible than normal to the scream of newspaper billboards that announced, SANTA SNATCH IN CITY CENTRE.

The story in the paper was short on fact and long on frenzy, queasily uncertain whether it should be outraged or amused. Tony, already on his way to Carol's office, quickened his step.

He found her at her desk, reading witness statements from the Santa kidnap. She looked up and squeezed out a tired smile. "Looks like you were right."

"No, I wasn't. I mean, I think I was, but this isn't him." Tony threw his hands in the air, exasperated at his inability to express himself clearly. "This isn't the next victim in a series," he said.

"What do you mean? Why not? You were the one who told me I should be looking out for Santa. And not in the sense of hanging up my stocking."

"There were two of them. I never said anything about two of them."

"I know you didn't. But it would have made the first two murders a lot easier if they'd been two-handed. And we both know that racially motivated fanatics tend to work in cells or teams. After what you said, I've had my crew looking at all our intel and we're not getting many hits on lone activists." She shrugged. "It may not have been in the profile but two makes sense."

Tony threw himself in the chair. "That's because I was ignoring my own cardinal rule. First you look at the victim. That's what it's all about, and I got distracted because of the eccentricity of the crimes. But I've looked at the victims now and I know why they were killed." He fished some print-outs from his carrier bag. "Tina Chapman used to be known by her married name. She was Christina Wallace." He passed the top sheet to Carol. "She taught French at a school in Devon. She took a bunch of kids on a school trip and two of them drowned in a canoeing accident. The inquest cleared her but the bereaved parents spoke to the press, blaming her for what happened. And it does look like they had pretty strong reasons for that. So, she moved away. Reverted to her maiden name and started afresh."

"You think one of the parents did this?"

"No, no, that's not it. But once I knew that about Tina, I knew what I was looking for with Jonathan." He handed over the second sheet. "Seven years ago, a five-year-old girl was killed by a hit-and-run driver. The car was a Porsche that had allegedly been stolen from a garage where it was in for a service. The garage where Jonathan Meadows worked. I went over there and spoke to the local traffic officers. They told me that there was a strong feeling at the time that the Porsche hadn't been stolen at all, that Jonathan had taken it for a ride and had lost control. His DNA was all over the car but his excuse was that he'd been working on it. His girlfriend gave him an alibi and nothing ever came of it."

Carol stared at the two sheets of paper. "You're saying this is some kind of vigilante justice?"

Tony dipped his head. "Kind of. Both victims were implicated in the death of a child but went unpunished because of loopholes in law or lack of evidence. The killer feels they stole children away from their families. I think we should be looking for someone who has lost a child and believes nobody paid the price. Probably in the past year. He's choosing these victims because he believes they're culpable and he's choosing these murder methods because they mark the points in the year where parents celebrate with children."

Within the hour, Tony and Carol were studying a list of seven children who had died in circumstances where blame might possibly be assigned. "How can we narrow it down?" she demanded, frustration in her voice. "We can't put surveillance on all these parents and their immediate families."

"There's no obvious way," Tony said slowly.

"Santa Garrity could still be a potential victim," Carol said. "We don't know enough about his history and there's nothing in your theory to say it couldn't be two killers working together."

Tony shook his head. "It's emotionally wrong. This is about punishment and pain, not justice. It's too personal to be a team effort." He ran a hand through his hair. "Couldn't we at least go and talk to the parents? Shake the tree?"

"It's a waste of time. Even you can't pick out a killer just by looking at them." They sat in glum silence for a few minutes, then Carol spoke again. "Victims. You're right. It all comes back to victims. How's he choosing his victims? You had to do some digging to come up with what you found. There was nothing in the public domain to identify Jonathan, and Tina had changed her name. That's why the motive didn't jump out at my team."

Tony nodded. "You're right. So who knows this kind of information? It's not the police, there's at least two forces involved here. Not the Crown Prosecution Service either, neither of them ever got that far."

Light dawned behind Carol's eyes. "A journalist would know. They get access to all kinds of stuff. He could have recognized Tina Chapman from the press photographs at the time. If he has local police contacts, he could have heard that Jonathan Meadows was under suspicion over the hit and run."

Tony scanned the list. "Are any of these journalists?"

DI Cassidy entered the Children For Christmas offices almost at a run, his team at his heels. A trim little woman got to her feet and pointed to her computer screen. "There. Just as it came in."

The e-mail was short but not sweet. "We've got Santa. You've got money. We want £20,000 in cash. You'll hear from us in an hour. No police."

"I thought I would ignore the bit about 'no police'," the woman said. "It's not as if we're going to be paying the ransom."

Cassidy admired her forthrightness but had to check she was taking all the possibilities into consideration. "You're not frightened they might kill Mr Garrity? Or seriously harm him?"

She gave him a scornful look. "They're not going to hurt Santa. How do you think that would go down in prison? You of all people should know how sentimental criminals are."

Carol's conviction that David Sanders was a serial killer took her no closer to making an arrest. There was a small matter of a complete lack of evidence against Sanders, a feature writer on the Bradfield *Evening Sentinel Times*. Even the apparent miracles of twenty-first-century forensic science couldn't nail this. Water and fire were notorious destroyers of trace evidence. She'd hoped that close analysis might fit together the cut marks on the tape and wire from the previous killings, but the fire had done too much damage. That meant there was no chance of definitively linking them to any materials still in Sanders' possession.

There were no reliable witnesses or meaningful CCTV footage. A couple of homeless men had turned up claiming to have seen Tina Chapman go into the canal. But the person pushing her had been wearing a Hallowe'en mask and the sighting had gone nowhere.

The only option left was to cling to Tony's conviction that the killer would strike again before Christmas. It was always hard to persuade her bosses to mount surveillance operations because they were so costly and because they took so many officers off other cases, but at least this one had a fixed end point.

And so they watched. They watched David Sanders go to work. They watched him drink in the pub with his workmates. They watched him work out at the gym. They watched him do his Christmas shopping. What they didn't watch him do was abduct and murder anyone.

Then it was Christmas Eve, the last day of authorized surveillance. In spite of the privileges of rank, Carol put herself down for a shift. It was already dark when she slid into the passenger seat of the anonymous car alongside DC Paula McIntyre. "Nothing moving, chief. He got home about an hour ago, nobody in or out since."

"The house doesn't look very festive, does it? No sign of a tree or any lights."

Paula, who had known her own share of grief, shrugged. "You lose your only child? I don't expect Christmas is much to celebrate."

The Sanders' four-year-old daughter had drowned during a swimming lesson back in September. The instructor had been dealing with another kid who was having a come-apart when Sanders' daughter had hit her head on the poolside. By the time anyone noticed, it had been too late. According to a colleague discreetly questioned by Sergeant Devine, it had ripped Sanders apart, though he'd refused to consider any kind of medical intervention.

Before Carol could respond, the garage door opened and Sanders' SUV crawled down the drive. They let him make it to the end of the street before they pulled out of their parking place and slipped in behind him. It wasn't hard to stay on the tail of the tall vehicle and fifteen minutes' driving brought them to a street of run-down terraced houses on the downtrodden edge of Moorside. On the corner was a brightly lit shop, its windows plastered with ads for cheap alcohol. Sanders pulled up and walked into the shop carrying a sports holdall.

"I think this is it," Carol breathed. "Let's go, Paula."

They sprinted down the street and tried the door of the shop. But something was jamming it. Carol took a couple of steps back then charged the door, slamming her shoulder into the wooden surround. Something popped and the door crashed open.

Sanders was standing behind the counter, a cricket bat in his hand, dismay on his face. "Police, drop your weapon," Carol roared as Paula scrambled to the far end of the counter.

"There's someone here, chief. Looks like he's unconscious," Paula said.

The cricket bat fell to the ground with a clatter. Sanders sank to the floor, head in hands. "This is all your fault," he said. "You never make the right people pay the price, do you?"

Carol collapsed into Tony's armchair and demanded a drink. "He didn't even bother with a denial," she said. "Being arrested seemed almost to come as a relief." She closed her eyes for a moment, memory summoning up Sanders' haggard face.

"It generally does when you're not dealing with a psychopath," Tony said.

Carol sighed. "And a very merry bloody Christmas to you too."

"You stopped him killing again," Tony said, handing her a glass of wine. "That's not an insignificant achievement."

"I suppose. Jahinder Singh's family can celebrate the festive season knowing their father's safe from any further consequences from selling solvents to kids." Before Carol could say more, her phone rang. "What now?" she muttered. She listened attentively, a slow smile spreading from mouth to eyes. "Thanks for letting me know," she said, ending the call. "That was Cassidy. Santa's home free. Two extremely inept kidnappers are banged up and nobody got hurt."

Tony raised his glass, his smile matching hers. In their line of work, making the best of a bad job was second nature. This wasn't exactly a happy ending, but it was closer than they usually managed. He'd settle for that any day.